MW01128596

TAKE ME

THERE'S A REASON IT'S CALLED THE DEAD OF NIGHT

WITH YOU

FROM THE AUTHOR OF DEBT

NINA G. JONES

A NOTE
FROM NINA

Here's a music playlist to help set the mood:

Every Breath You Take – The Police
How Deep is Your Love – Bee Gees
Night Fever – Bee Gees
You Should Be Dancing – Bee Gees
It's Too Late – Carole King
You're So Vain – Carly Simon
Killing Me Softly With His Song – Roberta Flack
I'm Not In Love – 10cc
So Far Away – Carole King
Can't Stand Losing You – The Police
She's Not There – The Zombies

Listen to this playlist on Spotify:
https://play.spotify.com/user/12135215332/playlist/0EynqplJcV1ju
AdVGNAG4y

TRIGGER WARNING

All of them.

Seriously. This is not a romance. This is not for the faint of heart.
Where you are about to go, there is no light.

TAKE ME
WITH YOU

There are no heroes in this world, only villains and victims.

PART
ONE

PROLOGUE

1978

I own the night. It's the only time I can walk freely without my mask. No, not the balaclava with which I shroud my face. It's the mask I wear during daylight hours, when I pretend I'm one of them. Those beautiful people with their perfect smiles and their echoing laughter. They mock me. They taunt me. But at night, when the streets are still, that's when I laugh. When I smile. It's when I take all the things from them that I never could have. When I crawl into their homes and into their skin. I wear their lives like a borrowed piece of clothing. Only by the time I give it back, it's tattered and damaged, and I must move on to the next home, one that hasn't been destroyed by my parasitic need.

But for those few hours when I am one of them, they have a taste of that pain. It's my turn to feel a concentrated dose of the joy they take for granted. The rush is fierce, like a dam breaking, the sensation of belonging overwhelming me. But the waters calm just as quickly, and then I am standing there, the shallow stream flowing at my feet, as the sun rises. And I wait, patiently, until darkness returns, so I can steal that rush again.

I am on the hunt. Vesper's at school. Her brother is at therapy, and her parents are on another trip. *Vesper. Evening prayer.*

It's ironic, the name. If all the world is a stage, and if irony makes for the best stories, then she was born for this role.

She's not the first. Not even close. But there is something about her that fascinates me more than the others. And there have been many.

I am obsession.

Every home I enter becomes the object of my fixation. So the fact that she has become all I think about -- despite all the other homes I prowl -- makes me impatient.

Patience. It's the most important tool in my arsenal. I plan every hunt from start to finish. I watch their lives through windows. I learn their routines. I enter their homes and go through their keepsakes and take small tokens here or there. Something they won't notice or will assume they have misplaced. I may move a picture. Eat something. Just enough so that somewhere in their subconscious they feel my presence long before I am standing in front of them. That used to be enough. Just being there, surrounded by their things, the vestiges of their daily lives. It used to be enough to look at the tokens I kept and remember the rush I felt being inside the walls I had watched from afar. But that rush faded a long time ago, vanishing in a spectacular eruption the day the one person who understood me died. Without her, the loneliness became unbearable and the rage swelled. It filled me until I could feel it creeping out of my skin, until I was so full of rage and pain that I had to put it on someone else to make it disappear. Watching wasn't enough. I had to hear their voices. See their faces. Steal their lives. So instead of just taking, I began to leave things behind: tape, rope, gloves, lube. Tools I would use later when I was ready for them. And if the police ever stop me, well, they won't find a kit on me.

I'm careful to make my targets seem random. I don't want to establish a clear pattern. My work as a contractor takes me all over Central California, where I grew up. I know the neighborhoods well. I know every shortcut and how all the streets connect. I know where all the freeway exits and ramps are for a quick getaway. Real estate agents call me to fix up houses. I'll look up their listings and pick a home they haven't had me work on. If I like the neighbors, I'll use those empty homes as a base to watch the area. Vacant houses at night are perfect places to hide. Other times, I just spot someone and the craving hits. So I watch them and see if they are a good fit. On paper it all looks random. But nothing is random.

I comb through Vesper's jewelry boxes on a chest of drawers. She still lives with her parents, but we aren't too far apart in age. Even though she is in her early 20s, the trinkets are a mix of adult pieces and tokens of her childhood, as are many things in the room. On a chair in the corner is a silk robe, the kind that would rest beautifully against the curves of her tits and ass, and on that same chair is a little teddy bear, weathered from years of being hugged. The chair looks old. The white, painted woodwork is chipped and grayed, the pale floral cushion is worn in the spot where she has sat countless times. I run my fingers along the faded flowers that have touched her skin. Then along the satiny robe. I pick up the teddy bear and examine it before placing it back in its spot, tilting it 45 degrees from its original position.

There's a picture board on one of her walls. The kind where you can pin stuff up or tuck the picture behind cross sections of ribbon. Many of the pictures are of her and her boyfriend. Mr. Soon-To-Be-Doctor. Mr. Perfect Smile and Charmed Existence. The board is stuffed with photos so they overlap many times over. Every one of them is of people smiling. All they fucking do is smile and it makes me sick.

You're not like other people.

These people don't know pain. They don't know loneliness. They might know fleeting discomfort, but they don't know the persistent agony of being an outsider. People like them have made me who I am.

I remember when I first spotted Vesper Rivers. It's an odd name, I know. Her mom is—was—a hippie. I wasn't hunting for anyone when it happened, though I always keep my options open. I was at the grocery store after a long day of work. Covered in sweat and muck, my clothes stained with paint and tar, I just wanted to grab something fast, and I was too tired from a week of prowling nights and working days to think about much else. That's when I saw her, walking through the cereal aisle. She had on a tiny top: a rust-colored halter with strings that wrapped around her neck. It was short, the waist of her shorts going just above her belly button so that when she moved, I'd see hints of her tight stomach. Her cutoff shorts barely covered her ass and made way for long, shapely legs. Her brown hair with hints of gold was long and feathered—a lot like that Farrah poster everyone has pinned up these days. But this girl, she was far more beautiful. Like an undiscovered gem just sitting in a pile of rocks and dirt. A long, elegant arm sloped down to a small hand. A boy. He must have been around eight. He couldn't be her son. She's too young.

"You like that one, Johnny?" she asked, bent at the waist to be at his level. Her voice, it was extra sweet for the little boy.

He nodded. His arm was crooked, one of his legs bent in awkwardly, and his mouth was contorted. He was different. Handicapped. And she was so kind to him. Maybe she wasn't like the others. Maybe she was something in between people like them and people like me.

That's when she felt me staring. I'm usually discreet. I've mastered watching people, hiding in plain sight, but she stunned me. She looked over, catching my eyes for a millionth of a second before I turned away. I couldn't let her see my face, and I was grateful it was covered in dirt and tar, hiding its subtleties.

I hastily went to the register with whatever was in my hands so I could get to my car before she got to hers. I waited for another fifteen minutes until she emerged from the store, a bag in one hand and the little boy dragging his feet holding the other. He was smiling. I don't understand how he could have been happy. I know how cruel this world can be to those of us who wear our imperfections on the outside.

She got into a white Grand Prix, looked like a '73. I later learned my hunch was off by a year. I took note of the plates. I watched her leave. Then I followed far enough behind for her not to notice me.

And here I am in her house a couple of weeks later. It's not my first time, either.

I snatch a picture I don't think she'll miss much as it was mostly tucked behind another. In it, she's sitting on a log, a lake as a backdrop. She's laughing, of course, her head thrown back to show her white grin. A necklace glints at her throat.

They'll smile at you then laugh behind your back.

I glance at the clock on her nightstand. It's embedded in this porcelain unicorn statue, and I hope for her sake that it's another remnant from her younger days. I need to get out of here. I don't want to cut it close and blow this one. Besides, I have a date I need to prepare for tonight.

I open up a small jewelry box, covered in multicolored rhinestones. There's a few pieces intertwined inside, but I notice the gold crescent moon attached to a necklace. It's the same one as the picture. It's mine now.

Like my last visit to her home, I have something for her. I pull out a roll of twine and place it under the seat cushion of the chair that holds her teddy bear. *Patience.*

CHAPTER 1

VESPER

"I'm doing some last minute shopping for the trip. Keep an eye on your brother. He's inside watching TV," my mother says as she walks to her car parked on the sidewalk. It's a hot, sunny day, so I've decided to wash my car in our driveway. My stepdad is paying for my school, but daily living comes out of my pocket, and I save money in every way I can, including car washes.

"Sure, mom," I reply unenthusiastically. Not because I don't love watching Johnny, no, he's my world. It's because he doesn't seem to be hers. I know all about that. I've pretty much raised myself, but Johnny has handicaps. He was born with his umbilical cord wrapped around his neck and, as a result, has cerebral palsy and a few other issues. He needs her. But she just came back from the Caribbean two weeks ago, and now it's off to Egypt with my stepdad for another two weeks.

She's oblivious to my tone, or she just doesn't care because she's already driving away. I drop my sponge and go inside to see how Johnny's doing. He's sitting crossed-legged in front of The Electric Company, bouncing up and down, and moving his good hand to the rhythm Easy Reader's signing. Johnny moves his lips, but nothing comes out. He's almost entirely mute. Sometimes when he's angry or elated, incoherent sounds escape his throat, but for the most part, he's silent.

"Johnny. I'm washing the car outside. Do you want to help?"

He either ignores me or is too enraptured by the show to hear me. "Hey," I say, walking in front of him to block his view. "Did you hear me, sweetie?"

He leans to the side to look past my legs. Clearly I am an annoying distraction. "Okay. Well, if you need anything, I'll be right outside. Okay?"

He nods without making eye contact, still rocking to the song. I ruffle his hair up, open the curtain so I can see into the living room from outside, and head back out.

It's blazing, and the cool, soapy water is a refuge for my hot arms as I dip my sponge into the bucket. I turn on my little radio and catch a Donna Summer song that's already halfway through.

That's when I feel it. I'm being watched.

The feeling is instant and it's certain. I stand up and turn to the street. It's a typical Friday afternoon. Kids are playing down the street, a few people are mowing the lawn, but it's the dark car that catches my attention. It drives by slowly, the driver's side facing me. The window is tinted and open just enough so that I can only see his eyes. And while he's far away, they are vivid. In fact, they are some of the clearest turquoise eyes I have ever seen. This is not the first time I have had this feeling. And this deja vu tells me maybe it's not the first time I have seen those eyes. I don't look away. Instead, I meet his gaze, trying to focus on those eyes. My stomach rolls with a mixture of nervousness and excitement. Eyes like that can only be part of something beautiful. And yet, that should be irrelevant. I should scoff at anyone showing interest in me, particularly in this manner. I'm already taken. And I am above random gawkers.

There's something else though, something familiar, but he's too far away for me to be sure. A few days ago, I was at the library studying for a test, and the same feeling struck me as I looked through the quiet basement level for nursing books. I had pulled out a book from a shelf and gasped when I saw a pair of eyes on the other side. They were just as clear as these staring back at me, with a distinct marker: in his left eye, there was a fleck of golden brown. In eyes that clear— like when the water at the beach is so pristine I can see my feet—golden-brown flashed like gold leaf. Just as fast as I caught sight of those eyes peering through endless rows of books, they were gone. A chill came over me and I quietly walked over to peek on his side of the shelves, but there was no one. I didn't even hear his footsteps. He was so quiet, I even wondered if I had imagined him due to the sleepless nights of studying that preceded the encounter.

Are those the same eyes? They can't be. Before I can assess any further, the window is rolled closed and the dark car turns in the distance.

I stare at the vehicle as it rolls away, wrestling with this new sense of paranoia. I'm stressed. I've got nursing school, work, a busy boyfriend, and taking care of Johnny. This is simply stress manifesting itself in other ways. I think about telling my mother or my boyfriend, Carter, but what can I say? I made contact with a mesmerizing pair of eyes at the library? That some guy drove by and gawked at me washing my car in a bikini and cut-off shorts? Sounds like the life of any remotely attractive female.

But there was something more to the paranoia. Something I wouldn't even fully acknowledge myself, yet alone tell Carter or my mother. This feeling of worry intermingled with something deeper— an intense feeling of being coveted. Not the disgusted feeling I get from a guy catcalling or trying to sweet talk me, but a quiet longing. I have been with Carter so long, I have forgotten what it is like to play the game. To enjoy those stares from men that lasted a little longer than they should have. I have made myself impervious to them, turned off my sexuality for anyone but my long-faithful boyfriend.

Except this time. This time, I couldn't turn off the curiosity. Wondering if the man I had seen or thought I saw at the library had come around to my side of the bookcase, would the rest of him been just as stunning as those eyes? Without a word, would he have pushed me against the books so hard they would have rained off the shelves around me? Would he have pinned me, and fucked me fiercely until I came, pulling me out of the routine and obligations I had found myself bound to? I fantasized a couple of times about those eyes when I slept with Carter, just to help get me over the edge. I liked dirty thoughts, forbidden thoughts. The more forbidden, the more aroused I became, but I could never tell Carter that. I didn't want him to feel inadequate. Besides, fantasies are private. They live in your head, not to be made real.

There's a tug on my shorts. Johnny can't call my name, so

I'm used to his touch. "Mmmhmm," I answer, my mind still off in the far-away thoughts. I decide Johnny is more important than a couple of meaningless encounters, and give him my full attention. "You hungry?" I ask.

He nods.

"Grilled cheese?"

He shakes his head.

"Cereal?"

He nods.

"Okay. I'll finish this up later. Let's get you inside." I lead Johnny to the door, but before entering, I cast one last look behind me to the now empty street. Just like at the library, I am left again with a hollow suspicion.

SAM

I'm itching for the feeling again. It's been a week since the last house and already I need more. It's gotten worse this past month, ever since I first spotted Vesper. But I'm not ready for her yet. There's still more planning to be done. The last home I hit, on the same day I snatched Vesper's necklace, quelled the urge, but it's back faster and fiercer than ever. I've never wanted anyone so badly.

For now, I'll have to settle for the Hoeksmas. I've been watching them for a few weeks. She's an ER nurse, he's a teacher. They have a pretty ranch in Rancho Sol. I know tonight she's not on call and they'll likely fuck. They're usually like ships passing in the night because of her schedule. So when she's off, they make sure to get it in. I'll wait until they're asleep and naked. She'll be tired from her three weeks of non-stop work, and he will be in a deep sleep from fucking.

I walk from my getaway—a car parked several streets away. It's past midnight and this residential area is quiet. Only a few lights still shine through the windows of the ranches and split-level homes with manicured front lawns. I blend in just fine with my dark wig and matching mustache. My passage is a series of canals that connect several neighborhoods. They are barren and dark and make getting from point A to B quicker. I use the canals to get from my car to a couple of streets down from the Hoeskma's house. For the next two blocks, I am a late night jogger in a black sweat suit.

I tuck my chin down as I proceed so if anyone does pass, they won't get a clear view of my face. These small adjustments are important. As long as no one ever gets a clear view of me, and I get away from the scene, they'll never be able to identify me. I am always changing, so any picture painted of who I am will be blurry.

The jog to the house is easy. I only pass one person, a man walking a dog who doesn't even bother to look at me. I turn towards the vacant house neighboring the Hoeksma residence, put on my gloves, and hop the wooden fence into their yard. Just as I predicted, all the lights are off, but their cars are in the driveway. They're sleeping in there, but it's still too early. I know the night. I flourish in the darkness. And for me, 3:15 is the quietest time of night. Far beyond most people's ability to stay up late, and too early for even the earliest riser. It's when you are secure in your sleep, in the safety of your warm covers, when you think you are most alone. That's when I come, when every last guard is down.

I wait patiently behind the bushes for hours, until every last light shining from the houses around me goes dark. It's finally about three and time for me to begin. Connie and Don use a window air conditioner and it roars loudly in their bedroom. I'll still be quiet, but I am less concerned that they can hear me over the white noise. Before I step out of the shrubs, I pull a black balaclava out of my pocket and slide it on. I head to a potted plant by their sliding glass door, where I hid a large screwdriver the last time I was here. I work the door, prying it open, trying not to make a sound, but the hunger is growing. The excitement is creeping up. Weeks of planning and I am so close to another house, another life, another rush.

Their glass door frame is thicker than usual, but eventually I am able to finally bend it, reach the latch, and jimmy it open. I take a deep breath, my hands shivering with the thrill, and slide the door. I listen for sounds of life. Nothing. There's a reason it's called the dead of night.

The sliding door leads directly into the living room of the well-maintained ranch. I have mastered moving quietly. I don't make a sound as I approach the sofa and lift a couch cushion where I have hidden duct tape. I take in the pictures hanging throughout living room one final time.

The happy couple. The nurse and the teacher. They sleep blissfully, taking for granted the life they have.

They want to hurt you again.

I creep to the bedroom door. Last time I was here, I oiled the hinges so they wouldn't make a sound as I entered. Carefully, I turn the knob. It's not locked, and I gently push the door open. It glides beautifully, not letting out even the slightest of creaks.

I approach the foot of the bed and watch them sleep. Don is on his stomach, a sheet haphazardly covering his bare ass, one leg hanging out of the covers.

Doesn't he know the boogeyman can grab it?

Connie is on her back, one of her tits is peeking out, her midsection and pussy are covered, and both of her legs are sprawled open. Her hair is spread across the pillow. She lies there exposed, secure that her husband can protect her. But my shadow rests across her partially nude body.

She's delicate. She's pretty. But she's not Vesper. I hate that she makes me do that. Each hit used to be perfect, existing as its own entity. Each experience new, unique with its own flavor. Now I find myself comparing each home to what it would be like if Vesper was there instead. She's stealing my thrill. I'll make her pay for that.

Connie and Don breathe slowly, their shallow breaths indicating they are unaware of my presence. I stand there for a few minutes, each one that passes adding to my power and their vulnerability. It builds. Until I am as charged as I can be without waking them, until I am throbbing with the unfulfilled craving. I pull out a handgun from my holster and a small flashlight from my pocket. I place the tape on the nightstand next to Connie.

Then I flash the light in her eyes.

She squints, shielding her eyes from the bright light. "Wake up," I growl.

"What? Oh my god. Don—?"

"Shhh," I say, putting the gun to her forehead.

Don stirs.

"Grab the tape," I say, shining at the roll resting beside her. She stares at me, her eyes like globes, her mouth agape, as she reaches for it.

Don raises his head, still disoriented. I shine the light in his eyes and he opens them but clamps them shut immediately, shielding his face. "What the fuck?" he mutters, scrambling to an upright position.

"Don't move," I keep my voice hushed, disguising its real tone. "I just want your money." This is the critical part. There are two of them and one of me. I need to pacify them. I need Don taped up. It's easier to control the mind than the body.

"Okay, whatever you want man," he says, trying to stand up. "Just please take what you want and go."

"Don't move," I command. "Connie, tape him."

She's petrified. Her hands quiver as she grabs the tape, but her eyes are glued on me. She can't see me. Not with the mask and the light in her eyes, but she's trying. "Tape his hands together, then his feet."

"Please don't hurt us," she begs, her voice quavering in terror.

"Just do what I say, and you'll be fine."

She tries to cover her nude body with the sheet.

"No," I say. "There's no time for that."

She pulls the tape open, barely able to rip it off the roll because of her nervous hands, but she finally gets it.

"Keep going. I don't want to see his hands at all." She completely envelops his hands in the tape. "Now his ankles. At least ten times around. Count them out loud."

"One…" she whimpers. She stops.

"Count them all," I grunt.

"Three…four…five…"

I wait until she's done. Until the main threat is lying on his side, bound. I rip the tape from her hands and tie her hands behind her back.

"It's gonna be okay," Don whispers to her.

"Shut up," I order. He's completely emasculated. I'm the man of this fucking house now. This is my fucking castle.

Once she's taped up, I pull Don off the bed and onto the floor. He hits the green shag carpet with a thud. Now, he can see nothing over the bed.

"Show me where your purse is," I demand, pulling Connie to her feet and dragging her to the living room. Now it's just us. Now

Don doesn't exist. I have conquered everything that is his. I grab a blindfold.

"But you said—"

"If you don't shut up, I'll fucking kill him," I rasp into her ear. There will be no more assurances of safety. Now I am in complete control. I bind her feet together as she sobs.

"You have a choice," I declare in a low gruff. I walk over to their fireplace and grab a poker.

"Oh my god," she cries.

"I hit him, as hard as I can, with this. Five times in the head, five times in the stomach. Or I fuck you." I wave the poker tauntingly in front of her. "How much do you love him?"

"Please don't," she whimpers, bowing her head in complete submission.

"Choose or I'll choose for you."

"Don't hit him. I'll do it," she answers in defeat.

"Well, it's not your choice. It's his."

"Please don't!" she begs, a little louder than I'd like. I tape her mouth shut and blindfold her. There's a few more things I need to do to make sure this script goes according to plan. I make my way to the kitchen and grab a stack of dishes, leaving behind Connie in the living room.

I speed back to the bedroom and find Don trying to chew off his restraints.

"Just take whatever you want," he repeats.

"You have a choice. I gave the same one to Connie." I hold the poker in front of me menacingly. "You either take five, full-force hits to the head, five to the stomach. Or I fuck her. You wanna guess what she chose?"

"You sick fuck!" he scowls. "You said you just wanted money."

"She told me to come here and bash your fucking head in. But I think I'll veto. I'd much rather have some pussy."

Don desperately tries to pull out of his restraints, but I pull him by his hair, extending his neck, and tape his over his mouth and eyes.

"Get on your fucking hands and knees." He holds his kneeling position defiantly.

"Hands and fucking knees," I repeat. "She has a chance to live." I place the gun to his temple. Without having to say another word, he obeys. I place the stack of dishes on his back. I whip a pillowcase off one of the pillows and cover his head. I use tape to secure it around his neck.

"If you try anything, I'll hear it. I'll kill you, then I'll kill her."

The pillowcase draws in and out with each breath. I realize combined with the tape on his mouth he might suffocate. I'm not here to kill. The threats are just another means for control. So I pull a hunting knife out of my ankle holster and cut a small slit in the fabric for more ventilation. That's as much generosity as he is getting from me. The stage is set, and it's time to make all of this mine.

I come back to the living room. Connie is on her knees, frantically turning her head, trying to get a sense of where I am. She has no idea I'm right in front of her. I push her down to the floor and she wails, but it's muffled under the duct tape. She's trying to say something. Probably begging. But it's pointless. I don't know mercy.

I pull off my sweatpants grabbing one of her tits to get me going. Normally, I'd be rock hard, but today I'm not all the way there.

A plate crashes. Son of a bitch. I run back to the bedroom. Don is still in place, one of the plates slid off the top. "Don't fucking test me," I snarl. I remember the lube is in her nightstand drawer. I didn't need to bring my own as they have a healthy supply.

When I come back to the living room, Connie is hopping towards the front door. Blindfolded, naked, and bound, I almost admire her tenacity, but anger is the overriding response. I grab her by the waist and pick her up in one motion. She writhes and kicks, but she's back on the floor in seconds.

I mount her, rubbing the lube on myself as I rub my head against her pussy. It won't fucking get all the way hard.

"Fuck. Shit," I hiss. She cries harder, afraid my words signal bad news for her.

This almost happened last time. And only one thing made my dick grow so solid I could come without even entering: thinking of her. That fucking girl. The beautiful one I saw at the grocery store. The one with the little boy who she looked at lovingly. Who had the nice life with the boyfriend and the parents. I close my eyes and imagine her: her champagne-colored eyes, her smooth skin, her firm ass and pert tits.

This is our house. We have this life. For these next couple of hours. I can have it all. She'll smile at me the way she does in those pictures. I'll be in on the joke instead of part of it.

Imagining Vesper's face twisting in a mix of agony and pleasure makes my cock grow thick and firm. I thrust. And I thrust, holding her name on the tip of my tongue. I can't give anyone a reason to warn her that she's next, so it stays there, begging to be uttered.

The warm clench massaging my cock is her pussy. And if this fantasy can feel this good, I don't know how I can handle it when the real thing comes. I barely hear Connie's cries as I come, erasing the last man who was in her. She's not even there anymore, she's just a placeholder until I can get the ultimate target.

I pull out, relieved, the unrelenting fire that rages in me momentarily snuffed. I don't bother to put on my pants. This isn't over. There's so much more I have left to do. I go through their house, tossing things around, trying to remember it all. Trying to somehow live their entire lives in these two hours. Connie has a lot of medical books. But she also likes old classics: Pride and Prejudice, Anna Karenina, Les Liaisons Dangereuses.

Don likes model cars. They don't have kids, but he keeps a lot of pictures of kids who I think are his nieces and nephews. I could do this gently. I could be quiet. But I want them to hear me tear their place apart. I want to continue to control them through fear. Their terror feeds me. And as long as they can hear me raging, they won't try anything stupid.

I open the front door. "I'm not ready yet," I hiss before closing it. It's just another red herring to make the cops look for someone who has an accomplice.

I have another go at Connie. Another reminder that Vesper is consuming my thoughts.

"Make it stop. Make it stop," I whine during my second bout of rifling through their things. Another distraction to make them think I'm delusional. I'm not delusional. I know exactly what I am doing. I show my face in the light of day. I am your neighbor. I am your brother. I am the guy who builds you that beautiful deck or fixes your broken front door knob.

By now it's 4:15 or so and I am famished. I open up the fridge and find some leftover chicken. I eat it on their back patio, relishing in the act of eating their—my—food. Everything of theirs is mine. This is my life as long as I am here. I glow in the act of eating outside, their neighbors oblivious to the goings on just feet away.

It's so quiet at this time, you would think no one even lives in this neighborhood. This is my hour. The darkness belongs to me. They shunned me. They forgot me. But I never went away. I am here. I am their living nightmare.

Once my belly is full, I know it's time to go. I can't stay past dawn. The early risers will be up and about. I leave the carcass on the patio table and go back in. I put my pants on and sweep the house for anything I don't want to leave behind before slipping out the patio door again.

"Hey!" A man's voice shouts from the street. It's okay, these things happen. I have my mask on. I have my gloves on. I don't even look back at him. Instead, I run in the opposite direction and hop a fence, then another, and another. I run towards the vast canal system I use, like a main artery to get me from one neighborhood to the next.

I lose that guy easily. Once I am in the brush, I catch my breath, pull off the balaclava, the gloves, the black wig and mustache, and tuck them all into my pockets as securely as I can. I pull off the dark sweatshirt and throw it in the brush, revealing a white t-shirt. I brush my light brown hair back, and walk back out to the street where my car is. I pass another obnoxiously early riser out with his dog. He nods at me and I keep my chin down, so he can't make out my face in the pre-dawn light, and give him a quick wave.

It's only a few more steps before I am in my car, calmly driving away, towards the interstate and my freedom. It won't be long until I have to feed the urge again. I don't know how much longer these morsels can hold me when I have been preparing a feast.

CHAPTER 2

VESPER

I lounge in front of an episode of Sanford and Son, waiting on a fresh batch of popcorn. Johnny is tucked in and my mom and stepdad left for the airport a few hours ago. It's just me in this quiet house on a Saturday night. I should go out more, but I often have to watch Johnny and I am usually tired from school and work. Carter and I even had plans to go out to a fancy dinner tomorrow, but when my mom decided on her way back from the Caribbean that she was going to book a last minute trip to Egypt, I had to drop them.

Once the popping sounds from the kitchen slow from their initial burst, I run over to pull the pot off the stove and melt some butter. When I reenter the living room, hugging my bowl of warm popcorn, Sanford and Son has ended and the evening news has taken its place. On the screen is a zoomed-in black and white sketch of a man's face, mostly obstructed by a ski mask.

"Police say the man attacked a couple in their Rancho Sol home," a reporter says. Rancho Sol is a subdivision, not twenty minutes away from here by car.

The image zooms out so it's hovering over the shoulder of the reporter, with the words "The Night Prowler." I fixate on the image. There have been a rash of break-ins all over Sacramento County. It's one of the reasons why Carter insists on staying with me when I am babysitting Johnny alone. But Carter won't be able to come over until much later tonight. I look over to the picture window that faces the main street and wonder what I would do if on the other side of the blinds was that masked face staring back at me. The cozy feeling of holding a fresh bowl of popcorn in the comfort of my home is overcome with the insecurity of the unknown.

The doorbell rings. The popcorn flies out of my arms and I fumble with it, saving it from tipping over, but not before making a small mess.

I tiptoe to the window, peer through the shades and am surprised to see Carter is here earlier than I had anticipated. I let out sigh of relief, placing the bowl on the coffee table, and open the door with a wide smile on my face.

"You're early!"

"I thought I'd surprise you." He gives me a soft peck on the lips that turns into something more, but then he stops himself and looks over my shoulder.

"Don't worry, he's in bed," I whisper mischievously.

"So does that mean *we* can go to bed?" he asks, pushing into the house with my body laced in his arms so that the door shuts behind him.

"I suppose so," I tease.

Carter locks the door behind him, still pressing his lips to mine, and picks me up by my butt. "That feels niiiice," he mutters against my lips as he leads me to my bedroom.

I pull away and press my finger against his lips. If Johnny wakes up, it'll be a bear to get him back in bed.

"It's like we already have kids," he whispers, nine-tenths jokingly, one-tenth annoyed.

Carter lowers me to my feet and pulls off his shirt. He is a catch: kind, loyal, a med student. Oh— and tall, blond, with honest brown eyes and a jawline most models would covet. We've been together for over three years. He was my first serious boyfriend. First everything to be honest.

I slide my tank dress to the floor, leaving myself naked besides my panties. He kisses me and sits on the bed, pulling me towards him by my fingertips.

The room is dark, but the light from the living room beaming into my bedroom is enough to illuminate him. His tousled blond hair and warm eyes glitter as they reflect the light. His long, lean limbs glimmer in the dark. He's everything I should want. He's everything I *do* want. But though I am going through the motions, nothing stirs inside of me. It's always the same. And for a while that was enough, but I have found myself wondering about more. Wondering about what it would be like to be with someone different. Someone who wasn't so safe.

Carter is hot cocoa with marshmallows. Sometimes I wish he'd be a shot of absinthe.

But I love him. And he is everything I could ever want. This is just a lull. So, I go with the routine, sliding my panties to the floor and mounting him.

"Mmmm, Vesper," he groans as I rub myself against him. I'm not wet, so I can't slide onto him. I keep kissing him, faking passion in hope things will turn. That his kiss, like a flame to gasoline, will light me up, but nothing sparks. I feel safe. I feel secure in arms. But today, I can't feel aroused.

I kiss Carter's neck, closing my eyes to imagine the ones I saw at the library. Imagining him coming into the restaurant where I work a few nights a week. It's empty, so most of the lights are off. I can barely make him out, but those eyes tell me everything I need to know. I tell him I'm about to close up. He says he just wants a piece of pie. I relent. I go behind the counter and turn away from him to reach into the pie case. Then I feel his breath on my neck. I startle, but I don't scream.

"Don't turn around," he rasps, reaching his right hand down my thigh, sliding it up and lifting my skirt. He pulls my panties to the side as his other hand reaches up and grips my neck.

"Don't say a word," he whispers, clenching his fingers around my airway. He tugs my underwear down roughly, so that it rests halfway down my thighs, and then he pushes his way into me. I'm wet. So wet. And I let him pump into me. Dark. Dirty. Forbidden. A secret I will keep from my family. I'll tell myself it's fear that keeps me quiet. But it's because I didn't fight. I let him take me. He smelled the need, like an animal sniffing out prey, and he pounced.

As the stranger grunts into my ear, I tighten around his thickness. A swelling in my belly overwhelms me, taking my breath away.

I open my eyes. "Carter!" I call out. That's how I convince myself that this is okay. It's still Carter inside of me. My skin touching his skin. His brown eyes I stare into. His name I call out when I finally come. He doesn't need to know I just let a stranger fuck me, using his body as a proxy.

"Oh baby," he utters, pumping himself inside of me. I watch the pleasure roll over his face as my orgasm weakens. If I had kept my eyes closed, if I had imagined the stranger, it would have gripped me. It would have taken my breath away. But I can't do that to Carter. So I rejoin him, and instead of that build up exploding like a bomb, it fizzles like a bum fire cracker.

Nonetheless, we come together. I collapse onto him for a second before rolling away and onto the bed, feeling unfulfilled. Feeling a tension between my legs that begs for a stronger release. Carter lies down next to me, perching his head on his hand, smiling, taking me in.

I feel guilty every time I do that. Every time I go somewhere else. I wouldn't feel so bad if it was a greedy act, something extra on top of my lust for him. But at this point, I need it. I need it to stay wet. I need it to come. I need it to engage at all.

After a trip to the bathroom, and getting dressed, I return to the bedroom. We don't have the luxury of mulling around naked. I watch Johnny so much it *is* like we have a child. And I love Carter for being so patient about that. A good-looking, smart, kind guy like him should be enjoying weekends out. Movies, parties, bars. But most of the time he's stuck with me, bound to responsibilities he never signed up for. I tell him he doesn't need to stay here with me, he can go join his buddies. He's in medical school and needs a break too. But he always ends up here.

Carter leans over and switches on a dim table lamp. "So, she's gone another two weeks?" he snickers. He really is patient, but he's not a saint. We're both so busy and I know it disappoints him that the little time we have together is often spent watching a special needs child.

"Yup. Pete has accrued so much time off, it's like they can't stop going on vacation. She keeps saying they're going to take him somewhere like Disney, but when was the last time they took him anywhere?"

"I just don't understand why you take her crap. He's not your responsibility."

I sit up sharply. "He's my brother."

"You know I didn't mean that," he rebuts apologetically. "I love him, too. But your mom takes advantage of that. She knows it's in your nature to take care of others, especially him. And she just dumps him on you. You're young. You should be letting loose."

"I've scolded her a million times. But they pay for my schooling, and I get to keep living here for free, and she holds that over my head. Like I earn my keep here by being his nanny. And you're right, I won't have him put in a stranger's care, not for the length of time she leaves." I tuck my knees up to my chest and wrap my arms around them. "She has the upper hand. And I hate even having this talk because it makes me feel like I think Johnny is a burden. I am happy to watch him. He's such a good kid. And I'm here bitching about my life, when he's the one who's been dealt the unfair hand."

"Hey," Carter rests a hand on my lower leg reassuringly. "It's okay to be frustrated. This has nothing to do with your love for him. It has to do with your mom using that and using you. You take care of everyone else. I just want to make sure someone watches out for you."

"I do have someone who watches out for me," I say with a gentle smile, resting my hand on his. I mean it, even though we only get to see each other once a week lately, and I can't be his primary focus with the pressures of med school, I know his thoughts are with me.

"I try. I know it seems like I'm always working or at school. But I will always be here for you. And I will make sure that you have fun and that you get to experience all life has to offer."

Carter's tone is exceptionally tender, and somewhat larger than this conversation calls for. Like he's making a proclamation. He sits up and reaches into his pocket.

"I was saving this for the dinner we had planned this weekend, then your mom made the last minute trip and we had to cancel. I was going to wait, but I don't want to wait anymore, not a second longer."

My eyes grow, my heart races. All the signs of what is about to happen are in front of me, but I won't believe it until I hear the words. He pulls a box out of his pocket and drops to one knee beside me on the bed.

"Vesper Rivers," his voice wobbles, a contrast to the relaxed tone he had seconds before. "You are the most beautiful, generous, selfless, kind-hearted person I know. I want to be the man you deserve. And I would be humbled and honored if you would be my wife."

"What?" I ask, unable to process the scene transpiring in front of me.

He chuckles nervously. "Vesp, will you marry me?"

"Will I—? Uh, ye—yes," I answer, laughing.

He grabs my hand and slides on a solitaire ring. We embrace. Any nagging doubts or guilt I had earlier washes away. This feels good. This feels right. I couldn't pick a better man to be by my side in life.

As I pull away to look at Carter, he's beaming. "I love you, Vesp."

"I love you, too."

We stare at each other for a few seconds, not knowing how to handle the enormity of this new commitment.

"Wait," he says, throwing his hands up as if a new idea just struck him.

"I brought some champagne. It's in the car. I didn't want to cause suspicion. Let me get that. Then I'll call my mom and dad quick. You want to call yours?"

"She's…" I swirl my finger towards the sky.

"Oh yeah, on a plane," he chuckles awkwardly. "Alright, be right back with glasses and bells on."

"Okay," I nod with an anxious smile.

Carter runs to the door, and then stops, turning to run back to me. He darts a kiss on my lips. "I love you. Thank you."

I laugh. He can be so adorable. "I love you, too," I respond, shaking my head. "Now go, get the wine so we can celebrate!" I shoo him towards the door.

Carter runs out of the bedroom looking like an overjoyed, floppy-eared pup as I admire my ring. Like most girls, my thoughts immediately go to the wedding. What will I wear? What other jewelry would match the simple, yet elegant gold ring? The necklace my grandmother gave me would go perfectly. I used to wear it all the time, but after I almost lost it during a trip to Lake Tahoe, I keep it in a jewelry box, only to be used for special occasions.

Well, a wedding proposal is a special occasion, isn't it?

I open the jewelry box, resting on the top of a tall dresser, fingering through a few earrings and other necklaces, but I don't see the crescent moon charm.

"Huh?" I mouth to myself, switching on a tall lamp just beside me to get a better view. But I still can't find it. My heart races. This necklace is precious to me. My mother was a carefree hippy when I was a child. I spent most of my younger years in a commune. My mother was often busy tending to her own needs, and my grandmother, a child of the greatest generation, did not approve. She would take the long drive north whenever she could to pick me up and spend the weekend. She doted on me. She was what a mother should be. I lost her when I was thirteen and it was utterly devastating. She gave me this necklace on my thirteenth birthday shortly before she died. My name means evening prayer, so she said every night she looked up at the moon and prayed for me. And that this necklace reminded me of her.

By the time Carter returns to the room, the joy of the proposal is overtaken by full-blown panic. I had upturned every jewelry box onto my bed, and the necklace was nowhere to be found.

"What's going on?" he asks, his smile quickly changing to a frown of concern.

"I can't find the moon necklace. The one my grandma gave me," I tell him, holding back tears.

"Okay, well just calm down. I'm sure it's here. When was the last time you saw it?"

"I—I don't remember exactly. But I know for a fact I put it in this box," I proclaim, presenting it to him. "I know I did. I don't wear it because I almost lost it a long time ago and I spent hours combing the shores of Lake Tahoe trying to find it."

"Well, maybe you put it somewhere else."

"No, I didn't," I snap. Maybe I'm going crazy. Maybe that man at the library was a vision. Maybe my memory is shot from the stress of classes and taking care of Johnny and my strained relationship with my mother.

I can tell Carter is disappointed by the shift the night has taken, but I have become a woman obsessed.

"I'm sorry Carter, but I won't be able to relax until I find this thing. It's all I have left of her. Something personal between us."

"I understand," he says, somewhat defeated. "How can I help?"

"You remember what it looks like?" I ask.

"Sort of."

"Wait I have a picture up here from the last time I wore it. It's really clear on there." I rifle through my picture board, looking for the picture I took at Lake Tahoe just before I lost it the first time.

"Okay, now I feel like I'm going insane," I mutter.

"What?" he asks.

"I can't find the fucking picture," I tamp down my urge to raise my voice. Waking up Johnny would only add to the stress, and my patience is as thin as a hair.

"Okay. Don't worry about it. It's a moon. I know what a moon looks like," Carter says with some levity. "Let's give it an hour. After that, you need to let the thing find you. That's how it works. Deal?"

"Okay, but if I don't, I don't—" I bury my head in my hands. I feel the metal of the ring dig against my finger. Shit. He proposed and here I am just sucking all the joy out of tonight.

"We'll go to sleep and tomorrow, when we're fresh and well-fed, we'll go on the hunt again. I promise."

I peek up through my fingers. "Deal," I pout. "I'm sorry. I'm ruining everything. This night was so perfect."

He runs a caring hand along the top of my head. "Hey, if I can't handle you through a lost necklace, what are you doing agreeing to marry me?"

I snicker.

"You'll find it. I know you will."

Carter offers his hand to me and I reach out for it. Seeing the sparkling ring on my finger is a pleasant shock. I made the right choice.

SAM

Tonight was just supposed to be recon. I wanted to watch, learn more about her routines. Find out if there will ever be a time the kid won't be there. But shit, it seems like the kid is always with her. You'd think she's his fucking mom. She was alone for a while, which was nice. I watched her slender silhouette through her bedroom window as she changed into a simple dress. I watched her fondly tuck in her brother. She moved to the living room. It's harder to watch her there as the window faces the main street. It's safer in the bushes on the sides and back of the house.

So I wait by her bedroom. She'll be back eventually. Then I'll watch her evening routine. Experience her quiet, simple life. When she's home without her parents, it's easy to imagine myself in the house, eating a home-cooked meal she made for me, watching her undress to join me in bed.

They'll always tease you. No one understands you like I do.

The intrusive thoughts interrupt the fantasy. She'd never want me. I'll have to take her. I'll show her she's no better than me. Just like all the others. They groveled at my feet. They begged. I was their god. They all think they're smarter than me, but they're not. They're just ants in a farm I can squash whenever I feel like reaching in.

An hour or so passes and she's back in the room. But instead of a sweet angel who I can admire putting herself to bed, she's with him. That fucking prince. The guy who has probably never known a true trial since the day he was born. I can only see their outlines with the lights off. I watch, huffing like an angry bull as she mounts him. It's mix of rage and arousal as it often is. Soon it'll be me, I tell myself. That makes it bearable. My throbbing cock begs for me to relieve myself in the bushes, but I resist. I want to save my nut for her. I want it to be so hard she screams as I puncture her. I refuse to relieve myself until I am inside of her.

They finish. They go about their business. It's the boring, monotonous stuff of living. Getting dressed. Going to the bathroom. The type of stuff I can watch mindlessly for hours if I allow myself. It lulls me into a hypnotic state. It's like watching a moving Norman

Rockwell painting, except now everyone's got beards, long hair, and bell bottoms.

The guy turns on a lamp, so I can get a clearer view. I have to be careful, but as long as I stay low and make no sudden moves, they won't know I'm out here. It looks like they're talking about something serious. It's intimate. I've never really known intimacy. Watching it makes me ache, and then it makes me angry. I'd rather be angry than feel longing.

Suddenly, Mr. Perfect gets up. Then he's on his knees. This can't be fucking happening. This cannot be fucking real. The ache burns. It's like being punched in the stomach over and over again. It's like someone reaching in and clenching my heart with a handful of hot, shattered glass.

As I have trained myself to do, I convert the longing into fury. And this time, there is so much of it that I boil into a blind rage. I need to expel this fire building in me. My instinct is to tear the bush in front of me to shreds. I tighten my fists as the lovebirds embrace, trying to contain the wrath that ascends in me like a flash flood.

Patience.

Fuck patience.

They mock me. They taunt me. Their white smiles and flawless faces show me the life I will never have. It's like they know I'm here and want to shove it in my face.

You can't trust them. Did you think you ever had a chance with her?

Fuck plans. I'm going to steal their joy just like they have so harshly snatched mine. He can't have her. I'm going to put my mark on her. I'm going to make Vesper mine. I'm going to be with them when they walk down the aisle. I'll be laced in every memory, every milestone.

I'm going in tonight.

CHAPTER 3

SAM

I wait.
And wait.
And wait.

It takes a while for Vesper to finally settle into bed. From what I could tell, she noticed that the necklace was missing. That's rare. Most people don't notice the things I have taken until after I've hit. I can tell what I took is important; it's nice to know the token I have of hers has so much emotional capital. That I'll always have an important part of her to relive what will happen tonight.

I'm not prepared. At least not as much as I would be if I came here tonight with the intentions of going in. But it's enough. I know the house. I left a roll of twine. The boy is there, but the parents are gone, so that's good enough. Mr. Perfect is there. That's great news. He won't be so perfect when I'm through with him.

My point of entry into the house is through her parent's bedroom. I cut the screen to access the window and pried it open when they were last out of town. I patched the screen up when I left, and they were none the wiser. So today, all it takes is a little yank on the seams of where I cut last to expose the window. And the window is unlocked just as I left it. I crawl in sideways, making sure that I am soundless. My heart races, but it's not nerves, it's being so close to something—someone—I have wanted more than anything ever before. It's the thought that this insatiable need will be fed.

But deep inside, I lament the thought of when this will end. It's always on to the next house, the next target. But she's the ultimate. The crown jewel. I'll have her once and then…what next? I don't let the thought steal my focus though. I've always managed and I'll manage after this.

My boots softly contact the burnt-orange carpet with each step. I pass the boy's room. He is sound asleep. I think about tying him up, but if he makes any noise resisting, I risk Vesper waking up. Then they'll have the jump on me. I'll make sure to keep them quiet so he doesn't wake. I'll use their protectiveness as a tool to control them. Despite what you may think of me, I don't want to scare the kid if I don't have to. He's had it tough enough. So instead, I reach in and close the door without a sound.

I pass their bedroom, the door ajar, and peek in. Doctor Handsome is shirtless and in track shorts. Vesper is wearing this white cotton baby doll thing. The way the pale blue moonlight hits her body, it's almost see through. I want to pounce her right there, but I have to keep to the script. It's what's allowed me to do this in dozens of homes without the cops having an inkling of who I am.

I head to the living room to take in the scene. One last time before the madness. When all is quiet and unharmed. Just before their untouched lives are sullied by my fingerprints. There are many pictures of her mother Joan, and her step-father, Dr. Peter Reynolds. Spain. France. Thailand. Mexico. There's only one of Vesper and Johnny. It's just them. He's sitting on her lap and she's squeezing him, tickling him. He's laughing, his body misshapen from writhing and his condition. She's looking at him with a smile. Is she smiling at him? Or laughing at him?

I don't understand. I don't understand how a pretty, smart girl like that could love that boy unconditionally. She must remind him how he's different. She must make him feel left out sometimes. He's not like them. And those of us who are different, they always find ways to remind us. Even if they are your brother or sister. Even if they say they love you.

As soon as you open your mouth, they'll think you're a joke.
The lurking doesn't last long. I'm jittery with the urge to

finally touch Vesper.

I didn't bring a gun. Didn't think I'd need it tonight. So I'm forced to improvise. I go to the kitchen and pull the biggest, sharpest knife from the knife block. I hold it up and slowly twist it back and forth, admiring the way the moonlight flickers off of it. It excites me, holding this power in my hands. I walk to the massive picture window that looks out to the neighborhood. Just dark houses. Quiet. Stillness. I am the king of the night. They all lie with their necks exposed. Any one of them can be mine. But tonight—tonight is Vesper's turn to learn what it's like when the sun has hidden and cannot save you with its light. I pull the curtains closed over the shades and it feels like nothing exists out there. Like the world is everything within these walls.

I'm not prepared as I usually am, so I wander about, looking for items I can use as bindings. Dr. Peter keeps a tidy garage, so I access it from the mudroom, just off the kitchen. He has a few climbing ropes perfectly coiled, hanging off a few hooks just to the side of the door. I lift them and slide them over my shoulder.

It's time.

I walk into the bedroom. Her closet door is open, overflowing with dresses and shirts and scarves. I grab a couple of the scarves and drop them on the bed at their feet. The fabric catches air and falls to the bed like a weeping woman. I gently place the rope beside it so as not to disturb them. I secure the knife with an overhand grip.

Click.

The flashlight shines at her face.

I study her as she opens her eyes, but shuts them at the sting of the blinding light. She tries to make sense of it all as she opens them again and rubs them. But she won't be able to. None of this makes sense.

VESPER

It happens so fast. I'm dreaming of sunsets at Lake Tahoe and then the sun, once kissing my skin, is burning my eyes. No, it's not the sun. I'm not dreaming. This is real. Is that Carter? No, it's...I don't know. I open my mouth to call Carter's name.

"Don't scream," a gritty voice whispers. I can't see what's behind the bright light. I don't have time to think or rationalize. I just sit there, stunned. But it only lasts a second before I rebel.

"Carter!"

He jolts up in response to the alarm in my voice. The intruder shines a light at him, that's when I get a better look, but it's not much. His face is covered in a mask so that his lips and eyes peek through. I see little flashes of residual light in my vision, making it hard to adjust to the darkness.

"Who the hell are you?" Carter asks.

The man grabs my arm and pulls me up. I let out a cry, but suck it back in when a cold blade rests against my neck.

"Oh my god," I sob.

"I just want your money. I don't want to wake up the boy. Do you?"

Carter puts his palms out, showing he's willing to cooperate.

"Take whatever you want. Please just don't hurt her."

"I won't. Just do what I say."

The knife slips away from my neck, but as soon as that relief hits me, there's a poke in my back, just where my heart would be if the knife sliced through my ribs. I kneel in between him and Carter. Even if Carter, a 6'4" former collegiate volleyball player with a great reach could get to him, I'd get caught up between them. I'd probably get stabbed.

"Tie him up," the devilish voice orders.

"We'll do what you want. You don't have to tie—"

The knife pinches my skin. "Do it."

"O—okay." I reach carefully for the rope. It looks like my stepfather's climbing rope.

"Turn around," the masked man directs Carter. "Hands behind your back."

Carter purses his lips, his barely-awake mind wrestling with his options, and turns with a protesting huff. I sob as I wrap the rope around his hands.

"I'm sorry," I whisper to Carter.

"Don't talk. Tie it tight," the man grunts. I can tell he's trying to disguise his voice.

"It's okay, Vesp. Don't be sorry. Just stay calm."

"Enough."

I nod and tie the rope as weakly as I can without being obvious.

"Feet," he grumbles.

I take the other rope and bind Carter's feet.

The man pushes me to the side and tosses the flashlight haphazardly on the bed, so that it shines away from us.

"You run and I'll take the boy," he warns. My thoughts go to Johnny. He had been in the back of my mind, but the scene had been so focused to this room. I realize I have to do whatever it takes to keep that man away from him, even if it means to fully cooperate. He just wants money. I'll give him everything we have.

I sit at the edge of the bed, trembling, stifling my cries as he redoes my handiwork, tying Carter in a complex series of knots, attaching the feet and arms so that he's hog-tied. He grabs a tie-dye scarf from the bed and covers Carter's eyes. It's the first time I get a full view of the intruder, head to toe. He's not short, but not as tall as Carter, maybe five-eleven or six feet. I can tell through the dark shirt and military-style pants he's wearing that he's built. Not thick and muscular like a bodybuilder. More lithe, like an athlete. Like a lacrosse player. Carter may have him beat on height, but this guy looks more solid, and I'm not sure Carter could take him. I know I'd certainly be no match.

Once he has Carter immobilized, he turns his attention to me, walking over to the chair I keep by the closet and lifting the cushion. There's twine underneath it. It doesn't make sense.

He walks over to me, remarkably light on his feet, despite the tall black boots he's wearing. He reaches down and turns off the flashlight and puts it in his pocket.

"You okay?" Carter asks. He's lying on his side on the bed, facing away from me, but he tilts his neck a little to address me.

"Mmmhmm," I mutter, afraid of upsetting the man tying my hands behind my back. He reaches for the other scarf and places it in his pocket. Gripping the painfully tight ligature around my hands, he pulls me to my feet.

"Show me where your purse is," he commands, pushing me out the door. "Move and I'll kill all of you. I'll slit the boy's throat."

He closes the door behind him and shoves me against the opposite wall. He pulls twine out of his pocket and ties it around the bedroom door handle, dragging the other end across the hall to the bathroom, and ties it to that door handle. It makes it impossible for Carter to open the door, and if he tried it would be noisy. He blindfolds me next.

"How can I show you anything?" I snipe. He doesn't answer.

My gut twists in sickness. This is too much work for someone who wants a purse. But I'm bound and Carter is trapped, and Johnny is still tucked in bed. I have no choice but to quietly comply.

He yanks me by the arm and drags me to down the hall. His hands grip my waist and he sends me launching onto a bed. We're in my parents' room.

"No," I whimper. I want to scream, thrash, fight. But my hands are numb from the binds and he's strong. And if I run, he could hurt Johnny.

He crawls over me, using his knees to separate my legs. I resist, but what I mount is met with effortless handling.

His hands run up my thigh, over the papery fabric of my nightdress. He rubs his fingertips on one of my nipples. I writhe underneath him, but that only seems to encourage him, as I feel his hardness stab against my pelvis.

With the adrenaline shooting through my system and my sight stripped from me, my sense of smell becomes acute. He smells of grass and the hydrangea bushes outside the house. He must have crawled through them. He smells faintly of soap, as if he had showered before coming here. His clothes smell as though they have just been laundered. This is someone methodical. He's not deranged and filthy. That fact sends a chill down my back.

His warm breath forms a trail along my neck.

"I've waited for you," he whispers. "You're so beautiful."

I don't respond.

"Shit," he hisses. "Don't move."

The weight of his warm body lifts away and I am left cold and alone. I think he's left the room, but I'm not sure. He has an uncanny ability to make very little noise. I deliberate if I should book it. I can make it to the neighbors and they can call the police.

But I am paralyzed with indecision. Unsure of what will lead to survival and what would ultimately cause more trouble. Finally, I decide to try to make a run for it. Even blindfolded, I can feel my way out of the house if he's distracted. I have to try. I roll to my side and get myself upright.

I keep my legs on the edge of the bed to guide myself towards the door. Then I start to run.

Smack. I take about four steps before I hit a firm body. I can smell him. I quiver in fear. Will he hurt me? Will he hurt Johnny for my disobedience? I almost drop to the floor in terror.

He doesn't say anything. Instead, he again handles me like a doll, and rests on top of me.

"I gave Carter a choice. I told him ten haymakers to the face, or I fuck you. Guess what he said?"

"He wouldn't." Carter would never let another man have me.

"He did," the menacing figure whispers in my ear. "But you have a choice too. You can veto him. I can go to the other room and punch him as hard as I can in the face fifteen times, or I can fuck you. You're going to be a nurse Vesper; you know his face will be destroyed. He'll never be the same. That is if he survives."

How does he know things about me?

"Make the choice," he snaps, not giving me much time to give attention to the fleeting thought.

I imagine Carter, helplessly blindfolded on his knees. Unable to see the punches coming. Unable to brace. Spit and blood splattering on my bed and walls. His nose ending up on the side of his face. His eye sockets being crushed. I can do this. I can take the pain for both of us.

I don't want to believe he sent the man back here to rape me. And in my heart, I don't. But if he did, I don't blame him. At least my scars will be on the inside.

"Don't hurt him," I beg. "You…you can…"

"I can what?"

"Do it."

"Say it. Say it exactly how I said it."

"F—fuck me."

He breathes heavily, the warmth of it fanning across my chest. "You did the right thing, Vesper."

He knows me. Is this someone I trust? Someone at the

restaurant or school?

His gloved fingers run along my lips. "I'm gonna come inside of you. You make me so hard, Vesper." The desire makes it hard for him to hide his natural voice, which is even raspier than the disguised one.

His lips trace along my neck. It tickles. It feels good. My mind zig zags in confusion. I don't want this, but my nerve endings don't know how to translate his touch. I hear him shuffle, and then when his hands are on me again, the cold leather is gone and I am met with warm fingertips.

"You have such a beautiful body." He pulls up my nightgown. I am exposed, powerless, entirely submitted. "I've wanted to taste your cunt since the day I first saw you."

That word, it shocks me like a live wire. I've maybe heard it used once before.

Wet softness grips one of my nipples. His mouth. I sob, eyes and lips clenched, trying not to let cries escape. Johnny has slept through all of this so far by some miracle, and this can't have been for nothing.

"You're so fucking soft," he gristles, his mouth still sucking on my breast, confusing my body. I can feel the blood rushing between my legs. I want to tell it to stop, but I can't. I am just as much a prisoner to my body as I am to him. His fingers make their way between my legs. He gently slips them between my lips. Fondling me. Like my body is a toy for his pleasure. "You're fucking soaked."

I shake my head, tears streaming down my cheeks.

"I'm gonna watch my come drip out of those lips when I'm done with you, *Vesp*." He says Vesp, almost mockingly. Like he knows those dearest to me call me that. Like he and I are familiar. "I was going to make you suck me off first, but your pussy is so ready. Do you feel how hard I am?"

I don't answer.

"I asked a question." The blade of the knife makes a surprise appearance against my neck. Fear slices through me like a lightning bolt.

"Y--yes."

"You made the choice, Vesper. You didn't have to do this. You wanted me to. You walk around in those little shorts. Hanging out in front of your house with that bikini top, teasing with your hard nipples. You wanted me to come here."

I have a moment of clarity. The man, the one driving by. It's the only time I wore a bikini top in as long as I can remember.

"You were here," I whisper.

"Many times," he taunts.

Before I can engage any further, he takes my breath away as he slides his fingers into me. It's stunning. He had violated me already, yes, but this—he's inside of me now. Even if it's just his fingers. He's penetrating me.

"Please," I beg.

"Tell me you love it."

I shake my head.

He keeps rubbing, his palm pressing against my clit. I feel that build up I felt earlier today. I try to take my mind elsewhere, to stop it. The reverse of what I had to do with Carter.

"Don't upset me," he grunts. The knife cuts into my skin. "Tell me."

"I love it," I answer through tears. I can't tell if his rhythm is making my hips slowly rock or if it's my body involuntarily conceding. But before I can humiliate myself, he stops, giving me time to catch my breath.

His fingers meet my lips again. I can smell the faint aroma of sex on his fingertips. "Lick it with the tip of your tongue."

I sheepishly dart out my tongue to taste a hint of the saltiness.

"I want you to see this," he says, whipping off my blindfold. Our eyes lock. My eyes have adjusted to the darkness, and I gasp when I see his. They glow. They are the eyes I saw at the library with the signature golden fleck. A turquoise so pristine it picks up the low levels of light in the room and reflects it like two small moons. I wasn't imagining him these past few weeks. He's real. He's terrifyingly real.

He still has the mask on, but I watch as he licks my cream off of his fingers. "It tastes better than I have ever imagined. We're going to do a lot tonight. I'm gonna eat that pussy over and over. But first, I'm shoving my cock inside of you."

"Please, I'll give you everything I have." I bargain as a last ditch effort.

"That's what I'm taking," he remarks in a sinister tone, reaching down to pull himself out.

I look down against my better judgment to see a swollen head. He's pent up and massively aroused. It's thick, thicker than Carter who is not lacking in that department.

"You're mine, Vesper. I'm going to mark you like a fucking animal."

It's inevitable. I made my choice. To take this sacrifice for Carter and Johnny. I take care of people. It's what I do. I can live with this, but I can't live with them being hurt.

He presses the head up against my slick lips. I gasp as he slides it up and down, lubricating himself with my wetness. And then he's done being gentle, pushing against my tight, nervous muscles to penetrate me.

I suck in a sharp breath. My mind races with thoughts in that brief moment. Earlier today, I was agreeing to spend my life with the sweetest man I know. Now I'm bound in a room with someone who has been watching me. A man I naively fantasized about. But now he's real. He's here like somehow I subconsciously beckoned him. He's inside of me. Nothing will be the same.

He pulls in and out, in and out. Fucking me. Stretching me. I moan through tears as his free hand roves along my body, squeezing, rubbing. His teeth tug on my nipples. The other hand still holds the knife. His hand clenches it firmly like he's stopping himself from using it against me.

The intruder presses his lips against mine. The itchy wool of the mask scratches against my cheek as I open my lips, letting him conquer another hole. He's kissing me, and I find myself so utterly dominated that I let him do so without a fight. What's a kiss when he's already pulsing his dick inside of me?

He wraps his arm around me and pulls me up, so that he's kneeling on the bed and I am sitting on him. He rocks me up and down. I am his toy, helpless, my arms still tied behind me.

My confounded body and mind war as the cock inside of me stubbornly insists on taking me to a place I don't want to go. I tighten around him. My moans get louder, a mix of pleasure, fear and defeat.

"I'm gonna fill you, Vesp."

"No," I mewl.

"Yes." His throat quivers as he chuffs. "I can feel you clenching on my cock." He squeezes my ass. "I think you're different," he taunts.

"Fuck you," I sneer.

"You already are." He pulls me tightly towards him, so that I am so full, so overwhelmed with him, that I can't fight it any longer.

"No…no…" I cry as I near climax.

Then from the corner of my eye, I see it: a shadow. My eyes go huge and it catches the violator's attention.

Johnny's silhouette is standing quietly at the door.

CHAPTER

VESPER

till inside of me, the intruder's body goes rigid.

There are a few seconds of taut silence. I don't know what to say or do. I can tell he's working out what he'll do and I am terrified he'll act on his word and slit Johnny's throat.

I try to sniff back my tears. Maybe I can convince him everything is all right and send him back to bed.

I lean towards the man and whisper. "Please, let me put him in his room. He won't bother."

It looks like he's considering it, or considering I can see almost nothing of his facial expressions, it feels like he is. But that only lasts for a few moments as a noise comes from Johnny's mouth.

"MMMMM…MMMM…MMMM…" With each repetition the nonsensical sound gets louder. It's the loudest I have ever heard Johnny. His equivalent of a scream. Sometimes when he's upset he vocalizes, but not to this extent or this volume. People look at him and they think he's dumb. They think he doesn't feel like us. They dismiss him as a "retard." But he has instincts just like we do. Even though he can't verbalize his feelings, he comprehends them. He understands right and wrong and he knows this isn't right.

"Johnny…shhh!" I try desperately to quiet him. But he gets louder.

The man rips himself away from me and charges toward

Johnny with a knife in his hand.

"No, please!" I scream. If my silence can't save Johnny, then I don't care anymore. I'll scream. I'll fight.

He grips Johnny by the t-shirt.

"Please, I can make him stop!" I cry.

A thud. Loud. Coming from my bedroom. Carter must have found his way to the door. It sounds like he's slamming against it, trying to break it open. The thumping is loud and repetitive and adds a layer to the chaos.

It's strange. As frightened as I was, as violated as I was, I felt I could manage this. Things were quiet. I knew I could pacify this stranger with sex. But in seconds, everything I was protecting has dissolved into chaos.

"I'll kill him," the masked man threatens with a throaty husk. He's gripping Johnny, but he looks down the hall. It's clear he's referencing Carter.

He drags Johnny with him, who is still vocalizing loudly and unrelentingly.

"No!" I yell, chasing after him with my hands tied behind my back, my inner thighs wet from his intrusion. I stop when I see him in front of my bedroom door, holding Johnny tightly against him, the other hand resting at his side with the knife. The door to the bedroom is buckling at the bottom. I think Carter is still bound. Otherwise he would have tried the window. There's a long way to go before it breaks. And when it does, he's going to meet his death. He'll be no match tied up against a man with a ten-inch kitchen knife.

"I'm gonna carve your boyfriend's fucking heart out," the man growls.

Johnny's going at full volume. There's too much panic. Too much noise. Too much chaos. Where is everyone? How can no one hear the nightmare developing within these walls?

The violator holds the knife to Johnny's neck. "Shut up!" he grunts. But Johnny is in a full blown tantrum, the worst I have ever seen. His crooked lips contort as he tries desperately to speak like the rest of us, but the same pointless sounds come out.

This whole thing is out of control. This man planned everything. He had us bound in minutes. He's lost control and he'll do anything to get it back. So I do what I have to do. We can all die, or they can live and I can give this man what he wants. I don't want to live if that means watching my brother and fiancé die.

"Take me!" I beg. "Take me anywhere. Somewhere quiet. I won't fight just please don't hurt them," I sob. "Take me with you. It's what you came here for. Please," I drop to my knees, completely broken, hoping to appeal to a shred of humanity in him. To understand I would rather him rape and kill me than take the life of the eight-year-old boy in his arms. It would be an act of mercy.

"I love you, Johnny," I say softly, my voice quivering as I restrain the scream of terror that wrestles to escape.

The bedlam drifts into the background like an echo. I have played my last hand. And either way, I will likely die. I close my eyes and bow my head. "Please," I utter, so low, there's no way anyone could hear me. I don't want to look. I don't want to watch him kill my family.

A hand claws onto my arm, the pain jarring me back to the physical world. The noises, the feel of a hand on my skin, they focus me.

"Get up," he growls.

SAM

I learned about sex from watching the animals. I guess we all have to learn it somewhere. There were stretches of time, long after the accident, when my mother would lock herself in her room, that the animals were my only companions. I fed them. I watched the stallion mount the mare with his huge cock and take her. She would neigh and fight, but he would conquer her. That's how it works in most of nature. The male dominates the female.

I guess as far as I can think back, I had a tendency to watch. I couldn't say much. Couldn't participate. I wasn't welcome. This was my way of knowing the world.

I guess this night is how Johnny will learn about sex. Fuck. And this is why planning is fucking important. Vesper made me act on impulse with that whole proposal charade. Johnny's room doesn't have a lock. I only had so much rope. Carter was the threat, or at least so I thought. It turns out the closest I have ever been to everything falling apart was from the will of a disabled little boy.

I don't relish scaring kids. Besides, with his issues he wouldn't be going far even if he did wake. His little useless fingers can't work locks. But I made a massive error. I have never heard him make a sound. I thought he was completely mute.

I considered letting Vesper put Johnny back into his room until he started making this god-awful repetitive whining chant. Like an excited donkey. The little fucker was getting so loud that I was going to have to bail or silence him. The shit hit a new level of chaos when the fucking Prince of Sacramento decided he was going to try and save Vesper. It was too late for him to save the day anyway. I'd already been inside of her. But I didn't come. Fuck. Shit.

Every time I hit a house, I strive for perfection. I am always learning from my mistakes, adjusting for the next one. If I fuck up big time, I feel compelled to go out right away and make up for it. It makes me more frustrated so that I become more brutal in order to ensure compliance. I don't like when things don't go the way I planned. Ironically, while this was not the night I planned to enter, I had almost reached utter perfection. The complete fantasy coming to life. Where I completely infiltrate their lives in every facet. Not just getting into the home, eating their food, taking their things, taking away their power. But becoming the man of the house, taking the woman and making her come all over my cock like her man doesn't even exist.

Vesper creamed up my fingers and cock. I didn't even need lube. Despite her protests, I could feel her pussy swelling around me, her body getting taut. I could hear her moans were genuine, even though she was stifling them. We were right there. Right fucking there. And then the kid came in. And everything went to shit—fast.

I wouldn't have hurt the kid. It's not like he could ID me or take me down. But, I would have killed her fiancé if he got out. I can't risk getting caught. His life is not worth my freedom.

Fortunately for me, it is worth hers.

The thought never crossed my mind to take her until she asked—begged. I don't do that. The destruction stays where I lay it. Nothing comes back with me that doesn't have to. That's how I have managed to do this for so long and completely outwit the cops. Hell, there's so many prowlers in this part of Cali, they're just starting to figure out which hits are mine. I've even got a media name now.

But this girl. I want more. I can't leave without finishing what we started. And then maybe, just maybe, I won't have to worry about what's next.

But this isn't in any plan. I haven't prepared for this. I never take risks. I run from them. I quit when things turn sideways. There's always another house. Another family. Another day. But there's not another Vesper. Just like she incited me earlier tonight, I act on impulse.

"Get up," I say, pulling her to her feet. She's wobbly; an emotional mess. This boy has her in pieces. Maybe she truly does love him in a way I thought didn't exist. Or maybe she just thinks she's going to die.

I drag them both in the main bedroom and lock the door.

"He stays here," I say.

Keeping one arm on Vesper, I slide out the window, then I pull her out, closing the window behind me so the kid can't even attempt to follow. I tuck into the hydrangeas and pull her down with me.

"If you scream, I'll stab you in the heart and leave you to die. They won't find me. But I will find your family. And I will kill them all. Understand?"

She nods her head. I stand up and look around. Carter's thudding against the bedroom door barely registers out in the yard. No one has heard anything. I pull her up and cover her mouth, digging the knife into her side, pressing it against her ribs so she understands I mean what I say.

Normally, I could easily hop the fences or use a stolen bike to get back to the canal, which is only three streets away, but she's a hell of a burden. This is why it's easier to go where the targets are instead of trying to move them from one location to another.

We shimmy sideways so I can lead her to the tall wooden fence that separates her house from her neighbor's, quietly lifting the squeaky latch so that we're in the neighbor's yard. We duck again behind some bushes. That's when she decides to go back on her deal. She knows her neighbors well (I've seen her chat them up on many occasions) and trusts they'll come save her. She thought she could draw me away from the guys, and then scream for help when she was closer to another house.

They're all liars. They want to hurt you.

If it were anyone else, I'd just let her go and make a run for it. I'd be pulling up to my house while the cops were still trying to figure out what was going on. No one is worth the risk of capture. She hasn't seen my face. She'd never see me again. But I want to keep her. She's already got me thinking about having her. About finally finding a way for me to have more than just the night.

I wrestle her to the ground, sealing her mouth shut so her screams are muffled. I would knock her out, but I don't want to damage her pretty face, so I take my knife. She squirms as I jut it towards her, but less so when she realizes I'm cutting off her nightgown. It's hard work, doing it with one hand while the other clamps down on her mouth. I'm getting sweaty and uncomfortable on his humid night and it's making my patience wear thinner. I nick her a few times, but eventually, there's enough for me to shove in her mouth, and then tie around as a gag. She's naked now, but I don't care because I'll make sure no one will see us. I blindfold her with the remaining fabric and throw her over my shoulder. It'll be easier to move her this way. I run from one yard to the next, ducking behind bushes to regroup. It's not even four yet, so people are still deep in their slumbers. Vesper tries to scream, but the gag muffles most of it, and I'm moving so fast that her stomach is bumping on my shoulder, causing her voice to break. If anyone were to get up to look for the sound, we'd already be at the next backyard.

When we get to the canal, I breathe a sigh of relief, lowering her to her feet. She's barefoot and naked, her hair is wild. She's moves her head wildly, completely unable to perceive her surroundings. She already looks feral. Seeing her body exposed and helpless out here makes me want to drop her in the brush and fuck her, but I can't risk getting caught out here. Not after all this work.

I huff as I pull of my sweatshirt and wipe away my sweat. Running with her over my shoulder is no small task.

"Come on," I order, with a tug of her forearm. She whimpers as twigs crack under her feet. I know it hurts, but there's not much I can do for her right now. She trips a few times over obstacles she can't see. We walk for ten minutes until we are able to emerge. I see my car in the distance. Just a few more steps and we'll be off. This is the riskiest part of all. I have to walk with a naked, bound girl down

46

a residential street. I step out, looking right and left as far as my eyes can see, just to make sure no one comes up on us by surprise. I don't have time for resistance, so I pick her up and jog us down the street. I pop the trunk, toss her in and slam it shut.

I lower myself into the driver seat with a huge sigh, laughing a little bit as I wipe the sweat off my brow. I don't know what the fuck I just got myself into, but the thrill of outsmarting these people and cops gives me such overwhelming satisfaction. The thrill of carrying a naked girl through two pristine Sacramento-area neighborhoods while people sleep soundly makes me feel like a fucking god.

I have her. The perfect girl. The girl who is a little like the rest of them, but maybe she's a little different, too.

I start the car, and pull out. The freeway is a block away, and once I'm on it, no one will hear her kicking against the trunk.

CHAPTER 5

VESPER

Where there's no light, there's no time. At least not how I knew it before. It could be just a few days or a week since I was dropped off wherever I am. I can't say where because I've been blindfolded since that son of a bitch body slammed me in the Johnson's backyard, cut up my nightgown and used it to gag and blindfold me. I thought someone would hear me. I thought someone would save me. I felt safe in my home, behind strong walls and locked windows, sleeping next to a man who had just made the commitment to take care of me forever.

A house provides the facade of protection. It's a sacred place, separating you from the beasts that lurk outside. But that's all it is: a facade. The reason your home is safe is because no one has wanted in yet. But if you are so unlucky, nothing can stop a monster from breaching those walls.

In the beginning, I passed the time worrying about Carter and Johnny. How long did it take for them to get out? Did they ever? I would think Carter's school would begin to wonder why he hasn't showed up to his labs. Are my parents on their way back from Egypt? Am I on the news?

I don't know. I am in a black hole. Over time, thirst and hunger have become more prominent thoughts in my mind. My lips are so dry, it's like running my tongue along sandpaper. My stomach cramps with hunger. I lie on my side, too weak to make the effort to stand. I fantasize about margaritas and a hamburger at The Firehouse, a tradition on Friday nights.

He left me here and hasn't returned. At least not that I can tell. I am in a constant state of discomfort. Naked in a place that is always just a little too chilly. My own hands rubbing the goose-pimpled skin my only source of warmth. As I become weaker with dehydration and hunger, I get colder still.

Yet, I am still alive. And with that there is hope. If he wanted me dead, he would have killed me. But then what does he want? He hasn't touched me again. He's not using me for any obvious purpose. Maybe he's left me to die a slow, agonizing, lonely death.

Then, footsteps. They creak above my head a few times, back and forth, like someone is up to something. I don't know if I should scream for help. What if he has abandoned me somewhere and this is my only chance to be discovered? What if I say something and incur his wrath? I have no choice but to take the chance.

"H…H…elp." I haven't used my voice in days and my mouth is so chalky I nearly choke on the sounds. "Help," I eke out.

The footsteps continue as I use my energy reserves to beg for help. I don't think I'm loud enough to be heard.

But then they approach a new area overhead and there's the sound of a door unlatching. My heart pounds with adrenaline, giving me a burst of energy I haven't had since the thirst began to overtake me.

Something thuds to the ground feet away from me. I scramble wildly trying to gauge where the person is. Terror creeps deep into my bones, but the need to survive is so strong, that it overrides the paralyzing fright. It's not bravery. Bravery implies there's a choice. "Wa-ter," I rasp.

Silence. Silence that makes those goosebumps surface. Then in an instant, the blindfold is whipped off my face. I've gone without seeing for so long, my eyes forget how to focus. I blink a few times, trying to find something to hone in on and recalibrate my vision. Instinctively, I do so on a bottle of water about fifteen feet away from me. The firmly built man towering over me wearing a black balaclava quickly steals my attention, though.

I shake my head and shrink my body in fear. I don't feel

human. I'm more like a caged animal. Like he's here to snuff me out. He pulls me to my knees. I look around and see I'm in a basement. A couple of short, cloudy, ground-level windows bring in hints of daylight. The light fighting its way in is bright with a tint of yellow; it must be a beautiful day out there.

I wait for him to say something, but he keeps silent.

He cups my chin and pulls it up to meet his eyes. Their clarity reminds me of the chunks of glass I used to collect at the beach as a kid. Still he says nothing.

He walks away and points at the water. I don't understand this game we're playing. But I am so thirsty.

I nod desperately. He turns away and heads back up the stairs, taking the bottle with him.

"No…no," I beg hoarsely. He leaves the door open behind him and I'm so despondent, I would follow with no regard for my safety, but I'm shackled by the ankle. Before I can try to understand his intentions, he's back, with a bucket in one hand and a white paper bag in the other.

It hits me instantly. The aroma of food. Despite the dehydration, I begin to salivate. I would do anything for that fucking food and water. I'm delirious with the need.

He places the bucket down and brings the bag to my face as if he wants me to peek in. I do. It's like he's been reading my fantasies. Burgers and fries. Oh god. Fuck. I begin to cry. I can't believe I'm crying over a hamburger.

He pulls the bag away and sets it back where the water was. He returns with the bucket. Inside of it is soapy water and a sponge.

He points at this and then the food.

I look down at my body. It's covered in scrapes and mud. I've defecated and pissed in another spot in the room and I have become numb to the scent of it.

"If I wash, you'll feed me?" I ask, with a sense of hope that belies the perverseness of the situation.

He nods.

"Okay. Untie my hands. I'll do it. I promise."

He shakes his head, putting the bucket down and dropping in his sinewy arm down to the elbow. He's not as covered as he was last time, wearing a t-shirt that shows his arms and jeans that are torn and covered in grease and paint, like he works in construction or something. My eyes run up along his arm, and that's when I notice a series of violent scars along the outer part of his biceps, like the skin has been ripped off at some point.

He pulls out the large sponge, soapy water running down his muscled forearm and back into the bucket.

He's not interested in me bathing myself.

You think you know hunger, but you don't really know hunger. Not the type that makes everything hurt. When you feel like the life force is being syphoned from your body with each hour. Where the rational side, the thing that makes you human and separates you from an animal is smothered by instinct. It turns you into the most basic creature, where nothing else matters but getting the nutrients you need to keep breathing.

"Okay. I won't fight. You can clean me. But can I please, just a sip. To wet my mouth?" My lips stick together with each word, making an awful suction sound.

He squeezes the sponge over my head so that the water rains down on me. It's warm; it's been so long since I felt warmth. And I let it run over my lips, trying to steal every last bit of moisture from it. I don't care about the bitter taste of soap, I'll take it however I can get it.

I focus on the promising scent of food, intermingled with the clean scent of soap as he pulls me up to my feet. It's not forceful, it's actually soft and in any other circumstances, somewhat seductive. He unties the rope around my wrists. He at least had the mercy to loosen them a little bit when he put me in here. They were so tight the night he took me, my hands had gone numb and purple. I probably would have lost them if he hadn't. But there are rope burns that are raw and red. He doesn't rub them, but again trickles the soapy water over the wounds.

He uses his bare hands to rub the slick suds along my body. They are a rough contrast to the slipperiness of the soap. I shudder. I haven't seen or spoken to a person in who knows how long. The loneliness eats at you. And it makes you hypersensitive to the presence of another person. His touch, though violating, is human. And just like the night he took me, my brain and body can't reconcile both sides of the equation.

He spends extra time on my breasts, massaging them, rubbing against the stiff nipples. I turn away when he does this, not that the mask gives me a view of his face at all. Just those eyes and a pair of plump lips, lips that were contrastingly soft and harsh when he kissed me that night. He glides a hand down my belly, past the patch of hair and rubs me down there. Cleaning, yes, but also toying with me, showing me he has all the control. That he can touch me how he wants.

I focus on the rich smell of warm food across the room, and not the carnal feeling his hands provoke.

He walks behind me, I try to turn but he pushes my face forward, and then bends me at the waist, spreading my ass apart. He scrubs it with the sponge vigorously, cleaning away the filth I have been unable to.

He comes forward again, and from the bucket he pulls out a razor. I flinch in horror. He puts his finger to his lips and points at the food, reminding me what my compliance will produce.

A few tears drop as I quiet myself, but I shake uncontrollably, afraid he'll cut me with it, like he did with the knife. But instead he shaves me: my legs, armpits, and most of my private area. He towels me off, brushes my wet hair and squeezes out the excess water.

Now I'm a clean caged animal.

I don't have time to care about my dignity. All I can think about is eating and drinking. He walks over to the food and tosses the bag at me. I pull out the water bottle and chug on it furiously, then I grab a handful of fries and shove them in my mouth.

A hand grips firmly on my arm. He puts up his other hand. *Slow down,* he's telling me. I'm a little embarrassed that I'm eating savagely enough for my kidnapper to have to show concern. But not too embarrassed as I shoot him a rebellious glare and finish shoving that handful of fries in my mouth without breaking eye contact. I do take his advice and slow down on the next bite. Focused on the deliciousness of the food, I don't pay attention to the work he's doing around me. I assume cleaning up my mess, but when he rolls a TV in front of me, it catches my eye. He turns the dial to ABC and adjusts the antenna. The image is grainy, with a line of static rolling up the screen intermittently.

I wonder if this is some form of entertainment he's trying to provide as I crouch there, damp and naked, biting out of my burger. It doesn't make sense considering his brutality during our last encounter, but when the anchors stop talking about the weather, it's clear what he's showing me.

"And up next, the latest news on the abducted Sacramento-area nursing student."

My stomach rolls with discomfort and I almost lose my precious meal.

"Who are you?" I ask.

No answer.

"What are you going do to me?"

No answer.

"Why won't you speak to me?! I've already heard your voice."

He turns and leaves, keeping my foot chained so I have no chance of escape.

As many fantasies as I had of eating a banquet all by myself, my shrunken stomach already feels like it'll burst, so I place the burger back in the wrapper. I don't know when my next meal will be, so it would be dumb to discard the food.

We're back with you, live on the six o'clock news. The family of a nursing student who was abducted on Friday evening from her Sacramento home, while her fiancé and young brother were bound and locked in separate rooms, spoke today.

They cut to a clip of my mother, sobbing in front of a bank of microphones. Pete and Carter stand solemnly behind her, rubbing her shoulders. "She's a good person. She was—is—going to be a nurse. She has plans to do good things…help people. Please, I beg you, just let her go. You can just drop her off and disappear. We don't care. We just want her back."

A man dressed in a beige officer's uniform takes the podium. He introduces himself as Sheriff Andrew Hunter-Ridgefield. He makes a brief statement that they are doing everything they can to look for me. He looks young for the position, and I wonder if he has what it takes to find me.

I look around for Johnny, but he's not there. They must have thought this would be too much for him.

I crawl towards the screen to get a closer look at Carter, the jubilance he carried on his face, no matter how tired he was, entirely gone. The chain yanks at my leg, keeping me feet away from the screen, so I am left reaching, but unable to touch the pixels that form my family. I had been complaining days ago about the burdens of a mother who made me become a mother to my own brother. A boyfriend who was almost perfect, but I had the audacity to believe not perfect enough. I fantasized about a monster over him, and now the fantasy is real. Maybe this is what I deserve.

The image of my family's press conference cuts away and back to the anchors.

Police are looking for this man.

On the screen is an almost comical sketch. It's a guy with a black mask. Two eyes and lips peek through. It's black and white, so there's nothing to indicate the color of his eyes. It could be anyone.

Police believe this is the work of the Night Prowler, who has plagued central California for about five years, first prowling and ransacking homes. However, police now believe in the past year, a rash of home invasions and rapes is the work of this same intruder who has grown increasingly violent.

It is believed he is roughly six feet tall with an athletic build. He may have a black sedan. It is estimated he is likely in his 20s. If you have any information regarding this case, please contact the Sacramento Sheriff's Office at...

Once the last sentence is being uttered, the man comes back downstairs and pulls the antenna off the set. Everything dissolves to snow and frantically I beg. "No! No!" I want to keep watching different news stations, see my family, and just be continually assured that I haven't been forgotten. But he doesn't give a shit and wheels the TV out of reach.

"Why did you do that?" I yell. "What was the point, huh? Am I ever going to see them again?" I ask.

He doesn't answer, but he pulls another water bottle out of his pocket and rests it right in front of me. Without further acknowledgement of my existence, he finishes cleaning up my mess, leaving a bucket and toilet paper in its place. Then he heads back up the stairs, closing the door behind him, and plunging me back into a world of solitude.

SAM

When my mother died and left me this ranch, I sold most of the animals. I didn't want to take care of all that myself, especially now being free to focus on the unpopular hobby I had picked up at a young age. While she was alive, there was always the chance that she would know; put two and two together. Figure out I wasn't always doing the things I said I did. And having her here, my fiercest protector, I felt obligated not to push the envelope too far. But then she died, and it was like a gasket blew in me.

Urges I had suppressed boiled to the surface. Anger stewed in me from being left alone. I began to crave access to the world I had shunned with her, a world she both protected me from and robbed me of, but I couldn't do it the way everyone else did. I wanted to taste, smell, and feel the things I had only watched until this point. I started doing the things her presence kept me from doing. Despite her faults, she reined me in somehow, and when she died, the strap snapped.

Now here's the ironic part: I got rid of most of the animals, only to find myself keeping the neediest of them all: a human woman.

I plan meticulously. It's what I do. Yet I found myself with a woman and no idea what I was going to do next. Of course, I know what I want. I'm a fucking man with needs, but I want it my way. When she begged me to take her, I thought holy shit, she feels this is different, too. I had a moment when I thought maybe she wasn't like the rest of the world that had rejected me and our connection was real. Then she started screaming, and I knew she was a lying fucking liar like my mother warned. She warned me women would only use me for my money. For the family name.

So I have a plan now. It took me a few days, but I realized this will be a lot like breaking a horse. First, I have to turn her into an animal. Take away everything that gives her power and strength. Reduce her needs to the most basic: food and water, sleep, sex. Second, I have to stroke her, get her to understand that compliance equals good things. It's the way you train any animal. I'll use food as a reward and other methods of positive reinforcement. Negative reinforcement, well, that's always in my back pocket.

She's been in the basement, but I've been working on

building her a shed deeper in the property, in the woods where no one treads. I can't keep her in the house indefinitely, it's too risky. So I've been working hard on that between my day gigs.

God I want to fuck her so bad. Her soapy pussy in my hands almost made me break my plans again, but I need to break her in bit by bit.

As my oatmeal sits on the kitchen table cooling, I listen to the police scanner set up on a built-in desk just beside it. I've often used it to monitor patrols to know the best times to strike certain streets. Now, I'm listening for clues about Vesper's case. There has been an increase in reports of suspicions persons all over Sacramento County. People are on edge. They've been patrolling her neighborhood and other neighborhoods I've prowled, hoping I'll strike again. That means they might think she's already dead and I'll need to go back out. It makes sense. Usually when women disappear like that, it's not good.

By the time I pull away from the scanner to address my dinner, it's cold and lumpy. I haven't been feeding myself well this week on account of being so busy. As I twirl the spoon in the pale goo, I get lost in its texture. Oatmeal will always remind me of my childhood.

"Why aren't you eating it?" my father asks. My throat tightens. "Just say it. I won't force you to eat it if you just say it. Just say 'no.' Say one word!" He snaps, losing his patience.

"Stop it!" mom scolds, coming to my side.

"You keep coddling him and he's never going to fucking learn. You're babying him. That's why he won't talk!"

"He's a sensitive boy. He'll talk when he's ready."

"Gloria, he's almost five years old."

"The doctor said he's fine. He has above average intelligence. In fact, he said he's extremely intelligent. And you badgering at him just makes it worse. It gives him a complex. Some kids just take longer to gain their verbal skills. He's special."

"Special? So that's what they're calling them now…"

I watch them argue. My mom knows I understand, but sometimes I think my dad thinks I don't get what they say. Dad looks down at me, and his eyes flare. He snatches the spoon out of my hand. "Eat it! Eat it!" He shoves the oatmeal to my lips but I clench them shut. The spoon hurts my lips and teeth, but I won't swallow. A sound comes out of my chest, but I can't get my lips and throat to join. I want to say STOP. It's in here, but I can't make it come out.

"See? It's there, you just have to stop babying him!"

"Stop it!" my mother yells, pulling his arm away.

We all look over to the entrance. Scooter, my older brother, is standing there. My dad likes Scooter a lot more than me. He speaks perfectly. Sometimes they go on fishing trips without me.

Dad sighs. "Come on Scoot, eat your breakfast. Everything is fine." He turns to the kitchen counter to grab his badge and gun.

"Okay," Scooter says skeptically.

My mother crouches down and uses her apron to wipe the oatmeal off my face. "You really should eat some. You'll be hungry later," she whispers, wiping my messy hair out of my eyes.

BOOM. BOOM. BOOM.

The pounding on my front door shakes me out of my thoughts. I scramble to turn off the police scanning equipment, pull it out of the wall and shove it into the cabinets above the desk.

I shuffle over to the door, peek past the curtains and see it's Scooter outside. Speak of the spawn of the devil. I wasn't expecting him, and I'm not particularly happy he's here. I open the door, and turn back towards the kitchen table, leaving Scoot to his own devices to follow me in and close the door behind himself.

"Nice to see you too, Sam."

Without missing a step, I give him a single, sarcastic wave.

"I haven't heard from you in what has it been? Three weeks? I keep calling and you don't answer here. I was about to drive up to the ranch this weekend to see if you were alive."

The ranch. It's mine. I hate how he thinks that he can just come up there. Especially now.

"I'm f-f-f-ine." *Fuck. Shit.* "B-b-b-been b-b-b-usy."

He tucks his chin in shock. "Shit man, you're way worse since I last saw you."

He's just like our fucking dad. Zero nuance and the sensitivity of a rabid fucking bull. The last thing you say to someone with a speech impediment is how bad they sound. You'd think he'd have figured that out by now.

"T-t-t-thanks asssss-h-h-ole."

I pull out my chair violently in a nonverbal sign of protest and sit down with a thud. The oatmeal sits there, the sickly blob reminding me of how different our lives have been even though we had the same parents.

He helps himself to a seat. "Okay, you've been spending all your time there, alone. Which makes no sense since most of your work is here. You're a ghost these days. And your stuttering is getting progressively worse…" His tone changes as if he's telling me a secret. "Is this about mom? You know, losing her was hard for me too."

"I-I-It's only an h-h-h-our." I open my mouth to continue speaking, but that familiar feeling of my mouth and throat tightening, of the words getting stuck on the way out—it's not going to stop. I'm too on edge being ambushed by him. I sigh and shoot up to my feet, stomp to the counter where there's a notepad and a pen, and write.

Don't wanna talk about it. How's work?

I plop back in my chair and slide the notepad to him.

He grins to himself and points at the pad and shoves it back to me. It makes me chuckle a bit too. I change the page and scribble the answer.

Fine. Lots of communities being built. Schools getting fixed. I've had to turn down jobs at this point.

"Well, that's good news," he says. "Been a while since I've been up to the farm. You have time to work on it?"

Scooter is so fucking greedy. I know it irks him that mom left me the ranch. We both got plenty after she died, but he just couldn't handle that small slight, that maybe just once I got the longer end of the stick. To him, the ranch was a place of refuge, a place where he'd come up and fish and ride horses on the weekend with dad. To me, that ranch was a prison. Despite that, I can't bring myself to leave it behind.

"Anyway, Katie wanted to see about you coming over for dinner. And your nieces and nephew want to see their uncle."

I wish he'd learn to take a hint. I jot on the pad. *Too busy now. Look at me. I come home covered in paint and plaster every day ready to sleep. Give me a few weeks for my projects to die down.*

"You keep avoiding us, we're gonna come here for dinner," he says. So entitled. And smug. Like everyone else, he thinks he's smarter than me because I sound stupid. I love the fact that he doesn't know who I really am. I love getting one over on him in particular, probably more than the entirety of society.

There are worse brothers than Scooter, but he's not a particularly good one either. And ever since mom died, and dad's been dead for years now, he's appointed himself patriarch of this family, the glue that holds us together. I wish he'd just let the shit crumble. We were a family, but we were on two distinct sides of an ongoing battle. And even when the weapons have been surrendered, battle wounds don't disappear. God, does he look like dad. Right down to the mannerisms.

Now that it's just us, he's always on my ass. Suddenly, he's the big brother who always wants to be around. The successful family man who has so graciously accepted the unsolicited task of checking in on his bachelor brother.

I point at myself and make a sleeping gesture. *Me tired. You, get the fuck out.*

"Alright, alright. I'm checking in with you every week. So save me the effort and pick up the phone."

I nod with a tired eye roll. I thought mom's death would give me freedom, but he's worse than her. At least she'd disappear into her room for a few weeks here and there.

I point at myself, make a phone gesture, then point at him. *Me, call you.*

I stand up, another nonverbal cue (I am very fluent in them), and he follows suit.

We walk to the back door that exits directly from the kitchen of my Sacramento bungalow, the city where we lived as kids. "I'll have Katie make you some real food. Can't believe you're eating oatmeal. That's one thing I don't miss about the bachelor life. You know, you don't have to watch out for mom anymore. You should get out there. You're a good looking kid." He grabs my bicep, the one that doesn't look like it was gone over with a cheese grater, and gives it a squeeze. "You've got money and a good job. Women lap that shit up…Katie has friends."

His disingenuous saccharine pep talk is unwelcome. He knows what happens when I get around women. All they want to fucking do is talk. I prefer to pay my women to fuck and stay quiet. He's spewing bullshit and he knows it.

He has no idea how much I get out these days. Besides, I have my woman. The one who I handpicked like a lone flower from a barren bush.

I wag my finger in the air and take a deep breath. "No." I manage that monosyllabic word like a big boy.

He releases my bicep, gives my shoulder a too-hard slap. "Well, see you soon."

I nod, edging him to the door. I watch him get into his car and pull out before taking a deep breath. If I hadn't come back to my place tonight, he would have gone to the fucking ranch. That was too close of a call. This is why I don't do—didn't do—kidnappings.

Five minutes after I am sure he's gone, I grab my things and drive back towards the ranch to finish Vesper's new home.

CHAPTER 6

SAM

Working on a client's front porch this morning, I can barely keep my eyes open.

"Awww Sam, you look exhausted," Ms. Dawkins says. "Can I offer you something to drink?"

I shake my head no, but then I put my finger up and shrug. *No, thanks. Wait, I've changed my mind. You know what? Sure.* Usually I make an effort to talk, but I've done work for Emilia Dawkins for years and I really don't have the energy for conversation. The stuttering gets worse when I'm nervous or overly tired. In her case, it's the latter: Mrs. Dawkins is old enough to be my grandmother. Even if I was attracted to her, I'm smart enough to never go after a customer. But normally, on a clear day like this, I'd be keeping an eye out for women at home while their husbands or boyfriends are at work, trying to narrow down who'd I'd like to hunt.

Ever since I took Vesper, however, I am the one being hunted. Conveniently, Ms. Dawkin's house is just minutes by car from Vesper's home. It's the perfect excuse to drive by on the way back and see what the police are up to — if they are finished combing the house for evidence, if there are patrol cars still sitting outside her house. I know how this all works. I just have to wait it out, let things cool.

Fuck it. The truth is, all I can think about is getting back to Vesper. Everything else, including keeping an eye on the cops, is just a distraction. I spent the entire night finishing her new home. I got maybe an hour of sleep. I just need to add some finishing touches. I can't wait to see her again. I have new gifts for her.

There's a school across the street and they've broken for recess. The quiet playground erupts with screeching children. That sound still makes me uncomfortable. I know it doesn't seem like it, but I had a soft spot for Johnny, mainly because he doesn't have a voice. I know what that's like. Well, at least until he decided to have a conniption fit. I don't blame him though. If I had a Vesper at his age, I wouldn't want to lose her either.

I glance over at the children playing. A group of them have formed a circle and are running in the same direction.

I stand in the middle of a circle of my schoolmates. My stomach hurts. I hate recess.

"Stu-stu-stu-stuttering Sam!" they chant. I nervously fidget, my eyes dart around looking for Scooter. He's playing with his own friends. Most of the time he doesn't talk to me at school. He has lots of friends; the older crowd. I think he's embarrassed by me. So at lunch, I usually sit alone. "Stu-stu-stu-stupid Sam!" some of the others chant.

Just before we broke for recess, Ms. Juniper called on me to read out loud. She said she wouldn't treat me differently. That my dad insisted on that. The class waits for me to get out a few sentences. It makes my stomach hurt. I'm afraid I'll pee in front of everyone because when I'm nervous it makes me have to pee. I pee the bed almost every night, and it makes dad angry when he finds out. When the kids giggle at me reading, Mrs. Juniper scolds them, but it just makes me more embarrassed. They wait and they wait for me to get through the paragraph. This time I didn't finish until five minutes into recess. This makes the kids really mad at me. At lunch, they like to call me names because they know I can't answer fast and they like to hear me struggle. It's easier to pretend I don't hear them.

When they tease me at recess, I stand there quietly, the pain in my stomach getting worse as they laugh and shove me.

When there's a break in the circle, I make a run for it. They all chase me around the playground, but I am fast. Faster than any kid at this school, even the older ones. I run past the teachers and off the playground. No one can catch me as I run into a yard and climb over a fence. I keep running and running, until the sounds of the school yard disappear.

I stop to catch my breath in someone's backyard. When I look up, I am facing a window. A woman is standing there, holding a baby. She's looking down at it, rocking it back and forth. I duck behind some bushes. I don't want her to see me and send me back.

She's wearing a white dress. It's loose and stops at her knees. After a while, she pulls down her top. She has big ones, and I feel something in my stomach that's not pain. She lifts the baby to one of them, and I watch the baby suck. I wish I was in there in her arms, but this is almost as nice. Quiet. No one making me talk. Alone, but not alone.

"Here's some iced tea!" Mrs. Dawkins hands me a glass. "I'm going to run some errands now."

I give her a thumbs up. I like my work. I am good with my hands and it allows me to keep my hobbies since I make my own schedule. I don't need the money. I just like being productive. These days, there's so much new construction in these developments, the bigger companies contract me aside from my own personal gigs. People trust my work, and my stellar reputation precedes me.

I can tell that people feel good about hiring me. Like it's charity, helping the guy who stutters. People assume I'm slow despite the fact that I can build a house with my bare hands. All because I'm different. Sometimes people recognize my last name and they ask about it, but I don't like to talk about my family. I think some of them assume I've been left out of the will and work to support myself. It's none of their damn business anyway.

Sure, they're happy to have me fix their things, renovate their kitchens, but that's as far as it goes. I'm still an outsider. I'm still that kid in the middle of the circle, it's just that adults have to act a little more civilized, and I'm a bigger boy these days.

A whistle blows, the kids form lines and are lead back into the school again. Quiet.

Now that I have Vesper waiting for me—I'm alone, but not alone.

VESPER

Two times the sun has left and the basement has turned pitch black. Two nights have passed since the man came in, cleaned me, fed me, and showed me the outside world through a television screen. Then he left without a word. I don't know when he's coming back, and that scares me. The food and water is long gone and only gave me enough energy to continue existing. But I'm still starving and thirsty, and he's the only way I have access to more food.

Hunger and boredom is a maddening combination. It makes you pray for anyone's presence to make you feel human again. At least when he's here, my body courses with adrenaline. It makes me feel alive when I don't have the energy from nutrition. It's the waiting that has become torture—not knowing my fate, suffering and growing weaker.

Sometimes there are footsteps and my heart skips with a jolt of excitement and dread. But then the house will go quiet again. My mind and body is constantly confused by this man who terrifies me but is also the person on whom I must depend for survival.

This time, when the footsteps come towards the door, it opens. My mouth produces what little saliva it can, like a Pavlovian dog, in response to his presence.

He comes down the stairs, a milk crate stuffed with random items in his arms. The smell of food instantly hits my nose and my heart rate accelerates. I try not to smile and look too eager. It makes me feel pathetic. But my eyes steal the attention from my nose when it follows the bare arms, slick with sweat, to a naked torso, up a muscled neck and to a masked face. He's wearing jeans again, torn up like the last time. He has streaks of dirt and paint on him, and his skin has a reddish golden tint like he's just been working out in the sun. What I would do to feel the sun on my skin again. I hate that despite all the horrible things this man has done, I can't help but notice his taut, athletic body. He makes another trip with a soapy bucket of water.

I watch in skeptical suspense as he goes about this business without acknowledging me.

Once he's settled, he lifts a gallon jug of water in front of me.

I nearly dance. I nod frantically, my throat clenching at the thought of moisture.

He points at the wash bucket.

"Yes—Yes," I submit without hesitation.

He walks up to me with the bucket, his frigid, golden-flecked turquoise eyes on mine as he rubs the soap along my body. I'm scared. Of my fate. Of what Johnny and my family are going through, but I'm not scared of this. He's done it once before and it wasn't the worst thing he's done to me. It's actually nice to be clean after being in a dingy basement.

Being more relaxed, my body betrays me as he cleans between my legs. Last time, I turned my face away in protest. Consumed with fear and rage, I was able to ignore the physical sensations. But being naked and alone for days on end, with nothing against my skin but cold concrete, his warm hands heat up every part of me they touch. His jeans smell of paint, but on his skin is the sweet aroma of salt and grass, and it reminds me of long days in Tahoe.

I act unfazed, but when I take a deep breath to calm myself, it skips nervously.

He rubs me everywhere. My body is conquered land; there are no secrets from him.

I take in the arm with the scars and see they run all along that side of his body, up his torso. Thick ropey marks crawl up his neck. The other side of his body is pristine.

He pours a jug of warm water over me to rinse off the soap, using his hands to assist the rinsing. My captor makes his way back between my legs, guiding the clean water to make sure it rinses all the filth away. And while his touch was soft but clinical before, this time, he rubs, letting his fingers go past the outer lips, but not breaching the entrance. Testing. Teasing. My stomach flutters with contempt and arousal.

"Stop it. Please," I beg as my knees weaken. He goes for a few more seconds, his hand invading me, but still nothing like the night we first met. Flashes of the feeling I had that night fill me with shame: How I let this man almost take me to orgasm, and how now, despite my resistance, if he wanted to again he likely could.

But he stops on his own accord, rinsing me off and toweling me. He hands me the water and I chug down as much as I can without getting sick. Instantly, life returns to my body.

"Can I watch more TV?" I ask.

He doesn't answer.

"I just want to see if my brother is okay. He wasn't at the news conference."

He shakes his head. TV is not on the table today.

I suck back a sharp sob, I don't want to cry in front of him anymore.

He walks over to the milk crate and pulls out a thick blanket. Softness. Texture. Warmth. What I wouldn't do to be able to sleep on that tonight. The floor is so cold and unforgiving. I've lost fat and with that, cushion, and my bones ache.

"What do I have to do? Just say it. I don't understand why you won't say it."

He walks over and lays it on the floor behind me. Then he comes back to face me, close, and that's when I see the bulge in his pants. It's menacing and I'm scared and yet the area where he last touched lights up. He leans in close enough for his hardness to graze me.

"I'm gonna taste your pussy," he whispers in my ear. His voice is gritty and low, the auditory equivalent of gravel.

I shake my head. I won't do this. This isn't who I am. He can strip me down, starve me, isolate me, but I am still Vesper Rivers.

He shrugs, pulling the blanket off the floor. Tossing it in the milk crate, going through the motions for a grand exit. It's so unfair, this is all nothing to him, but this basement is my world. That blanket could be my bed. It could shield my naked body so I can maintain a shred of dignity. It could hug me. A simple hug, even from a blanket would be a lifeline right now.

A sense of panic rises in me as he walks towards the stairs. He's the only person I can talk to or touch. I don't want him to go. I don't want to sit in this endless boredom, staring out the tiny window that is far out of reach. I've run out of things to think about. I've slept away more hours than I can count. I don't know how much longer I can keep going without food. I feel like I'm hanging onto my sanity by a hair. I have to stop him from leaving me in here.

"Wait! Can we bargain? Can I have one more thing?" He stops, but doesn't face me. He's listening.

"Food. I'm so hungry. I can't keep going like this. The blanket and the food. I know you have some. I can smell it."

He's silent for a few moments. Probably to fuck with me more than trying to mull it over. Then he shakes his head.

"Oh come on!" I shout, hot tears falling down my cheeks. I'm so angry I'm letting myself cry over such mundane items. I've been reduced to an infant, relying on someone for my most basic needs and unable to communicate through anything but tears.

He comes over and stands a foot away from me. Without a word, he looks me up and down, scanning my naked body like it's a meal. I've gotten somewhat used to the nudity, but the way his eyes scour me feels more intrusive than the bathing.

"You'll have to let me lick your cunt for the blanket. But if you want to eat food, you'll have to swallow my cock first." He reaches down and unzips his pants, pulling out his thick, engorged penis. For some reason I salivate, causing me to gulp. Sustenance, company, sex, it's all becoming intermingled. One associated with the other.

If I had to guess, I've been here for many days, maybe weeks. I've had one high calorie meal, but my hip bones are jutting out. I am weak. I am tired. I've had just enough water to keep myself alive and I wonder if my kidneys might go soon. The blanket is nice. It's a luxury. But food, food is life. And I am going to do anything I can to survive.

I don't have any more energy to bargain or even speak, simply nodding in consensus.

"Can I just have a bite? Just something to start? My head hurts." His crystal eyes, strong and unwavering, meet my sunken light brown ones. "I'll do a better job for you if I have energy." In case he doesn't have a human side, I appeal to his carnal one.

He walks over to the milk crate, his hard dick still hanging out, bouncing as he walks, and pulls out something. I stand taller with excitement. It's a bag of potato chips. He opens it and takes out a handful, then folds the bag, placing it back in the crate before walking over.

He bobs his head at me and I open my mouth. He feeds me one chip and my mouth bursts with salty goodness.

"Mmmm," I moan shamelessly. I think I see his lips curve

into a smile that he quickly fixes. Another. Another. I get ten chips. Ten glorious, salty, crunchy chips. Enough to make my mind think it's getting more food and trigger a second wind. The small dose shifts my mood, putting me in an unlikely post-snack high.

But the feeding is only a minute, and now I have to work on the down payment I collected.

He points to the blanket.

I lie down, watching him stand over me, making me feel so small. He finishes undoing his jeans and lets them fall to the floor. He's not wearing underwear, and now he's completely naked. His legs are thick with muscle, though not as tanned as his upper body.

You're still Vesper, I remind myself.

But am I? I've traded sexual favors for a meal and a blanket. That's not who I am. I clench up, thinking about my family and Carter. Carter who I am betraying by agreeing to this. I should have fought more. Now that I have a little bit of energy from the food, I should fight this raw deal.

The man, completely naked, except for the black balaclava, rests his hard body against mine. His cock presses against me, and I wonder if he's going to penetrate me instead of following our agreement.

"I changed my mind," I say. "I don't need this stuff."

He ignores my words. "I gave you a choice and you made it. Just like your boyfriend did that night when he told me to fuck you instead of saving you himself."

Like a cold rush of water, that memory comes back. I didn't believe that it was true. That Carter would tell an intruder to fuck me instead of taking the hits himself. But I don't know anything anymore. I am weak, weaker than I think. Those chips have already disintegrated in my stomach, and the gnawing hunger returns. A cynicism and mistrust I've never had for anyone overtakes me. Maybe Carter betrayed me that night. Maybe I put my body and life on the line for him and he hadn't done the same for me. And if he didn't fight for me, then why should I feel guilt over this?

I bite my lip as tears roll down my cheeks. *Fuck, Vesper, keep it together.* But keeping it together requires energy I have to conserve. The man watches me cry. He licks a tear, like my sadness sustains him. "I'm gonna fuck you with my mouth. I'm gonna make you cry, but not like this. I'm gonna make you cry for me."

He lowers himself along my trembling body, grazing his teeth against my skin, alert to his touch. His skin and mouth is warm and forgiving compared to the harsh concrete. He sucks on my breasts and my hips swivel. I tell myself it's resistance, but it's also like he's pulling some sort of trigger that I can't control.

I open my mouth to object, but instead, short, tense breaths escape. I shake my head no, but he doesn't see; he is entirely fixated on the rest of me—my body, my skin, my taste, my breasts. I am entirely coveted. I realize he's starving too, consumed by hunger so deep that he can't control himself. A hunger he will do anything to sate. He's been watching me. Craving me. The hunger intensifying so that it's all he can think about. Just like starvation, until you've felt it, you can't understand the things you'd do just to get a taste.

He bites my stomach, hard enough for me to flinch. I hold in my whimpers. I don't want to give him a reaction.

"I know so much about you, Vesp," he breathes into my pelvis as he works his way down. "So many things. But watching you was never enough. Now I'm finally going to be able to taste the flavor of your pussy when you come on my mouth." His perverse words burn through me like shrapnel.

I reach down to push him away just as his hot mouth hones in on my pussy, but my hand claws on the top of the mask.

"Don't even fucking try it," he says, pinning my hand down to the side.

I wasn't.

He makes gentle strokes with his tongue, his masked head weaving as he makes good on his promise to taste me.

I writhe around him, fighting the swelling sensation his mouth brings. My mind resisting what my body wishes to grant: Pleasure. Relief. Comfort.

I am still Vesper.

My squirming only makes him work harder, finding my clit with his tongue, massaging it, his lips suctioning softly. It only takes seconds before I am gasping for air, my body contracting every muscle in anticipation for a release. But he stops just seconds before, leaving me breathless and enraged. I had accepted the deal, I had prepared myself for what was to come, and now he was pulling away, leaving me wanting. I am not supposed to want this.

"Tell me you want me to make you come."

"No," I protest through clenched teeth.

"Your pussy is flushed and open. I can smell it. Taste it."

"Fuck you," I say.

"You want to be a stubborn little bitch, fine by me," he says, pulling away and kneeling in front of me. "Get up and suck my cock."

I give him a snarl befitting the animal I have become.

"Sounds like you don't want to eat," he adds sardonically.

I've come too far in this whole twisted deal to be left empty handed. I know what is to come, but I protest with stillness. He grabs me by my hair, pulling from the roots, onto all fours.

"Earn your fucking meal, Vesp." He says it like he knows me. He thinks he fucking knows me. But he's nothing more than a twisted voyeur. He sees what he wants when he watches, not what really is.

His cock awaits at attention inches from my face. I could bite it. But that's just a fleeting thought. I want to survive this, not get my head bashed in by this freakishly strong psycho.

"Take it in your mouth."

My pussy throbs, begging for the fulfillment it was promised as I trepidatiously purse my lips around his wide shaft. "Take it all the way, Vesp," he rasps, pushing his hips so that he hits the back of my throat. I gag, which prompts his acerbic chuckle. He pulls back and then in again. Out and in. Out and in. Fucking my mouth.

"I bet Carter never fucked you like this," he mocks. "That little bitch."

Tears leak from my eyes, but at this point, I can't tell if it's from choking or despair.

"Your ass from this angle…fuck, Vesp." Underneath his intensely throaty voice is the soft hum of relaxed pleasure.

I peer up, remaining on all fours, like an obedient pet, as he takes my mouth for his pleasure.

"One day I'm going to fuck that ass and watch my cum drip out of it. And you'll be begging for it."

I want to clamp down so badly, especially as my jaw tires. But I battle through. I need the spoils of my efforts.

He's all rippled muscles, and sweat, and filth. Eyes that

reveal no soul or depth, clear as a demon's. His round lips framed by black fabric. So many times I imagined a version of this as Carter was inside of me, never thinking it could be a reality. Thinking I was safe from my own twisted fantasies.

He groans, extending his neck and hips, increasing the pace of his thrusts.

"Your fucking mouth," he grunts, pulling out and gripping his cock in his calloused hand, pulling my hair to angle me upwards. He jerks faster and lets out a deep groan as he comes on my face, neck and breasts.

I don't fight him, it's far too late for that now. He cleansed me, and now he's dirtying me with his cum.

"You look fucking beautiful," he moans. It's not sarcastic or mocking, he says it the way a man would after his girl has made herself up. "Lick your lips, Vesp," he orders, still holding his cock and my hair.

"Lick," he repeats, rubbing the still-hard erection against my nipple dripping with his cum.

I dart out my tongue, tasting a little of the saltiness.

"More."

I do it again, this time taking a little more.

He looks down on me with pure lust. Eyes that see only me. A woman he selected and painted with his cum. His art. I ache below, my pussy still waiting for her turn. But I also ache at the fact that at this moment I could feel a smidgen of anything but total and utter rage.

I wish he would relieve me. I don't like him. Oh no—I hate him. But just like food, I'll take his mouth right now, just to make the pulsing stop. Just to have the touch of another for a few moments longer before I am alone again for hours or days. Of course, I can't say those words. I won't.

He stands up, his normally grounded stance a bit wobbly, walking to the wash bucket. His ass is firm, like that of someone who doesn't shy away from lifting heavy things. He grabs the towel, dipping a portion of it in the soapy water. He wipes my face, breasts and neck of his semen.

He puts his pants back on and grabs a brown paper bag and a jug of water, dropping them in front of me. Despite starvation, my nerves are too taut to eat. All I can think of is the feeling between my legs that won't go away.

He collects everything, so that he can make it in one trip and without saying a word, he walks up the stairs, leaving me to enjoy my earnings.

But I can't. Not until I make the sensation of being on the precipice disappear.

SAM

She's stubborn. Sometimes when a mare kicks too hard you have to pull back. Sometimes pushing too much only promotes resistance. I left her alone so she could realize how badly she wanted me to finish her off. Next time, she'll know better.

I wanted to wait a little longer before getting myself off. My tongue in her pussy would have given me enough fodder for a day's worth of orgasms. Problem is, this woman is like an antidote to my plans. She wanted to make a deal. She's learning faster than I anticipated. I just couldn't help upping the ante.

Fuck was it worth it, seeing her smooth, unmarred skin covered in my cum. Rubbing my scent on her body. I didn't shower on purpose. I want to come back later and smell myself on her. A reminder she's mine and I marked her.

She didn't charge the bag of food like I expected. I think I know why. So when I get upstairs, I decide to prowl my own house, trench crawling to one of the small basement windows, peeking in just enough so that she won't see me.

She's already fingering herself when I get there. Lying back on the blanket, her shapely legs spread open, her eyes closed. She's thinking of me. She's letting herself cave into what she wants. She's obstinate so she won't give me the satisfaction. I'll take it anyway.

I watch her truth. That's why I like looking through windows. When they don't know you're looking, that's when you see who they really are.

Watching her play with herself to thoughts of me gives me a fresh hard on. My sexual appetite is strong, usually requiring three orgasms a day just to pacify the urges. My cock is as rock hard as it was when she was sucking on it with those full lips minutes ago. I reach down, and jerk myself off in unison with her.

I time it so that when she's bucking under the touch of her gentle fingers, I'm coming to the sight of it.

She thinks she can keep secrets from me. That her act is convincing. That whole charade is for her, not me.

I see through windows. And I see who she really is.

CHAPTER 7

SAM

I've decided I'll be taking fewer jobs from now on. I won't drop off the face of the earth. No, that would be too suspicious. But I have money. Family money. Work was never something I needed to do, but a strong work ethic was instilled in me and Scoot by our father. I can't just sit around. But now I have someone under my watch, someone who distracts my thoughts all day while at work. Today, when I nearly hammered a nail through my finger thinking about the sight of Vesper finger-fucking herself, and the taste of her wet cunt, I realized I can't keep burning the candle on both ends. My freedom is the most important thing, and keeping it requires precision.

I finally finish Ms. Dawkins' new porch and head back to the farm. On my way back, I cruise along the block adjacent to Vesper's house. There are no signs of what happened weeks ago. The crime scene tape is down. There are no patrol cars stationed outside. I make sure not to drive directly along her block, in case detectives are observing the scene in unmarked vehicles. Vesp's still on the news, there's still a search. But I am already seeing the signs of what people think they know: she's dead. I don't think they have a single clue about who took her or where to find her.

I gave Vesper enough food for a day. I've been re-feeding

her. She got too thin and lost that apricot hue to her cheeks. She's been obedient. I'll give her just enough to keep her a little hungry so she stays that way.

Besides, I have a new idea of something I can give her.

I grab a cold beer from the fridge as soon as I enter the ranch and kick my feet up on the coffee table. I'm giving myself a few minutes of rest before I take care of my other responsibility. I'm always thinking about her. Always. It never stops. Even right now I want to go in there. Ever since I brought her here, it's a constant battle against immediate gratification. One I feel myself losing.

I watch my feet twitch atop the coffee table, anxious to get going on her next gift. The sugar to my salt. But I'm also dreading what I have to do to make it. It's like pulling off duct tape from someone's mouth. You can go slow, pulling every minuscule hair off their face, tugging at the skin, prolonging the suffering. Or you can do it in one harsh yank, causing a brief blaze of pain. So I go with the yank, slamming the glass bottle down on the coffee table, ringed with decades of bottle stains, and head upstairs to the room I haven't entered since my mother died.

I take a deep breath and turn the old brass knob. The hinges yawn as I push the door open. A draft of stale air blows past me as I enter. I know she's dead, but I still expect to see her, sitting in the corner like she so often did. I don't know this room any other way. Now it's just a memorial. The best and worst of her still lining these walls. She and I were rejected by our family. A shameful secret. Perfection was necessary when you carried the family name.

I don't look at anything but the things I came in for. Going into the small crafts room connected to the bedroom, I pull out her trusted sewing machine. I had watched her so many times make something out of nothing with it. Because I didn't say much, I learned to watch. To study. People. Habits. Tasks. I learned how to sew from watching her. I run my fingers along the rolls of fabric, trying to find something that matches Vesper. I regret tearing up the night dress she was wearing when I took her. It was perfect—both sexy and demure. I don't find that exact white fabric, but I find something similar, a crisp cotton fabric with a thin line of lace in the palest pink. Like the color of her pussy before I make it flush with need.

I look through patterns, hoping to find something I can work with. I find a longer dress that I can make short, just as short as the one I gagged her with. After cutting the fabric, I sit at the sewing machine, thread it, and press the pedal. That rhythmic churning fills my ears. I haven't heard it in over a year now and my thoughts drift to the past I try to forget.

A state trooper car rolls up to the park, where I have been watching a man trim grass for the past fifteen minutes. The sound is loud and repetitive. I like it. It calms me. It makes all the anger and sadness easier to forget. But when I see the car, I know I'll be paying for the little break I took. Dad walks over to me. He used to run over. But this is getting old to him.

"Let's go," he says sternly, curling his finger.

I don't fight him, and instead follow him into the car, sitting in the back with the metal grate between us.

"You keep doing this shit, Sam, they're going to kick you out of school. Whoopings don't help. Talking doesn't help. You can't keep running away from school like this!"

I sit quietly. Most parents would like a kid who doesn't talk back, but to my dad, nothing makes him angrier.

"Why? Tell me why! So help me god if you don't, you're gonna get a lickin' tonight. I have had it with this bull."

I don't like whoopings. "T-t-t-they..." I stop. I don't like talking in front of him. He makes me feel bad.

Dad glances back in surprise and pulls over.

"I'm not moving until you finish your thought. Why is it that you talk to your mom, but not to me?"

Because she doesn't stare at me like I'm a disappointment. She doesn't get impatient. She doesn't hit me. She doesn't even notice the stuttering and so when it's just us, it's barely there.

I play with my fingers and look down. I don't want to tell him. He'll think I'm a wuss. My dad is tough.

"You're making your mom crazy because you're a bad boy. You're misbehaving, it's making her sick. You want to make her sick?"

I shake my head.

"So tell me."

"T-t-t-hey c-c-c-all me n-n-n-n-names."

He sighs. For the first time, it sounds like he feels sorry for me. He adjusts himself to get a better view of me in the backseat.

"Sam, in this world, people are always gonna see you as different. You can run away, or you can figure out a way to stay. But I'm

not gonna pity you. I'm not gonna coddle you like your mom. It's my job to make you tough. Turn you into a man someday. You're probably gonna hate me for it. But it's what you need."

He turns around and starts driving. "The school day is almost over so I'm taking you home. Mom's sick, so you go straight to your room or play out in the yard. Understand?"

I nod.

He drops me off in front of the house with a threat. "Don't let me find you running off from school again, Sam. So help me god."

I run into the house. Save for the sounds of birds chirping outdoors, it's dead silent inside. No snacks are waiting for me. Mom's not sitting there with that look on her face of worry she has when I run off. Sometimes she gets sick. She goes into her room and doesn't come out for a long time. Dad has to make us dinner or sometimes the Waverlys next door help out. And then sometimes mom gets what we call the jitters. Her eyes go wide, she drives up to the ranch, and she sews and sews for days without taking a bath.

I open the fridge for a snack when I hear howling. Not like a wolf. It's lower and it goes up and down. I put my glass of milk on the counter to follow the sound upstairs to mom's room. The howling gets louder, but it's less of a howl and more like the sound of a ghost. The hairs stand on my neck. But I crack the door open anyway.

She's in bed alone, curled in a ball. Crying. Crying like I've never seen anyone cry before. She's making all sorts of sounds like she's in pain. But I think the pain is inside. The way mine is. Her crying is loud and makes me scared. I'm not supposed to look in there. I'm not supposed to bother her when she's sick. Dad will get mad and he's already mad at me. So I go downstairs, make my peanut butter and jelly sandwich, and take it upstairs with my glass of milk. I sit on the floor outside of her door and listen to her cry as I eat. I don't know why I do it, but I have a sinking feeling and I want to make sure that she's still making noise. That if she stops, it will mean something bad has happened.

As I am eating my sandwich, the downstairs door slams. "Sam?" my father shouts. He's not supposed to be home for a while, and I get nervous and knock over my glass of milk. I panic, embarrassed of him seeing me here, but also afraid of being in trouble.

I stand up, trying to collect my plates when the door opens behind me.

"Sam?" my mother asks; her voice is stuffy. Her face is pink and puffy. "How long have you been out here?" I don't say anything and

stare at her with worried eyes.

"Come here," she says, grabbing my little hand in hers and ignoring the mess. She closes the door behind me.

She bends over as she holds my hands in hers. "You're home early. You run away again?" she asks.

"Yes," I answer.

"The kids teasing you?"

"Y-yes."

She shakes her head sadly. "You're not like them, Sam. You'll always be different. Like me. This world is rotten. You know, I'd leave it if it wasn't for you. I'd just go to sleep and never wake up. But you're smarter than them. You're faster. Your family is important. And they're threatened by that. So they look for weakness. But I'm gonna protect you. You'll see. Even your dad is like them. Your brother. I'm gonna keep you safe from these monsters."

The door flies open. "Dammit Sam. What's this mess? I told you to leave your mother alone. She needs rest."

"He can stay here with me."

"And watch you cry all day? No, Gloria, rest and when you can manage to stay out of bed for more than five minutes at a time, you can rejoin the world."

"You're so cruel," she cries.

"Here we go again. The world is cruel. Everyone hates you. You're turning him into you and I won't have it."

"You hate me," she cries.

"Don't pull that," dad says. "I'm here, aren't I?"

"You only care about money. That's all you care about!"

"Oh for Christ's sake, you're a mess."

Dad yanks me by the shoulders and pulls me out of the room, closing the door to the sound of her cries.

He crouches down to me. "You wanna be like that?" he asks, pointing at their bedroom door.

I don't know what to say. She is the only person who is nice to me. But no one wants to be locked alone in a room all day. Saying no feels like I'm turning on her.

"Well, trust me, you don't. So go wash up and do your homework." He gives me a shove and a slap on the bum, sending me on my way.

"Christ this place is a mess," he murmurs to himself, picking up the leftovers and addressing the spilt milk I left behind.

VESPER

It's only been one nightfall since he last visited. During that nightfall, I had the best sleep I have had in as long as I can remember. With a full belly and wrapped in a cozy blanket, I watched as dusk turned to moonlight. The things the man did to me would flash in my mind, but the feeling it elicited was confounding. I didn't want to play with myself when he left, but my body sang for it. I meant it when I said stop, but I didn't think he would. He's my tormentor. My captor. My words shouldn't matter to him, and yet there are times when he seems to care about my needs. When he did stop, I realized I'm not sure I ever wanted him to. He started a physical cascade that needed to be realized. Now, my stomach knots at the thought of him spreading my legs, fondling my breasts, rubbing my body with his wet, soapy hands. But that sickening feeling, it links to something deeper—the feeling of my body tingling, betraying me, betraying what I know is right.

That sense of the forbidden. The thing I sought when I'd close my eyes while Carter was inside of me. I'd imagine scenarios of doing the wrong thing. Letting a man who I had just met take me without asking. That secret, it's what allowed me to enjoy sex with my sweet Carter at all. Now that desire is still a secret, but it's a living one.

I loathe myself for thinking of my captor's torso, lean with muscle, glistening with beads of sweat. How his scent, distinctly his, ignited something animal in me. It lingered on me so that when I wrapped myself in the blanket, it rose to my nose as I drifted into a slumber.

Even in my dreams he stalked me—a nightmare mixed with a fantasy as he fucked me at knife point, and I woke up to my hand fondling myself again. I came. Again. Then I slept peacefully the rest of the night.

I disgust myself. My weak will. How I have traded sexual acts for food and fabric. I used to yearn to see my family again, but now I fear the day I see them. They won't be getting Vesp back. They'll be getting back a whore who played with herself after a masked stranger came on her face and chest.

Only weeks have passed and I find myself thinking more about this man than Carter. Carter's become a distant dream now. An idea of a person I will never see again. He's home. I can't even bring myself to think of Johnny. It hurts too much. My world now revolves around a person I don't know. Every basic need I have is at his whim. It's easier to think of him than the world I have left behind.

I listen to the man's footsteps upstairs. If only everyone else could have the privilege of hearing their god above them. I haven't had a real conversation in weeks and he only speaks to me to taunt me during sex. Still, I find myself now looking forward to his company, whatever it brings. He doesn't hurt me. Strike me. Torture me. He barters. He makes deals. Sometimes it feels like a game. I'll take anything to pass the days in this dim, damp prison. The solitude is just another torment.

When the door to the basement opens, all those feelings of peace I have with him fly out the window. I still don't trust him, and my fight or flight response always kicks in first. Only when I know the reasons for his visit can I put the panic at ease.

I come to my feet, the shackle at my ankle clanking. That area is always tender. I wonder if removing the shackle is up for negotiation.

The wood creaks with each of his steps. Slow. Confident. He's come down here silently before, so the cadence of his steps is intentional. It's like, even with his descent into my prison, he's trying to play with my mind. Today, he isn't shirtless, but his t-shirt and jeans are weathered. He must work in construction or utilities. This is the only thing I have been able to gather about his identity thus far.

I use the blanket to shroud myself. Before I was exposed. Perpetually open to him. Nothing has changed, but the blanket gives me the illusion of autonomy.

He walks past me, takes my waste bucket out of the basement and returns.

Then he approaches me and pulls the blanket off of me. I fight, tugging one end of it.

"You said it was mine!" I shout.

He gives it another good yank and throws it to the floor behind me, signaling that this blanket has one purpose, and it is not to shield myself from his gaze.

The sea-hued eyes glare back at me. I try to study them, try to imagine what's under there, but so much of his face is shrouded in black. This man has taken everything from me and I don't even know what he looks like. I wonder if that's a good thing. That maybe there's a chance he'll let me go if I can't ID him.

He walks up to me, slips his hand around the small of my back and pulls me close. He hasn't presented me with anything. Maybe he's just here to take.

He runs his hand up my back and yanks my hair, exposing my neck. He dips his nose to my collarbone and inhales deeply. He's already aroused, pressing his hips against me so I feel what's to come.

"I watched you play with your cunt yesterday, Vesp," he says menacingly. He swallows and takes a deep breath as he lightly presses his lips against shell of my ear. "I know your secret now. You're a pretty little angel on the outside. But inside…" He shudders. "Inside you're a whore who likes it when I spray my cum all over your tits."

Those words hurt worse than the things he did to me physically. In that moment, when I did that shameful act, I thought I was alone. Even then I felt dirty. But I thought I at least had that sliver of dignity left.

He has stripped me of everything. Not just the life I had, but the basic right of privacy. With the things he says, sometimes I wonder if he can read my mind. Maybe there is nothing left of me that is my own.

It enrages me. More so than I have felt since I arrived here. I have been starved and isolated into compliance. Tuned into a pet. But the very human feeling of embarrassment is enough to spark a fire and bring back Vesper Rivers.

Although I'm quivering inside, I put on a brave face hoping to regain at least a smidgen of that dignity he stole. "What did you bring me today?" I ask smugly. He yanks my hair a little harder to get a better look at my face. His eyes wander along my features, revealing his confusion to my response. "Let me be clear: anything you think you see is just me trying to get things from you. You don't even have the balls to show your face or speak to me. You're just the boogeyman. You're not even a person. None of this is real," I snarl. "The only way you can get a girl to suck you off is to steal her and bribe her. You're a pathetic little peeping tom." As those last words escape, I gasp in fear. When the dark pupils overtake the clarity of his eyes, I know I have poked a beast.

He takes one jagged breath before I find myself breathless, being driven against a cold, hard wall behind me. I gasp for the air that was purged from my lungs while I jerk away from his grip. I recoil and writhe, trying to escape, but he grips my hair tighter. A cold blade is pressing against my neck. It hurts, and for the first time in a while, I am genuinely terrified. Not just the constant uncertainty and fear that simmers in the background, but a heart-pounding, breathless fear.

"You want to play this fucking game, Vesp? You want to lie to my fucking face? I've given you choices. I've been easy on you, but now let *me* be clear: I am going to use your body in every fucking way I can imagine. You're gonna scream for me. You're gonna beg me to fuck you in every hole. Because that's who you are, Vesp. The gifts are there to make it easier for you to come to terms with it. But it's inevitable. You have no control over it, just like you have no control over the fact that you need air or water. I broke into your house and fucked you while your boyfriend was tied up like a little bitch and you were in your own little fucked up slice of heaven. I have news for you, Vesp. When you're fucked up like me—like that—heaven and hell aren't very different."

It's the most he's ever said to me at once, his chest vibrating against mine with every sharp word, his voice as biting as shards of glass. Despite our discord, our heaving chests move in unison. His solid cock—either not affected or even motivated by his anger—digs into my stomach.

His eyes lose their intensity, as if he's even shocked by his little diatribe. He's made a point not to say much to me like it's some rule he's created and I think he just broke it. He steps back and thrusts away from me. I reach down and hiss at the pain in my ankle. The tender skin broke when he pushed me and it burns like hell. He glimpses down at me wincing and walks over to me with the knife still in his hand. I recoil from him, still fearing that this could be the end. He kneels and I observe him as he pulls a key out of his pocket and unlatches the leg. A thin trail of blood runs down over the side of my foot.

I haven't had that freedom since he put me down here. My ankle burns from the cool air that instantly rushes the wound, but it also feels lighter having lost the heavy collar. I think about making a run for it, but this guy is freakishly strong and fast. He's thrown and carried me like a rag doll. It's better to earn his trust so I can find a better opening if I survive the next few moments.

He doesn't say a word but instead, tugs off his shirt, his chest still rising and falling, his uneven breaths filling the silence of the basement. There's no negotiating tonight. I don't have any fight left. They call it fight or flight, but there's another option, when the fear is so paralyzing that you submit. In fact, I'm even somewhat grateful that after the harsh reminder of his power, through his own anger, he let me relieve the pain in my ankle. The masked man unbuttons his jeans and lets them fall to the ground. His athletic thighs are peppered with hair that trails up to his cock which stands tall, undeterred by any previous protestations.

He comes at me, white-knuckling the long blade. I stiffen in anticipation, and he throws me over his shoulder, like a possession. I am weightless and inconsequential in his grip. He carries me past a corner I could never reach with my chain, to another part of the basement, full of tools and a work table. Thoughts of torture cross my mind and I scream, kicking and flailing.

"Please don't hurt me. I'll do whatever you want." He lowers me to my feet and I make a run for it, but he wraps me by the waist in seconds. He heaves as he throws me at the steel work table, causing a loud thud, and bends me face down against the frigid surface.

I wriggle underneath him, but he's like a boulder. He presses my cheek against the table and kicks my legs open.

He yanks my arms behind me and itchy twine wraps around my wrists.

"Remember this?" he asks hoarsely as he works on tying my hands.

My tears fall on the metallic surface below me, the glinting knife rests a foot away from my face. Will it be the last thing I see? He reaches over with the long strip of twine and wraps it around my nape so that if I pull with my hands, I tighten the grip around my neck.

"I'm sorry," I plead. "It's true, okay? I was embarrassed.

What am I supposed to say? That I like it? That makes me fucked up."

But he's in some sort of rage-induced trance as he completes the intricate bindings.

"You can fuck me all you want, just please don't kill me. Please."

He tugs on the twine connecting my hands and neck so that I straighten enough for him to put his lips against my ear. "Shut the fuck up, Vesp," he whispers.

"Oh god," I cry.

He slides his other hand over my ass and squeezes viciously. I let out a sharp cry. Then he slaps the same spot, a distinct clap filling the air. A singeing pain throbs on the spot. He thrusts his hips violently against me, teasing his rigid cock against my ass and gripping the twine like a horse's reins.

"I can get what I want in many ways. Let me remind you of that."

He slips a couple of fingers into me and back out, slipping them along my slit. It's too easy. I hate that I don't clench and dry up. He's a monster, he's wicked. But his warm upper body presses against my back and contrasts the cool air of the basement. His heart thuds like mine. He's something—someone—other than the barren, unforgiving, concrete shell that is usually my only company.

He grabs the knife and I whimper as he reaches around to run the sharp tip along my collarbone, then down to my breasts. I try to suck in and make space between me and the blade, but it's useless as he presses the point against the tip of one of my nipples, sending waves of heat and fear down my stomach and to my clit. He runs it down my stomach, and inner thigh, stopping there to lightly drag the blade over my femoral artery. He knows I am a nurse, that I understand the message this sends.

My lips purse as salty tears run over them. *Please* sits just below the surface, but I know it won't make a difference. Without a word from me, he slams the knife back down on the table, so loudly I jump. Then my shoulders relax a bit with the immediate threat being gone.

"Now, tell me, Vesp. Tell me how your pussy feels," he commands.

I'm hyperventilating so hard it's difficult to get any words out. He gives the twine a sharp tug that pinches at the soft skin of my neck.

I open my mouth, but the words stubbornly won't come out. They squeeze my throat, my mind strangling the body, fighting the disloyalty it displays every time this man touches me.

He bends me over the table again, the icy surface shocking my skin. His warm, soft tongue and lips are just as terrifying a weapon as the knife when they make a slave out of me with no threat. I moan and pucker my hips against the rhythmic lapping and sucking of his tongue. My mind and body begin to melt into one, the body snuffing out the protests of the mind. There is so little good down here. So few moments of pleasantness or pleasure. Of contact. Warmth. Excitement. This is one of them. It's wrong. It's weak minded. But my mind and body are weary. They just want to remember what it was like to feel at peace and not waging a constant battle.

So I let myself slip into a state of complete arousal. Not just passively accepting his mouth, but actively enjoying its adventures. And just when I do, proof I am certain, that he can in fact peep into my mind: he stops and pulls me halfway up.

"Tell me how it feels."

My pride awakens, strapping in for another fight. It's one thing to silently accept that pleasure. To play with myself during a dream or let myself enjoy his tongue inside of me. It's another to say it. It's the ultimate act of voyeurism, to force himself to hear my feelings, my secret thoughts.

My pussy throbs, again being close to the highest of pleasure during a time when I am at my lowest. But I can't.

He lets go of the rope suddenly, so that I fall forward onto the table. The soft sound of his footsteps head away from me. He's going to leave me here, bound, for I don't know how long. So that I can't even relieve myself of the heat that has built between my legs.

I turn my face towards him. His bare, muscled back and ass are shaded by the shadows of the dark space. The shiny blade extends from his hand, and for a moment he looks like an ancient warrior. "Wait! Wait! Please don't leave."

He keeps walking, about to approach the corner and

disappear.

"It—it feels good. It feels so good," I call out through a tense throat. My stomach twists in a mixture of arousal and humiliation. He stops, but he doesn't turn back.

"My pussy is throbbing. It feels like—like I'm hot and there's a cool wave coming my way and it's just right there…right about to crash over me. But I need you to do it. Your lips and mouth…I did almost come that night in my house. It scared me. I used to think about you. I didn't know it was you. But you saw me at the library, right? And I thought you had the most incredible eyes. And I thought of looking into them instead when I fucked Carter. I think you're a sick fuck. But maybe that's irrelevant because I'm here, and…" I almost chuckle through my stuffy voice.

Before I can finish, he's striding towards me. He yanks me up to my feet by the twine and spins me, so that I'm face to face with those piercing eyes.

"I want to see you," I mutter.

He shakes his head, his eyes colder than the metal table edging into my ass.

He grips his cock in one of his hands. Like him, it is unforgiving and brutal as it savagely burrows into me. I let out a cry from deep within as he pistons his hips. I'm grateful that my arms are tied, because if they weren't I'd wrap them around this man who is filling me—the ultimate betrayal to everything I ever thought of myself. But my legs are free, and without seeking my permission, one wraps around his warm bare leg. His slick chest slips against my breasts as he grinds against me.

I moan, allowing myself complete abandon. He has stripped away so much of me that it's impossible to feel shame in front of him at this point. He is my shame. He owns that too.

I want to call out a name, but I have nothing.

"Who are you?" I cry.

"The Night," he rasps.

I let my body collapse around the sensation of him inside of me, resting my face against the curve of his neck. His smell, a heady dose of masculinity, intoxicates me, allowing me to get completely lost in The Night. It's his firm arms that hold me together as I increasingly go weak around the swollen cock inside of me.

"I'm gonna come," I pant. The wave begins to crest. He grips the neck binding and tugs it back so that our eyes are inches apart. I told him I imagined the owner of those eyes fucking me. Now, he's reminding me this is not just a fantasy. This is real. This is a dream. This is a nightmare. Like he said, maybe sometimes they're the same thing.

He twists the back of the binding so it closes around my windpipe. The wave crashes over me. Spraying pleasure onto every inch of me. Each thrust just another little wave colliding against me. Like someone in a desert who has stumbled upon a great shore of relief, I drink up the salty water, knowing it could kill me, but all I care about is the instantaneous relief of now.

He grunts and plunges deeply into me, taking himself to the climax he couldn't achieve weeks ago.

I think it's over. I'll come down and feel the guilt I used to feel after playing with myself to my stepdad's dirty magazines. But he pushes me back on the table and spreads my legs. The warmth of his cum slowly drips out of me, the ultimate mark of a beast on his conquest. He uses a finger to wipe some off of me, taking the creamy mix of us and rubbing it on my nipples, glossing them with our filthy sex. He sucks on my breasts, cleaning up the filth with his mouth.

It's so fucking dirty. So repulsive, and yet, I can't help but watch it greedily. Watch him worship upon the altar of this whole fucked up thing. He lowers his face between my thighs and mouth fucks my still blooming pussy. It only takes seconds for me to come again. My thighs clench The Night as it consumes me.

"Oh god," I call out, knowing that there is no such thing down here. At least not the one to which we say our evening prayers. Only Night.

CHAPTER 8

VESPER

I'm not sure what's next as I watch Night (I guess that's what I'll have to call him from now on) get dressed. He hasn't released my bindings and I worry that what we just did hasn't quelled the rage. That maybe the two body-quaking orgasms were simultaneously my punishment for my venomous talk and the reward for my submission. Maybe he'll leave me here for days, bound, forcing me to start over again to earn that balance we had just begun to find.

Evening has descended so that all I see are shadows of the masked violator getting dressed. Revulsion and attraction brew in me. Though the revulsion isn't just towards him. Never have I felt that level of abandon with another human being. Like two feral people relying on instinct, void of morality. He has taken away every sense of decency from me, so that there is literally nothing left to hide. Carter loves me. He is kind. He is sweet. He accepts me for who I am. Or does he?

Vesper must be good. She must be kind. She must take care of everyone. Because otherwise, who would love her? Her own mother barely did and her father has never laid eyes on her. Who would love a girl who is impure and dirty? A fiend with whorish desires? Not Carter. He loves the perfect Vesper Rivers. Normal Vesper Rivers. I was lucky to have such a handsome successful fiancé. Asking for anything more was greed. I always understood that.

Maybe Night is right. Maybe I have always been hiding, making myself easy to love by giving others what they needed and never asking for anything in return. What else could explain how my body betrays me?

Once he's done getting dressed, Night throws my blanket over my head.

"What—what are you doing?" I demand.

He bear hugs me and drags me a few feet, before deciding it's easier to do the customary fireman's carry instead. Draped in the blanket and still tied, I have no idea what's in store. Has he reached the endgame with me? Have I lost my luster now that he's fucked me? Is he going to kill me and move on to another new, shiny toy?

I feel bodies rock as he carries me up the stairs. The door creaking open and the warmth of the upper level instantly stifling me under the blanket. Footsteps I have become used to hearing from underneath the baseboards. The sound of a door swinging open. Then another.

Cooler night air. Crickets creaking. Complete darkness.

We're outside.

"Where are we going? Please tell me. Please don't hurt me." I don't fight. In this position, I can barely breathe. If I flail, the noose connected to my hands tightens. I listen for clues. The sound of grass crinkling underneath his shoes. The crisp scent of nature that lingers on Night sometimes. A hint of animal stench. A farm? Is that why his jeans are often smudged in paint or oil and ripped?

Then it dawns on me that this is my first time outdoors since I was captured. I had hoped I would find a way outside again, even if it was under captivity, but I never knew how. Yet, wrapped in this blanket, I am still a prisoner, still confined. Just like looking at the sun beaming through those tiny basement windows, the scents and sounds are just a tease. Days ago, the blanket was the best fucking thing that ever happened to me, wrapping me in its warm embrace, lulling me into erotic dreams. Now it's just another prison, hot and claustrophobia-inducing.

Just when the panic begins to set in, that perhaps this really is a march to my slaughter, there is the sound of another door opening. It slams shut behind us.

Night sets me to my feet. He folds the blanket over from behind to keep my face covered, but expose the bindings, which he loosens and removes. I moan from the relief and shake off my arms. He takes the blanket off, but it's so dark I might as well have my eyes closed.

He slaps me on the ass, which sends me forward a bit before pulling the door open. In any other circumstance, it could be considered playful, but everything he does is designed to belittle. I try to peek outside, but it's like a pool of black ink. The kind of dark you forget exists when you live your nights by the glow of street lamps and TVs playing through your neighbor's windows. From the chorus of crickets coming through the door, I am sure we must be in the middle of nowhere.

"Where are you going? Wait!" I can't believe I'm begging him not to leave, but that basement has been my cocoon and suddenly he's thrust me from those walls and is leaving without a word. The insecurity frightens me.

He flips a switch beside the door before slamming it shut. A few latching sounds follow. I'm too disoriented by the sudden bright light to pursue his whereabouts. Besides, what I see shocks me. I'm in a tiny windowless cabin. Well, it's more like a shed, but it's freshly painted white, down to the wooden plank floors. On a twin bed, its head pushed up against the center wall, pristinely made with white sheets and covered with a pastel-toned quilt, there is a pale pink nightgown, one that looks a lot like the white one I wore when I was taken. The one he cut up, and me along with it, and used to bind and gag me. Next to that are two newspapers and a note. I run to them almost as quickly as I did that first meal, desperate to understand my new surroundings.

This is your new home. You are expected to use the attached facility to clean and groom yourself daily so you are always ready for me.

I've seen your room at home. You don't have as much here, so I hope you can keep it tidy. Maybe if you had less clutter, you would have noticed the things I had rearranged and took from your room in the weeks before my final arrival.

93

I gasp, remembering the moon necklace and the photo. During the saddest, lowest times, when I was starving, I thought of how grandma said she would look at the moon and think of me. I sobbed, wishing I had that necklace to hold onto, to feel like the only person who ever really understood me was somehow still connected to me. This son of a bitch had to have taken it. I know it was in the jewelry box. I have to get it back.

As usual, your composure and compliance will mean a pleasant experience for you. Acting like a bitch means that that won't be the case. Then again you like it rough. I don't care. I'll get what I want either way. I like it when you don't fight. I like it when you do. This is for you, not me. Though I will admit there are traits about you that attracted me to you out there—that flush in your cheeks, your lush hair, your healthy body. I'd prefer for you not to be starved and sullen. But it won't stop me, as you have already experienced. So, let's agree that it's in your best interest to make the most of your time here. It's in my best interest to keep you looking like the girl I first took.

Eat. Rest.

Your quality of life is entirely dependent on the choices you make.

After the initial moment of rage, I snicker at the sardonic tone in the note before flicking it onto the bed. It's oddly…human. All this time, he's been a caricature of a kidnapper. Just elements of this idea of a person. But here, I hear a bit of the real asshole in him. That smug son of a bitch. I eagerly grab the two newspapers that he made no mention of in his note. Since he showed me the segment on TV about my kidnapping, I have had no concept of how my family or the outside world is reacting. I had time to think about his intentions since that day. My verdict is that since he won't talk to me, at least in not any way that a normal human would converse with another, it was his way of explaining the direness of my circumstances. That I was his captive, that he knows who my family is, and that the police seemed to be clueless about my whereabouts.

The paper to the left is dated the day after my kidnapping. On it is a recent picture of me. Carter took me to the coast for an overnight trip a few months ago. This picture was one we took along one of the bluffs. My hair is windswept and I'm smiling.

NURSING STUDENT KIDNAPPED IN TERRIFYING HOME INVASION the headline reads. I flip to the article, reading about how Carter had given up on the bedroom door when he realized he couldn't get enough leverage while being hog-tied. He screamed and screamed until a neighbor—the very ones I tried to scream to when I was taken—heard him when one stepped outside for the morning paper.

Authorities were desperately searching for me.

I was believed to be the victim of The Night Prowler. I remember hearing about him on the news that night, but beside the fleeting chill anyone has about news of a criminal on the loose, I hadn't given him much thought. To be honest, his wasn't the only name on the news. Despite the sunny weather, beautiful houses, and well-mannered neighbors, the Sacramento area had been plagued with prowlers for some time now.

I hadn't known much about his crimes, but the article went into detail. About the pattern they believe he followed. That he may have prowled dozens if not hundreds of homes, ransacking them, taking tokens and peeping through windows for years before finally escalating to attacking homeowners about a year ago. *Hot prowl.* That's what they call it when a prowler enters a home with people inside. It takes a level of brashness many criminals do not possess. Most criminals just want your things and minimal confrontation. The hot prowl, that's instigating complication.

I cringe at the unmitigated brutality of his crimes. At me for allowing myself to enjoy this monster in any way.

He is why we fear the night. He is the real monster kids imagine in the closet or under the bed. A shiver races down my spine thinking about how I have found a way to be somewhat comfortable with this man.

As if to twist the knife in my gut, the article states that he has never been known to kidnap, preferring to leave without a trace, making him elusive to the cops. Maybe if I had said nothing, he would have fled. Maybe I did bring this upon myself. But I had no choice. He had Johnny. I throw the paper down in frustration, sick and angry at myself. If I had paid more attention, maybe I would have been able to notice someone had broken in. If I had just screamed in the house when he shined that light in my eyes, maybe he would have spooked and left. I let him force me to bind Carter. There were so many times along the way I could have done things differently.

I grab the next paper and skim the date. It's been just over four weeks if this is today's issue. I can't believe a month has already passed. But there's a wisp of hope in that—it's a month and I am still alive. I can survive this. This time the headline on the paper is about some political race. I flip the pages to find the many articles about me and how the world has stopped to find me. It takes me several passes through before I find a short one.

NO NEW LEADS IN THE CASE OF THE MISSING SACRAMENTO NURSING STUDENT

The Sheriff of the Sacramento County Sheriff's Department, Sheriff Hunter-Ridgefield, claims they are still working vigorously behind the scenes, but have shifted their investigation from a large scale search to old fashioned police work, with evidence from the scene and witness testimonies so they can be more targeted. It feels like code for "we have no clue." Forgive me if I sound cynical.

Besides that update, there's not much news in it. In fact, the article is about how The Night Prowler has yet again stumped the police and they don't believe he has committed a crime since taking me, but he has been known to go through periods of dormancy, so much is uncertain. Yet there is one development that makes my heart skid to a halt.

When asked if she thought her daughter was still alive, Rivers' mother confessed that they had "given up hope on that possibility."

Four weeks. Four fucking weeks and she's already cast me off as dead. She's finally free of the burden. The daughter she didn't plan on as she fucked every man in our commune. She had to guess who my father was and he wouldn't even think of accepting me, knowing the odds. She was a hippie, but it was never about love and peace with her. It was freedom. From responsibility. From the world's expectations. Now she's free, married to a doctor of all things. And I'm the one who's a prisoner.

I'm already becoming a byline in the paper. They think I'm rotting somewhere in the desert. No one is looking for a living woman. The only person who knows I exist, who I matter to, even in a twisted way, is the man who took me.

I crumple up the paper and let out a frustrated yell as I roll it into a compact ball. Then I pull it apart and rip it petulantly, already breaking the rule of keeping my new home tidy. Tears roll down my cheeks as I realize that I must come to terms with the fact that this is my new reality. Maybe one day I'll be found or run away. That day could be tomorrow. But in the meantime, if I don't accept and adapt to the present, I'll lose my mind before that day comes. I'll be as torn and rumpled as the paper that litters the pale knotted-pine floor.

So I wipe the tears, bend down and pick up the shards of paper. I've already made my stand earlier, and I think that's enough rebellion for one day. As I pick up the pieces, I feel the soreness from when Night was inside me earlier. I quiver with the memories of the indecency. I grimace at my depravity in lusting for him. I take the fragments of newspaper and hide them under the bed, so if someone ever finds this place and I'm dead, maybe they'll piece together that I was once here.

I push against a small door to find a very small washroom. There's no modern plumbing. There's makeshift wooden seat which I presume leads to a bucket underneath. It's too small a hole to fit even an entire leg through, so I don't entertain the thought of a grand escape. There is a basin full of water and another empty basin. On a small wooden shelf are fresh towels. On one wall is a small, faded mirror, ornately curved in shape. My face shocks me. It's thin, and my hair is wild. A bright red streak colors my pale neck from when he held the sharp knife against it. I run my finger against it and smudge the blood against my cheeks and lips like makeup. It's just a surface cut from the contact of the knife. It won't even scar. I know because I had many of these when he took me and they're all gone now. Erased from memory as I surely will be in a few months.

There is a pull cord and of course, I curiously yank it without thinking. Water rains down on me and I startle. It's some sort of makeshift shower. The water isn't hot, but it's warm enough, and already being naked and needing to cleanse away the earlier activities, I pull down the cord all the way and let the water fall on me.

A shower, even one as primitive as this one is an absolute

luxury. I wash away the blood and evidence of the brutal sex we had, but the pink ligature marks on my ankles and neck stubbornly remain.

Blocked from my view earlier by the towels are small bottles. Shampoo and soap.

As the lukewarm water cascades down my skin, I think of the cute little abode in which I find myself, feeling a twinge of gratitude. This entire thing required thoughtful planning. *Stop, Vesper. This is no different from the basement or a cage.* But it is. He could keep me wherever he wants. Instead, he built me a home. He's given me a way to clean myself. A place without windows which means that at least I am safe from his prying eyes when I am alone.

He's stripped me of my dignity, but he's also giving it back to me in small pieces. If I behave, I can keep this.

Once complete, I wrap the towel around my body and use the small antique brush resting beside the empty basin to comb my hair. It's the first time in weeks I've felt comfortable. I don't know how long it will last, but this is the way things are now. Here, I still exist. The old Vesper Rivers will have to be stowed away, protected by the new one, so that when she is free again, she will still be whole. This is survival.

SAM

She looks like those jewelry boxes, a beautiful girl surrounded by pastel colors, confined to her perfect little world. She doesn't know I can still see her. Of course I would make sure to install peepholes throughout the little cabin. I'm me for fuck's sake.

She read the articles and cried. She understands now. It's only a matter of time before major resources are pulled from her search. There will be a little girl taken somewhere, a murder, then another. And with each of those she'll be pushed a little further towards the back burner. I saw how it used to bother my dad when a case couldn't be solved, but you can't pool your focus on one person forever. It'll get to the point where they will require a mistake on my part to find her. I don't make mistakes. Vesper understands that the only person who can take care of her now is me.

I won't mention that I can see her this time. I shouldn't have the first time. But I went down there and smelled myself on her skin and the visions of her writhing on the floor as she moaned flooded me and all my plans dissolved. Already burning from the heat those thoughts stoked, she opened her smart mouth and ignited them. She had the nerve to lie to me and I had to humble her.

I am always on the brink, living on the balance of wanting to hurt her and fuck her. It's why I have to hold the knife so tight, why I allow myself to give her little cuts, to let blood. It satisfies the rage just enough, but I could slip and then it could be over.

And I don't want it to be.

Fuck.

That's the thing about keeping a person alive. In a way you are just as much a hostage to them as they are to you.

CHAPTER 9

VESPER

Tap. Tap. Tap. Taptaptap.

A bird on the skylight above my bed awakens me. I didn't notice it yesterday. I'll still get sunlight. That was thoughtful of him. I watch the bird attack the glass for no ostensible reason. "Keep trying bird, you'll see there's no point," I groan aloud.

If I don't look down, or move from the bed, with the white walls and sunny skylight, this almost feels like a vacation in the woods. But the soreness between my legs, on my neck and wrists; the aching muscles and tender spots from when he slammed me against the wall, they are a reminder that these moments are an illusion.

I used to wake up with a day full of chores, constantly feeling overwhelmed. Now, I lie in wait for Night. There are no monotonous tasks, no mundane errands. My survival rests on the most basic acts here. Choosing to eat, sleep, bathe—everything is a delicate balance in this power struggle.

At first, I forced myself not to think about Johnny. It hurt too much to think about how he was coping, what I was missing. But lately, days go by before he comes to mind. Survival doesn't allow for excess or luxuries. All my energy must focus on the present. But when Johnny does sneak in, it still hurts, not just because I miss him, but because of the guilt I feel in becoming used to a world without him. I wonder if I am becoming my mother, and it scares me, so even in those increasingly infrequent moments when I allow myself to recall Johnny, I have to force him away.

On this morning, when if I squint a certain way things can almost look normal, I feel him, the memories of him, trying to force their way to the surface. I sit up, the sudden movement a way to distract myself, and cry out as soon as I see the balaclava-clad face. He's just sitting there, in the corner of the room in that perfectly void silence he has mastered. I don't know how long he's been watching me.

"Oh fuck!" I scream, catching my breath. You'd think by now, nothing would startle me, but this shit never gets old. "You scared the shit out of me!" I say, like he's an old friend, like he cares, like his intentions were anything but to frighten me, hoping that if I act familiar with him, he'll see me as a person and not just a toy for his sick pleasures.

I brush a wild lock of hair away, and my heart slows a bit as I lock into his blinking eyes peeking through his mask.

I know what he's here for. I think the cat and mouse game stopped yesterday. Instinctively, I cross my legs under the blanket, the one I earned through oral sex days ago.

"How long have you been there?" I ask. It's pointless, but when you have no one to talk to, you try.

He points to a tray that he must have carried in. On it is fruit, water, and a few hard-boiled eggs. I'm hungry, but he keeps me fed enough now so that I don't act like a stray around food.

"Thanks," I say begrudgingly.

He stands up, and my breath hitches. We may not use money, but nothing here is free. I notice he's dressed well today. At least compared to his t-shirt and torn jeans. Today, he's wearing a buttoned down shirt, with a fresh pair of jeans and boots.

"You look nice," I add, trying to ingratiate him though the words taste like sour milk on my tongue.

He doesn't respond. Instead, he unbuttons his shirt as he stands over me, those eyes paralyzing me into submission. He rests the shirt gently on the weathered wooden chair behind him, revealing just a white tank underneath, his muscles suggesting his physical domination over me.

His heavy boots clunk loudly against the wooden floor as he

slowly strides towards me. I know he does this on purpose. He uses every tool, including sound, to create the ambiance he wants. He is capable of becoming a ghost when he likes.

But today, he wants me to recognize the tension of each step. There are only three needed in this small space before he is standing beside me. He whips off the cover and I gasp. I'm so used to being nude, that I forget I am still covered in the little pink nightie he gave me. He reaches down, softly guiding his hand along my cheekbone and then sharply gripping it to turn my eyes up. His other finger runs along the fresh scrapes on my neck. Then at the neckline of the dress.

He's already hard as he does this, the bulge in his pants taunting just inches from my face.

He pulls a little on the neckline to show me something. Blood. One of my cuts must have bled in my sleep. I don't know all the rules and if that's going to upset him enough to cause some kind of punishment, but he seems to move past it for now, letting the dress fall back against my skin.

In a sudden burst, he reaches for my ankles, turning and pulling me to the edge of the bed. I pant, as he meets me on his knees, positioned between my thighs.

"I'm sorry. I didn't know I was bleeding."

He doesn't heed my words as he pushes up the hem, running his fingers up and down my lips, triggering me to squirm in a mixture of arousal and discomfort. I told myself I had to hide the old me to get through this, but she claws to the surface. She won't let me completely lose myself in the moment yet.

He takes his rough hands and clamps them down on my thighs, his disciplinary glare saying it all.

I nod.

"How does your pussy feel?" he asks.

"Umm...do you want my honest answer?"

He half grunts.

"It's sore. You're thicker than Carter." It's the truth, but I add that in there to stroke his ego.

"Don't fucking say his name again," he snaps. "He doesn't exist here."

I nod sharply.

He gently unbuttons the tiny pink buttons on my nightie,

halfway, so the limp fabric falls open, exposing my breasts.

"Play with your tits," he orders.

"O-okay."

I close my eyes and reach up for them, taking deep, staggered breaths as I fondle them. At first, I'm almost too nervous to feel anything, but as my breaths calm, I am able to escape into my touch.

"Open your eyes." He commands.

I take a beat before following. He's right there, still in front of me, forcing me to look into those eyes. Eyes that have stolen everything. Eyes that have taken me to starvation and filth and then back to life. Eyes that terrified me. Eyes that have watched me come so hard my entire body convulsed.

I hate that they're beautiful. I hate that they are the kind of eyes you could stare at for hours, studying the nuances in their coloring, and how the hues of green, blue and gold change with the light. How can someone so sinister be blessed with something so stunning?

I get lost in them for a moment, slowing my hands.

"Don't stop, Vesp. Only when I say."

I continue, looking into those eyes as I please my own body, so that I can't associate them with pain at this moment, only carnal pleasure.

He reaches into his pocket, pulling out a glass figure. He pushes my legs further apart so I am exposed to him, taking the pointed tip and running it along the wet flesh.

"You want me to fuck you," he says assuredly. "Your pussy puckers open. It never lies. It wants to swallow my cum again."

The cabin is quiet, making me self-conscious about my breathing which is heavy and ragged.

He runs his finger along the entrance, and I feel empty. A yearning inside wants him to slip those fingers in and fill the vacuum.

"If you think you're sore today, wait until tonight," he taunts. "I want tears."

My lip quivers as I desperately hold in a tear at the rim of my eye, but when he flips me onto my stomach, I let it fall out of his view.

He pulls open my ass cheeks, I hear him spit a few times, then run his wet hands along the hole. Carter has never even asked for this. I've never explored that area. I wrestle for oxygen as he presses me into the mattress. I flail my arms, desperately reaching behind myself and only catching air.

"The more you fight, the more it will hurt. Take a few breaths." He pulls my face out of the mattress with a sharp yank of my hair.

I pause, realizing the fight is futile. I have to go along with this. Become the girl who adapts. I resist old Vesper's pleas to continue fighting and let my shaky hands claw on the bed sheets.

He presses the glass against the hole first without breaching the entrance. Then slowly, he slides the glass tool into my backside. I cry against the sheets from the pressure. It's not as painful as I thought it would be, but the invasiveness breaches my soul. He glides it in and out a few times, being surprisingly gentle, until the pressure subsides and the feeling becomes something I can't quite label. It's totally new and my brain and body are unsure of the verdict.

"Good dirty girl," he grunts. It's the first time he's ever complimented me, and it's surprisingly reassuring. It calms me to know I did something to get on his good side. Night spins me onto my back again and comes to his feet. His body shines with a thin layer of perspiration from his efforts. His cock is still rigid through his pants.

"You don't take this out of your ass, only I do. You don't make yourself come when I'm not here today. That pussy, mouth, and ass is mine to fuck. You can play with your tits; you can do anything but come. If you do, I'll know. And I will make you bleed."

I sit there, stunned, unsure how I'll be able to sit here all day with this thing in me.

"Acknowledge me, Vesper."

"Yes," I mutter.

He looks down at my face, streaked with tears, a physical response from the earlier intrusion and steps closer to me.

"You will like this." He says it as though it's a comfort. I don't take it as him meaning tonight, or just having sex with him. He means all of this. Eventually I will like this life. What kind of mad person takes someone from their home and believes they will ever like it? That's when I realize his weakness. He believes that one day I'll want to be here, and if I can get him to believe that, then I might have the chance to regain my freedom.

SAM

"Here you go, Sam." Katie hands me a cold beer with a warm smile on her face. Scoot wins. I don't want him snooping, so this means I have to visit him and assure him I am a perfectly functioning member of society.

"Thanks," I say with a smile. I lean back on the porch swing as Scoot takes his beer from his wife's hand. Katie's alright in my book. She tries really hard to get me to like her, but she doesn't understand I don't really like people. So the fact that I don't despise her, well she's reached her limit with me. "Dinner was g-great."

"My pleasure. I'll be right back."

She leaves me and Scoot on the porch to enjoy our drinks. "See? This isn't so bad is it?" he asks.

"Never ssssaid it was."

"You sound a lot better than the last time I saw you."

That's because today you didn't ambush me shortly after an unplanned kidnapping.

I shrug. Whenever anyone calls attention to my stammer, even to compliment a lack thereof, it gets worse. He and my dad never seemed to have understood that very simple concept.

Across the street, a woman comes out onto her lawn with tiny shorts and a green tube top. She's not wearing a bra and her nipples shoot right through the fabric.

"Yeah," Scoot sighs. She just moved in a few weeks ago. God bless America."

"She m-married?" I ask. It's a force of habit, wanting to know every little fact about people. Storing it into my mental database to come back to later in the event I'd like to pay a late-night visit.

"You interested?" he asks, surprisingly.

"No. Just don't want her husband to k-k-k-kick our asss-es."

Scoot lets out a hearty laugh. "You gotta use the technique you know, pretend to be looking at the bushes on her lawn, or admiring the kids playing on the street in front of her. Check her out on your periphery." He nudges me with the hand that's holding his beer.

Ha, he thinks he can offer *me* tips on watching people.

Yeah, she's hot for a woman in her forties. She knows it. She's probably always been hot and fed off of that attention. She knows we're watching. She's the kind of woman who likes that. She bends with her ass out a little extra. She sticks out her chest. I like to watch the one who really doesn't notice. Who smiles about a pleasant thought that crosses her mind. Who doesn't know the strap of her tank has fallen off her shoulder. Who undresses in front of the mirror and examines her flawless body looking for faults only she can see. Even the modest ones though, in public, they know on some level they're being watched. It's why I do what I do, to get rid of that extra layer of self-consciousness between us. The most intimate way two people can be together is when one doesn't know the other is watching.

Suddenly, the neighbor looks up, Scoot and I both expertly pretend we weren't just discussing her.

"Hey!" She waves. Her eyes move to me, she puts down her watering can and makes a beeline across the street. *Fuck. No. Fuck.*

I tense up dramatically. Scoot notices. "It's cool man. Relax. She's nice."

Don't tell me to relax. I can't fucking relax. It's never fucking worked and yet he's always putting me in these impossible positions.

"Heeey! How are you?" she asks Scoot.

"Good, Milly. Getting some gardening done?"

"Yeah, thought I'd do so before your party starts tonight."
Party?

Scoot looks over at me sheepishly. "Well, it's not a party, just a little thing in the backyard..." he dismisses.

"And who is this, fella?" She runs her finger up and down in my direction, oozing with overdone sexuality.

"Oh, this is my brother, Sam."

"Nice to meet you, Sam," she says, putting out a limp hand for me to take, like she's a lady. I nod and give it a gentle shake.

"Do you live around here?" she asks.

My throat clenches, a bead of sweat rolls down my temple. I don't have a way out of this.

"Y-y-y-y-y-yes."

Her smile drops a bit and she tilts her head. "Ooooh that's nice." I can see in her eyes; she's trying to figure out what the fuck is wrong with me. She's thinking I'm a retard. Just like all the kids used to call me.

"I just moved in from Savannah, Georgia, just a few weeks ago. It's been a big move," she transitions smoothly.

"Milly is getting a fresh start here," Scoot adds.

"Divorce," Milly confirms, wagging her tongue and pretending to tug on an invisible noose around her neck. "They say California is where you want to come to start over."

"Everyone's flocking here," Scoot replies, guiding the conversation for me. "Our family though, we're originals. Back generations, been here almost as long as this state has."

I nod to maintain some modicum of participation in the conversation.

"Scoot!" Katie calls from the house. "Can I borrow you for a sec?"

"I'll be right back," he calls tensely, knowing that I would rather be set on fire than continue this conversation alone.

Milly eases herself against a wooden support, waiting for me to say something else. But I can't. It'll only get worse.

"Scooter invited me to the party, but he didn't mention he had a brother!" she says, playfully shoving my knee.

I give her a shy chuckle. With Vesper, I've spoken clearly more frequently than I ever have. I no longer have to wait for a new home to enter so I can feel that rush that tunes me like a dialer searching for a crisp channel on the radio. My notes are always off, my words spotty, but when I'm focused on survival, sex, or anger, it's like someone turns my tuner to the right spot and the words come out like a perfect melody.

"Well, I better finish up my gardening." She finally relents.

I smile and nod.

"I'll see you later then?"

I nod again and give her a friendly wave.

She baby-waves at me before spinning on her heel and shoving her hands in her pocket.

Milly sways her hips as she crosses the street. A recent divorcee out on the prowl. I can smell the desperation.

At any other point in my life I'd be carving out a plan to get into that house and make her regret all the attention she ever begged for. But all I can think about is the pretty girl sitting in her room, with her ass stretched, waiting for me to fuck her.

SAM

Scoot failed to mention that the family dinner he had invited me to had grown into a neighborhood cookout. That's him in a nutshell right there: always pretending to give a shit, when he doesn't at all. He doesn't really know me or understand me. He thinks he can just keep prodding and pushing and I'll become like him. He knows this is my nightmare. A social gathering, where I have to talk to a bunch of people, some of whom I have never met. But if I leave he'll end up coming over to apologize and that's the last thing I need.

Just to add to the inherent misery, a few of his neighborhood friends who are cops are here tonight. I'm not worried they know who I am. In fact, when I do have to interact with these guys, I get a kick out of knowing they have no idea. Who would think Scoot's little brother is The Night Prowler? But cops in general, they remind me of my dad, and I'd rather keep my contact with them to a minimum. I've kept my ear out for chatter when I was around them, but the one time work came up, Katie butted in and playfully ordered they not talk shop.

I know it would seem like the thing to do would be to get chummy with the cops at the party, but I've always been reserved around them so the change in behavior would be odd. It's best not to talk. Any seemingly innocent piece of information could slip and implicate me down the line. I could place myself near the scene of a crime on a certain day or mention something about The Night Prowler that only the man himself would know. Some of these guys, they are like hawks, always scanning people, always hunting. So while everyone is drinking and socializing, I find a way to hide out upstairs where the kids are playing, like a fucking weirdo. Now I'm the stuttering creep who hides from the party with kids. I can't fucking win.

When the sky begins to swirl with shades of blush and umber, I decide I've played this game long enough and hope to make a quick exit. By the time I get downstairs and peek out into the backyard, it's clear everyone is trashed. Tiki torches are lit. Pot and cigarette smoke wafts in the breeze. The off duty cops always seem to lose their sense of smell at these shindigs. And these suburban folk sure like to get loose on the weekends. I debate whether I should risk slipping out without saying goodbye.

"Saaaaam!" Milly slurs. I roll my eyes before turning to face her with a plastic smile, and am surprised to see her arm wrapped around Scooter. Her legs wobble on top of her high heeled clogs. I wonder if he's fucked her already.

"Hey, where the hell have you been?" he asks playfully. "I was just about to take her home. She's had a little too much. Why don't you escort her for me?" He winks out of her line of vision.

"I-I-I was j-j-just leaving."

"Oh come on! Take me!" she says, throwing herself into my arms. "Your brother told me so much about you. I feel like I know you already."

"Thanks, Sam," Scoot says again, shooting me with a finger pistol and backing out before I can protest.

She's sloppy drunk, and a hint of her nipple is hanging out of her top. She disgusts me. Scoot thinks he's throwing me an easy lay, but I don't want these scraps. She's just delaying the delicacy I have back at the ranch.

Now I'm stuck with her and I have to play the whole gentleman thing, so I walk her across the street.

"Hey, I want to show you something," she says, playfully pulling me to the side of the house, dark with shadows from the half-set sun. She stops and there is nothing in particular to show me, in fact we are in total privacy with most of the neighborhood being at my brother's.

She pushes me up against the house and presses her weight against me. She reaches into her pocket, pulls out a joint, and lights it.

"Here, have some," she whispers mischievously.

I take it from her, suck in some, but don't inhale. I don't want a foggy mind right now.

"Shot gun me," she laughs, digging her body against mine.

I shrug, taking another puff and blowing the smoke at her.

She purses her lips and sucks it in, coming closer, closer, until her lips touch mine. She pulls back and smirks. "You're really cute. Your eyes, I saw them from across the street," she giggles. She runs her hands up my right arm and the side of my face. She touches me like she has the right. I clench my fist, stopping the hand from grabbing her throat. "I like the scars. It makes you look tough. What happened? Your brother said it was an accident, but he didn't tell me what," she asks as she unbuckles my belt.

What happened is none of her fucking business and my scars are not a novelty.

My dick is hard, but that's because it's still waiting to complete what I started with Vesp this morning and the slightest contact gets it at attention.

She kisses my neck. "You know, Scoot told me about your stuttering. How you get nervous around women and it's so bad it almost makes you mute. I don't understand it, you're gorgeous. Who cares about what you have to say? Anyway, I think it's kinda cute how you get all tongue-tied…"

She's thinks this is all a fucking joke. My speech impediment. My scars. As if those appeared out of nowhere. As if my scars don't come with memories of intense agony. Or a lifetime of never being taken seriously because the complex thoughts in my mind are butchered fragments by the time they reach my lips. Now both of my hands are balled and trembling, the ember on the end of the joint singeing the palm of my hand before it goes out. My breathing deepens as she lazily plops her body against mine. She smells of sweat-tainted perfume, beer, and cigarettes.

"You know, I don't care," she says in her best messy seductive voice, as she runs a finger along the rough skin on my shoulder. "You're still sexy," she adds, yanking down my pants. "Oh wow!" she starts laughing. Laughing at my cock.

I grip her hair at the roots and ask "What the fuck is so funny?" The beast is out. It shouldn't be. Not here. Not so close to Scoot's house.

Milly's body goes rigid against my pull. Her lazy breathing stops suddenly.

"Nothing," she answers soberly. "I mean it's really nice. I was shocked at ya know, its girth," she says, like a kid trying to get herself out of trouble.

"You think this is all funny? Huh? You want to tell all your southern society friends about how you sucked off a twenty-something stutterer who looks like he was dragged along the back of a truck?"

"I—uh—I didn't…"

"Then do it," I say, pushing her down to her knees and shoving myself in her mouth. Let's see if she can laugh now.

At first she resists, but it's not much. I've had fighters. No, she relaxes and starts running her mouth along my shaft. It's a mouth and it feels good, but I don't want this. I planned on the perfect tableau. I have a better mouth and pussy waiting. A perfect one. Clear-eyed, not drunk and sloppy. Modest, not this tramp who expects every man to fawn over her sexuality. Someone who is subtle and nuanced, not this fucking human equivalent of a blow horn.

"Get the fuck off of me," I say, pushing her to the ground.

"What?" she asks, wiping her saliva off her chin. I'm a little surprised she's mounting a resistance.

"Go suck Scoot's cock. I'm not interested. You're tired and pathetic." I throw the joint at her face.

She stumbles onto her feet, and into the path of a floodlight, where I see mascara running down her cheeks. "What the fuck is wrong with you?" she asks. "One second you're nice and shy. The next you're fucking kinky." She wobbles a bit, but finally plants her feet. "You know what? You should be begging me!" she yells.

"Shut your fucking mouth," I sneer, stabbing a threatening finger in her direction.

"Fuck you. You're pathetic. Too scared to talk to girls," she mocks in a baby voice. "I was being nice, you know? I can tell your brother was trying to push us together. Fuck you! You fucking freak!"

I should walk away. There are off duty cops at that cookout across the street. But it's like she has a fucking handbook for how to set me off and she followed each fucking rule step-by-step. I grab her forearm and pull her back into the darkness, slamming her against the house. My fingers wrap around her neck and squeeze, squeeze, squeeze, doing what I always wanted to do against anyone who has ever called me that or something like that. Wanting to make her shut up. I asked her to be quiet and she wouldn't. I didn't ask for her to suck my cock. I don't want her pity. I don't want anyone's pity. It's me who should pity them. I rule them. I haunt their fucking streets and they don't even know it.

At first she fights, clawing, gurgling, but she begins to weaken under my grip. My power in the dark puts her beneath me, where she belongs. She thought she was doing me a fucking favor. Like I'm some fucking charity case. But right now, I am her god, holding her very breath in my hands. I stare into her eyes, they are huge and pleading and I have no desire to let go.

My nieces and nephew spill out of their house and it breaks me out of the trance. I loosen the grip around Milly's neck. She gasps for air.

"Shhh!" I lean in close with my finger over my lips.

"Listen closely. I know where you live. You aren't from these parts, but this is my home. This is my fucking city. You know who we are. No one would believe you because you looked like a drunken fool leaving the cookout. I am a son of this city. And if you tell this story to anyone, you won't survive to repeat it. Understood?"

She nods frantically, but I keep my hands on her neck to control her.

"Do I sound scared of women now, bitch?"

She shakes her head as if she can't agree fast enough.

"Now, close my pants and belt for me."

She does as I keep a threatening hold on her neck.

I walk to her back door. She can barely stay on her feet now, quivering like a plucked string. She opens the door with a shaky hand.

"You really should keep that locked when you leave the house." I suggest wryly.

She stumbles through the door, trying to close it behind her as quickly as possible. I stop its momentum with my hand.

Her body shakes as she stares into my eyes. I put my finger to my lips in one final reminder. *Shhh.* I make a slicing motion with my thumb at my throat and smirk, letting the door close on me.

I exit the yard, wound up tight. So tight I could pop at any moment. This fucking party, this whore thinking she's better than me. My dick is throbbing so hard, my head is light. The whole fucking time I was here I wanted to be there, inside of Vesp. I am buzzing on adrenaline and sex and I need to release this stew inside of me before it spills over in a way I don't want to.

Fuck all these people. Fuck their houses. Their yards. Their little families that hide their repressed sexualities. Fuck Scoot for talking about me to her and making me out to be some sort of pathetic fool. Fuck him for conning me into this fucking cookout.

I head to my car feeling like I'm on fire. Like if someone were to touch me, their fingertips would burn off. Vesper is going to get it. This is her fault. I came here because I have to hide her. She's complicating my life. I had a system. I would have normally just taken the whore. Let her blow me. It wouldn't have been ideal, but it would have gotten the job done. But now, nothing else is good enough. It has to be her. I realize what truly made me mad looking at sloppy Milly was that I'm starting to feel sloppy. Vesper makes me messy.

As I head to my car I catch a glimpse of the kids playing down the street. All the adults are at the cookout and the kids have been allowed to roam after hours so mommy and daddy can play. I spot my nephew riding his bike. I used to love riding my bike when I was a kid. Physical pursuits have always been my strength. I don't need to talk when I use my body. My brain has trouble telling my mouth to communicate, but it's as swift as a whip when it commands my body. Growing up, the kids could poke holes in everything else I did, but I was always faster and stronger. Even my dad was proud of that. He used to call me Lightning when he was in a good mood towards me.

Watching him cools me down a bit as I lean against my car. Everyone says little James looks like I did at that age, with his light eyes and blond hair. I'll admit it's true. He's quick too. And he doesn't have my disability. He's a happy kid. Watching him is sometimes watching a remake of my childhood. Sometimes it hurts to watch, other times it's wistful. Today it's the latter. I smile, watching him pop wheelies on his one-speed like I did long ago. The boiling in my blood simmers and I take a deep breath. It's just then that I see a kid run and push him from the side, sending him flying off the bike and onto the pavement with a crack.

CHAPTER 10

SAM

*T*he doorbell rings. Scooter runs over to answer it. It's not for
me, it's never for me, so I don't bother.

"Hold on," he says to the kids at the door. "I'll be right
back."

"Mama!" he calls out.

"You know I don't like yelling, come over here and speak to
me like a gentleman," she scolds from the kitchen.

Captain Kangaroo blares on the TV set, but I can hear his
whining from the kitchen.

"But mooooom. I don't want to take him. He's annoying."

"He's your brother. You should never, ever pick other kids
over him. You are going to be all you have some day. You're supposed
to protect him when kids pick on him. If it upsets you, you don't get
rid of him, you do something about it."

"I'm tired of it. I'm normal mom. Why do I have to deal with
his stuff all the time? I just want to hang out with my friends and not
have to worry about him."

"Scooter, this conversation is over. Either you go with Sam
or you don't go at all. Case closed."

There is a pause before he comes out to the living room. He
opens the front door. "I'm coming. I have to get my bike from the

garage. I'll meet you guys out front. Sam's coming too," he sulks.

Scoot shuts the door, and mutters as he walks past, "Come on Sam, grab your bike, we're riding out to the creek."

I jump up, pretending not to hear the disappointment in his voice. I wish Scoot liked me more, but I am happy to play with the older boys, even if they pick on me sometimes. They're not as bad as the other kids my age because they don't want to make Scooter mad. I make it a point not to say much around them. I just want to be by their sides.

I follow Scoot, but he races to the garage and grabs his bike suddenly, hopping on it and sprinting away. He waves the boys ahead of him. "Go! Go! Go!" he yells. They all laugh mischievously and jump on their bikes, sprinting as fast as they can.

"Wait!" I call out, trying to get some junk off my bike.

I'm confused, but I take it as a challenge to catch up, so I pump the pedals. They are far ahead and make a sharp right vanishing from my sight. My smile turns into a frown when I realize this isn't a game. They're trying to lose me. They don't want me, not even Scoot. I start crying. The wind blows the tears off my face as they leak from my eyes, one by one.

But I am fast. Faster than all of them. I will catch them and show Scoot he can't lose me because I am better than him at this. I turn the corner and see them. I stand on my pedals for leverage, my thighs burning, the tears fading away. I push hard, my lungs on fire. I'm gaining. Getting closer. Closer. The sadness turns to victory in knowing that these much bigger boys can't outrun me on their best day.

I'm going to win.

Then there's a screaming sound. No, not screaming. Screeching. The smell of burnt rubber. Before I can look over, I feel my body thud against the metal and glass. It's not pain I feel at first, more like an earthquake rumbling in my body. I can feel my insides shake. I actually see the man's eyes through the windshield—confused, scared.

"Oh shit!" I hear one of boys shout. The man looks back at them and then at me. That's when the aching starts. He's going to stop and help, I think. I understand he's shocked. I am too. I groan as I look up at the boys racing my way. Maybe they don't hate me after

all.

But the car lurches back, and since I can't move, I just roll off the front onto the ground like a sack of potatoes. He drives forward and around me, the front tires barely missing my head. He's going to leave me here, but as the car screeches again, I feel myself moving, and when I look down, I see the leg of my pants is hooked onto something, a part of the bike, which is jammed under the car. The bike sparks as it pulls me along the asphalt.

This time the pain is instant, as my clothes grind against the pavement and turn into nothing. And then next, the skin on the right side of my body. I don't remember how I got free. I think I passed out way before that.

SAM

I don't feel myself walking over there. I just hear James crying, like an echoing chorus in my head. It sounds just like my own cries when they would change the bandages at the hospital on my raw skin. He's bleeding, but it's not him I'm walking over to. The kid who did it, the little prick who thought it would be funny to blindside a kid on the bike, he already made a beeline to cut through a yard because he's too much of a pussy to face the mess he made.

I have the mask in my hands. I don't remember grabbing it from the car but I guess I did. Rage is exponential and that piece of shit bully picked the wrong time and the wrong kid to fuck with.

I know this neighborhood like the back of my hand. Every yard, every fence. This is one of my hunting grounds. I cut ahead of his path, my face shielded in a mask that will haunt him for the rest of his miserable life. I wait in a bush until I hear the oversized kid in his undersized shirt walking through the yard. When he's within reach I grab him, throw him to the ground, and cover his mouth.

"Listen you little piece of shit," I curl the collar of his shirt in my fist, lifting him up and slamming him back down. "If you ever push another kid again, I'll cut off your little dick and make you eat it. Understand?"

My vision adjusts to the darkness and I see the glowing whites of his bulging eyes.

He tries to choke out a response, or a cry for help, but nothing comes out. Not so tough now.

"And if you tell anyone about this. Your mother, your father, anyone…I'll come into your house one night and I'll fuck your mother. I'll make her scream for help and make your father watch. I'll make you watch. You understand?"

Now he's crying like the little bitch he is.

"One day when you're older, you are going to realize who I am and you are going to know these were not idle threats. Now go home, you little shit," I say, pulling him up to his feet. I push him away and shove his butt with my foot, so he falls on the ground. "How does it feel to be pushed around by someone bigger?"

He runs off, and now I'm fucking hotter than plasma hot. Levels of anger and pent up sexual frustration are mixing together into a violent stew. I take a deep breath and toss the mask into the bushes. By the time I am back on the sidewalk, flanked by perfectly manicured lawns and well-maintained houses, I am one of them again. I decide the best cover is to go back Scooter's house, show him a cool and collected Sam. He's in the kitchen, holding ice to James' head.

"What happened?" I ask.

"Some kid pushed him off his bike. He hit his head. He won't tell me who."

"Something tells me it won't happen again," I mutter.

"What's that?" Scoot asks, particularly interested in the clarity of my voice. The smoothness in speech that only comes in rare moments, when I'm scornful and singularly focused, or when I'm ready to fuck. Everything suddenly is clear. When the darkness eclipses me, the words flow without interruption.

"Where've you been?" he asks teasingly.

I nod towards James, implying what I've been up to is not for kid's ears. That's not technically a lie.

"Oooh," he grins. "Oh, to be a bachelor," he rues.

"Oh," I respond dryly.

"He'll be fine, he's gonna be strong just like Uncle Sam, one day. Uncle Sam builds houses, he lifts logs and stuff. You're his spitting image, so you have a lot to look forward to, kiddo," he assures the boy, roughing up his hair and sending him on his way.

"I'm going home. Tell Katie thanks."

"Shit, what did Milly do to you?" he remarks, regarding the flow of my words. He leans in, "Did she fucking cure you?"

I chuckle, not because his joke is particularly funny, but because this night has been ridiculous and it's just beginning. "You have no idea," I quip.

CHAPTER 11

SAM

I peel into the driveway of the ranch house. You would think the drive would have cooled me down, but no, I am burning hotter and more ferociously than when I had that little piece of shit pinned to the ground, than when that woman treated me like some sort of fucking exhibit.

I run into the house, pull off my shirt, tear apart drawers for another balaclava, and come upon a white one. It's hot tonight and the fact that I have to wear this fucking thing pisses me off even more. I imagine her recoiling in horror if she were to see my face, my scars the physical manifestation of a person who never belonged. At least until the accident I could be silent, and blend into the background, but after, these wounds planted a flag in me. Marking me for ridicule and curious stares.

They'll laugh at your face. They did this to you.

I pull a knife out of my drawer. I don't know what my plans are for it, but I want it in my hand, something physical and sharp to grab and ground me in reality because I am spinning.

I don't like this feeling. She was supposed to be the perfect target, and the second I got off the script and brought her here, I have been battling. Thinking about her. Wanting to pull off the mask. Wanting to tell her my story so she understands why she's here. Why

I'm here.

But she's a manipulator. Because like my mother said, like Milly reminded me today, I am different. I will never be one of them. At best, they'll pity me.

My victims have always been disposable. That keeps me safe. Knowing if I had to, I could get rid of them—carve their throats with a knife, or pull the trigger at their chest. It makes me a god, and the power I emit at those moments is so strong my targets will do what I say. But with Vesper, I can't do it. I can't entertain the thought of being alone here again. Of not having a taste of a life I could only peer at through windows. And that means an unassuming nursing student, of all the people I have dominated and tarnished—she's the one who could ruin me.

I need that back. I am the arbiter of life and death. I am going to remind her who is in control. I am going to remind myself. She won't play me or manipulate me like women so often do.

I march through the woods, the branches yanking at my tank top, the fibers ripping so that by the time I reach the door it's shredded. Heaving, I remove the wooden plank and unlatch the door, thrusting it open so that when it hits the wall it makes the tiny shack reverberate. Her eyes are huge as she sits there, huddled in the corner, paralyzed with fear. I look down at myself, my white tank covered in dirt and speckles of blood from the scratches I earned during my trek.

Don't trust them, Sam. They'll hurt you. They'll use you.

I am a monster. Monsters don't live under the fucking bed or the closet. They don't appear in a puff of smoke. No, monsters are like me: the quiet guy who walks a drunk woman home, a protective uncle, that unassuming guy with the friendly smile who fixes your porch. We do our work in the dark, we lurk in the shadows, but we roam during the day, scouting our next prey.

Girls like her don't want the beast. They want the idea of one. They want to be safe and still revel in the thrill. But there's no safety with a monster. Because monsters consume. They take your body, your soul, and your innocence.

I've been playing a careful game as I figure this thing out. Thoughtfully stripping her down to her most basic so I could build her up. But it's really no different than it is any time I walk into a house. At first, I ask for their trust. I tell them I'm only there for money. I give them the rope to tie their lover. Then once I have them secured, I don't need their trust anymore. I take. I rule. I conquer.

Tonight she will graduate. She's got the cabin, food, and her little pink dress. She's got her dignity back.

This will be her final lesson.

I don't have to get any more riled up to speak her like I usually do, oh I am at the fucking summit already.

"Get the fuck out," I command.

She stares at me in complete bewilderment. I watch the wheels turning in her head; I like that she doesn't run right away, that I already have that hold on her.

"I said get out!"

She jumps, then stands on shaky legs, walking past me and slithering through the narrow space I have left for her in the doorway.

"You want to fucking leave me, Vesp? You want that perfect little life you had? Then go. If you can make it to a road out there before I catch you, I'll let you go. You can go pretend that life is still for you."

"A-a-a-and, what if you catch me?" she asks, her voice quivering in terror. There's a twinge in my gut watching her shake.

"You already know."

She doesn't move. She's still waiting on my orders. Maybe I haven't given enough credit to the strides we have made. Maybe she really does want me.

Don't do it, Vesp. Show me I don't need to do this.

"I'll give you a head start. Thirty seconds for you to run out ahead. This is your chance to go home."

Run, Vesp. Run so I can break you.

"I—I'm scared," she admits through a shaky voice.

"We all are," I answer. "This will be your only chance. Take it or leave it. You have a choice."

She won't make it far. It's dark and she'll run in circles. There's acres of untouched forest out here. But that's beside the point.

"You have ten seconds before the offer is rescinded."

I want her to drop to her knees so I can finally take a breath. I want her to run so I can break in her ass. I want to terrorize her, but I want her to want me.

I countdown. *10...9...8...*

Her eyes jump around, she's going through all the scenarios. And that right there—that shows me there is still so much work left. Because she should have begged me to let her stay.

3—

She bolts. It's sudden and almost takes my breath away. I am disappointed that she's chosen to leave, but I'm fucking thrilled that I get to hunt her. I get to redo that perfect night I lost when I broke into her house and things went to shit.

I count loud enough, without yelling, so that I hope she hears each second passing, wondering if she's one second closer to rejoining that world she thinks she's still a part of, or closer to facing her new destiny.

25 Mississippi…26 Mississippi…

I can still hear her tearing through the trees, stumbling in the pitch black of the night.

30.

I stab the knife into the side of the cabin leaving it vibrating as I follow the sounds. These woods are an extension of me. I used to roam here as a boy on weekends and long summer days, and as I got older it became a refuge from the ranch house. I walk confidently, but don't run as it's easy to trip out here and I need to hear her.

There's a splash and I know exactly where she is. I start running. The sound of snapping twigs and my own panting fill my ears so that I've lost her sounds. As I get closer to the brook, I spot her moonlit outline, coming to her feet. She starts to run again, but I've tackled her to the ground before she can even take three steps.

She wrestles me, displaying strength I had forgotten she possessed. She makes the catastrophic error of kicking me in the stomach. It knocks the wind out of my sails for a second as she drags herself through the mud away from me. But that small moment of freedom that kick afforded her only adds to my fury. I grab her ankle and pull her back. She claws at the mud that crumbles underneath her fingertips. The earth won't help her. This, right here, is nature. This is the order of things.

What's left of her pale pink dress glows in the moonlight, reflecting light where there is only absence of it.

I pull up the dress and mount her back, but I want to see her face. I need her to look into the eyes she claims to dream of. I roll her onto her back. She flails at me and I grab her two hands and pin them underneath one of mine.

"Vesp, this is what happens when you try to leave me."

I reach down and feel for the plug I put in her ass. It's still firmly lodged in her tight asshole. There's only one way to fuck in the ass, in my opinion, and that's rough.

I pull it out and her body tightens as she moans. All I have thought about was popping that ass cherry. Now I am dangerously pent-up.

"Please. I didn't want to run. You…you made me…" she pleads through shuddered breaths.

"No Vesp, you wanted to. You wanted to leave me, after I've been good to you. After you told me you wanted me. But you're a liar. A manipulator."

"No-no-no. That's not true," she sobs.

"Vesp. Shut up and take your punishment." I spit into my hands and coat my cock, so hard and sensitive to the touch. "This won't be long, but it's going to hurt like hell."

I use my available arm to hoist her pelvis up against my hips for leverage. And then I begin to push into her asshole. She groans as I push my way in. It's so fucking tight, and when I finally get halfway in, she screams. She tries to wriggle away.

"Don't!" I grunt, securing her hips.

"Oh god," she wails as I push all the way in. I stay there. Living in that moment eternal, where my dick is gripped by her virgin ass. "It hurts. It hurts," she weeps.

Her cries subside into gentle sobs.

"You've never been fucked in the ass, have you?"

She refuses to answer.

"I asked a fucking question." I push my hips against her for punctuation.

She shakes her head and the glossy trail of tears twinkle in the moonlight.

"Breathe," I tell her. "I've had your mouth and your pussy. And now I'm taking your ass. You'll be all mine, Vesp. Filled with my cum in every hole."

I run my hands over her breasts, up her shoulder and gently brush her hair.

"One day you will beg for me to fuck you in the ass. But I have to break you in, first. So right now, this is all about me and I don't give a fuck about how you feel."

I slide the soothing hand down from her crown and over her mouth, pressing down. Her eyes expand in panic and I pull out and thrust back in. Fucking her into submission. Her thick, vibrato screams struggle to make it past my hand. Vesp's asshole chokes my cock so hard, so unrelentingly, that it's pulsating inside of her in seconds, releasing a huge load into her, dominating a part of her no one else has ever had.

I pull out and roll over onto the cool mud next to her. She doesn't move, but she's whimpering, trembling.

My mind is clearer now. And a part of me begins to wonder if this was fair. I shouldn't care, but Vesper makes me think of things differently. Unlike the others, she is my responsibility. She is my ward.

I roll over, and she puts her hands up like I'm going to hurt her.

"No…no…" she mumbles.

"Shhhh," I offer, scooping her up in my arms. She wraps hers around my neck and cries into my chest, her body shaking uncontrollably. I've hurt her. Probably because of things that happened earlier that had nothing to do with her.

She kept the plug in her ass. She did what I asked earlier, so it's only right I give her something to show I appreciate the compliance.

I carry her back to the cabin and sit her on the chair. I'm shocked at what I see. It's not just the mud and the torn gown. She's covered in blood, like I slashed her with the knife. I look down and see I am too.

I point at her, without the distraction of anger or sex, I'm afraid of what I'll sound like if I speak.

Her eyes are hollow, as if she's still wondering how she ended up here, and looks down. She touches the dress and follows it down to the hem, her fingers trail her thighs.

"I'm…I'm…sorry," she mutters. I watch as she musters all the strength she has to tell me what she feels is a disappointment. "I have my period."

Christ. How did I not think about that? Maybe it's because I didn't have a sister, or I've never lived intimately with a woman. But I've been around animals, and blood is just another part of life. I don't blame her for it.

So I use this as an opportunity. To show her that if she stays, if she's honest with me and doesn't try to manipulate, then I can be something gentler. I can give her the things she needs if she gives me what I need.

I reach for her hand and bring her to her feet. I switch off the light in the cabin so we can't see, all we can do is feel. Finally, I can remove this mask in front of her so I can fucking breathe.

I pull her dress off and then my clothes, letting the ravaged cloth fall to the floor.

I lead her by the hand to the bathroom, pulling the cord on the pressure shower so the fresh water I loaded in it today falls down on us. It's still warm and feels so soothing compared to shock of the frigid brook water. My hands rove along her body, washing away the blood and filth, running my hands through her hair, stringy with mud.

I lather my hands with soap and clean her pussy. She hisses when I clean her ass and my cock twitches at the recent memory of squeezing into that tight space. It's hard again. So hard. I press against her to show her how fucking hard she makes me. How much I want her all the time. How she makes me do things that aren't like me. Like this—trying to fix her after breaking her. So I can keep the best parts of her, but kill the parts that are holding her back from our full potential.

And now I'm back in that space, where everything feels clear and my body is relaxed and I'm not the freak who stammers over every syllable. And yet, I still choose not to utter a word because I don't trust what I might say. Instead, I slide my hand back over her pussy, slipping a finger along the tender flesh.

VESPER

I'm at a loss. I can't understand the game I am playing. I have spent my time here trying to earn his trust and I took the bait and ran. Of course it was a test. What other choice did I have? I had to try.

I knew things were bad when he barged into the room, wielding a knife, looking like he had been through some type of war. The black pupils swallowing the clarity of his eyes. It was too much to take all in. I thought maybe he was going to kill me and was giving me one last chance to save my own life. I don't know what I thought to be honest. He came in so fast, like a tornado.

I tried, I really did. But it was dark and my feet hurt, and I kept bumping into things. So instead of freedom, I ended up on the ground, my mouth covered as he sodomized me. The pain was horrific. He said one day I'd learn to like it. Nothing that excruciating could ever feel good.

Now he's here, showering me, as tenderly as if he were cleaning an injured bird. You may judge me for accepting it, but I don't live in the world of options you do. I need to reinforce his gentleness. I need comfort. And it's so fucked up that the only person who can give it to me is the person who hurt me. At first, it's hard not to recoil from his touch, and the throbbing, burning pain in my ass reminds me of the assault that just took place. But his hands, they wash it all away, they pacify. His calm breaths and total silence are now a contrast from the gristly voice that made sudden and drastic demands. It's like I'm here with someone else.

Could it be that a part of him feels sorry for what he did?

It's so dark in this cabin, I can only make out a faint silhouette of his body, but I see something I never have before, an outline of his hair. Roguish. Wild. Just like him. He's unmasked. Though I can't see his face, I still feel like he's exposing a part of himself to me.

He caresses me between my thighs. I can feel him harden. I shouldn't want this. I should be repulsed. And I am. But I am also eager to be in his graces, and the opportunity to encourage this kindness brings a hint of hope amidst complete defeat.

I want him to contrast the brutality with this tenderness. To know that things are right again now that I've taken my punishment. To make this plight bearable. I want to connect. To speak to the soul I know must live deep within him. To erase the memories of the agony I felt as he bore into a part of me no one else had ever even touched. To feel safe with him, if only for a short while.

With any other man, I would wonder if the grisly display of

my womanhood repulsed him, but not this man. He is raw—all flesh and blood, bones and sinew. A pure predator—as if he was pulled away from society and its norms. As if he had evolved only enough to look like us, but inside, he doesn't understand what it is to be human.

I reach up and land the tips of my fingers on his face, but he grabs my wrist and puts my hand down at my side before I can even really feel him.

I don't say the words. It would hurt too much to know I consented to him. The silence convinces me that the old me still lives buried deep inside.

But I need to feel good somehow.

I grab his shaft, without his prompt or his demand, running a slick hand along the length. I guide my hands up the mounds of his abs and then across his shoulders. One side smooth, the other rippled with uneven, marred skin.

Again, he takes my wrists and pushes my hands away.

We stand under the water, face to face, not touching for a moment. He takes a step closer, and his need presses against me.

A flood of emotion pours over me as I begin to cry. It catches me by surprise. I'm losing her. She doesn't have the will to keep fighting the conflicting feelings that echo inside of me all day.

With no words exchanged between us, he pulls me against him, and then up against the wall. Soap and the smell of damp cedar fills my nose. The contrast of the civilized and the wild. I drift between those two worlds every day now.

We kiss, roughly, our faces twisting and turning, my heart threatening to leap out of my chest. I don't know what this is. I don't understand it. But every part of me wants it. To feel so strongly desired. To be cared for. To always be the singular focus of his attention. He's brutal, but I am the focus of his obsession. Not forgotten, not second place. It's something I have craved since I was a little girl, to be wanted. Even with Carter, nothing could come before his medical school program. Out here, Night may be my god, but I am his angel.

His body reverberates, like he's holding something back, something fighting to escape as he lifts up one of my legs. This isn't like it was out there, dirty and malicious. This is something else.

He reaches down and slips fingers into me. I moan as they send a rolling wave of pleasure up my belly. He drops to his knees, propping a leg on his shoulder, and eats me out. I swallow water and air as I gasp, little tiny streams fall down my forehead, eyelashes, and nose.

He stands before I can come. His nose pressing against mine. His warm breath huffing against my lips. Our bodies locked in on a single breath. Rhythmic, like a heartbeat.

No words. Just the music of our breaths, and the pitter patter of the water hitting the teak below our feet.

We both slide down to the floor. Still face to face, buckling under the weight of this complicated, fierce thing. I lie on the wet surface and he shields me from the trickling of the water.

I wish I could see him, the faceless man who haunts my dreams and waking hours. If I could, maybe I could understand him better. Maybe I could understand myself.

But he's just a shadow. As real as the fantasies I used to make up to draw me out of the monotony of my relationship. Or to pretend to know what it felt like to be something more than everyone else's rock.

The water runs to a slower trickle, the way the droplets fall from the trees after a heavy rain. He enters me. It doesn't feel like a violation. Or part of a bargain. It's hard to reconcile this was the same man who brutalized me not an hour ago.

But logic has no place in my life any longer.

We break the silence with our moans and groans. He rocks in and out of me as I dig my fingers into his taut back. And it's only a few seconds before I am trembling underneath him, tears mingled with shower water so that I'm not sure if I'm still crying.

He lets out a growl as he comes inside of me. Every time he does, it's like he's injecting me a little more with his sickness, making me a little more like him.

He stays there for a moment, hovering over me. I reach out to touch a tendril of his hair. To prove this really happened, that the man behind the mask exists. He lets me for a beat, but then he comes to his feet, standing over me and under the shower head which is now slowly dripping over him like a leaky faucet.

He walks out and I crawl towards the door on all fours,

hoping he'll slip and switch on the light so I can see his face, but he just opens the door. The sound of crickets floods the cabin. A hint of moonbeam sneaks through the doorway so I can make out his movements. He simply grabs the heap of tattered clothes on the floor and his boots, holds them at this side, and walks out into the wild, dripping wet and naked.

Then he latches the door.

PART
TWO

CHAPTER 12

*I*t's noon, but the house is dark. All the shades are drawn because mom doesn't want visitors. I'm still in pain. They put new skin over the skin that was stripped from my side and it's still healing. It hurts when I move. Mom, dad, and the doctor explained to me that they had to put me in a coma. I always thought comas were bad. I didn't understand why they would give me one on purpose. But they explained it let my brain rest and heal because it was swollen. I guess I'm glad I slept through a lot of the pain. My cheek was torn open, the skin hanging off my face. Scoot said some of the kids threw up when they caught up with the accident.

The man ran over a cop's kid. He's in big trouble now.

They wouldn't show me my face at the hospital. On the way home, I tried to sneak peeks at my reflection in the car window, but the glare made it hard to see. When I got home, I begged Scoot to bring me a mirror. Mom had covered them all with blankets. He snuck in at night and brought me a hand mirror. It was pretty with vines carved along the handle and up the frame. I saw the reflection. A red, raw scar running from my ear to the corner of my lip. The stitches were still in and it made me look like Frankenstein's monster.

They tell me it will heal a lot, and by the time I am a grown up, it'll be a line, not red and swollen like it is now. But all I can imagine is what the kids will say when they see me. At least I was normal on the outside before.

There's a knock on the door. Mom comes rushing in and puts

her finger up to her lips. She closes my bedroom door so it doesn't make a sound. She crouches as she walks past the window and over to a chair beside my bed. She's pale and sweaty and her eyes are always moving around, searching for something.

When I got home last week, a bunch of people came over with food: cakes, pies, casseroles. I was excited to have all these sweets. But mom kept inspecting them all. She said she found things like bugs, and poison and that she wouldn't let anyone hurt me ever again. That we can't trust our neighbors anymore. They tried to kill me once and she won't let it happen again.

The doorbell rings again and mom jumps in her seat, like someone just set a firecracker off next to her.

"Mom, why d-d-do you think they want to hurt m-me?"

"Because you're going to be someone special when you grow up and they are trying to kill you before that happens," she whispers, rubbing my hair away from my forehead. "I finally understood. W-w-when I saw you at the hospital…" her voice starts to shake. Sometimes when people cry, they sound the way I always do. "All the tubes and you were so still…" Her tears fall onto my bed sheets. "I understood. The teasing. The way they lured you out there. It was a set up."

It's easy to believe what she's telling me. That they don't want me because I am better than them. That I will be famous one day. That this was a way to take me down, the way that The Joker is always trying to take down Batman.

"I'm going to protect you. I won't leave your side again. No more trips to the hospital for me. They know I know. And they are trying to make me forget so that I won't protect you."

The knocking and ringing stops. She turns to the window and peeps through the shades.

"See? Someone left something at the door. I'm going to get it and inspect it. They keep trying to sneak in poisons."

"But ma. D-d-dad is a cop. He arrr-ested the man who r-ran me over."

She smiles sweetly, grabbing my hand in hers. "Oh my little Samuel. That's just his job. Your daddy is one of them too."

VESPER

I don't startle anymore when I wake up and find Night sitting in the corner of the room, watching me in silence. This time, it's late, the skylight above still black from the night sky. Usually I sleep through his entrance. He can be silent when he wants, but tonight, I am restless. Once I see his silhouette, watching me, I can't even entertain going back to sleep.

It's been weeks since he chased me through the black woods, tackled me to the mud, and attacked me. Weeks since he tenderly carried me back to the cabin, showered me, and then made the pain he caused go away on the wet shower floor. That hasn't happened again. No, the sex has been rough, as if he's trying to erase that night from my memory. As usual, my compliance is rewarded—with orgasms, food, clean clothes, fresh water. I never quite know what is coming my way…a knife held against my throat, being bound or blindfolded, gagged, or sometimes it's just raw. He comes in and he takes, he gives, and he leaves.

If you had asked me months ago, would I be used to anything like this, I would have laughed at the notion. Or maybe even recoiled in horror. But no, this is my life. I have come to terms with it.

You will like this he once said to me. Like isn't a word for this. This is not buttered toast or a cup of tea. You don't like this, you breathe it. It lives and grows in you. You hate it or you pine for it so strongly that, without it, you find yourself wanting to pull out each and every hair at the root, one by one.

When he misses a day or two, I get anxious. So anxious I find it hard to breathe, and I worry that he won't come back or that I have done something to upset him and awaken the rage he showed me that night. He is my only person now. So I cling to his presence desperately, even if I know the second the opportunity arises, I will unlock the old Vesper out of her dungeon and I will run.

He still hasn't shown me his face. I find it insulting, that after all I have given him, he can't show me that respect.

Night knows I am awake, but he does nothing. He doesn't move or utter a sound. I wonder if I've disrupted this routine of his. If he wanted me awake he would have awoken me. So I decide, at my own peril, that if he is going to intrude on my sleep, I will intrude on his Vesper-watching time.

"Why do you do that? Watch me?" I ask, still on my back, gazing up at the skylight. "Oh, that's right, you don't talk to me. Well, you do, but only when you want to fuck or boss me around," I snipe cavalierly.

"Well, I like to talk. I miss having conversations, you know. Maybe one day we could have one?" Thanks to that night, in the shower, I know there is a mote of humanity in him I must tap into. It's rare I get him like this. Still and quiet. So I must take the leap.

"Okay, I'll take that as a *not tonight, Vesp.*" I imitate his rough voice. I chuckle to myself and I just know deep down inside he wants to, too.

"Sometimes, I can see the moon through the skylight. Thank you for that by the way…the skylight. I miss feeling the sun on my skin. It's the closest thing I have to that." I pause, unexpectedly finding myself choking up. The wooden chair creaks as he shifts his weight in it.

"Anyway, do you know what my name means?"

I wait for a response, like I could trick him into speaking with me.

"Well, I'll tell ya. It's Evening Prayer." I pause politely giving him a chance to respond as if this were a two-way conversation. "My mom and I aren't close. I grew up for about the first thirteen years of my life on a commune. She was always more concerned about herself. I was just a product of her exploration." I add air quotes to that final word. "She had so many partners, she wasn't even sure who my dad was. Not surprisingly, no one stepped up to the plate. Years later, she got pregnant with my brother. She gave birth to him with one of the women at the commune—they referred to themselves as goddesses—assisting her, and there were so many complications. That's when she realized she had to leave. His condition was one that required more modern interventions."

I'm not used to one-sided conversations. It feels like I'm rambling. But as he sits there silently, I'd like to think he's listening, maybe even intrigued.

"She moved us down to Sacramento, and within a year she was married to my step-dad. She has that way about her. She's so fucking selfish and yet she gets who or what she wants. Maybe it's because she makes no apologies or has no shame. Me, I'm full of those…" I sigh, wondering if this is too much. Maybe there are parts of myself I should shield from Night. I can't tell anymore if this is the new me, the one who has adapted to survival, who has accepted her current station, or the old me, a wounded girl, just wanting everyone's love and approval.

"My little brother, Johnny, sometimes I hate her for how he is. I can't help but think if they had just gone to the hospital sooner, things could have been different for him." Tears glide down the sides of my face. I haven't really thought of him since the first few weeks. It just caused too much pain. But I've decided tonight will be the night when I'll let myself feel a little self-pity. "She's no better about him than she was with me. So I try so hard for him to see that he's loved and he's not a burden. And now he doesn't have me—"

The chair creaks again. I think I'm pushing a button so I stop. I wipe the tears from my eyes and smile. "Oh yeah, this was about the moon. Wow, I really went off on a tangent there. So my grandmother, she was so different from my mother. And she lived by Sacramento, so she couldn't see me too often. But when she could, she would take me away for a weekend here and there. She was so warm and kind. She's the person I try to be like most, especially with Johnny. She died not too long after we moved off the commune. I've never felt pain like that. Just a hollowness. A loss that just sits there. She used to tell me that whenever she saw the moon, she'd think of me, because of my name. And she'd say a little prayer for me."

I sigh, sitting up in my bed.

"Then she gave me this necklace. It was this pretty gold pendant of a moon. It was her way of always being with me. So when I was feeling sad, I would hold it and close my eyes to feel like she was still here. But I don't have that anymore. Now it's gone. Now I'm truly alone."

The words flowed out of me from a place of honesty. I lost myself. And only then do I realize the massive risk I have taken in sharing that story. That I am accusing him of not just stealing a necklace, but of trying to replace something with his presence that is irreplaceable.

The wooden chair grinds across the floor as his shadow

grows tall.

I hold my breath, wondering if I've set him off. If he's sees my words as a manipulation and not just a desperate woman just being human in the face of insurmountable circumstances.

This time, he's not silent as his boots stomp heavily against the creaky floors and he slams the door and latches it behind him.

CHAPTER 13

SAM

I wanted to say something.

So badly that my lips trembled and I could barely sit still.

I'm not sure what I wanted to say, but as she went on about her life, told me things that no amount of peering through windows could ever reveal, I wanted to speak to her.

I head back to the main house and upstairs into my bedroom where I remove a plank from the floor underneath my bed. In it is a box full of all the tokens I have collected from all the houses I ever entered wearing a mask. Each one jogs a memory of that particular home, family, and story I had concocted for them based on the clues lying around their house and what I saw through their windows.

When you are as prolific as I am, it can all become a blur, but these souvenirs help me remember. But now, as I hold up a small jade statue of an elephant, I realize that there are things—no matter how much I watch, no matter how many times I scour these people's homes, no matter how invasively I insert myself into their lives—that I will never know. That even for those moments when I am in their home, pretending to be in their skin, it's always bullshit. It's why I can't stop, because I never fucking get what I want. I keep striving for perfection: that perfect prowl where everything runs seamlessly, but it's never perfect because when it's over, I'm still back here, a man hiding behind a mask with a box of shallow tokens.

The realization angers me. Counterintuitively, it motivates me to go back out there and take my anger out on these people. But the actual desire to do it—to peer through windows and coordinate break-ins—has simply vanished with Vesper's arrival. This whole thing—this supposed fuck up I didn't plan for—might be becoming the thing I have been tearing houses and families apart searching for.

I didn't ask questions.

I didn't force her.

And yet she revealed herself to me.

I hold up the necklace she spoke of. Understanding the story behind it gives me a sudden rush that I am holding something more than just gold, something priceless in her eyes. Of all the things I could have taken, I grabbed the most perfect thing.

I didn't like the way the story made me feel. It was unfamiliar and uncomfortable. That's why I wanted to say something. But unlike the other times, I didn't feel a surge of rage so distracting and singularly focused that my mouth would just spew out verbal darts—precise, directed, piercing.

No, my mouth trembled, my tongue felt heavy, and I knew that if I spoke, she would hear my weakness.

She's a liar, they all are.

I almost let her get in my head a few weeks ago, when we showered together. I started it as another way to toy with her, but as we wilted to the floor, I wasn't sure anymore what was real and what wasn't. I wasn't even sure who was playing who.

I drop the necklace back in the wood box, and look down at the open floorboard. It's always felt like a suitable hiding place, but now it feels exposed. It never really belonged here, anyway. There's only one room in this house where this box truly belonged, and for the past year, I was too much of a fucking mess to go into it. I hold the box under my arm and run down the stairs and outside to my truck. I rifle through my tools until I come upon a claw hammer.

I take it up to my mother's room, pull away one of her many bright, complicated tapestries and pull out a plank from the wall. This will be the new home for my box of stolen memories.

Vesp's not getting the necklace back. I won't allow her to know her words carry meaning with me. As far as I am concerned, that necklace is a talisman, and I'm the only one who can hold its power.

———————————

There's noise outside my window this morning. I look at my clock and see it's early, only just after seven. I get up from bed and see a moving truck outside through the transparent curtain. There's a couple of men carrying boxes as an old lady directs them. I pull aside the curtain so I can peer at my new neighbor, watching suspiciously, just like my mother does. Were these people sent to kill me? At first I didn't believe her. But then she showed me a razor she found in a pie. So now I'm a little scared that the man who hit me will escape jail and come find me.

Dad said the man won't get out for a long time. I don't press him because mom says I can't tell dad about what she's been saying. Some days she trusts him, and other days she thinks he knows things he's not telling her. She says I should always love and respect him, but that he may have been hypnotized or something. So for now, it's our secret.

My curiosity gets the best of me and I tiptoe downstairs. Scoot and dad went fishing around dawn, so it's just me and mom. The house is quiet and I think she's still in bed. I don't make a sound on the way to our front window, where I watch the people moving up close.

There's a girl standing in their driveway, which butts up to our lawn, jumping rope.

She's singing some sort of song, I can't make it out, but I hear her cheerful voice muffled through the window. She's wearing a baby blue dress with white ruffles and pretty white socks that have ruffles too. I want to be friends with her. It's been so long since I have been outside, but the stitches are out of my face and I can walk fine now. I only have a few bruises left.

Normally, I would be shy, but there's something about the way she hums the song when she jumps rope, like maybe she'll be the one person who treats me different.

I open the front door and step outside, still in my P.J.'s. With my chin down, I drag my feet as I make my way to her until I am standing close, but I don't say anything. I'm afraid the words will come out funny because my heart is beating so fast.

"Hi," she says.

I don't say anything back.

"You live in that house?" she asks.

I nod.

She doesn't stop her staggered rope-jumping as she speaks to me. "My grandma is moving into this house but I don't live with her. What's your name?"

I move my lips and hardly a whisper comes out.

"S-sam."

"How come you're out here with no shoes or shirt on?" she asks.

I shrug.

"My grandma said I could ride my bike as long as I wasn't alone. You have a bike?"

My heart sputters at the invite. But I know my mom would be so angry if I rode down the street on a bike again. Especially after what happened. Nevertheless, I nod to let her know I do have a bike. Really, it's Scoot's.

Her rhythmic jumping stops and I look up to see what's changed. She drops the handles to the floor. "What happened to your face?" she asks.

Now my heart sputters for a different reason. Will she laugh when I try to speak? Is she part of the group of people trying to hurt me? Is this a trap?

"I had an aaaaa-cident."

"How?"

"C-c-c-car hit m-m-me."

"Wow," she says, her eyes going wide as she reaches to touch my face. I jump back. I've never had a girl touch me before, and I regret that I don't let her. I want to tell her to touch me, it's okay now, but I'm too embarrassed.

"How come you talk like that?" she asks.

The question is so straightforward, but I don't feel so bad when she asks it. It's like she wants to know about me instead of just already thinking she does.

"It's a sp-sp-sp-eech—" Right now, the word 'impediment' might as well be supercalifragilisticexpialidocious, so I change

direction. *"I st-st-st-uter. B-b-b-but I go to classssss-es for it."*

"Oh," she shrugs. *I wait for her to laugh, to tell me to beat it. "So, you wanna ride around?" she asks.*

A friend. Could she be that person? The one I always thought was out there, who wouldn't gang up on me? And she's so pretty.

"Sam!" a panicked voice calls out from the front door of my house. "Sam!" mom says more firmly as she marches towards me. "You're not supposed to be out here."

She's wearing a housecoat and looks sleepy.

"Sam, you need to be home resting," she puts her hands on my shoulders.

"I'm f-f-f-ine."

"Sam, what have I been telling you?" she whispers. Our little secret.

The girl watches our back and forth.

"Hello," my mom says with a nervous sweetness in her voice. "He is a very sick boy and he cannot play today."

"Oh," the girl, whose name I don't know, responds.

My mom drags me back home, and my heart sinks watching the pretty girl in her ruffled socks disappear from my eyes.

"Mom, I want to play."

"What have we discussed?" she snaps, pointing her finger at me. "It's not safe out there! You think that pretty little girl moving in next door was a coincidence? She is the perfect plant for a boy like you."

"She was n-n-nice!" I protest.

"Sam, honey, girls will be nice to you to get things. They will use you to get money, or connections. You are special, but they don't understand that. Little girls are shallow and they would rather be with a boy like Scoot. He's simple, but he's like everyone else. You are complex."

"This isn't f-f-fair!" I argue, a tear coming down my cheek. "I t-t-t-thought she liked m-m-m-m-me..." the sobbing makes my chest shiver and the stammer act up.

"Sam, you cannot fight me on this. Those people are strangers. They could be planted here by the CIA—anyone! I'm trying to protect you."

"I want to go outside! She was nice. She was going to be my

only friend!" I shout, frustration finding a way to break through the tension in my mouth and chest that holds back my words.

She looks surprised for a second and a little sad.

"That's it!" she says throwing her hands up in the air. "I am your mother and I will do whatever it takes to keep you safe! I don't care what your father says. I don't care what anyone says. We can't stay here anymore. It's too easy to find you. It's too easy for you to be manipulated and lured out there."

She grabs my hand and yanks me up the stairs and into my parent's bedroom, pulling a few suitcases out of the closet.

"Wh-wh-wh-ere?" I ask.

She tosses a large suitcase on the bed and unclips it. "To the ranch. You'll be safe there. I can home school you. We can stay there until you are old enough to protect yourself," she says, her face covered in sweat, her eyes bouncing around like two ping pong balls.

CHAPTER 14

VESPER

I know this morning will be different when I open my eyes and see the newspaper on the chair that usually seats Night.

These breaks from the monotony are welcome surprises, like bits of treasure. Since that night when I spoke to him and he stormed off, he doesn't sit around watching me much, instead, he comes in only to take what he needs from me, or give me my essentials.

Lately, during the few seconds it takes him to put his clothes back on, I have been hastily begging him for things that I believe will help me long term: books, magazines, music, origami—fucking anything. I'm starting to feel different, like my mind is slipping in a way. I have no stimulus other than fucking him, and I'm afraid eventually something will snap. I think about him all the time. What he's doing out there. If he's still going to houses. If he's been with other people. I think about what will happen if he gets into an accident and dies out there. I will slowly starve to death and no one will ever know what happened to me. My mind has to breathe, to see a glimpse of a world that has to do with anything but him.

He hasn't heeded those pleas, and the newspaper might just be another veiled message, but it's full of stuff I can read.

So when I see this paper, I almost trip rushing out of bed to devour its contents, ignoring the small breakfast waiting for me on my bedside table. Naturally, the first thing I do is look for stuff about me. I skim front to back, back to front, multiple times. Nothing, not one fucking article. Based on the date on the paper, if it's even today's issue, I have been here for about four months.

A tear trickles from my eye, but I wipe it before it can trigger a flood. I am numb to my former life. It's just a memory at this point. I read the entire thing front to back, not leaving one article—even the most boring financial crap—unread. It's funny how I used to bitch about all the textbooks I would have to read for school. What I wouldn't give now for an anatomy textbook to pass the hours.

Setting the paper down, I feel as satisfied as someone who has just consumed a gourmet meal.

But as I sit there eating my breakfast, staring at the beam of sunlight that pours down to my bed, a dull panic sets in.

Will Night visit me today? Do I have to face another day trapped in these walls with nothing but silence?

So I start humming to myself. A song I used to sing to myself as a little girl.

Jimmy crack corn I don't care,
Ole Massa gone away.

My head bobs side to side, then I tap my feet. But I bore with that after a while.

"What the fuck are you going to do today, Vesp?" I ask. "Stare at this wall? Or this wall?" I point to identical adjacent walls. "No, you'll just wait here for the psychopath with the annoyingly perfect body and terrifying temper…" I let the words drift away, talking is boring when you're alone. My attempt at comic relief isn't working on me, only reminding me how tragic this all is.

I look around the small, but well-appointed space, as if something new will pop up. Of course, nothing does. Nothing ever happens unless he does.

So there's only one thing I can do at this point with myself, one way to entertain my idle hands and mind.

SAM

I watch Vesper, eager to see her reaction when she realizes that she's pretty much forgotten. Her case is already as cold as the brook running behind the cabin. The flyers stapled to every tree and telephone pole have become faded and tattered. She now gets an infrequent mention in the news or an occasional small article. But while her case was headline news for the first couple of months, there hasn't been anything to report. They don't have a body, they don't have leads, and The Night Stalker has gone dormant. And if there's no new information, you don't make the paper.

Last time I gave her the paper, she had a little meltdown. Knowing what I know now about her relationship with her mother, I think I know what part of the article set her off. I watched that raw moment, fascinated by the different stages of emotions as she reconciled her mother had already proclaimed her dead.

I thought it was odd too, to be honest. Most people are quite the opposite. Their loved one is dead and they medicate themselves with hopeful denial. When they finally believe their daughter is dead they usually wait before publicly announcing it. But her mother seems to have given up on her almost as quickly as she was snatched.

This time she wipes her eye once. Just one tear. I have tasted those tears, consumed her grief. She's running lower on them now, usually stone-faced unless we are in the heat of fucking. Then her face contorts and animates with pleasure, pain, and fear. That one night she told me the story of the necklace, I got something in between that. I liked it. I hated it. It's too much of a gamble to let her get under my skin like that again.

She starts to hum a song. It's faint and distorted by the time it breaches the cabin walls. But still, it stirs up a sense of a memory. I reach into the depths of my mind to recall the details, but I can't quite recollect.

She starts to talk to herself after she quits the song. She's been doing that more. Pacing back and forth, saying nonsense to herself sometimes. I can't quite hear her unless she's loud and in this case, she's not. But she's animated enough to make me laugh. I've been thinking about giving her things so she doesn't go crazy, but I'm still not sure I want to give her the power of entertaining herself yet. I like being her sole source for that. When I am certain I have her fully, I'll consider it.

I fall into the zone of watching—it's a calm, almost hypnotic state as the intrusive thoughts, which have been less frequent in the past few weeks, fade away when I view the mundane through an extraordinary lens.

But what she does next, violently rips me out of the trance. She sits in my chair—I call it that because despite me never stating she cannot, she never sits on it—and pulls her feet up, spreading her knees apart.

She pulls out one of her plump tits, tits I have feasted on so many times and yet still cannot get enough of—and massages it with one hand. She dips her head back, running her pink tongue along her lips, like an invitation, or a taunt.

She pulls up the little nightgown I made her to replace the one destroyed the night I chased her, exposing her shaven pussy, so I can see the pink wet lips, and begins to finger fuck herself.

I've watched many people masturbate. Usually they're quiet, save for a few climaxing moans, because there is no one to put on a show for. Until this point, I was certain she didn't know I was watching. But she's loud, her body fucking her hand vulgarly, as if she wants men to watch and jack off to her. The contrast of this lovely, innocent woman, so vulgarly fucking herself, simultaneously pisses me the fuck off and gives me an angry erection. She shouldn't be entertaining herself like this. I own that pussy. I own her sex, period. Yet she's finding a way to circumvent that.

"You sneaky little bitch," I sneer under my breath.

Then she moans my name. Well, not Sam. But my alias, one that we stumbled upon the first time we fucked to completion. I'm not there and she's still fucking me. My rage converts to an almost emergent need to come with her, so I pull out my cock and grip it, biting back my own moans as I watch my handiwork: a woman reduced to just a few needs—me being one of them.

"Fuck me, fuck me!" she says as her hips rise up against the chair, her finger fumbling with her tanned nipple.

"Oh fuck, Vesp," I grunt from my belly as my dick builds up to its precipice.

Her moans burst through the cabin walls as I move my hands faster to meet her, the cabin wall catching my cum. Though I wish it was her pussy or mouth, knowing I made her come without even being there is intensely gratifying. And yet, it's not enough. It never is. There's never enough sex. There have been days I fucked her four times, and then had to switch to her ass or mouth because her pussy was swollen from all the fucking. Yet, she's always ready for me. Always coming.

I fix myself, determined to go in there and give her a dose of the reality she's been fantasizing about. But first, I want to study her. She pulls down her dress, a glazed look in her eyes, as if she doesn't understand what's overtaken her.

Vesper stumbles to her feet and fixes herself, trying to erase the evidence of filth. She looks around suspiciously as though, perhaps, it was so immoral that God may have come down just to judge her. She takes a deep breath and runs her hands along her brow and passes them over her head with a great sigh.

"Woah," she mouths. "I am so fucked."

I laugh. She can be funny sometimes.

But then, seemingly out of nowhere, her facial expression changes. Instead of shock, confusion and disgust take over. She takes another deep breath, as if trying to settle something. Then she sprints over to the water closet, which I can't see from the peephole I'm using.

CHAPTER 15

VESPER

The twisted mix of relief and shame I feel after playing with myself to thoughts of my captor are eclipsed by sudden dizziness. The walls swirl around me, the floor moves under my feet.

He's trying to kill me. He's poisoned my breakfast.

My stomach cramps and I run to the miniature bathroom, sticking my finger down my throat, coaxing my meal out. My stomach is relieved instantly, but I break out in a cold sweat, terrified of what will come next. I slam the door, and sit with my back pressed against it, determined to never let Night in. I can't catch my breath as I gasp for air, gripped by a new kind of terror. I'm going to die. I know it. I just do. I had allowed myself to trust him, that if I gave him what I wanted, I would survive, but he's using the very key to my survival to kill me.

My vision tunnels, the poison must be doing its handiwork and I only pray that I threw up enough to halt its progress. I try to calm my breathing but my chest only tightens a bit more every time I suck in air.

Then I nearly stop breathing all together when I hear his footsteps in the main room. Without thinking, I scramble on all fours and reach for the razor. A paltry weapon, but it's my only option. I thrust myself at the bathroom door just as he tries to push it open.

"Go away!" I cry. Using all the strength in my legs to push against him.

He pounds on the door, each thud making my heart bang against my chest.

"Fuck you!" I shout, through sobbing and hyperventilation.

He begins his campaign against my barricade, pushing the door steadily. My heels burn as they desperately scrape against the floor. But he's too strong and he manages to open it enough to stick his body halfway through.

"Nooo!" I scream, turning onto my knees and lunging at the door, pushing it hard against his body. He grunts, and pushes the door back in one explosive motion, sending me and the door flying back. The door comes swinging back towards him and he pushes back at it again, this time so forcefully that it cracks and splinters. Facing him and on my ass, I push myself away from him, against the opposite wall. It never get less frightening: a strong, masked, man heaving over me. As anonymous and soulless as any monster in a campfire story. All I can do is brace myself against it.

Night grabs me by my shoulders and pulls me up.

"You son of a bitch!" I shout, flailing the razor at him. I get maybe a swipe and a half before he grabs my wrist and pries it out of my hand. He throws the razor against the wall, and it bounces a few times before resting by his feet.

"You're trying to kill me!" I shout. "You're trying to kill me!" Everything is slipping away. I feel myself growing weak. "I hate you!"

I use every bit of energy I have left to kick and wrangle myself out of his grip. I'm well fed now, and stronger than when he had me starving and living in my own filth, even with his poison inside of me.

"You promised you would take care of me if I was good!" I scream. "I've been good!"

I've barely even looked at him thus far, overwhelmed with panic and the sensation of dying, but at that point I notice his frustration. His lips puckering as if he's fighting the urge to say something. His eyes wide and glazed in a way I have never seen.

With no weapons, and rendered almost incapacitated in his grip, I butt him right in the nose with my forehead.

"Fuck!" he says, letting go of me to grab his nose.

I manage to pull the bathroom door open and get to the main door, but he pulls me back by the pretty little nightgown he gave me. Both his arms wrap me as I leave the ground and slam down onto the bed. The joints creak and crack under the force, and I am breathless despite the padded surface taking much of the impact.

I start screaming as loud as I can, choking on the force of it.

Night rears his arm back and slaps me. Hard. So hard everything, including me, goes silent.

He grabs my shoulders and shakes me. Like someone trying to get someone's attention. His eyes are fiery but huge, pleading.

I've learned to read him, his eyes and gestures a language of their own. He's trying to get me to just calm down and look at him.

I grab my cheek, flaming hot and pulsing from the slap and begin to wail. He's never hit me before. It's one of the reasons I guess I trusted him or believed him. I know, it's ridiculous considering all he has done, but the cuts, the bruises from the bindings, those were all unintended consequences, or so I thought. But this slap, I've never been hit like that in my entire life. And it works, to an extent, to get me out of the complete spiral I was being sucked into.

He shakes me again, less forcefully, and I open my eyes, still holding my cheek.

He shakes his head. Over and over again. *No.*

No what? You're not trying to kill me? You didn't just try to poison me? No—don't you scream again or I will hurt you?

But I don't ask. I don't want answers. I don't want to talk, I just want to keep believing he's poisoning me.

He stays on top of me. Both of us still panting from the wrestling and screaming. And he does so until the poison wears off, my vision clears, my breathing slows.

When he's confident that I won't run or go apeshit again, he slowly slides off of me. Night keeps his eyes on me the entire time as he backs away and plops himself on his seat. He turns it to face the corner, like a punished child, bows his head and pulls off his mask. With a great sigh, he runs his hands through his wavy light brown locks and then buries his hands in his face.

This is it. I'll finally see the face of the person I have been living with and fucking for months. The sadist who broke into my home, spied on me, stole my grandma's necklace, raped me over and over. The person who I wait for every day and miss when he doesn't visit. The person I fantasized about, not understanding the full repercussions of wanting a man like him. I'll see the face that houses those eyes, beautiful and evil.

I sit up, waiting, resisting the temptation to peek and perhaps cause him to rebel and mask himself again.

But just as I am convinced he will show me that we are something more than just a prisoner and a sick, twisted psycho, he bows his head down and pulls the mask over his face again.

I snarl as my expectations sink.

If he had just given me that, reached out to me a bit, I could believe that this morning was a mistake. A panic attack, food poisoning. But he has made it clear with that small gesture that all I am is his fuckhole.

He stands up, straightens out the chair, and heads to the bathroom to inspect the damage to the door. That's just a few seconds. On his way out, he grabs the used plates and utensils.

Night kicks the door open with his foot, and before leaving, he turns and give me one final look. I can't read it. I'm conversational in his language, but not fluent. Maybe I could be if he'd let me see more than his lips and eyes. But I can feel it's a new look. One laced with disappointment, perhaps regret. Though those aren't words in his vernacular, so I must be projecting.

When he leaves, I throw myself back on the bed. Just like him, I run my hands over my face and through my hair trying to understand how a morning that had started out so quiet, had dissolved into a hurricane of chaos. I'm losing my mind, I think. And he won't help me keep it. This fucking newspaper, designed to taunt me, to remind me no one cares, is not enough.

I don't care how many times he shakes his head. I know what happened. And that sickness I felt after I ate his food was real.

So I do what a person in my position, someone who is weak and left with nothing but an empty room, the clothes on her back and her body does in protest. I guess I should be grateful to him, he's trained me to endure a physical agony I never imagined. If he wants me dead so be it, but it won't be quick. If he doesn't, well then he's going to have to listen to my fucking demands. If anyone is going to kill me, it'll be me.

Today marks day one of my hunger strike.

CHAPTER 16

VESPER

I think Night was angry at me at first. He didn't come back for two days. Punishment I suppose. No food or fresh water. I was annoyed because a hunger strike only works if your captor tries to actually feed you. The hunger was sharp, but nothing like what I experienced down in that basement. On day three, he left breakfast for me. When he came back in the evening and it was untouched, he petulantly grabbed the tray and stormed out, leaving me alone.

I still feel sick. Whatever he put in my food, it hasn't worn off. Usually, I'm fast asleep when he brings my food in, but this morning, I've woken up feeling ill and am dry heaving over the makeshift toilet as he comes in.

I swing the door closed for privacy, but once he sets down the tray, he pushes the door open. He always has to counter any act of independence. I pretend I'm just washing up. I don't look at him. I don't say anything. I simply sit on my bed and stare at the sun through the skylight.

Night gets my attention when he pulls out a pad and paper. My heart almost screams with joy. I'm supposed to be mad at him or at the very least indifferent. So I pretend to be unimpressed by the first signs of possible non-sadistic interaction.

He quickly scribbles something on a pad and holds it up.
I didn't poison you.

He had to have.

I scoff. "Well, I don't believe you."

He huffs and scribbles again.

You're no good to me sick.

How romantic. "Yeah, well maybe you wanted me dead, but I wizened up and threw up the crap you gave me. And I won't eat your food again. I'd rather starve to death."

You're losing your grip on reality.

When I read that "concerned" note, I start to laugh. At first it's an ironic giggle, but the more I think about the hypocrisy in that statement, I start to laugh hysterically. I'm not trying to piss him off or even mock him, but is he really claiming I'm the one who doesn't operate in reality?

He puffs his chest and stands up, circling away from me in frustration. I try to stop laughing. I am terrified, genuinely. But my body or mind has gone rogue and the laughter won't stop.

"You—" I laugh again. "Put me here—I haven't had a two-sided conversation in months. Or read a book. Or watched TV. One minute you won't speak, the next you're asking me how my pussy feels. If I am losing my mind, it's all your fault!" Like that, the switch flips from uncontrollable laughter to manic rage.

In one quick motion, he turns, grabs a piece of toast from the tray and holds me by the neck, smashing the food against my mouth.

"Eat!" he orders through gritted teeth.

I claw at his arm. My mouth hurts from the impact, and the little buttery crumbs that do reach my tongue are so tempting, but I purse my lips in defiance.

He pulls his hand away and I spit out the bits of bread lodged in my mouth.

"You see?!" I scream. "I'm supposed to trust you? I'm supposed to believe you don't want to kill me when you've been killing me little by little every single day? You can beat me, you can strip me. Put me out in the woods. But I won't eat!" I screech at the top of my lungs.

There's no logic in my protest. This strike started out to keep me alive, but he might kill me right now. No. This is about something else. I'm still not sure what. It's not survival, that's for sure.

He picks up the tray and flings it across the room, juice, toast and hardboiled eggs exploding every which way.

"You want to play this fucking game?" he points a finger at me. "You have no idea how bad things can get. I'm gonna give you one day to reconsider. Because if you don't, you will know what it really feels like for me to want to kill you."

He marches out of the cabin, slamming the door so hard I swear he's dislodged the frame.

I let out a desperate scream. I don't know what I'm doing or why. I don't know if this man cares that I live or die. And it hurts more than anything to think he might actually care more than my own mother. The man who mocks me with articles reminding me that I am one of the forgotten. The man who keeps me locked in a room. I'm supposed to believe he wouldn't dare poison me?

The mess he left torments me. Not in the way that I want to pick through the debris to eat it, but in that it roils my stomach. I run to the bathroom and vomit bile.

"Nononono…" I whisper to myself with a sudden realization, the thought so traumatic, that perhaps I've deluded myself into thinking of grand poisoning conspiracies.

In nursing school, we had to take a psychology class. I remember learning that sometimes people disassociate to protect themselves from their reality. As I crawl into bed, that thought sits on the surface. I'm unwilling to fully uncloak it and examine why I would make myself believe I was poisoned, and exactly what aspect of my reality am I trying to mask.

SAM

I don't want to hit her or torture her. We had a good thing going for a while. A routine. We gave each other what the other needed. She was complaint and it seemed accepting of the circumstances. Then one minute, I'm watching her masturbate to thoughts of me, the next she's in a frenzy claiming I've poisoned her.

She had asked me for weeks for ways to stimulate her mind. Maybe I fucked up and was too hard on her. But now, if I give her something, it'll make her think acting up reaps benefits. No. Four months and I'll have to go back to square one. No contact. No food. No water. Until she breaks again. Hopefully this time, it'll be even harder on her and she'll realize she needs me. That she's happier when she just accepts that.

But I still don't get it. Yes, she was acting a little odd, but not much more so than what I see average people doing alone. Average people talk to themselves, they cry alone, they do all kinds of weird things when no one's looking. Her demise came so abruptly.

I keep rethinking my strategy. What if starving and isolation completely break her and I'm left with just a shell? No, I want her, the parts of her that fit into me. Maybe, in trying to kill the parts of her that get in the way, all of her is dying.

It's been two days since I tried to force feed her, and in my desperation to communicate, I even brought a notepad. I felt like a little bitch scribbling that shit to her. Like I have to explain myself. But she's just stuck in her head.

I haven't gone back. Not to watch her, not to feed her. I needed time to carefully think of how I can steer her back onto the right path. But it was two days of agony, not touching her, smelling her, tasting her. Not even getting a peek at her silky skin and long, wavy hair. She thinks she's the only one who wants company. That disciplining her isn't an exercise in discipline for myself. But all I ever fucking wanted was to be a part of their lives. A part of someone's life. Indispensable. Why is she suddenly fighting what seemed inevitable?

I trudge over to the cabin, first canvassing it. There's a trail of ants leading up to the wall where I threw the food. They are crawling in and out of the slats, collecting little crumbs. I take my boot and scrape it against the colony. I enjoy destroying their little collective. I'll have to clean the cabin sooner or later, it'll start to stink and I like to take care of the things I build.

I make my way to one of the peepholes facing the main room. She's not in there. So I go to one facing the bathroom. There she is, looking pale and weak, hunched over the waste hole like she's gonna vomit. She heaves, but there's nothing left. I can't tell what came first now. Maybe she is really sick and it's giving her a real reason to believe I've poisoned her.

She staggers to her feet, her eyes red. From gagging? Crying? I don't know. She pulls her hair out of her face and goes back to the main room. I follow her trail to another peephole.

God, she's a fucking mess, and yet I still savor being this close to her. She sits on the edge of her bed, burying her head in her hands and shaking no. A breeze hits me and a foul odor wafts over. The eggs. She's been sleeping with that stench. I don't want to subject her to it, but she's not given me much of a choice.

She takes a deep breath and sits upright, slapping her palms on top of her knees. A new look of determination is in her eyes. She stands up and walks over to the corner where my chair is. I can't see it from this angle, but she reappears in my line of vision when she brings the chair close.

"What the fuck?" I mouth to myself as she stands behind it and mutters some words to up above. But I don't have much time to make sense of that when she plunges herself down onto the edge of the chair, landing on it with her stomach.

"What the hell?" I ask, my feet twitching, ready to run in there and stop her feeble attempt at suicide.

She does it again. I can tell there's not enough force behind it to do anything other than bruise. She has no idea the strength it takes to hurt oneself.

For a nurse, she's sure displaying an incredible lack of understanding of how the body works. The level of trauma she'd have to inflict to kill herse—I stagger back away from the peephole when it all clicks. Vesper's not trying to kill *herself.*

CHAPTER 17

VESPER

Sitting in my cabin, alone. Hungry. Tearful. Amongst the stench of old eggs and sticky juice, I watch the ants assemble. They invade my home, but it's just an illusion of a home. A home is a place where you can come and go as you please. Where you can cook a meal, or entertain yourself with books and invite guests. No, this is a prison designed to look like a home. These ants make it look so easy to leave as they form a continuous black trail from one slat in the wall to another.

Not having seen Night or having bathed or eaten for days, things become clearer, like some form of meditation. All I've had is the water from my bathroom and yet the nausea and dizziness come back every morning.

If he wanted to kill me, the man who mercilessly chased me through a forest, who fucked me at knife point—oh he would have found a much more fulfilling way to off me than with poison. Oh, he's poisoned me alright. Just not with chemicals, but with something far more insidious.

It's taken me days to chew on that reality, taste its bitter flavor on my lips. In the framework of whatever this is, killing me is the sensible conclusion. Being the father to my child is unfathomable. But this world I'm in: where my mother and the so-called sane world has already given up on me, and the man who stole me looked shaken up by my breakdown—a man whose presence I miss after two days of total solitude. Nothing is the way it's supposed to be.

But I am still Vesper Rivers. Underneath the yearning for the physical response to the stranger's touch and the company of his silent shadow, I still understand this is not the way I am going to bring a child into this world. He can have me. I can be his slave. His lover. There is something in me that grows in his shadow, like moss. But not a child. A child cannot know a father who hides behinds a mask with no words. Who relishes suffering and violation. And I can't accept that the fight is over. Because if we come together to create a human being—something from nothing— then we are forever united. He would have a part in my greatest creation.

So as I watch the ants, all bearing the weight of crumbs so many times heavier than their own bodies, I understand I have a weight of my own to bear. A load so much greater than I ever thought I could manage. I don't want this to be a slow death. I want it out now. Then, at least, we can go back to the way things were before that morning when I first felt ill, where it was just a simple disaster and not this complicated catastrophe a child would bring.

I come slowly to my feet, feeling heavy from the lack of nutrition and the weight of the impending mission. I've thought of ways to do it. He never leaves behind utensils made out of anything other than flimsy plastic. So I decide on the chair. I knew someone whose father saved his own life using a chair. He was home alone choking, and he flung himself down onto the edge with enough force to send the piece of steak flying out of his windpipe. If he can do that, I can do this. If that doesn't work, then I'll find something else. I will find a way.

I pull Night's chair from the corner of my room. The last time I touched it was when I sat on it, my legs splayed open, and came to thoughts of him. It was gratifying, that moment I climaxed screaming his name shamelessly. But as the high settled, the tide of shame washed in. When I felt sick and Night walked in, old Vesper burst out of her holding place, demanding to rebel, to not let this monster swoop in and pretend to be her savior.

Maybe it'll be easier to just let her die. I can't keep fighting two wars at the same time: one with myself, the other with him. And I can't get rid of him.

166

I thrust myself over the chair, it hurts, but no more than walking into a piece of furniture. I can't bring myself to push past that limit, where I can inflict physical trauma. That must be a sign I am still sane. But I have to do this. I don't want this growth inside of me. I don't want that growth to become a person with a soul that will never know what it's like to have the sun kiss its face.

I thrust myself on the chair again, it's harder, but nothing more than a mediocre punch to the stomach.

I take a deep breath and collect myself.

You have to kill it. You have to.

I muster up the strength to give it another go, but the footsteps start. Hard and fast. Just like the night he came in sweaty, dirty, and angry and fucked me in the ass. My stomach burns at the memory and terror. I position the chair in front of me as some pointless barrier as he unlatches the door. He flings it open and his wild eyes jump around, the mask scrunches at the smell I have become used to.

He points at the chair.

I shake my head, stalling for an explanation as to what I am doing.

He walks up to the chair, yanks it away from me and holds it up between us, slamming it down with such force a leg cracks.

He wants me to explain the chair. Of course he's been watching me. Of course. But I can't find the words. I always thought they would be words said to Carter with joy. This is a horror.

I just keep shaking my head through tears.

"Vesp, don't fucking tell me—" he stops short, his lips pursed with rage. Even he can't bring himself to accept that this world, one that he has managed to shrink to just him and me, has instantly grown so much larger.

"I—I don't know. I don't know. I think…maybe," I sob.

He lets go of his vice like grip on the chair's back and paces away.

"No… no…" he grumbles. "Fuck!" he punches a wall. He spins back and points an accusatory finger at me. "You little lying cunt! Saying I poisoned you. For what, Vesp? You wanna get rid of it? Be my fucking guest. In fact, I'll make sure of it," he snaps. "You don't get to make this kind of call without me. You're just fucking lucky we're on the same page."

He makes a beeline to the door but brakes suddenly. Without turning he speaks. "You think you're too good to have my kid? No, that's not what this is about. This is about me not being ready to share you. I've only just begun with what I'm gonna do to you." And with that he slams the door behind him, leaving me to imagine horrifying visions of what's to come next.

"You can't live out here!" dad says to mom. I should be in bed, but I saw the lights of his car shining from far away. I thought he might be angry that we left and I wanted to hear what he would say.

"I won't let anything happen to Sam again. He's safer out here."

"What about school? Scoot? Us!"

"You can come up on the weekends like we do anyway. Scoot will be fine. He's a strong boy. In the summer and during school breaks he can stay up here the whole time. We are still a family. I'm just doing what I have to do."

"He's my son. I get a say in where he lives."

"Oh come on, you've always treated him like a burden. I thought you'd be thrilled."

"That's NOT fair, Gloria. We have different ways of doing things. I'm just trying to make him stronger. He needs it."

"This is the way it's going to be."

"Listen, you need to rest. You're exhausted."

"Stop patronizing me. You all want to keep sending me to these places. I'm not crazy! I just know things, and they have you so brainwashed, you don't even see what's really happening."

"If you were so good at protecting him, why'd he get run over on your watch?"

There is a pause. Even I feel a little sick. It's not her fault.

"How dare you!" she shouts.

"Gloria—wait—I didn't mean it."

"You probably wished he had died. Then you could send me away. Then our families could pretend that I don't exist, that he doesn't exist. Then we wouldn't tarnish those glorious legacies."

"Oh just stop it," he sighs.

"I'm the only one who understands him, who knows what it's like to be different."

"Okay, let's say I go home now. I need you. I don't know how to get Scoot off to school in the morning, or make his dinner or… and what about Sam? He needs school."

"Oh you mean the place he runs away from every day? Do you even listen to him? Ever? Or do you just impose your will on him?"

"Be reasonable."

"I can home school him. You might think I am only good for folding clothes and food, but I went to Bryn Mawr."

He sighs. "You know what? You want to live up here with him, fine. You think you can do a better job, fine. I'm sick of fighting you and him. I'm sick of your paranoia. I love you, but I can't keep doing this."

"I love you too. This has nothing to do with that. And I hope you'll see what you've been blind to."

"Yeah. You should call Scoot tomorrow, explain you won't be coming back."

"I'll talk to him. And I'll see him this weekend. We're still a family."

"Uh huh," dad says.

The screen door squeaks open and slams closed. I run to my window to watch the lights drive off into the dark farmland. When he's nothing but a speckle as tiny as a star, I creep back to my bedroom door. After a few minutes, the sewing machine starts churning. She just sews and sews and sews. I walk down the hall towards the room. The door is cracked open so I peek in. The room looks different than it used to, the walls and windows now covered with quilts she made. On one of them, there are a few newspaper clippings pinned up. I recognize they are about my accident.

She catches me looking in.

"How long have you been awake?" she asks.

I shrug.

"Well, your dad came and it's all working out. He'll come up with Scoot on the weekends. I think he's coming over to our side."

I push the door open and point to the wall of articles.

"Oh. That's just a little project I'm working on. Trying to

gather evidence about the accident, link the different people involved. But I don't want you to worry about that. That's for mama to take care of."

"The w-windows?"

"Oh that's to make sure they can't see in here," she answers matter-of-factly.

CHAPTER 18

SAM

I whip my mask off before storming into the house, sucking in air as I pace, balling up my fist and banging it against my forehead over and over. *Think. Think. Think.* But I don't think with her. I have stretches of what seems like control, but it's like holding onto a ledge for dear life. And then I can't hold it any longer and I slip. I show weakness. This—my impulsiveness in grabbing her on what was supposed to be a quick hit, in fucking her over and over without the thought of consequences—I didn't make a plan. I keep patching shit together. I can't let this complication grow. I can barely plan for Vesper, let alone a child.

A child.

I'm not like those families whose windows I peek into, like a moving portrait, framed by their windows. I am a reject, and I don't want to make another me. I'm too far gone to pull things back and make a life.

I crouch down to the floor when the realization hits me. She was right, my mother. I could never be normal. They would all shun me. Hate me. Not because of the way I was born. Or my speech patterns. Or because the world was conspiring to kill me. No…I made it happen. I fulfilled her prophecy. I have become something so inhuman, that I can't ever have the thing I have been chasing. The very act of chasing it, of forcing it, has made it something I could never, ever grasp.

This child has nothing to come home to. The visions I had of making Vesper mine, all those fantasies I had as I placed myself in Carter's shoes, they were only meant to live in my mind's eye.

I'll always be the stuttering freak with the scars and the trail of screaming victims behind me. My most prized one, being the mother to this child.

I bow my head and take one deep breath before standing up and making my way to the shed. I rummage through the instruments until I find a suction hose. I pull and straighten it out to inspect its length and when I am satisfied, I grab a shop vac, some tape, and head back to the main house. In a frenzy, I grab duct tape and seal the hose to the vac. I take a moment to sit back and look at my work. I've never done this before, I've only heard about what women have done.

Before I can go any further, I realize I need assistance. So I barge into the kitchen and rummage through the cabinets. Usually a beer man, I look for the hidden bottle of whiskey and take a generous swallow, shaking my head at the burn.

I need more. A back up plan. I run to a downstairs closet and fling off a jacket from a metal hanger. I uncoil it so it's long and sharp, but keep the hook intact. Gloves. Whiskey. The vac. The hanger. Fuel for the generator. Cords. Lube.

This is a plan.

I speed back to the cabin, sweaty and buzzed. I've gotta stop this spinning out of control. My freedom is the most important thing. And with a baby, I will lose that inevitably.

VESPER

I hear Night before he comes in. That's usually the case when he doesn't care if I know. He moves measuredly, exuding a false calmness. False, I know, because of the sweat dripping down his exposed clavicle down to his low slung jeans. His chest moving up and down tells me his heart is racing. The bottle of whiskey dangling from his hand tells me this man who has nothing to fear, who has never kissed me with the scent of alcohol on his breath, needs to calm his nerves. His mask—the dark face I have come to know as his—is saturated with sweat, but stubbornly, he won't remove it.

Without an utterance, he puts the bottle on the floor and ties my hands behind my back. Oh god, this is it. What I feared would happen when he learned I was pregnant. I have become too great a liability. It's why I couldn't accept the changes my body was screaming for me to hear.

"What are you doing?" I ask. "Please. No. I'll get rid of it. I'll find a way."

He goes back out and returns with a broomstick in hand. He grabs one of my feet and I pull it back, he grabs it again and forcefully yanks it towards the stick, tying an intricate knot to bind my foot to it. Then he does the other, so that my legs are forced open.

"Please, tell me what's happening," I sob, the heat of all my anxiety forcing sweat to bead all over my body and soak through my pale pink dress.

"Please!" I scream. Begging, trying so desperately to reach something inside of him. There must have been a time when he was a child himself. Innocent. Unmarred by the world or even the terrifying changes that manhood can sometimes bring.

"I'm so scared," I cry, a confession to my god.

He picks up the bottle of alcohol and presses it to my lips.

"No!" I protest.

He grabs my face and squeezes my cheeks, pouring it in. I gurgle as my mouth floods with the spicy liquid. Despite my best efforts, I manage to drink some. And it works, sending a warm shiver down my arms and spine, but only for a moment. The adrenaline roars through the dull warmth as he lifts my dress up, pouring some of the whiskey over my stomach and privates.

"What—" I stop the questioning, suddenly understanding what is to come. Oh god, he's going to try to do this. "If you're going to do this, please, I'm a nurse—almost. How? Please just tell me!" I scream, but he's focused on his task and as far as he's concerned, serving me the alcohol has taken up all of his mercy.

He leaves again. I've stopped screaming. Instead, I wait, my staccato sobs synchronizing with the erratic rhythm of my chest. When he returns with a shop vac, jerry-rigged to a suction hose, I begin to wretch in horror. I slide up as far against the wall as I can.

"You're…gonna…kill…me," I sob. "I'll bleed…to death," I plead amidst the choking.

He yanks the broomstick, pulling me to the edge of the bed.

"I'll knock you out if I have to. Your choice," he menaces.

I obey, understanding that that's always the simpler route with him. I wanted this. I wanted this baby out of me. Maybe if I had begged to save it, the outcome would be different, but I didn't fight. I invited this death into the cabin.

He steps outside for a moment, coming back in to switch on the shop vac. The deafening whirring punctuates the chaos in the room. To be heard, I have no choice but to scream.

"Please, there has to be another way," I wail as he pours whiskey over the hose and coats the end of it with lube. I fight back the vomit crawling up my throat, a smoky vignette clouds my vision as the terror threatens to knock me out.

He pulls the chair to the foot of the bed. I make another attempt to distance myself, but he grips the broomstick to keep me close. The lamp that illuminates the room, goes in and out as the vac steals its energy.

"Oh god," I plead under my breath. I am seconds away from being siphoned clean of an embryo. I didn't fight for it. I gave up on all hope as soon as I realized I had it in me. And maybe that's where I went wrong. In thinking that my only option was to purge myself of this parasite. Maybe this isn't a curse. Or Night's poison. Maybe somehow it's the key to unlocking this puzzle in front of me.

"Please!" I shout. "I want the baby. I want it," I sob hysterically, sweat and saliva dribbling down my face. I am reduced. Stripped of pride and agency. This baby is all I have. It's my only tool. My only promise of hope. That in the midst of having everything taken, I have been given something.

"I want to keep it. I want your baby," I shout, louder, afraid he can't hear me over the blaring of the vac. "We can—" I stop myself. Never have I referred to us as a unit out loud. A team. We've never had a shared cause. We've had things we both wanted and bargained for. I could feel the betrayal he sensed when he realized I was aborting his child. I've gotten so good at reading his non-verbal cues. He dreamed of having me like I dreamed of him. He dreamed of a life with me. We saw the child as a hindrance to our individual goals. But what if this child can get us what we both want? "We can make a family," I sob.

He holds onto the tube, it's close, so dangerously close to my shivering thighs. I tense every muscle in my body that wants to flail and panic. But he's thinking and I can't set him off with rebellion.

We are still like a picture for what feels like minutes. Night disappears into darkness and reappears each time the light fades and returns. Darkness. Light. Darkness. Light. Each time the light flickers the whir of the vacuum fades and strengthens, like a warped record.

I await the verdict, shivering, until he stands up and flips the switch to the vac. The roaring goes silent. A silence that is deep and haunting compared to the insanity of the screaming and machinery that bounced off these walls just seconds ago. I fall back with relief as I sob with my entire body, crying so hard it hurts. I'm going to live, and I'm going to have this man's child. Any illusions I had of returning to my previous life have been incinerated. Of course, I never had a chance to go back to who I once was, but this is the moment she officially dies. And I mourn Vesper Rivers. As I cry, Night unties each limb gently. His shadow eclipses the light and I open my eyes to find him standing over me. Shirtless, glistening, his eyes are softer than I've ever seen them. He rubs the pad of his thumb against one of my tears and raises it to his lips, subtly running his teeth and tongue against the sadness. I calm down, studying the clear of his eyes, and the way he stands there, his posture relaxed, telling me he won't hurt me today. I don't take my eyes off of him, waiting with shaky breaths to see what he'll do next.

I want him to crawl into the bed and hold me like he did that night he carried me to the shower. To make the pain he caused go away.

I want him to tell me he wants me to have this child, and he will be good to us now.

I want him to fill me with his poison again. He likes the taste of my sadness and I like when he injects me with his venom.

He is my danger, my greatest threat. When he's on my side, I know that I am safe.

So I wait, hoping he'll give me a greater sign that I am protected from him, by him.

Will he pull my legs apart and taste me? Or pull out his cock and make me ease his tension?

I wait.

Finally, he moves. His eyes, the colors of the beach during high summer, staying honed on mine, as he reaches down, over his face, and pulls up his mask.

CHAPTER 19

VESPER

I study Night's face so hard, it's almost too much to take in at once. It's like getting too close to the television set, until the moving images are just tiny squares of reds, greens, and blues. His eyes are even brighter against his flushed skin and eyebrows. His lips, often only partially revealed through the mouth hole of his mask, are round and pouty. His jaw, angled, but not sharp—still youthful. Not a mark of stubble in sight. His hair, little wisps of gold mixed into brown, is tousled from the mask. As I put the pieces together, I can step back and imagine him freshly showered and hair combed. He would look like a harmless young man. A shockingly handsome, harmless young man. The proverbial boy next door. But as if his body is displaying a physical manifestation of his lacerated soul, his otherwise pristine face sports a glaring imperfection—there is a thick scar that runs along the right corner of his mouth, up his ear and then out to his temple. While it roams across his cheek like a fault line, it's faded and flat, telling me this is an old scar. His neck on that side, mostly hidden from me, is a collection of uneven skin and jagged scars.

When I am finally able to draw back and look at the collection of his features and his faults—the reds, greens, and blues—what I see before me is a physically beautiful man. The scar does nothing to sway my opinion; instead, it adds a layer of texture and intrigue to someone with eyes like ice and skin as smooth as sand when the water washes away.

I don't know what to do next. All this time I have held onto his anonymity as a sign that none of this is real. That he doesn't see me as worthy of knowing him in any way equal to the way he knows me. The mask told me he didn't trust me. The mask reminded me I was a prisoner. It reminded me I was just a guest here. But I see him now. He's unveiled himself to me, and I almost wish he hadn't. Because what I see is a face I could trust. A face that belies everything he's done. He is a person. He is someone. He is not a monster.

And now that I see the whole picture of this young man, I want to know about his scars, all of them, inside and out.

"W—why now?" I mutter.

He stares at me blankly, as if he's not sure himself.

I sit up, never letting my eyes leave his face. I don't know how long this will last. He might put the mask back on, and then I'll be the only person here again.

"I'm done fighting," I declare through my still-wavering voice. I am. I can't keep waging battles against both him and myself. A battle where winning is losing and losing is winning.

Again, he just stares back, but his chest sinks with an measured exhale.

"I don't know what to do. I just—I just want you to say something to me. Tell me how it's going to be. Tell me what's on your mind. Why did you stop? Why did you pull your mask off? Do you want this?"

He won't speak. He's already shown too much. But I have to keep this dialogue open. I am more to him than he is willing to admit, and I have to remind him of that. And if I'm not, I have to convince myself of that to believe I can survive this.

I slowly come to my knees, so that I am nearly face to face with him.

"I can't read your mind. I don't even know your name. But I feel like I know you—like you know me—more than anyone I've ever known."

I raise a trembling hand to his face, to the side that was hurt a long time ago. It's a risk. This could all backfire terribly, but I don't know any other way. I only know how to care for people. It's always been my instinct. I've seen the power tenderness has. If there is any sliver of a soul inside of him, he craves it somewhere deep inside. Maybe that's why he took me: underneath all the animus was someone who just wanted what he saw through each of those windows.

I move my hand so slowly, there are moments I wonder if I'll ever reach him. I wait for him to slap it away and storm out, or to throw me on my stomach and take whatever he wants. But he's frozen as my palm and fingertips rest on his cheeks.

"I don't know what I'm doing," I confess. "Please tell me you do. Because I'm not supposed to want this, but your face…" I say, dipping close, so my lips graze his. "You terrify me, and yet I could look at you all day long…"

I plant a soft kiss against his pillowy lips. He's stern, and I stiffen, confused by his lack of response.

"No," he says.

"Oh, I—" I stumble on my words. Feeling embarrassed and exposed. Rejected by the man who stole me. Maybe there is nothing inside of him that craves to be needed like I had hoped.

I pull my hand away but he snatches my wrist. I gasp.

"No—" He yanks me towards him in one sharp movement, so that my body, cool from the damp nightgown presses against his hot chest. His cock is pressed against me, everything about his body is a *yes* despite his words. "I…don't know what I'm doing," he confesses.

He grabs my ass so hard I gasp, launching me off of the bed and into his arms. I wrap my legs around him, letting him carry me away from the bed. The smell of man and sex and whiskey overtakes the stench of the old breakfast across the room. The pale walls and floors fade into a blur as the colors of his skin, hair, and eyes sharpen. He kisses me so hard, my lips sting and I kiss back just as hard, trying to return the pain he makes me feel: Agony doused with pleasure. Sin blended with deliverance. Captivity leading to a type of freedom I never had outside of these walls.

I wrap myself around him, touching him, trying to get as close to him as I can, so that I can become a part of him, a part he could never destroy, but at the same time, I want to keep watching him. He's more than the fantasies I imagined when I thought about who would be under that mask. His face tells a story. I want to know it. I want to know him. Then I could make sense of this all.

He thrusts me up against a wall, expelling the breath from my chest, as he bites and sucks on my neck and shoulder. I graze my lips against his lips, his cheek, his temple, the salt of his glimmering summer skin seasoning each kiss. It's messy and desperate, but it's so good to be on his side. When he wants me, he wants me wholly and completely. I thought being loved was the most gratifying feeling. No, it's being obsessed over. It's having someone so infatuated with you that they would risk everything to have you. That is a high that love can't touch. Love is a slow burn, a stockpot simmering to soften the heart. But this—this is a flash flood, it's the smoke billowing when a steak hits a hot pan. It's threatening, but its fierceness is the very thing love dilutes.

He pulls away roughly, taking a sudden breath, like he has just snapped out of a trance.

I give him a questioning look as I catch my breath. But it's not even a second before he is spinning me against the wall and slamming me so hard against it, my cheek throbs from the impact. He's trying to set things back. To before that night in the shower, or just minutes ago when he showed me his face. He's trying to deny this. I have so many times bowed to his will without resistance. I've bent over, sucked, gagged, and braced—a passive participant as his prisoner of lust. I came, I dreamt about it, I waited for it through hours of soul-crushing loneliness. Part of that allowed me to hold on to the old Vesper. I could say that despite it all, he took, and I reluctantly abided. But she's gone now. I want more. I can finally admit that. In order to truly survive, I have to be all in. I have to get past the facade of this entire thing. For him to show me the hand he's been hiding, I'll have to show him mine.

As he peels the damp dress away from my backside, I twist away from the wall, to face him again. I glare into those eyes that are so clear they don't reflect my image. The act of rebellion sets him back just long enough for me to grab him and pull him into me, assailing his lips with mine. He lets out a heavy breath as he reciprocates for a moment, but then he pulls away again. I can feel it—his muscles tensing under my grip, nearly trembling, trying to stop himself from going down the path. The one where we truly see each other.

He turns me again, this time pressing his forearm against my upper back, frantically unbuttoning his jeans with the other hand. But I wrestle his confinement, my slick skin allowing me to slip out, again facing him. I push his arm to the side and weave my hand through his hair, pulling him towards me.

"No—" he says.

I suffocate the word with my mouth. He twists and moans into the kiss before sharply pulling away again. This time, picking me up and throwing me down on the bed, face-down.

I am a woman determined. He'll have to render me unconscious if he wants it this way. I know that inside of him he doesn't. I can taste it in his frantic kisses. I wriggle underneath him and twist onto my back as he tries to pull himself out.

This time, he lets me go, only to give himself enough time to take off his pants, so the next time he comes for me, he'll have two free hands. I struggle onto my feet in those moments. In seconds, he is standing across from me, the bed dividing us. He is completely nude, his tanned, muscled curves, leading to a frustrated erection. This headless body I have seen many times before, seems so different now that it is part of a person. His shining, heaving figure lurks, like a jungle cat waiting to pounce. But this time, instead of waiting on him, I run across the bed at him, pouncing him fearlessly, so that he has no choice but to catch me in his arms. He spins and stumbles back onto the bed, underneath me. I pull off my dress, exposing my already-swollen breasts to him. He sits up, wrapping one hand around me and the other bracing our weight against the bed.

"Don't," I whisper. "Let me see you."

"No…" he says, a hint of vulnerability in his voice. Normally so verbal when he fucks, he's almost silent during this frenzy.

I slip my tongue through his boyish pout and slide him inside of me. It's effortless and breathtaking at once. We both exhale into each other's mouths. I wrap my legs around him, pinning him to me, claiming victory over his stubborn attempt to fight this.

He's as deep in me as any man could ever get, and I grimace and moan at the painful filling of my pussy.

"Oh god," I cry. "I can't hold on." It's too much, he's too far inside of me.

As his hips weave against mine, he slides his hands up my nape and tugs my hair, pulling me away from him. For a moment I think he's going to come in for a last second maneuver, throw me on my stomach and fuck me in the ass, leaving me without an orgasm as a punishment. But instead, he watches me—my face, my body— riding him. In that moment, I get that chill, the one only he can give me, where I am singularly coveted. I am the only woman on earth. I am his. I don't have to compete with anything or anyone for his gaze.

He sits taller and slides both of his hands under my ass, boosting me up, so that he can worship my breasts. My breaths skip as his lips glide over the tender nipples. They ache, but his mouth finds a way to give them relief and draw out pleasure. It's impossible to hold on any longer as the pulsing deep in my core grows to a crescendo. I let out a series of wails, wrapping my arms around his head, smothering his face in my breasts. His cock thickens against my spasming walls, and a flood of his warmth releases inside of me. He collapses underneath me. My body goes soft, as if gripped and constricted until the moment of death and then released to see another day. I wither on top of him, skin to skin. Our bodies breathe like two parts of one living being.

He keeps his head turned away from me. I know he's confused. I know he's upset that he let it all get this far tonight.

I reach over and play with his tendrils. I've wondered for months what I would do if I ever got to see all of him. All I want to do is this simple ritual, a way to stay connected after something so intense and confusing. Until this point, every time he fucks me, he walks away. It feels like I'm being thrown overboard, left to fend for myself in a harsh, unforgiving sea. But this small act, it keeps me above water. And, if my gut is right, it's doing the same for him too.

He's still here. Hours ago he was a terrifying nightmare in a mask, and now he's lying next to me, asleep, his golden wisps of hair and gentle expression marred with a fissure like that of a wounded angel. I had dozed off by his side, I'm not sure how long ago, but his arm finding a way around my torso woke me.

Once the initial grogginess wears off, I realize that the door to the cabin is unlocked. It can only be locked from the outside and he's still in here with me. This could be my chance, to slip out from under him. If he startles, I can tell him I was just going to the bathroom. If I could just free myself from his grip, I can quietly slip out the door and get a head start.

But something is holding me back. Well, many things.

What will I do when I get back? I'm not so sure I want to get rid of this baby anymore, but the idea of facing the world—facing Carter—with another man's child, no relationship could survive that.

Guilt. He's beside me, suddenly looking so vulnerable, and—I can't believe I am saying this—he finally trusted me. Let me see him. And I would be betraying him. If he caught me, which is likely, I would never get that chance with him again.

But I have no idea what life holds for me in here. Of course nothing is certain, but I can't just stay here in this shack forever. I have a brain. I matter. This can't be my life. Maybe last night changed things. If I can win this small battle, I can keep winning little ones until I can figure out what I want to do next.

I stare at the door, fully torn, paralyzed with fear and indecision. I should leave, but it's a fool's errand if I do. I wouldn't make it far, and if I did by some miracle, I'm not ready to face my old life. There will be a better time.

Just to test, however, I slowly slide from under his arm. He doesn't even flinch. When I creep towards the bathroom however, and the floor creaks, that's when he shoots up. I can barely make out his frantic silhouette as feels the bed for me.

"I'm here," I whisper, softly putting my hand on his shoulder. "I have to use the restroom."

He stills, but I can't see the details of his face. He finds his flashlight and scans it around the room.

"Are you leaving?" I ask. It was nice to have someone sleeping beside me.

He doesn't respond.

"You should stay. It's already very late."

He flashes the light up and down at me, I shield my eyes, then he shoots it over at the mess on the floor. Now that the alcohol has dried, it stinks. I've gotten used to it, but apparently he hasn't.

"We can use the shop vac. You did bring it all the way out

here."

He doesn't say anything, but he hands me the flashlight, guiding my hand towards the mess. He pulls off the suction hose and switches it on. I shine the light on the mess at first, but playful instincts take over. He has to have a sense of humor somewhere in there. So I flash the light on his butt instead. Frustrated, he turns to scold me for my lack of focus to find me giggling. He looks down and sees where the light is aimed. He rolls his eyes, but I can tell he's not really angry, and points back to the mess.

"Okay," I say.

Once he starts again, I move the light, at his heavy penis, flapping to and fro as he manipulates the vac.

He stops again, widening his eyes and thrusting his hands towards the mess.

"What? It's pretty!" I chuckle.

He just looks at me deadpan, like he can't believe my immaturity at this moment.

"Fiiiine," I sigh. "Killjoy."

I shine the light on the mess. He nods and mouths *thank you* before finishing up.

When he's done, he rounds up his stuff. In the midst of that, he hands me a bag of something. Jerky. I devour it while he finishes his work. I'm sure he's leaving, but I've already suggested he stay and I won't beg. He places all in his things in front of the door and takes the flashlight from me. He points the beam to the bed, to me, to the bed.

Get in.

I slide onto the bed.

He jerks the flashlight to the other side of the bed.

Move over.

I do.

He gets into bed. I pretend not to be shocked. He's just tired and doesn't want to hike back. I glance toward the door. His stuff is a blockade. He wasn't planning on leaving.

I lie down, and stare up at the dark skylight. This time, he drapes his arm around me. Not an accidental gesture during sleep, but a conscious choice. I could tell myself it's affection, but I know better. This time, if I move, he'll wake up instantly.

CHAPTER 20

W e've been in mom's room for two days. She won't let me leave. Some weeks she's normal, then others, she gets a signal and we have to hide. Then she just sews and sews. I asked why once, and she said it's all she can do now, it makes her feel less scared. She says the sewing machine drowns things out.

When she's calm, she reads to me, makes me do math and history, just like school. I get to play outside in the forest for hours. But when she's like this, when the people are getting close, she just gives me books and makes me sit in the corner on the floor, so in case they can see through the fabric and paper, they still won't see me through the windows.

Dad used to come every weekend with Scoot. But they started arguing more and now he only comes once a month.

"Mom, I'm hungry."

"You still have food, don't you?" she asks without looking up.

I look at the plate strewn with crumbs beside me on the floor.

"You have to pace yourself!"

"I'm bored."

She sucks her teeth and stops the machine. "I'm sorry you're bored. But sometimes we do things we don't want to do, and this is one of those things."

Sometimes I don't believe that people are coming to get me. We've been here for a year and I haven't seen or heard of anyone.

She won't let me make friends or go to the neighbors. The few times she's let me leave the ranch was with her and we don't speak to anyone, we just go to the stores to get what we need.

"The animals, m-m-om. They need to be w-w-watched."

"They'll be fine. Now here, read your book," she says, passing me Green Eggs and Ham. It used to be my favorite. She would read it to me before bed and tickle my nose when it was my part to say "Sam I am." It was the first book I could read aloud the whole way through without stammering. But now, she just gives it to me when she needs me to be quiet.

I flip through the pages and roll my eyes. I can recite the book backwards and reading it is pointless now. I begin to get angry. I want to scream. I want to go out and play. This isn't fair.

"I do not like it in this r-room. I do not like it on the floor. I do not like this anymore!" I scream.

Mom scurries over to me and sits next to me. "Shhhh! You have to be quiet." She rubs away my tears. "Heeey, that was so good what you did there. Did you just make that up?"

I nod.

"That was a good poem!"

"When's Scoot com-m-m-m-ing?" I ask, my mouth quivering with sobs.

"He's—oh no," she mouths, jumping up to her feet, looking through all her materials. "Do you have your composition book in here?" she asks.

I hand it to her. She goes to the back, counting the days on the calendar.

"Crap. He's coming today." She glances at the clock. "He'll be here in an hour. I need your help Sam, we need to fix this mess up and get everything back to normal," she says.

I'm happy to have dad and Scoot back, and to be out of the room, so I begin cleaning up the scraps. Mom doesn't like dad to know about the times we hide. He gets angry and threatens to take me back to Sacramento. But I know he never will. He doesn't want me around all the time like that.

We run around the house, cleaning, vacuuming. I put on my boots and run out to tend to the horses and goats. They made a mess and have run out of food. As I walk out of the stalls, I see my dad pulling up in his pickup truck with Scooter in the passenger seat. I stand there with a bucket in my hand, waiting for them. Dad stops the car and Scooter jumps out of his side and runs at me.

When he gets close, he punches me in the shoulder. "Ewww, you stink."

"I-i-i-it's t-t-t-he ami-ami-ani-mals," I say. I want to sound perfect for dad, and it always makes me worse.

Dad walks over. He's not wearing his uniform today, just a pair of blue jeans and boots with a striped shirt. "Hey, son," he says, rubbing my head. "Mom inside?"

I nod.

"Looks like she's put you to work, that's good. You can't just read books by yourself all day. We have to keep working on our project, okay?"

"What project?" Scoot asks.

Dad pats him on the back. "Go get your mother, will you?"

He looks at us suspiciously but runs towards the house.

"How's mom been? Acting strange?"

I shake my head. I need to protect us from spies.

"I worry about you here."

I look down at my feet, at the bits of manure stuck on them.

"Alright, well, I won't force you out of here. But you should tell me if she's hiding anything."

I can't tell whose side he's on.

"Let's get in the house. You need a bath. Have you eaten?"

I shake my head.

"Well, then you need food too. You are gonna need all the energy you can get for tonight."

VESPER

He's locked me in again. The room has no trace of evidence of the previous week's insanity except for the crack in the bathroom door. I thought I had at least chinked his armor, but every day is like a new one for him. I never know who will be walking through that door. But before I can further analyze my predicament, hunger burns through my belly. The bag of dried meat he gave me was just enough to hold me through the night. Just as always, I know nothing. I don't know when my next meal or visit will be. Time doesn't exist here.

I make my way to the bathroom. I ran out of water the day before and in a moment of wishful thinking, I yank on the chain from my shower, hoping for a trickle. I don't expect the water that drenches me. "Shit!" I hiss as I jump back. This is good, though. He filled my water stocks!

I look down at my naked body and decide I should just finish the job, pulling the cord all the way and hoping into the stream of water. I open my mouth, hydrating myself and my baby.

My baby. Our baby.

I clear my mind of the thought. The responsibility I am undertaking. I don't want to think about how I am using this child as a tool for my own survival. Or how I am bringing it into a terrifying and uncertain world. I can't afford to labor over moral ambiguity. I can only focus on what needs to be done for survival.

I close my eyes and soak in the warmth of the water when I hear footsteps. He wants me to hear. He can be a damn ninja if he wants, so when I hear him, it's because he's either taunting, doesn't care, or maybe in this case (I hope), showing some kind of deference to my space.

I push the door open with my toes to peer out as I rinse off.

He's there, in his full glory, face exposed, dressed in a well-worn t-shirt and jeans, setting a tray of food on the table. My stomach goes queasy, unsure of how to act around him after last night. Now that I can see his face, he's so human, and it's like I am getting to know him all over again.

He must know I am watching, but he doesn't acknowledge me. Maybe it's weird for him too. Then he moves out of my line of sight. He can't be leaving so soon. I turn off the shower and grab my towel, chasing towards the door like a curious puppy. He's already gone.

I sigh with disappointment. I have to build on last night before he erects his walls again. But the door reopens, and he's back, this time with another small table.

I freeze, standing there, dripping wet, wrapped in my thin towel, caught staring at the door from which he departed.

"Good…morning," I utter awkwardly, like some girl who is

seeing a boy she first kissed the night before.

He nods. This is the first time I have gotten to see him in the light of day. Some of his thicker scars are almost opalescent with the sun shining through the skylight. But the sun shines on his other features just as brightly, and he is even more handsome than I thought.

He sets the table against a wall and steps back out. I wait patiently, wondering what he has up his sleeve. This time he returns with...a record player. A record player!

I haven't felt like this since my grandmother surprised me with a trip to Disneyland when I was ten. I desperately try to play it cool, but a smile fights its way to the surface, and then I'm just grinning like a fool.

He places one album upright, behind the player, against the wall. The soundtrack to Saturday Night Fever. It's a small glimmer into who he might be. I doubt he had time to go buy it this morning, so it must be from his own collection. I never would have guessed.

I run over to the record player, but he puts a gentle hand on my forearm and points to the other table.

Eat.

Of course. The excitement had made me forget the pain for a moment. The plate is loaded with fruit and bacon—a rare treat—hard boiled eggs, toast, oatmeal and pulpy orange juice. This is a feast by the standards here. I grab the toast first and take a few eager bites.

"Thank you," I say through a full mouth.

He doesn't say anything, but looks at me, almost coyly, from the corner of his eyes. As I shovel oatmeal into my mouth, I observe the small pleasure he has afforded me. Maybe something did change last night.

Unlike my other feedings, he doesn't leave, instead, he sets up the record player and then sits in his chair. Once I have enough food in my belly to slow down, I figure I should say something for the both of us.

"You like the Bee Gees?" I ask.

He shrugs.

"Did you see the movie?"

He nods.

"Did you like it?"

He shrugs.

"I saw it with"—I stop myself before mentioning Carter—"friends. It was fun. I actually had a friend who was obsessed with the movie. She's in love with John Travolta. She saw it, I think, ten times. One night, when we were studying and needed a distraction, she taught me one of the dance routines."

He raises his eyebrows a bit, I can't tell if he's feigning interest or not.

"It would be nice to have a name for you, you know?" I ask. "A real one."

He shifts in his chair and doesn't acknowledge my request.

I am stuffed like a piggy by the time I scoop up the last bite of food and fall back on the bed. "Ugh, I think I'll explode," I say. The satisfaction of the meal only last seconds, before my new friend, morning sickness, returns. "Oh no," I mourn, covering my mouth as I run to the bathroom. I bend over the waste hole and nearly all of that delicious food purges from me.

I rinse my mouth out and exit the bathroom, feeling wobbly on my feet. I don't look at him. I don't know how to navigate anything relating to his child with him, so it's easier for me to pretend it didn't just happen. I walk over to the record player, and slide the record out of its sleeve. The fuzzy sound of the record brings a childlike joy in me as I wait for the song to start.

I feel him behind me. Still draped in a towel, I know what he wants. He places a hand on my shoulder. It's almost tender. I turn to look at him, ready to drop my towel and let him do to me the things I must allow to keep the gift he brought, but when I look into his turquoise eyes, they shift over to the bed. There's a bag there.

"For me?" I ask.

He nods once.

I dip into it, and pull out several beautiful dresses. Some long, some short, all flowing and floral. I had been wearing nearly the same dress for so long now. It seemed like the least of my worries, but having these pretty dresses, all for me, reminds me of the little things I miss from out there.

"They're beautiful," I say. "I'm going to try them on."

He steps back, leaning against the wall with his arms crossed, watching me as I slide on a lightweight floor length white

190

dress with pale pink and blue flowers. I spin around so the hem takes flight.

"What do you think?" I ask.

He gives an approving frown.

I lay the dresses out onto the bed as How Deep is Your Love begins to play. I hum to the song as I stretch out the beautiful fabrics in all their glory. For a moment I allow myself to feel good. To think that one night and a pregnancy could change this baby-faced terrorizer. And in that moment of momentary peace, he comes up behind me.

"Shhhh…" he whispers in my ear as he wraps an arm around my waist.

"What are you doing?" I ask, my relaxed demeanor already dissolved into trembling terror.

He doesn't say a word, but places a dark cloth over my eyes and ties a knot behind my head.

CHAPTER 21

"*W*ake up," my dad whispers as he shakes me. I rub my eyes, looking around for a fire or some other reason he would be waking me up this late into the night. But it is dark and silent. There is no sign of danger. No emergency.

"Put these on," he says, passing me trousers, boots and a sweatshirt.

"Wh-wh-wh—"

"Shhh! I don't want to wake your mother or Scoot. I'll explain when we're outside. Don't put on the boots until we're outside, they'll make too much noise."

I follow his orders, tiptoeing down the stairs, sitting on the porch steps. The sky is clear, the moon shines bright and tonight it's silent except for a few crickets.

"Let's go," he shoves me to my feet. I follow him along the dark pasture and towards the woods. As we near it, I stop.

"Come on, Sam."

"Wh-wh-what are we doing?" I ask.   He's   been making me build something with him, in the woods. It's supposed to be our secret. But today he doesn't have any tools or supplies with him. The woods seem blacker and scarier than they have before. Tonight feels different.

He sighs and crouches down on one knee. "Your mom wants you up here. When it comes to you, she's always gotten her way. I know you want to be with her, so I won't take you away, but I will *make sure you become a man. You will learn the things my father taught me. I've been too easy on you, and you need to toughen up. And like everything we do here, it's our secret. You tell no one. You understand?"*

I nod.

"I mean it, Sam. You tell your mother, it stirs up problems. You know what happens when she gets stressed. I'm doing this for your own good. You won't always have her and you need to learn how to fend for yourself. Now let's go."

He pulls me along, finally shining a flashlight in front of us. We walk and walk, past the brook so I know where we're headed. Once we reach the lake, he stops.

"Take off your clothes," he orders.

I don't move.

"Do it," he says, louder.

I strip down to my underwear.

"I want ten laps tonight."

I look over at the water, black except for a few strips of silver moonlight. It looks cold and like there are millions of monsters underneath. He's trying to kill me, just like mom thought.

"No," I murmur.

"Get in!"

I shake my head.

He grabs me by my arm and drags me into the water, taking himself in up to his thighs so that his pants are soaked. The water is frigid, shocking me out of my sleepiness.

"We'll be here all night if we have to, Sam. You get to the other side and back. Ten times and if there's time, you get to go back to sleep. Now go!" he shouts.

I start to cry. I don't want to do this. I want to be in the house, where mom says it's safe.

"Your tears won't work on me. This is exactly the issue. You're a pussy, Sam! But you're going to be a man by the time I'm done with you."

He stands over me, arms crossed, an unforgiving giant shadow. I have to swim or he'll never take me back home. I've played so many times in this lake. But it's huge, and I've never had to swim across it without breaks, and definitely not ten times.

I dive under, kicking and pulling the water, until I hit the top again and suck in air. I do it again. And again. Every time I think I'm going to reach the other side, I've barely made any progress. I keep pushing until I've made it to the other side. I want to stop and rest on the flaky rock face on this side of the lake, but I'm afraid I'll cramp up if I stop. I turn over and make it all the way back to him. This time I do rest at his feet, panting for air.

"I...can't..." I beg as I roll along the smooth pebble.

"One," is all he says.

"Puh-puh-lease."

"One."

He nudges me with his foot, so that I crawl back out until the water is up to my chin. I swim again.

Two.

Three.

Four.

When I reach him for the fifth time, each limb feels like it weighs a hundred pounds. I cough up dirty water that I inhaled along the swim. I don't have any more in me. But he just says "six," over and over until I understand that this is not a choice.

When I get to the opposite side of the lake, I rest myself against the rock face, Everything hurts, my lungs burn, my head spins. Everything is dark except for the dot of light on the other side: my father holding a flashlight like a beacon. I take a deep breath and stroke against the water, towards his light.

I wish he was dead, I think to myself as my body begs for me to stop. And then suddenly, as if a giant grabbed my leg and squeezed as hard as he could, it locks up. Pain worse that what I remember from my accident shoots along the back of my leg. I cry out and swallow a mouth full of water. The pain sets alarms throughout my body, but I can't move. I flail my arms as I sink underneath, the moon shrinking. I try to get to the top but can only do it for a second between the pulsing behind my leg. I swallow more water. It rushes up my nose and down my throat. I sink lower and lower. I hold my breath, wondering what mom will do when she sees my dead body. She was right.

The moon is gray down here. I watch through the waves of the water. It's quiet even though I am screaming. Noises don't come out, just bubbles. Empty words full of air. My words were always my weakness.

Then there's the sound of something strong boring through the water, like those big drums. An arm wraps around me and I shoot up to the surface like a rocket. I gasp for air, but it's not enough. Every time I try to breathe, I just wheeze and choke.

"Relax," dad says as he drags me the second half of the way back to shore. "You're gonna be fine."

He lets me go and I find myself on my knees, vomiting water and silt. Finally, I can breathe again. It's over. He's made his point. I'm more confused than ever. If he wanted to kill me, he would have let me drown.

I roll onto my back, panting, shivering, wearing nothing but my white briefs.

"I wanna go h-h-h-home," I sob.

"You're gonna be fine, kiddo," dad says, brushing my hair out of my face as I sob.

"See? You're tough. You've got it in you. Your mom wants you to think you don't. But you are powerful."

His words don't sink in, but fall on top of me like raindrops. I feel them, I hear them, I understand their purpose, but they glide off of the surface. I just can't make sense of this all right now.

"Alright, get up," he says, pulling me to my feet. I stagger up, still lightheaded from almost drowning. I scan the ground for my clothes.

"This way," he points to the water. "Seven."

I look at him in disbelief. I didn't hear him right. There's no way.

"Seven," he repeats.

VESPER

He's leading me, through the forest, unresponsive to my pleading and questions. I trip and wince in pain every time I step on a small twig or rock, until finally, he swoops me off the ground and carries me. Cradles me. The only other time he carried me that way was when he chased me through this very forest the night he almost let me go.

"Puh—puh—lease. Just tell me you aren't going to hurt me," I plead through panicked breaths.

He shushes me harshly.

I cling to him, knowing any trip with him could be my last, and yet he's the one holding me protectively in his arms so that gripping him is instinctual.

Finally we stop. When he lowers me, my feet rest on damp pebbly soil. I dig my toes into the cool mud searching for clues.

He pulls off the blindfold. In front of me is a lake or a massive pond. The shallow bay is just inches from my feet gently beckoning me to dip my toes as it lilts forward and back. All around it's surrounded by forest. I haven't been outside during daylight hours in months. I haven't felt the sun directly on my skin since the day he took me.

I turn to face him, unsure of how to receive this gesture. There has to be a catch, there always is.

"Why are we here?" I ask, not expecting an answer as usual. But he pulls something out of his pocket. A small notepad and pen.

For your mind.

I chuckle half-heartedly at his response, but he's not laughing.

I scan the open area as my heart rate slows back to normal. I feel so free right now, standing at the shoreline as the wind catches the skirt of my dress.

"We're out in the open. Do other people come here?"

He uses his fingers to make a large circle, then points to himself.

"This is all yours?" I ask.

He nods.

"Wow."

He shrugs, unimpressed by his station. But it stokes my curiosity. This young man with scars along his face and body, who likes the Bee Gees, who owns a huge property, who invades homes and does horrible things to his victims—it doesn't add up. And yet, I can't ask, at least not yet. I'd rather let him drop these little breadcrumbs for now.

I look back at the water and suck in the fresh air, closing my eyes, so I can relish the sun on my skin.

He picks up a stone and skips it on the water, the sound of it breaking me out of my meditation. He looks so...*human.*

He catches me watching him. I look away, as if there's anything to hide from him. He waves his hand in the air to regain my attention.

"Hmmm?" I ask.

He points to me and the water.

"You want me to go in?" I chuckle.

He shrugs. *If you want.*

I want to. So badly. To submerge my body in the brisk water. For my throbbing breasts to feel weightless.

"Are you going in?" I ask.

He shakes his head.

"Well, I don't want to go in alone!" I protest.

He waves me off. *Go. Go. Go.*

I bite my lips together skeptically. "Ah, what the hell. It's so hot out here."

I walk towards the water, but when the hem of my dress gets wet, I stop.

"I don't want to wet the dress," I lament.

He gives me a smart ass look and makes a sweeping motion upwards at his own torso. *Well, then take it off!*

It's different out here. Under the sun, in the full light of day. That's all psychology though. He's seen parts of me I didn't even know existed. Bits of me tucked into boxes inside of boxes stacked in shelves buried deep inside of my soul. My bare skin is just another shroud. So, I take a calming breath and pull it off. I tread into the cool water, up to my hips, meekly cupping my breasts. I take one more look back at him, my teeth chattering, hoping I can get a smile out of him. I must endear him to me. The more moments I create between us, the less he can see me as his prisoner.

But he's not smiling. No, he's watching me, adjusting the waist of his jeans. He's already thinking of the things he'll do to me. His sexual appetite is insatiable, aggressive, ever present.

I dive the rest of the way in, deciding to swim underneath for as long as I can. In those moments, submerged in the lake, moments that seem to slow in the resistance of these dark waters, I am free. So I stay under as long as I can, conserving my breath through each stroke. When I surface, I gasp as the water cascades down from my hair over my face. I'm farther into the lake than I thought I'd be. I look over at him, picking up another stone, and over to the opposite side of the lake. I could make it over there. I'd have to climb some rocks, but I would have a massive head start.

I dip under again, swimming further away. Testing my limits, and his. I emerge again at the point where I can no longer hold my breath. This time he's waving me in, now the small shape of a man in jeans and a t-shirt. I look towards the other end. Maybe four or five more strong swims and I could get to the other side.

"Come on!" I shout playfully, covering in my tracks in case I don't make it across.

I dip under again and swim hard, harder than I ever did during my trips to Tahoe, where I learned to swim as a child. Where I almost lost the necklace. A necklace he still has. A reminder that no matter how many dresses, or records, or trips to the lake, I'm still his captive. So I kick harder, stroke harder.

If I make it to the edge, I don't know what I'll do. But I have to try. I say I won't fight, but there's still something in me that won't die, that doesn't quite want the outside world anymore, but doesn't want this. If I could stay here, right in the middle of this lake forever, weightless, with Night watching over me while skipping stones, I would.

This time, when I break through the sheet of water, there is no one standing at the edge of the lake. There's just a tiny heap of pale yellow and blue—his t-shirt and jeans. My eyes race to the mild disturbance in the water. Small rhythmic splashes growing in size, coming in my direction. He's an incredibly fast swimmer. The predatory way he hardly breaks the water or rises for air informs me that I found his limit. I choke back the urge to beg for forgiveness or plead. Despite every primal instinct in my body commanding me to flee, I take a breath and swim towards the monster. This time, I don't glide through the cool water, instead my body feels as heavy as lead. No matter how hard I kick, it feels as though I'm barely making progress. Fear is real. It's not just an idea. It's heavy. Massive. Dense. It weighs me down, but I drag it and myself towards him. When he is a few feet away, I tread the water, and hope it will hide how I am trembling beneath it.

"Boo!" I giggle when he launches his head and shoulders out of the water.

Sheets of water glide down his face as he swipes his hair back from his eyes. He's panting, his eyes are focused and tense, the pupils two tiny black dots submerged in ice.

I don't feed the monster by reacting with fear. Apologies and pleas would be a confession. I was just teasing him. He wouldn't come out here, so I had to find a way to get him out here. Like playful lovers.

I splash at him, as if I could diffuse his anger like flames.

"You're a fast swimmer!" I shout over the crashing water.

It doesn't work. He grabs my forearms. The false smile melts off my face.

"I know what you were doing," he growls. I never know when he'll speak, but I do know when he does, it's rarely good.

I try to yank my hands away, but his grip is immoveable.

"I was just trying to get you to come out here and loosen up a bit," I pout. "What was I going to do? Swim out of here naked? And what? Go back home with your child inside of me?" I snap with indignation. "I don't have a life out there anymore. Don't you get that? You, this baby, this is all I have now. You know my mother has already written me off as dead. And Carter—I can't go back to him. Not after what we've done. We…we have something I didn't have with him."

This is just a speech, I think as I recite the words. A way for him to let his guard down around me. But I never planned these words, they come from one of those hidden boxes that I sometimes hide, even from myself. As I say them, I know even I'm not sure where the lies and the truth diverge.

"You wanted me. You dreamed about me. You told me the night you came to my house. About fucking me. Having me. Well, here I am! But you won't talk to me. You won't tell me your damned name. One minute you treat me like your girlfriend, the next you threaten me. You're the only person stopping yourself from having what you want."

This time when I snatch my hands away, he lets me go. I swim towards the shore, amazed that my little fit worked. This time I pace the swim back, exhausted from the sprint out and the wading.

I don't look back, afraid to see his reaction behind me. As I near the edge, I stop where it's just deep enough for my shoulders to peek out of the water, listening to the carving of the water behind me. I don't want to leave the pond. It's been so long since I've been outside that despite the scene I put up, I am appreciative he brought me out here.

I don't look back for him. I'm still nervous. All this time with him and I still can't anticipate his reaction. It reminds me of playing jacks as a kid, the way the little jacks bounced unpredictably along the ground. Whenever I throw something at him, I have no idea how it might fall.

I close my eyes and take a soothing inhale as he nears me. He grabs my arm and turns me around to face him. There's still anger and mistrust in his face, but it's wrestling with a softness. One that might be sick of constantly questioning my intentions. But as he pulls me closer, the darkness takes over.

He kisses me hard, biting my lip so that it smarts like a wasp's sting. I whimper, pulling back, and then tasting the blood, I do the same to him. Our lips covered in the metallic crimson, we make a silent blood oath as I wrap my legs around him. He grabs my ass and stands up, streams of water plummeting from our entwined bodies as he walks me to the shore, lowering us into the bed of smooth rocks beneath us.

He presses his weight on top of me, squeezing my face in his hand, his lips tinted with diluted blood. Through gritted teeth, his throbbing cock pressing against me, he confesses, "If you leave, I'll have to kill you, Vesp. I don't want to do that. Don't make me do it."

He's killed me a thousand different ways. Stolen countless breaths and hopes. Slaughtered the girl who had plans to marry a nice doctor. Killed the dream of helping people for a living. Snuffed a piece of her soul by pulling her out of her little brother's life. Pillaged her pride. And out of those tiny little deaths, someone else has been born. Someone who sees that underneath his threats, there is vulnerability. He's begging me not to leave. It's not romantic or laced with syrupy sweet words. No, it's wrapped in barbed wire and cutting threats. But at its center is something he is protecting, something I have found a way to reach in and touch, even if it means being sliced and pricked along the way.

"Then tell me—show me—who you are," I answer against

his lips.

He grips my wet hair and pulls it taut so that my neck tenses. "I am—" He bites my neck, my collarbone, my shoulder. "I am—" He glides his tongue against my nipple, grazing the swollen bud with his teeth. "I am—" he works his way down my stomach running his teeth and lips against the spot that holds our creation.

My clit throbs, hoping to be next. To feel his hot mouth contrast the cool water evaporating off of the sensitive flesh.

He yanks my legs open. "I am—" he bites my inner thigh, sending shooting pain up to my center, followed by electric aftershocks.

"Tell me," he commands, "who you are," hovering his mouth over my pussy. Taunting with heavy breaths that match mine.

I don't know who I am anymore. I've been torn apart and pieced back together so many times, I don't recognize this pregnant woman lying naked on a shore, fucking with abandon like a forest animal.

So I say the only thing I am certain of. The only thing that is completely true at this moment. The fact I am resigned to. There are many things that are uncertain, but there is one thing that is sure.

"I'm yours," I rasp.

He tugs on one of my lips, plump and waiting to be relieved of the tension building between my thighs.

"Again," he grits.

"I'm yours," I gasp.

The words light him like a fuse and he glides the tip of his tongue between the threshold of my opening, toying with his property.

"Again," he murmurs.

"I'm yours," I chant breathlessly.

He runs the point of his tongue along my clit. I let out a moan, so he does it again. I try to wrap my legs around him, but he pushes them open again, reminding me who belongs to whom. He pushes them back, exposing my lower half entirely to him. Like meat on a spit, I am presented to him for his consumption.

His lips and mouth lap me up, the sounds of his mouth fucking me contrasting the patterns of nature in the background.

My moans elevate, my breath catches in my throat, as he

buries his face in my ass and pussy. And then he stops just short of relief.

I watch him helplessly as he rises to his knees, his cock tall and ready, and takes me by the waist, flipping me onto my stomach. The cold, smooth pebbles shock the skin of my breasts and stomach. He pulls me up on all fours, the hard rocks banging up my knees and digging into my palms.

"You're right, Vesp. I've wanted you since I saw you. I could taste your cunt before I ever put my mouth to it. I could feel you wrapped around my cock before I ever fucked you. I could see your pretty eyes looking up at me while your mouth was wrapped around my dick, before you ever swallowed my cum."

He rubs the head of his cock along my pussy, already blooming for him, pulsing like a heartbeat.

"And I thought I could have you once and it would make the hunger stop. But each dose just makes me crave you more. And the more I have the more I want."

He presses the tip of his head inside of me and pulls out. We both groan and heave together at the promise of what's to come.

"I'm losing control, Vesp." He rubs his hand between my legs and rubs his own cock, using my cream to stroke himself.

"Who am I?" he asks in that voice, dirty and broken. "I am the person who has nothing to lose but you."

He pushes himself inside of me, and even though I am ready, it is so sudden and hard, I nearly cry as I gasp.

"I am a man who has risked everything to have you."

He pulls out slowly and plunges into me again.

"You are the only thing, Vesp."

He draws himself out and buries himself inside of me.

"And *you*…are my obsession."

His obsession. Wanted. Needed. Craved. The most important person in his world. It's what I felt when his eyes first met mine. It's the most thrilling thing to be told you are precious. That you are so valuable it puts you in danger. Nothing of such high regard can exist in this world without causing a storm. When a man covets something so strongly, he is its greatest threat.

He keeps himself deep inside of me, pulling me up tall so that my back is pressed against his chest. He holds one breast as the other travels past my womb and down to my clit. He weaves his hips against mine, the hand on my breast traveling up to my neck like a snake, the fingers coiling around my delicate nape.

He squeezes; threats mixed with pleasure. My guardian and my stalker. My lover and my enemy. A stranger. The father to my child.

"I want to make you feel everything, Vesp," he grunts in my ear.

"You do," I eke out, already feeling countless contrasting sensations. "Give me all of it," I beg. He closes his grip so tightly I can't speak another word. My muscles lock around his cock and burst around him, sending pulsing waves through my legs and belly. I wheeze against his suffocating hold on my neck, and it prolongs the intensity of the bursts that radiate throughout my body. He grunts as his warmth fills me, one hand staying on my neck, while the other secures me firmly against him. *His.*

Night slides out of me, comes to his feet, and walks over in front of me.

"Show me," he says, his dick still not settled. I know his needs already. I know mine.

I lick his thickness, coated in the mix of us as he softly caresses my hair. He watches me, his hazy eyes betraying the sexual dominance he displays.

When he's satisfied, he pulls away, walking into the lake to freshen up. I watch him, naked, my knees red and marked with rock indentations, his cum dripping out of me onto the mix of stone and mud below. I look across the lake. Physically, the swim is a possibility, but the world beyond these woods seems like another dimension.

I don't know if there is a world between that cabin and Sacramento. But I do know one thing: we are both hopelessly bound to the other, holding each other afloat. And if one of us snaps the line or sinks, the other will drown.

CHAPTER 22

VESPER

W hen we've washed up, Night reaches for the blindfold and
puts it in his pocket, gesturing his head back to where I
assume we came from.

"I, uh…if we're going to do this again, which I would love,
I'm going to need shoes."

He nods in agreement, reaching for his notepad.

Need a ride back?

"Please," I sigh with relief.

He lifts me off the wet rocks, my long white floral dress
draping along the ground. I wrap my arms around him. Unlike the
walk out here, I'm not scared or distrustful. I'm hungry and tired, both
more than usual with the hormones raging through my body, so I can't
help but nuzzle my nose in his neck and rest my eyes.

"Why is it," I ask through a yawn, "you only talk
sometimes?"

His body tenses at the question. And as usual, he doesn't
answer. His reaction, the way it's automatic like that, even after all
that we have shared, finally helps me realize this is not some
psychological warfare. It's another breadcrumb I have to find. There's
a story there.

I doze off in his arms to the gentle rocking of our bodies over
the terrain, eventually feeling myself being lowered onto the bed. I'm

utterly exhausted and drift into a deep sleep as he lays a sheet over me.

It's not until I hear the door being latched a couple of hours later that I wake up. My stomach sinks when I realize I missed him. I'm finally discovering him, and it makes me eager to see him again to find if I can uncover new mysteries.

I look up at the skylight, a dusty blue and orange haze swirls in the sky. My stomach growls loudly just as I notice the food he's left behind. A couple of sandwiches, tea, milk. But it's what's next to it that steals my attention: A copy of Green Eggs and Ham. It's old, the edges and spine peeling and tattered. A token of his childhood, perhaps? I nearly race to it, curious for another crumb. The book falls open where there's a note.

Don't ask me that question again. You will never get an answer. But here is something I will give you. I flip the small paper over. There is no other writing. At first I think he's referencing the book itself. Maybe he considers it a gift. But when I look at the pages in which the note was tucked, I think I see the answer he is willing to give me. Circled in black ink are the words "Sam I am."

He's no longer "Night," "My Captor," or just "Him."

Sam.

A name so innocuous and kind. One befitting the boy next door facade. Not the name of a monster.

With each new puzzle piece he gives me, I am building a new picture of him. Over the one of the wordless, masked animal who hurt me. Slowly this new image is growing over the old one, making it harder to recall.

SAM

Why did I take her?

It was because I wanted her. More than I've ever wanted anyone. Because as much as I told myself she was one of them, I saw the way she acted with Johnny and knew there was more to her. I did it because having her felt good. More than good. Getting into her house and having her was the pinnacle of my craft.

So if having her is what I've always wanted—what I combed houses and personal possessions for—why am I fighting it? If I am greed and she is my indulgence, why shouldn't I suck every last bit of juice from her? I've risked it all to have her, so I should get it all.

The lake, just watching her out in the water, the pink flush in her cheeks from the air and sun, I fucking liked it. For a moment before I freaked out, it was nice to just skip rocks and be with her. But that part of me that can't fully believe she isn't just one of many who have set out to hurt me awoke fiercely. I had to threaten her, to watch the calm in her eyes morph into fear. Fear is the glue that holds us together.

But there are other things that could keep her here. The baby. The sex. And something else—I can give her everything she needs. No one has ever taken care of her like I have.

It's not like she has a choice, anyway.

I'm tired of fighting. Of not letting it just feel good. So from now on, if she doesn't give me a reason to, I won't bring fear to the table. It'll always be in my holster, but I will use it sparingly. After all, this was the goal, to break her down, strip her to a doll I could keep for my pleasures. But she hasn't become a shell, she's only evolved into something that can survive this, keeping all the best parts of herself and shedding the shit that disgusting world makes you carry around. When I sit there quietly, my mouth heavy with the words I want to say to her but can't, I feel it's me who's being stripped down.

If I try to talk to her when I'm vulnerable, she'll hear my voice and the words will stagger and it'll ruin her illusion of me. But I decided I would give her something else. My name. It's the biggest risk yet. But it's a commitment. With that knowledge, she can never go back out into the world. It'll keep me from getting too complacent. And I want to hear her say my name.

I pull out a few more records to bring to her cabin. She was right about needing stimulus. I think she's proven she deserves it. And I've seen how quickly being good to her has endeared her to me. I love music, and it'll be nice to share it with her.

As I head out the door, my phone rings. I wait for the answering machine to pick up.

"Hey Sam, it's me," Scoot says. "Call me when you get a chance. I need to ask you something."

He always does that, leaves some vague message so I'll have to call back. I shrug it off and step out of the house.

I walk through the woods, my flashlight shining the way to the little white cabin. At night, with no windows or light, it's nearly invisible out there. But I could find it blindfolded.

I walk up to the door, making myself heard so she has a moment to prepare, and pull up the latches. When I open up, she's sitting on the bed, her dim lamp shining a light on her. The one record she has plays faintly in the background. She's holding the book I left behind—clutching it. Like she's been waiting all evening for me to come to her.

It feels good to know she waits for me like that.

Her golden brown eyes gaze at me expectantly. She glows right now. My own little angel in a white box. My seed growing in her. She's pure, fertile ground on which we could grow a life. She's everything. Vesper stands up, hugging the book to her chest and walks up to me.

"Sam?" she coos.

My name, rolling off her lips, like a blessing, sends shivers through my stomach.

I nod.

"Is this yours?" she asks, tilting the book in my direction.

I nod.

"From childhood?"

I nod.

"I wish I had a book with my name in it when I was a kid. There aren't many Vespers out there," she chides.

You are the only thing, Vesp.

"Do you want it back?" she offers.

I shake my head, reaching into my pocket. Sometimes writing shit down is as exhausting as stumbling over the words, so I am conservative with what I say. It encourages me choose my words wisely.

For the baby, I jot down.

Her eyes brighten at the words.

"Thank you, Sam," she says with a soft smile.

I remember the records in my hand and hand them to her.

"Oh this is great stuff," she says, flipping through the sleeves. "Will you stay and listen with me?"

Of course, but I only shrug so as not to show her how much

the invitation means to me. I make my way over to the chair as she pulls out a Pink Floyd album, one of my favorites.

"Come sit on the bed with me," she insists. I've become so used to watching her. From windows, and peepholes, and chairs in the corner of the room. Never a participant in her daily rituals, always a spectator, only breaking through that barrier to take the one thing I wasn't satisfied to only watch. I always thought the world was different when I wasn't in it. That there was a secret everyone was hiding from me and that once my presence was known, people acted differently. But I know Vesper so well, and she's not much different when she knows I'm watching or when she doesn't.

Her perfect fiancé, Carter, he didn't know her like I do. He only knew the pretty parts she wanted to show. I know all of her: her beauty, her cracks, her strength and weakness, her filth.

So I ease myself up from the chair and sit up against the wall, on her bed. She starts the album, bobbing side to side along to the first song.

She sits on the opposite side of the bed, facing me. She lies on her back with her knees bent, listening to the music. Of course I don't say anything to her. She doesn't say anything either. I wonder why she wants me here. Why would she want someone who has done the things I have done to stick around? I used to think for her it was just about sexual desires, things that were too depraved to be fulfilled elsewhere. But right now, there's none of that. It's just the most innocent version of us.

It doesn't mean I don't want her. Her dress has slid up her thigh, revealing her smooth curvy leg. There's always something deep inside of me, churning. A craving that never ends. A dragon I'm always chasing. When I first discovered the thrill of coming, it became an obsession. Locked up in my house, not allowed to have friends or leave the ranch, I'd jack off until my dick was raw. And it grew with my other proclivities. It's a beast I can't feed enough. It's why I need her here. She's the one who can keep me sated. Stop me from the inevitable disaster I've been working towards.

But for the first time, I control the urge. I'm not sure I can explain why, but I think it's because for the first time, just being around someone feels good too.

This could be the life I stared at on photographs on stranger's shelves. That I watched through windows. Every week, we'd lie here and her stomach would grow a little more. And she'd have a baby, with my physical gifts and her gift of gab and unassuming beauty. And I'd be able to start everything over, retire my mask and not be so fucking angry all the time.

"I think I have a fever," she starts, sitting up fast.

Before I can think of how to address her sickness, she runs over to the record player and pulls out the album. Oh, she means *that* type of fever.

She starts Night Fever.

"I think I remember the dance my friend taught me," she says, preparing herself for the chorus to kick in.

She starts to dance. From what I recall, it looks just like the movie. I bite my lip. I don't want her to see me smile. I don't like drawing attention to my face and the ropey scar that extends from the corner of my mouth, so thick, I can feel it tug on its corner when I curve my lips. And Vesp she has to understand I'm still a threat, but god, is it hard to keep in the urge to laugh around her sometimes. Most people are insufferable, so usually it's easy to keep a straight face.

After getting through the routine once, Vesp dances over to me.

"Come on! Loosen up!" she says, grabbing my hands.

No way. No fucking way in hell.

I shake my head and give her a sour look, like I'd rather eat shit, but she keeps pulling. Finally, I yank back in protest, so she falls onto me, landing between my legs, so that we're face to face.

It's uneasy, the feeling I have. Normally, I'd turn her on her stomach to make it stop, but this time, I just stew in it. I want to see how she plays this hand.

She keeps her eyes locked on mine at first, but then they travel along my face. I tilt my head so she won't look at the scars. Usually, she makes me forget they're there.

"I wish I didn't think you were so beautiful," she mutters. "It makes me think I'm crazy."

I know exactly what you mean.

But the tenderness wears off when the voices, which have been quieter as of late, begin their reminders.

She's playing you.

You're a freak.

She's just saying that to get what she wants.

I grab her hand firmly and pull it away from my face, shaking my head no.

"Sam." It throws me off for a second, my name coming out of her lips. "It's true."

I come to my feet, frustrated by her insistence at trying to get to me. She's making me weak. So I do the only thing I know to get my strength back. I listen to the urges. I cut the bullshit with the higher functioning and listen to my body.

I slam her up against the wall. The record skips and gets stuck on the same verse. It's jarring and unsettling.

"There is no beauty here," I whisper through tight lips, pushing her down to her knees. "Suck my cock," I growl.

But it's her eagerness to do it that confounds me. The way she pulls her dress down to expose her swollen tits, the nipples puffed and alert. They way she doll eyes turn lidded with lust. The way she locks them on mine as she runs a soft tongue on the tip of my dick before covering the shaft with her mouth.

There used to be a fight, one where she would finally allow herself to answer to her dark secrets. But now, she doesn't shy away at all. I may have actually done it. Gotten her to be truly free of the bullshit out there. Maybe this isn't a ploy on her part. Right now, as her warm mouth draws pleasure from my cock, I don't even give a shit.

I come in her mouth, and like I've trained her, she sucks and swallows every last bit of my cum. She stands up and meets my eyes again, undeterred by my attempts to regain control. She runs her fingers through my hair, just like girlfriends do to their boyfriends.

"It's true," she says. "Come to bed with me, Sam."

My stomach twists at the way her pout massages my name. Is this what it feels like? To be one of them?

She takes my hand and pulls me to the bed. I pull off my shirt and jeans, but not before going to the door, and slapping on a padlock to keep us in. I'm not that big of a fool.

211

CHAPTER 23

*D*uring the day, especially when it's sunny, being out on the water feels so different. It looks like its own little paradise, not a place that makes my heart race at the sight of it, knowing I'll be trapped in it until my muscles cramp and water seeps into my lungs. I rest on the shore, letting the sun heat my skin, until I grow restless, picking up a stone and skipping it on the water. Counting the skips. The most I've gotten was ten.

Suddenly, the urge strikes me. It happens all the fucking time. All I think about is fucking and coming. Scoot's in college now, I bet he gets to fuck girls all the time. But I'm stuck here. Never allowed to leave for more than a specific errand. My mother adamant that this is my world here. That I have everything I need on this property.

I pull myself out, trying to silence the ever present need. I close my eyes and visions of tits and pussy intersperse with scowls. They don't want me back. So I have to imagine myself holding them down and taking it. It doesn't take long for me to come. I wash off in the lake and head back to the house, the horses and goats need tending.

I get back to the stalls, seeing my house a hundred or so feet away. Mom's pacing back and forth working in the kitchen. She's been a bit calmer this past year, maybe because I'm 16 and taller and stronger than her. But whenever I talk about visiting Scoot in school, she gets sick so I let it go.

I lead the horse I used to ride to the lake and back to a trough and secure it while I go to get the others.

Off in the distance, I see a puff of dust, a car driving up or long driveway towards us. My heart races. We don't get visitors other than dad or Scoot. I've come to think my mother's thoughts that people want me dead are just delusions, but when I see the visitor coming towards us, I am overcome with a sense of dread and mistrust.

"Mom!" I shout, running towards the house. "Someone's coming!" I'm on the porch in seconds, meeting her at the door.

"Come on, get inside!" She motions me in. "Go upstairs. Hide in my sewing room. Let me handle whoever this is. No matter what you hear, don't come out."

"Mom, I can protect us," I say.

"Just do what I say!" she scolds. I run up the stairs, and into the sewing room. But instead of securing the door, I keep it cracked open to listen.

A minute or so later, there are male voices. I can't make out what they are saying. But only seconds later, my mother is screaming "No!"

All of her instructions become irrelevant as I race to my room and grab a bat, running down the stairs to help her. But I stop in my tracks when I see her sitting at the kitchen table, sobbing, two uniformed officers standing above her, one with his hand placed gently on her shoulder.

I open my mouth to ask, but the words gets stuck all the way. Not even a syllable can make it out.

"Ma'am," one of the officers says to get mom's attention. She looks up, her eyes red and swollen. He points to me. Her eyes widen, her instinct to keep me hidden overriding whatever other emotions she's feeling.

"You both can go. Thank you," she says.

After a few assurances, they leave, each tilting their hat to me on the way out, their somber faces affirming what I already know.

"Sam...your father."

"He's d-dead?" I ask.

"He made a routine stop and a car hit him. Oh god," she says, collapsing so that I have to catch her.

I feel nothing.

"Scooter...he doesn't know yet. They're so close..." she weeps.

"I'll c-call him," I say, leading her to a chair.

"The police just came. Dad was hit by a car. He's dead." That's how I tell Scoot. It comes out so clear and crisp. I'm not sure if it's numbness or peace I feel, but this trance I'm in lets the words come out smooth. I'd be lying if I said I didn't feel a twinge of satisfaction in being the one to deliver the news to Scoot. It's the first taste of the thrill I have in delivering misery to people like him. Scoot chuckles at first. But I don't protest, I just hold the receiver in silence as he keeps asking me if this is a joke. Until he stops asking. Until his distraught cries burn my ear. I listen to his wailing. Feeling like a stranger in this family, full of people who cared for a man who wished I was never born. Who dragged me out of bed for years to torture me and make me run until I puked, or carry unfinished logs so that my back was ripe with dozens of cuts and splinters. The man who screamed at me for not being like Scooter. Who looked at me with such disappointment. Who I knew gladly let me live at this farm because he was ashamed. In a family full of generations of success, I was a failure.

I can't muster up a single tear.

Scoot takes it upon himself to call the extended family. People who I haven't seen since I was little, my mother and I tucked away and forgotten, her sickness something to be hidden behind closed doors. Her own brother, a prominent Senator, hasn't visited her since before we moved out here. Scoot would be on the next bus up, getting to us early tomorrow morning.

After so many tears, my mother goes to bed with a handful of pills. Our family is strange, but they found a way to stick together despite the obstacles, and maybe when they shouldn't have.

I tend to the animals and sit on the porch as the sun sets. I wouldn't have to worry about his bullying, or the sick feeling in my stomach when he'd walk into a room. Even when he wasn't mad, I could feel him judging me.

And that's when I realized the gift he had left me with. He introduced me to the night. When the world is quiet and calm and I don't have to worry about people hearing me speak. When mom is tucked in bed on her sleeping pills, so I don't have to worry about making her sick with worry. I used to dread the night when he was here, but now I don't have to share it with him. It's all mine.

I wander towards the woods that lead to the pond, when I stop halfway. I've been in those woods countless times. I've swam in those waters, run through that brush, climbed those trees. I want to see something new. Something forbidden. I grab my bike and ride it down our long driveway that winds for over a quarter mile towards the mailbox that marks the end of our property. I bike hard, my lungs pumping air, my legs burning, just like the afternoon that car slammed into me. I ride as fast as I can, like a prisoner escaping a jail, but as I near the end of the driveway, my stomach contorts painfully. I ignore the feeling of nausea, pumping the pedals, the mailbox getting closer. I pass it. The road is just ten feet or so, but when I reach it, I slam on the brakes, the rubber burning against the chrome. I turn the bike skidding it on its side so I don't go flying over the handle, stopping right where the driveway meets the road.

I stand there, gasping for air, trapped by an invisible barrier. I don't even know if I believe the reasons my mother has kept me here all these years, and yet, I'm frozen. Back there is where I'm safe. Where I don't worry about the way I sound or look. But every year, my thirst for what's out there grows stronger, and I imagine all the things I would be experiencing if I wasn't stuck here.

Once my breathing calms, it's silent. Of course there are crickets chirping, but that's just white noise to a kid who's been living here most of his life. Besides the new moon, there's no light. The road is black and uncharted. The night can cloak my scars. It can cloak me, so I can see what it's like out here, how people act before they see me and change.

I let my bike fall to the ground. I need to be able to duck off the road if any cars come by. I choose to run right, just a slow jog. Dad used to make me run miles in the woods, through the trees and branches. They'd smack me in the face, cut me, and I'd fall. He'd make me get up and keep going. Mom would notice the marks sometimes, but she believed they were from my days alone in the woods.

I run for a half an hour until I come upon a small house with one light on. I suppose these are some of my closest neighbors, though I've never met them before. My heart pumps faster, not because of the jog, but because of the thrill of becoming a part of someone else's life.

I creep to the window on the first floor where a light flashes, dim and blue, like it's coming from a TV. A man is sitting on the couch with a woman. They look a little older than my parents. I'm scared they'll see me, so I duck every few seconds, and when I do peek in, I only see their top halves.

The woman stands up and leaves the living room. It looks like she says something to the man. After she leaves the room, another light switches on. I follow her to the kitchen, where she grabs two beers from the fridge. She switches off the light before coming back to the living room. I could watch the banality of their lives all day, the little moments of interaction I wish I had with other people. Just as the woman sits down, lights beam onto the road in front of the house as a car turns the corner. I crouch out of sight as a car pulls up to the house.

"Thanks for the ride!" a girl says, slamming the car door behind her. She's got on a short dress and little boots with heels. Her hair is straight and long past her elbows. She jogs into the house. I peer just enough to see her enter the living room and kiss her mother and father, before disappearing from the room again. Seconds later, a light switches on upstairs. It's like fresh meat being waved in front of a dog, I have to have my fill. I run back, hiding behind a tree so I can get a better view of what's up there. I see hints of her at the window, but I'm too low. Desperate to get a better look, I climb the massive tree, its mature branches extending close to the house. I choose one and park myself on it, hidden by the dense foliage.

She's still in her dress, but she's kicked off her boots. She's giggling on the phone with someone, twirling the long cord around her finger as she lies on her bed. I wonder what she's saying and who's on the other line. Is it a girl? A boyfriend? I've never really had friends. Definitely not a girlfriend. I think I could be a good boyfriend if she gave me a chance. I pretend I'm on the other line, muttering things to her and pretending the reaction I see through the window is to my words.

"Why don't I take you out to the movies tomorrow?"

"We'll get dinner first. Wherever you want to go?"

"Is that what you want to do to me? But your parents will be

217

home."

While I'm up there watching this pretty girl, I forget about the solitude. This is no different than opening a book, or turning on the TV. That's not true, it's better. This experience is one of a kind and in the flesh. Time disappears up here until she hangs up, and I have to end the conversation. It snaps me out of my state, but I wait for what's next.

She sits up, looking at her vanity, the mirror edges bordered with polaroids of her huge social circle. She reaches back, twisting around to reach for her zipper. My heart and stomach dance in anticipation for the show. Finally, her fingertips find it and she drags it down. The dress parts to show her small back, and she bends over to slide it off. Underneath, she has a lacy bra, two small thin triangles covering her small chest. Below, she has on pale yellow panties. She opens a drawer and pulls out an old t-shirt, placing it on the bed. Then she reaches back to unclip her bra. I let out a breath as she reveals her breasts. I've seen breasts in magazines Scooter slipped me, but nothing is like the real thing.

Hers are small, very small, barely coming off her chest, but the nipples are puffy and my dick aches at the sight of them. Her hip bones peek out from the waist of her panties. She's very delicate and smooth. I know all the things I would do to that body if I could. But no matter how satisfying the illusion, it's still not the real thing. I can't go in there and suck her little tits. So instead, I reach down to the urge that never seems to quiet and grab it. Under my breath I urge her to wait on putting on her t-shirt until I finish. As if connected to my thoughts, she stands in front of the mirror, and runs her hands through her hair. Admiring her own body, a hand makes its way to her little breast and she softly pinches her own nipple. I didn't know girls did this. Touched themselves like boys do. She takes her other hand and places it over her panties.

My dick tenses up, I bite down on my lip so as not to moan. This is the most intense it's ever felt. For the hundreds of times I've jacked off, this is different. I am not alone.

I jerk my cock, holding on to the tree with the other hand so I don't fall. So close to coming. And that's when she stops and furrows her eyebrows like she senses something. She drops her hands and turns to look out the window. She squints, coming closer. I freeze, hoping that the tree will shield me. But when our eyes lock, I can see her slowly make out my outline in the darkness.

She screams at the top of her lungs. A horror movie type scream. I scale down that tree as fast as I can. I'm booking through their yard and into the woods before I even know what's happening next. I run through the untamed trees and fallen logs, the many nights my father forced this upon me, a lesson I never knew I needed. I get a satisfaction knowing this was never his intention. This is my rebellion.

I run and run until I am back on our property, but as I near the house, I remember my bike is right by the road. If the police come, it could be suspicious. I cut back and grab it, riding it all the way back to my house. I wait at the porch for a few seconds to calm my breathing. Mom can't know I was out. I slip through the front door, up the old stairs that anyone else would cause to creak, but not me, I've learned how to move in silence. I slip into my bed, and when I lie down, the jitters hit. I laugh to myself that I pulled it off. My heart still quivers at the thrill. At the image of that girl touching herself. I grab my dick to finish the job, still riding high off of the adventure.

Now that dad is gone, the night is mine.

VESPER

This pregnancy hasn't been easy. My morning sickness has been violent and unrelenting. My breasts persistently throb and I am always exhausted. Ironically, Sam has been the one to take care of me, spending nights here and taking me to the pond whenever he can. Floating in that cool water seems to help me recover from the rough mornings. He doesn't blindfold me, and he gave me a pair of shoes so I can walk alongside him. Discreetly, I've paid attention to the path. He changes it around a little bit every time, sometimes walking us in circles, but every day I get a little better at figuring out how to get to the water.

Sometimes he leaves me for hours, but now he tells me via notes why: work. He's out there, in the world, working, probably interacting with people and they don't have the slightest idea of who he is.

But he has been ever the doting father and lover. Preparing my meals, spending evenings with me listening to records. He brings books which I read out loud to us and the baby. They say kids don't fix what's broken, but me carrying his child has triggered a seismic shift in the way things are here. Maybe conventional wisdom doesn't apply to unconventional arrangements.

Today is another morning, just like the others in the routine that started fourteen weeks ago.

Sam rises out of bed, his back facing me. I don't make a peep, but I watch him, and just past him, against the wall, the crib he presented me with the night before. It's exquisite. I could tell he wanted to downplay his pride in making it, but he wasn't very good at it.

Actually, it was kind of cute, the way he brought it in, matter-of-factly, looking down before casually passing me the note. *It's not finished yet. I'm going to paint it whatever color you want. Just let me know.*

"Did you make this?" I asked.

He nodded.

"It's incredible," I muttered, as I ran my fingers along the freshly sanded, blonde wood.

He shrugged modestly.

"Actually, can we keep it like this? The room is so white, I like the wood against it."

He gave me a half smile and nodded.

The sun beams in from the skylight on his naked taut frame. His skin, so smooth and tan from his days out in the sun, abruptly grows violent and marred on his left side. He is a puzzle made of pieces that don't fit. Handsome yet scarred. Intelligent yet animalistic. Full of stories, yet taciturn.

The breadcrumbs. He's been scarce with them since he gave me his name. Though a few days ago, while walking a new, longer path to the lake, we came upon old wooden structures. They were overgrown and neglected, but I could still make out their shapes. A wall, pillars, horizontal beams. If I wasn't mistaken, it looked like an obstacle course of sorts.

"What's all that?" I asked, pointing to the ruins.

He was quiet for a moment. I could see the internal debate

about what he could share. Finally he stopped and pulled out a notepad.

It's a playground. Old one.

"A playground?" I asked skeptically. His answer felt like it was hiding something, but he didn't acknowledge my skepticism, so I added it to the list of crumbs. I also decided it was a better use of my efforts to stay concentrated on its relation to the lake in the event I found myself out here.

Sam turns sharply as if he knew all along I was watching.

He scribbles on his pad. *Work today. Want to show you something first. Do you need to puke first?*

I chuckle at his lack of tact. But no, this morning, I'm feeling surprisingly stable and curious.

I get up, rinse myself off, and put on one of my dresses.

"Ready!" I declare.

He lifts up a bandana, folded into a narrow strip, gesturing to his eyes. *I'm going to blindfold you.*

"Why?" I protest, my gut sinking for new reasons.

The look in his eyes tells me this is not up for discussion. He's been too good to me lately to suddenly want to hurt me. It must mean he's taking me somewhere new. So I throw my hands up in the air and relent. This could be another breadcrumb. A potentially huge one.

"Fine, but this is stupid."

I climb on his back as he instructs me to. The first thing I notice is we make a left instead of a right outside of the cabin. But being blindfolded, it isn't long before I lose track of distance and space. Suddenly, a smell hits my nose as a door creaks open, the sound of a goat bleating and huffing comes from beyond the threshold.

He sets me on my feet. The door creaks again as he closes it behind me. Then he pulls off the blindfold. I look around the small barn. A horse is tied up on one end, in a stall. Two small goats trot over to us.

"Oh my god!" I howl as one tries to gnaw at the hem of my dress.

He swats it and makes a hissing sound.

"We—you—have animals?"

He generously gives me a grin and nods.

"Do they have names?"

He nods, pulling out his pad. *Small goat, Trixie. Other, Hilda. Horse, Beverly.*

"Wooooow," I gasp, petting the goats who have since stopped trying to feed on my clothes. He gestures towards the horse, who he pats gently before letting her out of her stall. She huffs a bit, letting out some energy. He saddles her up and motions for me to mount her.

"Really?" I ask.

He gestures more forcefully. *Yeah, hurry up.*

I go towards the horse and try to hoist myself up. My belly isn't too big, but it's surprising how hard it is to keep my balance and work around it. He catches me as I fall back. The second time he gives me a hardy boost and I manage to awkwardly slide my body onto Beverly's back. He mounts her in one swift motion behind me, and reaches over me to show me the blindfold. It has to go on again. Once he's done that, I feel him give her a gentle kick to the hip and lead us out of the barn. We trot gently for a while, in this odd limbo where he extends another part of himself to me, while still keeping me shielded from any true knowledge of my circumstances.

But it does feel nice, the gentle rocking of the horse, the wind in my hair. How is it in this moment, I feel more at ease than I did in my previous, safe life?

After a couple of minutes, he pulls off the blindfold. We are on a trail in the forest. It emerges to open field. I can see roving fields for miles. Then hills with trees. No roads, no houses. Is this what is beyond the lake? Is my escape plan a hopeless endeavor?

I try not to panic. This could be another direction. I have no idea how we got to this area. I can't let despair sink in when I've found a way to maintain hope. Instead, I choose to appreciate the bright yellow sun blazing my cheeks and the occasional huff of the Palomino under us. There was a time my world was just a fourteen by ten box. It's already become so much larger.

Once we're done, he blindfolds me and takes me back to my cabin which is now regularly stocked with basic food to keep me happy when he can't make me a fresh meal.

Back by evening, he says.

I wave him off with a smile and he latches the door behind him. Taking the rare opportunity to possibly eat something without losing it in the morning, I grab a box of crackers, an apple, and snack on them while listening to my ever-growing record collection. I'm biding my time here, but I have to admit, even now that I have things to keep me entertained without losing my sanity, it's not the same when he's not here. Human company is as essential as air, water, and food.

Eventually, after filling up on snacks exhaustion hits and I doze off to the sounds of Carole King.

VESPER

The intense pain in my abdomen jolts me from my nap. Though it's been longer than a nap as I can already see the bright sky dimming through my roof. I grab at my stomach as panic sets in.

For most of the time after I learned of my pregnancy, I didn't care about this baby. It was an obligation. A tool. But a feeling of dread comes over me, and suddenly I want to do everything in my power to keep it alive, not just for my protection, but because this baby has filled me with promise. I was just starting to get to know him or her. Just beginning to feel something grow inside of me. Watch its mere existence change a monster into the kind of man who would take me out for a surprise horseback ride. It can't leave me. Not after giving me a glimpse of that life, in between a girl confined to a cabin all day, and one out in the world, trying to please a mother who never wanted her.

I tell myself it's going to pass. I'm (almost) a nurse and I know there many reasons for abdominal pain. But as I feel my innards contracting, I can't avoid thinking the worst.

I run to the door of the cabin, slamming my palm against it as hard as I can. "Sam! Sam!" I cry out, knowing my voice is simply echoing through the trees.

CHAPTER 24

I *listen at my mother's bedroom door for the sounds of the sewing machine to die down. Once she's asleep, I'll do what I've been doing for almost a year now, slipping out into the night, living a second life. The one I can't when the sun is up and shining, when my mother's only remaining sliver of sanity comes from knowing I am home with her. Ever since dad died, she lives more in the tiny world inside her bedroom walls and less in the one outside of them. While I go through the motions all day, tending to the ranch, reading, riding, doing things to keep my hungry mind occupied- I am living less and less during the day and more at night.*

I convinced mother that it would be safe for me to go to a local college during the day. I'm strong now, stronger than her. But if I am even a minute late returning home, it sets her off into a frenzy. I don't have to worry about that when she takes her pills and sinks into a deep sleep. My time belongs to me again.

The whirring stops.

"Sam! I'm taking my pills and going to sleep!" she calls out, thinking I'm in my room. I wait a few beats, then open her door.

"Good night," I say. Ever since dad died, my stuttering has improved even more at home. I keep quiet at school, staying to myself. I sit in the back or on a bench on the quad and watch everyone else. Socializing, smiling, communicating. It all comes too easily to them, the way the words just pour out of their mouths. Now that he's gone, the constant tension I used to feel in my neck and throat has eased. I

think I can do it. I think the words can come out of me with maybe a stammer here or there, but I can't bring myself to try. It's been so long since I've tried to make a friend, the thought of it makes my heart race and my palms sticky with sweat. So I watch. It's better than being alone at home. I fill in the blanks from a distance, pretending to be part of their conversations.

That's what I was doing yesterday, hypnotized by the moving lips of a cute girl talking to a guy, when someone called out my name.

"Hey, Sam!" It's distant, the voice, as if muffled by a smothering pillow. I'm so caught up in what I'm watching, I think it's just another part of the fantasy. "Sam!" the voice is right beside me now, and a hand slaps my back. I jump to my feet ready to defend myself. My mother's beliefs have been ingrained so deeply in my psyche, that even now that I'm not sure any of it was real, I don't trust anyone.

I spin around to meet the person accosting me. Scoot.

"Wh—what are you doing here?" I ask.

"I'm seeing a girl here. She used to go to school down by me, but she transferred. What are you doing here?"

"I'm taking classes."

He tucks his chin in a bit, as if he's taken aback. Scoot went back to school a couple of weeks after dad died. He calls home every week, but I never told him about this. I don't know why.

"Well, that's great. What for?"

"Thinking electrical engineering," I say. "Mom d-didn't say you were coming home."

Scoot's smile morphs into a frown as he breaks eye contact. "I didn't tell her. Ya know, I was just going to visit for a night. I didn't want to make a thing of it."

A thing of it. Mom is my burden to carry. Scoot does everything he can not to be bothered by us. Just like the rest of the family. The only difference is he has no choice but to at least call once a week.

"Yeah," I answer.

Scoot glances down at his watch. "Shit, I'm already running late. I'll call later this week." He slaps me on the shoulder. "I'm happy for you, man. You look—you sound— good."

I give him a reassuring nod and watch him jog off.

Now that mom's gone to bed, my heart vibrates with anticipation. I have to be patient, make sure she's deep asleep. But this ritual, it makes me feel a type of thrill I have never known before.

I hop into the shower, a productive way to pass the time. Just as I am wrapping a towel around my wet body, I hear the house phone ring.

"Shit!" I hiss. It's unlikely she'll wake up. But a late night phone call will send mom into a frenzy of paranoia if I don't grab it. And who the fuck is calling at this time? No one calls this house, especially after eight.

I race to the phone. I hate the fucking phone. It reduces me to my greatest weakness.

"Hello?" I answer.

"Sam, it's me," Scoot replies.

"Oh, ss-something wrong?" I ask.

"No, I mean nothing serious. You have any plans tonight?"

He's expecting me to say no. He knows how things are. And that's true as far as plans I can express openly.

"Mom's asleep."

"Good. Listen, that girl I was meeting today when I bumped into you — I want to go out with her tonight. But she made plans with a friend who doesn't want to be the third wheel. Will you do me a favor and come out tonight?"

A date. It's something I've craved. To know what it's like for guys like my brother. It's what I imagine as I watch people, inserting myself into the Sears catalogue snapshots of their lives. But now that it's here, presented to me, I don't know what to do with this. I'm so much better in my thoughts than I am in person. In my thoughts, words flow effortlessly. My curious scars vanish from my face. The nagging feeling that I'm being silently ridiculed withers away.

"Come on, Sam. You are finally getting out there. You're going to school. You can't always do what mom wants. Don't let her control you."

Control. My chest tightens at the word. It's only been within the past few years that I've begun to realize that what I've seen as caring for mom and her protecting me—maybe it's been a way to keep me here, surrounded by nothing but trees and animals. Safety is a prison.

"Uh…okay," I say.

"Sweet. She actually lives closer to you than Sacramento. I'll come get you."

"Okay. Pull up to the…d-driveway. I'll meet you out there."

It's hard not to fidget as we pull up to Cindy's house. That's the name of his friend. Almost as soon as he puts the car in park, the front door opens and two girls come prancing out, their long hair swishing side to side as they take bouncy steps towards us. It's hard to make out their features in the night, but I see shapes. Curves and slopes. Nothing hard or sharp. Lithe limbs punctuated by round edges. Their nonsensical chatter gets louder as they near the car.

"Hey guys!" one of the girls says as she opens the back door.

"Hey Cindy," Scoot says playfully. She's got flaxen hair. Long and wispy, so that it looks like a halo when the light shines through it.

The other girl slides in behind her and slams the door shut.

"Hi," she says in a less familiar tone.

"This is my cousin, Phoebe," Cindy adds.

The confines of Scoot's car are tight and I wonder if it's too much to spin around completely to get a look.

"Hi, I'm Andrew, but everyone calls me Scooter. This is my brother, Sam."

"Sam doesn't get a fun nickname?" Cindy asks playfully.

"I guess my dad never gave him one…" Scoot thinks aloud.

I take this as my cue to turn around. And when I see Phoebe, it's like a bucket of ice water is splashed on me. It's been almost a year, but I would never forget the face of the first girl I watched. The thin girl with the tiny tits. Except this year, she's filled out a little more, her body sprouting breasts I can see through the low neckline of her top.

I think she sees the look on my face, or maybe they all do. Or maybe they're all staring because I'm supposed to say something but I don't. It's your turn Sam, say something. They are all waiting. But the shock of my worlds colliding makes my throat tense in a way I haven't felt since the last time I saw my dad. So, all I do is give a friendly nod.

Fuck. I already blew it.

"Well, I hope you guys want to party," Cindy says, waving a little baggy in the air.

There's not much to do in these parts at night. I assumed we'd go back down to the city, but instead, Scoot turns up the radio and we drive back towards our place.

As I'm still trying to figure out if Phoebe will recognize me when she gets a better look, Cindy asks where we're going.

"My family has property out here. There's a pond and we can party without worrying about police or anything. I'm trying to be a cop one day, I can't get in any trouble."

I'm not sure I like the idea of bringing them back here. This is my home. My land. Scoot was always just a visitor. I don't like how he didn't ask. How he has just invaded my ground zero, the place where the rest of the world doesn't exist.

We drive up to a dirt road that leads to a gate with the sign No Trespassers. They are trespassers, I think to myself as he pulls it open. We drive down the rear access road as close as we can. But there's about a quarter mile left to go on foot.

He gets out the car and we all follow.

"I'm not dressed for this!" Cindy laughs.

"Give me your hand," Scoot offers before leading the pack.

Immediately, I see Phoebe struggling through the dark forest, the foliage I can run through with my eyes closed. I should offer but I don't want to speak. I'm all wound up now because this is all too real. It's easier to be the guy hidden behind the window, but when she can see me, I don't know how to handle myself.

"Do you mind if I...?" Phoebe asks coyly as she reaches out for me.

I shake my head and give her my arm. She must have no idea.

Now she's touching me and I've never had a girl touch me. Not skin to skin. In my mind's eye, I've touched dozens of real women. Watched them in their most intimate moments and imagined running my tongue up and down their wet pussy lips. But this is different. Because she's not the same person as she is when no one is looking. No one is. I don't like having to deal with these different layers. They confuse me. They make me think too much. Then suddenly, my throat gets tighter, and the words get lodged, and I'm the fucking idiot with the scars. Has she even seen my face? I mean really seen it, the ropey thick scar that runs along my cheek? Or the rough marked skin on the arm she's not holding? Evidence of the time my life changed. When my head hit the pavement, and I woke up, weeks later, as someone else.

I'm so lost in my head that she's just an accessory during the walk. When we get to the clearing where the water is, I barely notice when she lets go.

We sit around a lantern Scoot brought as Cindy pulls out a joint. I've never done drugs. I've never done any of this.

She passes it around, and when it gets to me, I pass.

"You don't say much, huh?" Cindy asks.

I look at my brother.

"He's the mysterious type," he chimes in.

"That's funny, because you looooove to talk Scooter."

Phoebe grabs the joint and takes a few puffs.

"You're more than mysterious," she adds. I tense up. Does she know something? "I don't think I've heard you say a single word."

Scooter can't cover for me anymore. They are stare at me. The silence of the woods, which isn't silent at all, only makes the void larger. I have to speak up.

"H-h-h-h-h-h-he t-t-t-t-t-t-talks f-f-f-f-or..." Oh shit this is bad. It hasn't been this bad since I was a little kid. But I'm too far in and I have to finish this sentence. "T-t-t-the b-b-b-b-b-b-both o-fffff usssss."

There's a moment of silence as I wait, my stomach turning with anxiety. I hold down the puke rising to the back of my throat. I can't do this. I'd rather watch. Participating is too painful. These fucking girls have it so easy. I bet everyone just worships them because they're beautiful and fit right into the cesspool of humanity. And the truth is, I want nothing more than to be like Scoot, who can just blend right in, and wanting it so badly is exactly what turns me into this mess of syllables and consonants.

After that one second that feels like minutes, when their wheels turn and they try to understand who this bumbling mess is in front of them, Cindy cracks a smile and looks over at Phoebe who seems relieved to see it. And they start laughing. They think I was joking.

I look over at Scooter as humiliation and rage swirl together and pick up speed like the formation of a tornado. I could kill those bitches right here if it wasn't for Scoot.

He looks embarrassed for me, for them. But he wants to get laid, so he has to be easy on them.

After a few seconds, the girls realize I'm not laughing and Scoot is only uncomfortably smiling along.

Cindy's giggling slowly stops. "I—oh my god—I'm so sorry," she says. "Scoot didn't tell me."

I nod, only accepting the apology on the surface. Phoebe looks too mortified to even muster up the words.

"Well, this is incredibly awkward," Scoot sighs. "Let's break the ice again?" he pulls out a bag of pills.

They each pop one. I'm so fucking pissed, I don't even know what it is, but I take it. I just want to find a way to disappear without the walls.

The night quickly descends into drug-fueled chaos. Cindy and my brother find a dark spot on the shore to hook up. Despite the darkness, the moonlight provides just enough light to show the outline of their intertwined bodies.

Phoebe sits along the edge of the pond, her eyelids barely parted, her body swaying. She smoked a lot and took a lot of pills.

I look over at her. I can feel her disappointment; it floats around her like a force field.

"Cindy, I have to pee!" she shouts.

"What?" Cindy calls out.

"Come with me to pee in the woods. It's scary out there."

The outlines of Cindy and Scoot part into two. He pulls her back down to him and she tugs away. I watch in silence as Cindy comes over and helps Phoebe up.

"Hurry up," she groans as they wander into the woods. On the way over, Cindy gives me a forced smile.

I look over to Scoot. He's wasted, lying on the ground, waiting for his lay to return. I look towards the woods where they went. The craving strikes. To watch. To listen. To see Phoebe when she doesn't know I'm watching. They are about twenty yards in. I can hear them giggling, yapping away, completely unaware of my presence.

"So is he?"

"I don't think so. Scooter said he's normal, it's just his voice. I don't think he's retarded or anything. Do you think he'd bring a retard to be your date?"

Phoebe laughs. "Ugh, I would kill him. To be honest he's really cute, I was pretty excited when I got in the car, but that was zapped right down when he opened his mouth. What about his face? Did you ask Scooter?"

"I didn't but he told me when he was explaining the stuttering. He says he was run over by a car and dragged down the street. He was in a coma and everything," *Cindy slurs in a slow cadence. The irony of then mocking my speech when they are so sloppy.*

"Oh my god. That's crazy. Now I feel bad."

"You should fuck him. Think of it as charity."

"Community service. Do you think he's a virgin? He's obviously not smooth with the ladies."

"It's the least you could do after laughing at him."

"Me? That was you! I laughed because you did first!"

They both begin laughing as if this whole thing is a joke. As if I am a joke.

"I'm gonna do it," *Phoebe declares.* "He doesn't even have to say a word."

"Do you think he stutters when he comes?" *Cindy giggles.*

Phoebe snickers. "I'm c-c-c-coming!" *she says in a husky voice.*

"Okay, let's go back. I want a round two," *Cindy says.*

I give myself a head start as they gather themselves and sit where I was previously, seething yet anxious. I am a virgin. And as much as I want to snap that Phoebe girl's neck, I'll take her pussy if she'll give it to me.

They emerge from the brush and Cindy waves coyly. "You two kids have fun!" *she says, fanning her fingers as she waves goodbye.*

Phoebe and I sit in silence as Cindy becomes just another shape in the darkness. This time, though, she's closer.

"We shouldn't let this high go to waste."

I look over at her. "Come on, then." I even shock myself at the drastic change in my speech pattern. Just hours ago, I struggled to eke out a sentence, and now I am confidently inviting Phoebe to the woods. And I think I know why. I'm the one in control now. I heard her words when she had no idea I was listening. I know what is to come. I'm angry and I am in charge. A calm rage has come over me, similar to the contrast of emotions I feel when I watch people through their windows.

Her eyes register surprise.

"Okay."

I stand and reach out my hand, taking her further away from Scoot and Cindy.

"Modesty. I like that," she flirts.

I don't let her say another word as I push her up against a tree and kiss her. Her body goes rigid but then relents to my dominance. I know she wants to fuck. I heard her say it.

She pulls away just long enough to say, "Who the hell are you, Sam?"

Bitch, you don't have the slightest idea.

I pull off her dress, and she's there, just like that time I watched her, except I can touch her. I can say the words. But all I want to do is make her remember me. Make her hovel at the thought of me. She'll never laugh when she thinks of me again.

She pulls my cock out of my pants and hoists a leg around me. I'm not nervous. I don't care about pleasing her. I don't care about my performance. This is about me. I push myself into her, and it feels good. It feels damned good.

"Fuck! Sam!" she cries out. I like the way she says my name. Not like a joke, but like I'm her master. Though, it's not enough. My head swirls with the drugs and the words she said. Her laughter. Her pity. The way she imitated me. My cock swells just like my anger.

"So, you think this is charity?" I sneer.

Her eyes, hooded with drugs and sex go clear with realization.

"You think this is a pity fuck?"

She tries to wriggle under me, but I hold myself firmly inside of her. "You're the only one who's going to need pity," I growl, each syllable, each word, as crystal clear as the anger I have kept deep inside of me all these years.

I pull out of her and turn her against the tree.

"Do you feel bad for me now?" I ask.

"Sam, stop! I'm sorry," she says. I cover her mouth before she can continue.

"What? I'm just a fucking retard. A harmless, little retard. I don't know what I'm doing."

She grunts and screams into my hand, the words dissipating into my palm. I spit into my other hand and shove my dick in her ass. Her cry vibrates into my palm, it's loud, so I press down harder. It's tight in there. I could barely get it in. She's bucking like an untamed horse, but she's a skinny little thing and my dad made me strong.

I pump a few times until I come in her ass. It feels like an explosion of every bit of energy in my body. I pull away and she spins around. It's dark, but I can see the sheen of her tears along her face.

"Can I go?" she asks. The false charm and sass have completely abandoned her. She's just a shaky, scared girl. Now she can be the object of pity.

I snatch her wrist. "Don't tell anyone. No one would believe you would they? You're trippin' out of your mind. And I'm harmless little Sam. I can barely get a word out, right?"

The power. It makes me something else. It makes me the person I hear in my thoughts. And now that I know the secret to being the person I only thought existed in my head, I'm never going to stop.

CHAPTER 25

SAM

I'm making spaghetti and meatballs. I am capable of cooking when I put my mind to it, and when I pull out one of my mother's old dusty cookbooks from the pantry. I usually feed Vesper well, to keep her healthy and attractive, but a pregnant woman has her cravings and I am sure this will be something that will make her light up. So I jotted down the ingredients I needed before leaving and picked them up on the way home. She'll appreciate the gesture. She'll appreciate me.

As I toss the meatballs and spaghetti in serving dish, the phone rings. I let the answering machine take it.

"Hey Sam, it's Scoot. Thanks for finally calling back. Of course it was on a Sunday morning, and you know we're at church. Anyway, give me a call. I just want to talk, okay?"

I've been avoiding his calls. I know I shouldn't, which is why I called on Sunday morning. I knew he'd likely be at church. That way, I could say I did, he'd know I was alive, and maybe he'd take a break from being on my ass. I made sure to give him all the necessary information I know he'd ask on a call anyway: I'm fine, working a lot, busy. It's enough to keep him from stopping by. It would take too much effort to drive the hour trip unless he thought there was an emergency. I've just been in a groove lately. I've found a state of mind that's a version of peace, at least when I'm here. The intrusive thoughts aren't constantly taunting me and I have a beautiful woman who is the closest thing I have ever had to a friend. We listen to music together, she reads to me, we go swimming at the lake. For the first time, I might have everything I need. Scoot brings me down; I just don't want to fucking talk to him.

With a pair of oven mitts, I grab the casserole dish and leave the house. As I hike to the cabin after a long day of work, that calmness takes over me. When I'm out there, I never feel at ease. I'm an impostor, and it is exhausting work. But with Vesp, she knows it all. She is the fusion of the things I want from out there, and the person I truly I am.

But as I get closer the house, I grow cold. My instincts tell me something is wrong. I've always been in tune with my gut, it's what has prevented me from being caught for so long. I think it comes from spending so much time in solitude. Vesper though, she's like a force field that throws off my calibrations. Taking her, keeping her— those things went against those instincts. But now, in the dark of the forest, they are strong and won't be ignored. I pick up my pace, but don't run. *I don't care. She's just a prisoner.* I have to tell myself these things. Because I can't afford to put her before me. If I do, I'll end up in prison.

When I open the door, it's clear my instincts haven't failed me.

Vesper is crouched on the floor, her arms crossed in front of her stomach. She's grimacing. The crotch area of her white dress is red with blood.

Blood.
The baby.
It's dead.

"Sam?" she says weakly.

I hear the casserole shatter as it hits the floor but I don't feel it leave my hands.

I didn't realize how much stock I had put in this: the idea of having a child with Vesp. How much I allowed myself to fall into a stupid fantasy. That I could have a taste of normalcy. That any of this could fix me.

She's looking away from a mess on the floor like she can't

bear the sight of it. I creep towards it and at its center, I see the small thing on the floor. It's a shock, the little boy, lying there. He has a little body, closed eyes— his tiny feet, ears, lips and fingers are formed. He's not ready to be out in the world, still translucent, still alien in many ways. Yet, he's perfect. He's not deformed or in pieces, he looks like he's sleeping in blood.

I did the right thing. I didn't abort him. I fed her. Gave her things to keep her occupied. Took her to the lake so she could breathe fresh air.

She did this.

She starved herself. She hit her womb against the chair. I bet that all caught up to her. Or even worse, maybe I trusted her to be alone and she's been playing me. Twisting my emotions all the while trying to find her own way to get rid of me inside of her.

This is on her.

I clench my fists as my body trembles with rage.

"Sam?" she asks again, this time a thread of fear in her voice.

I lunge towards her and stop when she cowers.

She did it on purpose while you were gone. She never wanted you. She would never want your child.

I want to hit her. I want to make her bleed and make her look like how I feel inside. I want her to sleep in a mess of blood and tissue. But I hold it in. Because something has been growing inside of me. Something I can't purge or abort. And it's changing me. But not everything changes—the rage that has slowly aged within me since before I could even speak. The impulses, the ones I can't control because something happened to me when that car collided with my body and my head hit that pavement. The emotions, because love is hate—my cruel father whom I so desperately wanted to look at me with pride, my mother who cared so much she made me into this fucking freak—so I can't tell the difference between the two. All that energy has to go somewhere. It can't stay in me. It has to go out. It has to be transferred.

I pull away from her and grab the chair—my chair—and I pick it up and slam it down on the ground.

She screams and pushes herself further into the corner, leaving a small trail of blood on the floor.

I do it over and over, growling, screaming, until the chair is just two detached arms in my hands. I throw them to the ground, but I am not sated.

"You did this!" I scream, pointing down at her.

"No…no!" she shouts.

But it doesn't matter. I have to do this. I don't know any other way. She thinks I'm trying to hurt her, but she doesn't understand that this outburst is keeping her safe.

I grab the record player and throw it against the wall. The plastic, metal, and wood explode violently. I kick the bathroom door open, so that it splinters and rips off the hinges.

"I'm sorry!" she cries.

"Shut up!" I shout.

I spin to face the crib, my pathetic display. A symbol of what a fucking sucker I am. I kick it over and over, the wood splintering and buckling under my feet. I tear up the whole place. This illusion. She doesn't want me. She doesn't want any of this.

"I didn't do it, Sam! I had a miscarriage. I wanted it too," she wails.

But I am blind. Nothing quells the rage. I want blood. Blood for blood. I want to kill. And I can't kill her. I can't.

I stagger out of the shed, marching back to the main house. I'm all instinct now. No. Instinct is about survival. I am rabid. Feral. I want to make pain.

I flail the door open to the barn and charge towards Hilda. Any other time, I would've chosen to kill a person over my goats.

Hilda and Trixie bleat frantically as I drag Hilda to the other end of the barn. Beverly huffs and neighs. The energy in here is frenetic, like they know everything that is to come.

I tie Hilda's legs up and hang her.

I hold the knife up to slit her throat, but instead of carving into her, without hesitation, I turn the knife onto myself, placing the blade against one of the many thick scars on my forearm, slicing into it, watching the old wound reopen. Slicing Hilda up won't bring the resolution I need. Someone has to be the recipient of this wrath, and a goat wouldn't even be close to worthy. But I am worthy. There is no blood at first, and then it flows at once, a crimson river running down to my wrist, palm, and then onto the floor of the barn. I walk over to the many tools hanging in the barn and find my weathered reflection on a sickle.

I find the next scar. I press the knife against it and I cut. I do it to feed the beast inside of me.

I cut into another scar. I feel the sharp edge slice into the sinew. I know it's painful, but it's nothing compared to the burning fire inside of me trying to escape through each wound I add to my body. I watch as the color of my skin morphs to scarlet, as the sheen of sweat becomes overpowered by the glistening of blood.

The animals cry and rustle as they smell the fury ooze out of me. Their cries feed the cycle. I try to make the feelings dissipate through these cuts, but with each new one, I see blood, and I think of it lying on the floor. Of the fantasy she held in her womb, of all the power she has, and I want to hurt her. So I have to do it again.

There is no relief. I still feel. I still rage. I still hurt.

When my torso and hands are too soaked with blood to find more scars, when I realize that no amount of cuts will stop my hands from shaking with the urge to hurt, I stop.

I amble over to Hilda and slice at the rope. She hits the floor on a heap and wriggles on her side until she is back on her feet. She staggers over to Trixie, screeching in terror.

I allowed myself to believe I could be something else, but this is how it always ends up. With screams. With fear.

All I want is her. All that can make this pain stop is the source. Like a fog clearing, I remember her. The girl who scrambles me up so that I can't figure out who I am when she's around. She makes me feel like I can reconcile all these mismatched parts of me. I remember her. Coiled on the floor, terrified. The pretty little smiling doll in the white dress soaked in blood, her face marked with terror and sorrow.

I left her back there.

Alone.

Terrorized.

And I can't remember if I locked the door.

VESPER

I stare at my home in disbelief. It's in pieces all around me. Like a small tornado ripped through and somehow left me unharmed. I didn't know what to expect when he came through that door. He had been different since he found out I was pregnant. That baby was my lifeline, I knew that. But I had begun to think it was more than that, that he and I were finding our own way. I've been the good girl, reaching deep inside of him to find humanity. I thought I had, and then when I did, I started to lose myself. What part was survival and what part was me falling for my captor? I couldn't tell the difference any longer. Not when I looked into those eyes, the color of the ocean and gold flecked shells along the shore. Not with that body, lean and tanned, resting naked beside me on my bed. Not when he brought me a new record, or swam with me in the cold lake. Or when he lay beside me as I read aloud. And especially not when he shyly brought the crib he built, a gesture so thoughtful, it's one most normal people wouldn't extend.

I had forgotten who he was. But as I sit here, still soaked in the remnants of our child, I remember. I saw the rage. I saw glimpses of the beast who starved me and locked me in a basement.

Yet, when the door creaks open on its own, when I realize that in his fury, he marched out without locking the door behind him, I don't run. I wait. There has to be more to this. There has to be a catch. It bobs back and forth in the gentle breeze for a while, and I realize he's not coming back. Not right away. This is my chance to run. To reset things. I've lost the baby. I can leave it all behind now. Slowly, I come to my feet, wincing from the occasional cramp. Thankfully, the bleeding seems to have stopped on its own and I am not hemorrhaging. If I was, I probably wouldn't make it through the night without serious medical attention. As I approach the door, I try to remember the steps I counted every time he took me to the water. He changed the route so many times, but I think I can do this.

I grab my shoes and slide them on, peeking out before I make a run for it. I pause at the door, recalling the last time I ran. The fear and pain as he chased me through the woods. I screamed. I begged for mercy. That person seems so distant from the man I spent the recent months with. I fight that twinge of pity for him. I try not to replay the look in his eyes when he realized we had lost the baby, shiny with tears he didn't want to shed. He wanted that child. It was my lifeline, but it was his too.

I brush away the thought and take a deep breath before taking off. The adrenaline pumps my heart so fast I can hear it thudding in my ears. I've been good, and I have been rewarded. He hasn't had to punish me in so long. But this—running off while he's having a fit—I might not survive what he'd have in store for me.

Despite all the planning and counting steps, with the panic and in this black night, I am lost. But I keep running, hoping I'll see something, anything to help me regain my bearings. I push through branches, twigs, and cobwebs, fear numbing the pain, until I come across something I have only seen once before and only during the daylight hours.

It's so haunting at night, it stops me in my tracks. The abandoned obstacle course, or "playground," as he told me. It's crawling with vines and overgrowth like jungle ruins. I remember the look on his face when I asked him about it. He was hiding something painful. This place feels hollow, void of happiness. Suddenly it becomes clear to me that if this was part of his childhood, then his was not a source of joy.

But as haunting as the tall, rotted structures are around me, this is a gift. I know where I am. It's still fresh in my mind from earlier today. I listen for sounds of him. Even though I know he can be deadly silent, I am reassured when I hear nothing. So I catch my breath and I make the final run for the lake. My refuge. My sanity. The place that I have convinced myself divides me from the rest of the world.

It takes longer than I expect to get there, but I waste no time trudging into the water, the skirt of my white dress dragging along the onyx glassy surface. Once I am waist-deep, I submerge myself and begin to swim into the black abyss. I know exactly how long it will take me to cross. I've studied it so much during our time out here. So just like the first time he let me swim out here, I go under, swimming until my lungs can't hold in another second, and rise.

Don't look back. He is my Sodom and Gomorrah. He is my sin. He is my darkest desire. The temptation is strong to mull over what I am leaving behind. A life where I am coveted. I am his world. He takes care of me. He pleasures me. I am his treasure. No one out there would ever take the risks he's taken to have me. He could have hit me tonight, but he didn't. He spared the rod. He's changing. I've changed him.

Keep swimming.

The further I go, the stronger his pull is. But this is my only chance. People like him never truly change. He is broken. But so am I. Maybe not like him, but our broken pieces fit together to make a mosaic of swims in the lake, late nights listening to music, the serene look on his face--both perfect and damaged--as I read to him, orgasms upon orgasms, that swirl of filth and arousal I feel when he takes charge of my body, silence that speaks louder than any words any one else has ever spoken to me. And the scars all over him. Different kinds. Some thick and long. Others short, like choppy brushstrokes on a painting. They cover part of him, like a painting of his story. A darkness he can't hide, no matter how hard he tries to silence himself. He was hurt. And I'd be hurting him again. I'd be sending him to jail. I help people. I take care of them. Even Johnny didn't need me as desperately as Sam does.

But I can't go back.

I know who he is. What he's done. What would that make me?

I come up for air and find myself at the center point of the lake. The spot I wished I could stay forever. Where I could keep the best parts of myself from both worlds. And I could keep the best parts of him.

I study the side of the lake I have yearned to reach since my first swim. I can't go back out to that world. I'm not her anymore. I just have her name, her skin, her eyes, her hair. But my soul? It's been completely altered. He's stained its purity with his darkness.

I turn towards the shore from which I came, part of me hoping he'll be there to force me back, but it's still and quiet. I look towards the other side that holds my freedom and I feel nothing. I stop treading water, and it feels so easy to let go. To let my body sink into the void. To watch the silver circle of the moon shrink as I descend into darkness. I don't feel so heavy anymore. I can just let everyone move on. I can stay here between both worlds forever.

As I go under the blackness engulfs me. This is freedom. No one can have me, but myself. I close my eyes, and take a breath. Instead of serenity, the water in my lungs shocks me. My eyes open wide and I jerk, awoken from this trance of helplessness. Down here, between two worlds, at its deepest point, it becomes clear. I don't want freedom if it means the life I had before all this. I can't imagine a life where Sam doesn't exist. This is the greatest test. The key to my new freedom. To show him I had the choice, and I chose him.

I push off the silty bottom and swim up as fast as I can before I lose consciousness. When I rise to the surface, I gasp and spit up water. The hollow sounds of my wheezing and gasping overpower the night sounds of the woods. I swim to shore, cough and vomit the water I inhaled, and collapse on the damp pebbles, rolling onto my back as I catch my breath.

He must be looking for me. I have to go to him before he comes to me. He needs to understand this is all my choice. I wobble up to my feet, fueled with the need to find Sam before he finds me. I run, this time having better bearings and a clarity of mind I didn't have when I was trying to find the lake. It takes me a quarter of the time to find my way back to the cabin. The door is still open. I glance in from a few feet away, still not able to bring myself to look directly at the event that upended everything. I could wait here. I could sit out front until he comes back. But I can't wait. I can't just sit here passively. This is a choice. From the very start, he's given me choices. Or the illusion of choices. But this time, it's all mine. I laid the options, and alone in the depths of the darkest waters, I made the decision to come back. I won't sit here and wait for him to come to me.

I have made the decision. And I have my demands.

I run in the direction where I know the barn was. I'm not sure how to get there, but I come upon what seems to be a worn path, probably cleared for his convenience for the daily trips to my cabin. I race down it, breathless, frantic.

He was terrifying when he last saw me. But I'm not scared anymore. I've run out of fear. I know he needs me, maybe even more than I need him.

I laugh in hysterical relief as I see a pale amber slits glowing in the distance. As I get closer, I see the outline of the barn in the darkness. I don't know what I'll find when I get there. Or if he's even there. But I sprint towards it, my dress wet and clinging to my body, my hair damp and sticking to my face and shoulders.

I almost call out his name, but I realize I know nothing about his life. I assume he is alone out here. That he has no close neighbors. But for all I know I could open that door and find a group of people in the barn. I don't have time to contemplate much further as the door bursts open, and out storms Sam.

Heaving. Sweaty. His shirtless body, clad in a pair of torn jeans, glimmering with blood. His golden brown hair is slicked back with haphazard strokes of red. His clear eyes glow against the dark night and the crimson streaks masking his face.

He is a monster. And I have run right back into his clutches.

CHAPTER 26

SAM

The last thing I expect to see when I frantically push the barn door open, is Vesper. I was ready to hunt her. To tear every last fucking tree down if I had to. I was going to go after her. And yet, here she is.

Vesp comes to a sharp halt when I lock eyes with her. She freezes as her gaze travels quickly over me and back to meet my glare. I'm so fucking wound up, it almost hurts. Every muscle in my body is knotted. My heart is on overdrive. My mind is filled with racing thoughts, still wanting to hunt the woman who has tracked me.

She's panting too. She's been running. Her hair is dripping wet. Her white gown is soaked through, so that I can see her tightened nipples pressing against the fabric. Streaks of mud stain her skin and gown. The blood. The deep red stain of loss, it's still there, slightly diluted by her excursion into the water.

The water.

She tried to leave. But she's here now. And I don't fucking understand.

"What have you done?" she asks, her voice wrapped with horror.

I look down at myself, at my blood coating my skin. I feel the burn of the cuts like little lashings all over my side. What she sees is who I am. I shake my head faintly at her question still holding every muscle taut as if she's holding a gun to my head and might shoot at any moment.

"That wasn't a person?"

I shake my head.

She nods, glancing over to the barn.

"Was it one of the animals?"

I shake my head again.

"Is that blood…yours?"

I nod, just barely. I'm not even sure if she can see it. I raise my arm and glance down, the layer of blood on my arm thick and gleaming like the shell of a candy apple.

She looks back at me, raising her palms just a little bit, smoothly, as if I'm the one with the barrel to her head.

"I'm here," she utters, her voice quivering and weak. "I'm here, Sam," she says more assuredly.

But her words don't mean shit. Words have done nothing but betray me my entire life.

"I tried to leave. I did. But I came back. Because I made a choice. I…" she drops her head down, and stifles a sob. "I don't know why. But I didn't hurt the baby. I liked spending that time with you in the cabin. You don't have to force it. I'm here. I'm here. We can keep doing what we were doing. None of it has to stop. But if you want this. If you want a life where you don't have to look over your shoulder, wondering if I'll run, then you can't take me back to the way it was. I just want it to stay the way it's been."

Every thought is telling me that this is somehow still a lie. That every nice gesture, every smile is just a way to deceive me. Who would want me? A demon, covered in scars, struggling over every other utterance. I crave things that aren't normal. I know this. My mother knew this. It's why she kept me out here. She was protecting me from myself.

But Vesp is here. I didn't run her down. She came to me. Do I reward or punish? Sometimes things aren't so clear. Maybe she gets that.

So I have to do both.

VESPER

This was a mistake. Coming back here. Thinking I changed him.

It's like he's under a spell, and I'm trying to speak to that tiny piece of him that can still hear me. Trying to coax him back to reality. He's holding a knife. I didn't even see it at first through the mix of light and shadows hitting his body.

No one will ever know what became of me.

They'll never know my story.

And even if they found me some day, would they know I came back? That I had a chance to survive and I ran right back into his path?

I run out of words. Words I'm not even sure are reaching him. I used them early on to pry out his humanity. But the person in front of me is dazed. Savage. Beyond language.

He stares at me for a while. I dart my eyes up at the moon and hope that if I have to go, I'll see my grandmother. Then maybe dying wouldn't be so bad.

He lingers. Stretching the moment out, his chin tucked down as he burns me with his intense eyes, glowing in the night like a mountain lion's. I wish I knew his secrets before leaving this earth. It doesn't seem fair that I don't get to learn them.

"Please…" I stammer. It's arbitrary. I don't think it'll help me, but I say it anyway.

Then I do something. It's not really a calculation. It's as animal as the man before me, unfazed by the wounds along his arm and chest. It's beyond language. If I can't speak to the part of himself he's imprisoning, I can speak to the one who's here right now.

I descend to my knees and bow my head. This isn't a standoff. This isn't a battle. This is acceptance. Acceptance that needs to go both ways.

I reach out my hand, not looking up. Hoping he'll accept. That my demands are humble, not defiant. I wait, but there's nothing. Just as I begin to drop my arm, a rough, soaked hand clenches it.

I gasp in shock. Terror and relief wrestle inside of me, unsure of what this means. I look up and my gaze meet his as he pulls me to my feet. My eyes shoot down to the knife in his other hand and I recoil instinctively. He looks down at it, and back up at me, dragging me closer to the barn. He plunges it into the old, cracked wood before slamming me up against the wooden exterior.

"I did this..." he mutters against my lips, "to save you." Grasping my face between his blood soaked hands, he presses his mouth to mine. A spiteful kiss laced with rage and surrender. Tasting of blood and perspiration. Victory never tasted so bitter.

But he pulls the kiss away as powerfully as he thrust it on me.

Sam grabs my skirt, finding a small tear from my jaunt in the woods and rips it open. He wipes a hand clean on the fabric. He slides his fingers inside of me, afterward bringing them up to his face to see them better. Fresh blood glazes his new fingertips--the remains of the life we created together still slowly trickling from me.

"I'm gonna take you like I did the first time you ran," he rasps in my ear. This time his reasons are different. Sam finishes ripping my dress open, so that the hot night air breathes on my humid skin, and he runs his mouth along my torso, leaving a scattered trail of blood wherever he touches me. The smell of iron and sweat crawl up my nose inciting a hunger, like the craving for meat. I curl my fingers into his damp hair, through caked blood. It doesn't even phase me. I've been so close to death for so long, it's just a part of my life now.

He stands back up, taking sharp, impatient breaths. His hard chest pushes against mine with each inhale. I reach below and feel his potent need. He lets his jeans fall to the floor, so he is just man — skin, hair, blood, muscle, sweat. Without wasting a second, he grabs me, dragging me into the barn.

It's so fast, but I see a trail of blood lead to the opposite direction, where I can't see, where his earlier violence must lay. He shows me into an empty stall.

"I want to see your body in the light," he grunts, pushing me down onto the thin layer of hay. "I'm gonna fuck you like an animal."

The itchy straw sticks to my wet skin as he mounts me. The musky smell of livestock wafts in the air, intermingled with our own natural musk.

He forces his way in. It's not gentle. He lets me scream as he opens me up, his first thrusts slow. Not for my comfort, but because he wants the moment to last. It allows me to relax around his girth, and to enjoy the feeling of his cock in my ass. And just when I have found that comfort, he pumps harder, pulling my hair like he's riding his horse.

He grunts and groans as he plows into me.

This is my punishment.

This is my reward.

Finally, all those times he took a part of me and replaced it with himself have come to this. Because I am deriving a pure, untainted pleasure from this. No guilt. No shame.

I made the right choice to stay. It was a gamble of the highest stakes and it's paid off.

I reach under and play with my clit, taking myself to climax just as he lets out a powerful moan, his cock pulsating within the tight grip of my ass. His fullness and the reverberating echoes of my orgasm drown out the dull cramps in my belly from the loss.

He rolls off of me and onto his back. Something has changed. His eyes are human again. His body not so rigid.

I know better than to expect him to say anything, so I do.

On my knees, I turn to face him. He looks up at me inquisitively.

"I'm here," I say one more time, before lying beside him, facing him in the fetal position. He doesn't react for the first few seconds, still tentative. But then he slides closer, reaching his arm underneath, and pulling me in close.

I run my fingers along the warm, slick blood on his arm. I've never had a problem with gore, one of the reasons I decided I had the fortitude for nursing. I trail along until my finger stops at the gaping wound, and then another.

"Sam…" I lament. He's hurt himself so many times tonight and I hurt for him. "We need to take care of these. I can stitch you up."

He doesn't answer, which is to be expected, but when I look up for confirmation, he's already asleep. His face is blanketed with serenity underneath the smudges of blood.

I rest against his bloody torso, matted in straw, until we both fall asleep.

CHAPTER 27

VESPER

Sunlight slips through the wood plank walls and shines into my eyes to awaken me. My stirring wakes Sam, who has wrapped himself around me. I still can't tell if it's affection or mistrust.

"Good morning," I wince. Despite the full night's sleep, I am still exhausted from the ordeal my body went through and have a strong hankering for steak.

He sits up, barn debris falling from his blood-stained nude body as he stretches. He gives me a curt nod. *Good morning to you too.*

The blood on his body has dried, but the wounds still glisten with congealed blood. He barely winces as he moves. I don't know how he handles the pain so well. "We need to get your wounds stitched. You've slept in this mess without cleaning them. You're going to get an infection. And I'm starving. I need iron. I need meat, please," I propose.

He looks me up and down, and nods thoughtfully. He comes to his feet and offers me his hand. I stand up, remembering I am completely naked. Modesty shouldn't have a place here, but last night, I told him I wanted things to keep growing. So I test him.

"I have no clothes here."

He points a finger up, signaling for me to stay put. He puts on his jeans and slips out of the stall, running out of my sight, and returns with his t-shirt. He beats away straw from it before handing it to me.

"Thank you," I offer coyly.

He leads me towards the picturesque farmhouse I had only seen for the first time yesterday. But instead of treating it like some forbidden fortress, he leads me up the stairs and through the front door.

I want to take it all in. The antique furniture I can tell was not collected, but has lived in this home for generations. Spots where there were once frames hung for many years, and removed, leaving just the trace of their outlines on the wall. But he takes me to the bathroom so quickly, I barely have time to absorb and interpret these pieces of him.

In the bathroom is a huge, claw foot, cast iron tub, with a flimsy pale yellow shower curtain draped around it. He turns on the water and gestures for me to enter first. I pull off my shirt and he his jeans and we enter together.

Filth and muck rinse off our bodies and down the drain. That's when I am able to get a full view of the damage, the deep cuts, possibly a dozen, all carved into thick scar tissue.

But even with the fresh wounds, once the blood is rinsed away, he doesn't look like a monster, but a young man, roughened with scars, but handsome enough for them to only add to his mystique. Nothing about him makes sense. He should have never had to do the things he did to get me, or any woman for that matter. Though I know by now, this has nothing to do with sex.

He cleans my hair and I clean his. Something he's done for me so many times before, but I've never had the chance to reciprocate. Between us, there's silence. Just the sprinkling of the shower water hitting the tub and our bodies.

"Am I staying here?" I ask. I'm used to doing the talking for the both of us.

He shrugs. He didn't plan for this.

He yanks the shower curtain open, giving me one last glance of his dripping naked body before closing it behind him. I finish and towel myself off, wondering where he went. He returns within seconds with a needle kit, thread and rubbing alcohol.

He offers it to me with a shrug. *Will this do?*

I nod and direct him to sit on the edge of the tub. I thread the needle and take a deep breath, rubbing alcohol along the wound and dipping the needle and thread in the solution.

I plunge the needle into side of his cut. He hisses.

"Sorry!"

He winches and nods, encouraging me to keep going. I weave across the cuts. These aren't small nicks and the skin is thick from existing scar tissue, so it takes tremendous pain tolerance on his end.

The experience is so wholly unpleasant for him, I cannot understand how or why last night he was the very person who opened his own flesh with a knife.

"What happened? In the barn?" I have to ask knowing he has no way to answer sitting here naked without a pen or pad. He doesn't acknowledge the question. I didn't expect even that much anyway.

Whenever I think Sam needs a small break, usually once I've wrapped up one laceration, but before moving onto the next, I rub his hair softly, and he allows himself to lean back onto me with his eyes closed, and accept my comfort. When I am finally done, he's covered in black stitchings, like an old teddy bear being held together after decades of ownership.

"You look like a rag doll," I laugh.

He snickers, walking over to the sink and running the water so hot it steams, and rinses off his face. As he does that, I tend to the small mess I made working on him. The door closes behind me and I spin around to see that Sam's left, but the sink is still running. On the large foggy antique mirror over the sink is a finger-written note for me: *Thank you. It had to be me so it wouldn't be you. I'm going to get meat. TRUST.*

VESPER

I wander through the house, first looking for something to wear other than the barn-scented t-shirt. His bedroom is right next to the bathroom, so the search is brief. The room is sparsely decorated and orderly. The twin sized bed and wooden desk in the corner hints that not much has changed here for a long time. Books line a shelf above the bed and bookcase on the adjacent wall. He is someone who escapes into fantasy. I pull open a small closet door, in it are many t-shirts and a few button downs. No surprise. But on the far end are a couple of suits. I touch them; the fabric isn't cheap. I know he has means, and that fact only adds to the mystery.

I glance over my shoulder and listen for sounds, just to make sure he isn't here before I tiptoe to a desk drawer. I slowly pull it open and there's nothing but a few pens and a notepad. It's clear this room is just for sleeping so I slip out and try the next room. The door is locked. I go from room to room, searching for clues on the upper level, but he seems to have hidden them in that locked room. This farmhouse looks like an innocent, sweet abode, with floral coverlets on beds, breezy white eyelet curtains, and old wood furniture. But every room lacks that worn-in look of a lived in house. The other bedrooms lack personal artifacts. Only Sam lives here, but it's like he's not really here.

I make my way downstairs to the first level. A cursory search tells me this will go nowhere, and he could turn up any minute. I look down at my shirt and realize the only things that likely survived Sam's tantrum are my dresses. Then sorrow pinches my heart. The baby. I couldn't bear to look at it. As far along as I was, I probably would have been able to tell the sex, but I have no idea. I've always been conflicted about the child growing inside of me. A symbol of my captivity. Of loss. But also a new life. A blessing. Hope. That baby changed things here dramatically. And maybe that was its purpose, to transform things here, not to live.

I've learned since being here to live in the pain, to go through it. Not hide from it or run around it. And going back there is just that. It's just another pain I have to live through.

I find a paper and pencil and leave him a note.

I don't want to wear t-shirts all day, so I've gone back to my cabin to get my dresses. I'll be back in a jiffy. I know your instinct is to chase me. And you can. But you'll just find me rummaging through a mess for my favorite things. Remember, TRUST.

I follow the path to the cabin confidently, reaching it in record time. I can tell an animal scavenged through some of my dry goods and the dish he dropped and I grow nauseous. Our baby. I run inside but it's gone. The blood spot is still there, but spread as if someone tried to clean it up. I tell myself Sam took care of it. I can't allow myself to think an animal came here and ate the tiny corpse. In another time, the mere thought of something like that would have turned me into a heaping mess of tears, but I am toughened now.

I solemnly pick through my things, hoping animals it didn't urinate on them. I rifle through the debris, mourning the record player and torn books. But I manage to pull out all of my dresses from the rubble. Some could use a cleaning, but they are in decent shape. I dust off some random crap from them, when the light glints on something. The Bee Gees record. The first thing he brought to me. It seems to have slid innocuously to the floor behind the table that was holding the record player, now on its side. I smile and grab it. A token of when things began to turn for the better. I think to myself that I will get him to learn the dance. And maybe one day we'll go to the movies together.

We can start over. We can leave here and then he won't have to hide me. We can't get to the place we both want to be until the shadow of our past isn't hovering over us.

I hold onto the record, thinking about my outlandish—or not so outlandish—proposal. Lost in thought, I hear Sam's familiar footsteps crunch against the scattered food on the steps outside my door.

I roll my eyes satisfied that Sam found me doing exactly what I said I would.

"What happened to trust?" I ask, as he enters, my back still facing away from the door.

The feet stop moving, and he's silent. But I am used to that. I have to look at him in order to communicate, either through gestures or notes, so I spin on my heels.

But the person in front of me isn't Sam.

We stare at each other for seconds that seem frozen. He seems just as shocked as me.

I still have that initial instinct to beg for help, but I think about Sam, and what will happen to him if I do. After all this, it feels like a betrayal.

As I stare the familiar face, searching my memory for who he could be. I haven't seen anyone other than Sam for so long, but this man's face feels relatively new. As if I hadn't first seen him that long ago.

He takes a big gulp; I can see from the way he struggles to speak that his mouth is dry.

"Are you...Vesper Rivers?" he asks.

Am I? I have her face, her body, her hair and eyes, but am I the girl that was taken months ago? I don't know anymore. If he's here to save me, he wouldn't be returning her, he'd be bringing back a stranger.

But lying doesn't seem like an option, and I nod hesitantly.

He lets out a heavy breath and stumbles back. "I'm...I'm sorry," he says, stepping back outside, feeling for the door.

"Who are you?" I ask desperately, confused and frightened by his reaction.

"I...I have to go," he stammers, shutting the door.

"Wait!" I shout, pounding and pushing against the door as he locks it. "Who are you?" I shout. But as I am so accustomed to, I am met with silence.

I pace back and forth, trying to place the face. It's so familiar. Then, with the intensity of a lightning strike it hits me all at once. I rummage through my things for pieces of the news clippings I tore during one of the times Sam taunted me. I had gathered some and hidden them under my mattress early on. In case I had died but someone found this place, there would be a clue. I scatter them on my messy bed, and frantically piece them together. And that's when I confirm what my gut already knew. There is an image of the press conference. Below, a caption listing the people in it from left to right. The man who just locked me back in my cabin is the man who is supposed to save me: Sheriff Andrew "Scooter" Hunter-Ridgefield.

CHAPTER 28

SAM

There's an unlikely calm in my truck as I drive back from the butcher. Is this what freedom feels like? I can't remember the last time I didn't feel like a prisoner to my urges. Last night, I realized this could be it. I might not have to live with the constant tension of waiting for the other shoe to drop.

I watched the house for fifteen minutes before leaving. Trust doesn't mean I have to be completely naive. But Vesp didn't leave. I could see her go from room to room through the windows. I expected that. She's starving to know more about me, and it doesn't upset me.

As I pull into the long driveway that leads up to the house, a sensation of dread usurps the fleeting semblance of liberty I felt during this short trip.

Everything looks just as I left it, but something is off. My sharp instincts kick on high alert. Did she play me? Is she gone, after all? I speed along the rocky driveway, bumping up and down the uneven road. I step out of the cab, surveying the vast open space that holds the house and barn.

Fresh tire tracks line the grass in front of the house. I could follow them to see where they lead, but I have to check the house first to see if she's still here.

I walk into the front door and he's sitting there, a bottle of whiskey in one hand, a gun pointed at me with the other.

This has been a slow suicide. Every action since the night I first snuck out and climbed that tree. Taking Vesper, allowing her to make me sloppy—that was just when I finally had the guts to pull the trigger.

"What are you doing here?" I ask Scoot, the name I've called him since as far back as I can remember. The nickname he used in his bid for Sheriff to make him sound more folksy. But most people know him as Sheriff Andrew Hunter-Ridgefield.

His scowl drips with disgust.

"What have you done?" he asks, his tone a mix of rage and despair.

"Where is she?" I ask.

"Oh wouldn't you like to know? Don't worry, the cavalry won't be rushing in here quite yet."

I take stock of all the things I could bash his skull in with if it came to that. But I won't. As much as I loathe my brother, there's a sense of loyalty that undercuts all that bullshit.

"I called you a few weeks ago. Then again and again. You didn't answer. You never just fucking answer," he grunts through tight lips. "The morning after the barbeque, I saw Milly packing her bags and leaving. I watched it as I had my morning coffee. I thought, well maybe she's going out of town. But I'm a fucking cop, Sam. I couldn't help but notice the look on her face, like she'd seen the devil." He rubs his face with both hands, temporarily removing the gun's aim on me. "But I didn't even think it had anything to do with you. Because you're my fucking brother, man. I let that shit cloud me. So I brushed it off after asking around. No one knew anything. But she's new. Maybe she just didn't feel like telling a bunch of strangers her business."

He pauses for a moment to absorb. I can see him cataloguing everything from our past, making the connections the way an experienced officer would. He's just like dad, and it makes me sick. It's like dad is still here, still fucking judging me, still looking at me like a disappointment.

"I'm busy. So I didn't think much about it. Honestly, I have been so fucking sick of chasing you down, trying to make you feel welcome, I thought I'd give you your space. Even when I called you a few more times, I just wanted to check in on my brother and if Milly came up, great. But it did irk me that she never came back. Like an itch I couldn't scratch. Until yesterday when I saw a moving truck and a crew moving her stuff out. Eventually she showed up. I could've let it go. I could've said it wasn't my business. God, I almost wish I had. But I crossed the street and went up to Milly, friendly-like. When she looked at me, there was this *look* in her eyes. First fear, then anger. I pretended I didn't notice, asked her why she was moving. Just friendly talk. She didn't answer me, just kept carrying her things to her car. I kept pressing, wondering what I had done until she snapped. 'Why don't you ask your brother?' That's what she said."

I sigh, hating myself for losing control like that. It's those little mistakes that lead to your sheriff-brother pointing a gun at you in your living room.

"It hit me in the gut, you know? Because I never really said it, Sam. And I try to show it. But I feel like shit for the way things happened. For being a little dick and racing off the day that car hit you. And I know you think that I kept my distance growing up because I was a shitty brother, but it was because every time I saw the scars on you, it made me sick to my stomach with guilt. And I have been trying so hard. Despite all the smugness, and the seething looks, and every fucking avoidance tactic under the sun. So when she said that, I felt sick again. Because I knew that there was something I didn't want to know."

My throat should feel tight. I should feel trepidation about any words that might come from my lips. But finally sharing a secret is a great relief. I finally feel like I can be myself. Suddenly, the invisible hand gripping my neck releases.

"Well, I'm glad you think I owe you my undying gratitude because one day you woke up and decided not to be a cock."

"God, you are such an asshole," Scoot groans. "I am so tired of your fucking 24-7-365 pity party. You're fucking unbelievable. You should be…BEGGING me right now."

"You have no fucking idea!" I shout. "No fucking idea what it was like to be me. You got to be free. Dad didn't wake you up in the middle of the night and make you swim until you'd drown because he hated you. Because he thought that your birth was the reason mom got worse with her fucking delusions. You only had to see mom a few hours a week, and then you both drove off and I was here! I was here being held fucking prisoner."

"I am so sick of this shit, Sam!" Scoot shouts, punching his pistol into the air as he jumps to his feet. "Here's the thing no one had the balls to tell you. Except dad, and it's why you hated him so much. You were a fucking weird kid. You always were. We all saw the strangeness. You weren't right. You were never right. And you aren't the first person to be different, you know. You can blame mom and dad, or me…but it was always there. Mom fucking knew it. Maybe she couldn't bring herself to see it that way. But, that's why she had you out here and that's why dad let it happen!"

"There it is," I chuckle. "Underneath all the caring and checking in, that's how you really feel. I like that! No bullshit. It's dad reincarnated."

Scooter jolts a step towards me, keeping the gun trained on me so I don't move.

"You're a sick fuck. I should shoot you right here. I came over you know, to find out what the fuck Milly was talking about. I sure as hell knew you wouldn't answer the phone if I called. You're not here and all the pictures are gone. I'd thought you'd finally lost it like mom. Something felt off. I go to the barn, and I see a pool of blood, trails of it throughout the barn, leading outside. I tell myself, maybe he's dead, maybe someone came here and did that to him. Because he's fucking weird, but he's not psychotic. My gut tells me to follow the trail into the woods. It's well worn. It's being used a lot these days, I can tell. Twigs were snapped along the whole way, like someone had been running. I thought I'd find you out there. And then I see her. I see the fucking girl who was all over the news, whose fucking picture is tacked up onto my office wall, who I have lost so much sleep over because we have nothing to go on, who was taken by a serial home invader and rapist and my brain is fucking exploding because suddenly it's all clear…" Scoot lets out a wail, agony so strong it's physical. "It's you. You check all the boxes. You knew how the police work because of dad and me. Your job keeps you mobile. You're strong and athletic. You're isolated so no one would notice your late night excursions. But there was one thing I didn't get…no one ever mentioned a stutter. Clearly that would be the first thing anyone would mention. Is anything about you even real?"

I glower at him, feeling a sense of satisfaction that I fooled that smart ass for so long. "Oh, very fucking real."

"I should fucking kill you!" he screams, prodding the gun in my direction, tears running down his cheeks.

I brace myself, but just like I can't do it to him, I know he can't pull that trigger.

"Whose blood was that? In the barn?" he asks. "She didn't have a scratch on her. Are there others?"

"No."

"Then whose blood is that!" he demands.

I shift on my feet as I stall. He wouldn't understand this, and I am in no mood to explain. The partly rolled up sleeves of my shirt move enough for him to see some stitches.

"What the fuck?" he mutters. "Pull off the shirt," he orders.

I don't move.

"Do it!" he waves the gun at me.

I sigh in protest as I pull it off, the t-shirt underneath doesn't hide the various tracks of thread along my arms.

"Did she do that?"

"No. It was me. I've never hurt her."

He stares at me puzzled for a few beats. "You are fucking deranged, man."

I snicker.

"Did you even think about the rest of us? The family name? I wanted to run for mayor, then maybe even governor someday. It's why I followed in dad's footsteps, to show that despite the money, I could do the hard work like everyone else. You knew that was my dream. My career will be over! Our name will be dragged through the mud if this gets out. "

If. The self-preservation of wealth and power trumps all.

"All the lives you've destroyed. And what about our family? What about Uncle Tommy?"

Our uncle, the senator.

"Oh you mean the family that made sure we stayed nice and quiet up here? Not a single one of them ever bothered to visit, you know? Even when mom died hardly a person showed up at the hospital. They just made sure mom was quiet. They made sure the money flowed. That we didn't embarrass our family. Yup, the

Hunters and the Ridgefields, great American families! They can't be sullied by a paranoid woman and her retard son! I don't give a fuck about what happens to them!" I scream with wild eyes.

Scoot stares at me for a while, like he finally saw the beast in me. The one I hid under chronic underestimations and manipulation.

"She didn't beg for help you know? I think she thought I was you and she made this comment in cutesy tone. I found her in that little shack in the woods. The place looked like a train ran through it. What the fuck did you do to her?"

I don't plan on saying anything, but he stops me anyway.

"You know what? I don't wanna know. I don't wanna hear a word of it. I know enough. I know what you've already done you sick fuck."

I glare at him. These words are empty. I want to know what he's going to do about this. Is this the end? I need to hear it.

"So what now?" I ask.

He paces in a roundabout way, rubbing his temples with the base of his palms, the gun still planted in his hands. He's a sickly pale green and it looks like he could pass out at any moment.

He snickers. "You've ruined my life. You know that?" he asks. "No matter what I do, you've ruined my fucking life. Every time I look at my son…" his voice weakens, "his eyes, his smile, the way he laughs, I'll see you. I'll wonder if he's so much like you that he'll become you. That he's got your fucked up sickness. But unlike you, I love my family, and I am not going to put them through this…I'll do anything for them." He sits down and buries his head in his hands, like he can't look at me for what he's about to say. Like he probably will never be able to look at himself again.

"I want you to leave town. I don't ever want to see you again. You're dead to me and every family member. You have your trust, stocks, real estate— you can work anywhere, you can sell this whole fucking farm for plenty. I don't want it, not after the vile shit that has gone on in here. Then we're done. I owe you one. Maybe you're like this because of me. The doctors said you might be different because of the way you hit your head. But no one ever told you directly. We thought we could ignore it and it'd be fine. You were strange anyway. But fine. You were different after that coma. Fine. I accept that maybe in some way I had a hand in this. But then we're even. And you are nothing to me."

I don't show it, but I couldn't be happier with the verdict. I don't have to pretend with him anymore.

"And you have to get rid of her."

"What?" I snap.

"You heard me. I don't mean take her with you. I mean there can't be a trace of her. The possibility she'd tell her story. She saw my face, Sam."

"No," I shake my head. "You fucking do it if this is your master plan."

"This is your mess, you fucking clean it up!" he shouts, raising the gun a little higher to remind me this is not a democracy.

He studies my face, the stone expression I had kept so artfully throughout our conversation must be lost.

"Oh, you fucker. You think you love her? You think you're even capable of that? You stole her from her house. Took her away from her life, her family. I'm sure you've raped her countless times. Like you did to the others. Maybe tortured her? Oooh, but this one's different," he mocks. "You think that's love? You think you even know human emotion? You're not even an animal. Animals don't hurt people for kicks. You're a monster. A real fucking monster. You're the boogeyman. You've already killed her, you understand? I've seen victims who couldn't come back from less. You've probably got her head so fucked, she can't function out there. But if you don't get rid of her, I promise, I fucking promise I'll come back here with the full force of the law. Fuck reputations. Fuck family. And fuck your fucking freedom! I'll make sure you fry, and then you'll burn in hell! And she'll be paraded out for the world to see. And she'll just suffer for the rest of her life. So take the fucking offer!"

Somewhere in his diatribe, he had come towards me, so by the time we're done, he's in my face with his finger pointed at me and the other hand pressing the gun at my temple. Spittle is dripping from his bottom lip, the tiny capillaries in his eyes look like they'll hemorrhage. Just like my dad when he'd get impatient during his "lessons."

He blinks in rapid succession, giving his concentrated rage a chance to dilute. "You can have a life, I just want mine back," Scooter says more calmly as he steps back.

Warm whiskey-scented jagged breaths huff against my face as he waits for my acceptance.

"Tell me you'll take care of this," he commands. "Tell me I'll never hear about you, or her again."

My mantra comes to mind. Nothing is as important as my freedom. I'm not the type who wants his name all over the papers for what he's done. This is my secret. Well, now it's Scooter's too. But I'd rather die than go to jail. Than to have the world that never accepted me justify it all with what I've done. Just like Scoot's doing right now. This is great for him. He gets to tell himself I was always a freak, and that he never liked me because underneath it all, I was this. I was always a psycho. It was predetermined.

"Okay," I whisper through clenched teeth.

"You need to be gone within three days. You can sell the house from out of town. Hire an agent. But you never step foot in this part of California again." He starts for the door. I can't let him leave without something to stew on. I understand now nothing I say will make him change his mind. He's backed into a corner with all this. He doesn't *want* to turn me in.

"Just remember, Scoot. You're no fucking hero. You're not doing this for her or me, or even Katie and the kids. Dad had his hero complex, but at least he believed his own bullshit. You're doing this so you can live the charmed life you've always had. You play cop so you can pretend to be a commoner. But when the true test has come, when you have to really be one of them and let go of all the things that make you so fucking privileged, you've proven that it's all an act. Just remember, you'll have blood on your hands. I've never killed a person, and my first time will be because you wanted me to."

He pauses, whips open the screen door and hesitates before turning back.

"Listen to you," he sniggers, "that voice as crisp as a whistle. It's all that hiding that made it so hard for you to speak, wasn't it? It must have been so difficult, holding this secret for so long. We have a task force on you. We know how far back you've been going into houses, peeping. It's been a long time." He squints, a mischievous smirk growing on his face. "But when you're you... when you're *really* you, when that evil shines, man you could talk a fish outta water."

"Maybe."

My curt answer turns his face red, the grin molding into a snarl. "I wish you were never born. You were a fucking mistake," he seethes.

"I know."

And with that, I am alone, finally free. Truly free. Not just at night, but in a few days, I'll be a man with nothing to hold him back.

No one besides my brother, his wife and kids, and me visited my mother regularly as she lay dying in the hospital. Her parents had been dead for years, her brother did come once, but was busy with his work in the Senate. Cousins sent flowers and cards. The younger members of the family hadn't even met her. She was a distant idea, an aunt they had probably heard about but had never met. That's the way it always was. She had the name, and the Hunters always took care of their own, but they couldn't be bothered with the shame. She reminded them that despite the wealth going back to the Gold Rush, the positions of power they held in local and national government, the homes and boats and Stanford degrees, that they were not immune to everything.

It was sudden and slow. She had a wound she had been hiding from me. She didn't want to go to the hospital, as her paranoia had hit a new peak. It wasn't until I noticed her face was grey and clammy, and the festering smell in her room, that I finally got it out of her. She cut herself in the barn on a rusted piece of metal, when she was in better spirits weeks before. It had become infected and her mental state plummeted with the infection. She was in bed a lot that week, but that happened so often, her illness getting worse with age, that I didn't notice how sick she was until it was too late.

"We can't go!" she weakly pleaded like a child terrified to go to the dentist.

"Mom, this is enough!" I shouted. "No one is going to hurt you in the hospital! It can't get any worse," I begged. The wound on her thigh reeked of puss, it was black where the pus wasn't overflowing, and the area surrounding it was swollen and a throbbing red.

I carried her out of the room, unsympathetic to her shouts and cries. My whole life I heeded her warnings, lived in a shadow to appease her, and now this very thing she claimed would protect us was killing her.

I sat in the waiting room as the doctors took her in. My instincts, the ones that I had honed over the years, allowing me to sneak into dozens homes and neighborhoods over the past ten years without being caught, they told me this would not end well. I knew eventually I would live a life without her. But I didn't think it would be this soon. My chest tightened at the thought of a world where I would be truly alone. A prisoner with no warden. A child with no mother. I was still that boy that nobody wanted but her. She wasn't perfect, but she was the only one who truly cared about me. No one else had ever showed me that type of unconditional love.

Finally, the doctor walked out. His face was solemn, and I knew my instincts didn't fail me again.

He spoke to me about sepsis, and how her organs were failing, antibiotics, making her comfortable, cautious hope. About preparing for her passing. That I should call people. Then he left me, sitting there, in shock.

I called Scooter and let him know he needed to come. And then I sat vigil for the next three days. Scooter couldn't do that. He had work and a family, and this wasn't for him. It was only appropriate that it should end with her and me alone, the way it had always been. On the last day she was mostly incoherent, sleeping as monitors beeped and IVs dripped. I could feel the life slipping away from her body.

It was on the third night, just after Scooter had left after a brief visit that she awoke. It was quiet in the wing. Most of the lights were dimmed, but her turquoise eyes shined as she blinked. I took her hand, not expecting her to have the strength to speak. But then she moved her lips, stuck and crusted from the lack of water. I wet them. The fog lifted from her eyes. She was lucid, and she knew.

"Sam," she rasped.

"Yes?" I replied leaning in to hear her better.

"I know," she breathed out.

"You know?" I asked.

She took a few heavy breaths, trying to maintain her

strength.

"Where you go...at night."

There was no point in denying. I was with a dead woman, and dead women can't tell your secrets.

"I tried. I tried to protect you."

"You did, mama," I assured her.

"You're different. I knew."

"No one's gonna hurt me, mom. You can rest. I promise I'll take care of myself. You don't need to protect me from then anymore."

"No..." she stopped, seemingly exhausted from the brief utterances. "Not them. From. You."

Her words knocked me back like a battering ram. Her precious boy. Her angel. All this time I thought she saw me as special, misunderstood. But she saw the darkness. Taking me away was about protecting me and everyone else...from me.

Tears streamed down my cheeks for the first time in as long as I could remember. She closed her eyes again and didn't utter another word.

As I sat there in the dark, next to my only true ally, I realized she was one of them all along. She made me this way. I was always alone. She saw me as a freak, too. And now that she was gone, I had nothing to keep me rooted to this world. If she lived to protect them and me from myself, well now a beast had been set free. For years I had spied on these lives, my mother's existence keeping me from breaching an invisible wall. I could walk through their homes, I could study their things, I could watch them through their windows, but I couldn't take their lives. I could not touch them.

After a couple of hours, as she lay there comatose, I leaned in and whispered into her ear the things I felt deep inside all these years but was too afraid to believe. She was all I had. She was mommy. She was my savior. But what I always knew was she was my ruiner. I blamed dad for everything. And he deserved blame. But I couldn't allow myself to be angry at her, the only person I had. And she used that against me. "I want you to know that I hate you, you sick bitch. And you've done nothing to save anyone, including me. If you hear this, I want you to know that there will be pain in your name. I promise you this. No one will be safe."

She never did open her eyes again, dying a few hours later.

CHAPTER 29

VESPER

I wait, seated, with my back pressed against the locked door of the cabin, staring at the sweeping blood stain on the floor, so many unanswered questions demanding answers. Why did the sheriff leave me here? How did he find me? Why wasn't he in his uniform? Where the hell is Sam?

It's all over, it has to be. So many instances over the course of my time here, I envisioned what it would be like if I was found. I imagined droves of police kicking down doors, or even a covert mission of officers sneaking in and swooping me away from the man who took me. I haven't been imagining that lately. No, instead it's been visions of what the baby would look like. Imaginings of my future, sometimes a happy one, sometimes something more tragic.

I understand the choice I made. I made it hoping that the Sam I see now is the one I'll continue to have, that somehow his sinister urges have been tempered. But I still don't understand what is unfolding around me. I didn't want to be saved, but now that I'm locked in here by the person who was supposed to drag me to safety, even against my wishes, I am beginning to believe things are far more complicated than I understood.

Time passes slowly. Yelling indiscriminately is of no use out here, so I wait, listening for any sounds of life outside the planks of the shack wall. Finally, I hear footsteps close by. I know Sam's gait when something is wrong. I know it like my own heartbeat.

"Sam?" I call out cautiously. "Sam!" I shout, pounding on the door.

He unlatches it and pulls it open, and I collapse into his arms. I don't know how he'll receive me. If he'll blame me for leaving, if he has any idea of what transpired. For all he knows, I ran away.

"Someone was here. I recognized him, I'm almost one hundred percent sure he's the sheriff. He might be back," I recite frantically.

Sam shushes me, running a tender hand over my head. He pulls back and nods like he already knows.

"You saw him too?" Dread seeps over me like hot tar as I think of what he might have done. "I don't understand. Did you—" I can't bring myself to ask. This fragile fantasy I built, the one where he could become someone better, hinges on a few words.

He shakes his head. *No, I didn't hurt him.*

He looks me in the eyes, the color of glacial ice, often so frigid, doing his best to warm them, to focus them on mine. He doesn't look away until I return the same calm focus, and then he nods measuredly.

It's okay.

"The baby, it's gone," I murmur.

He nods and tilts his head towards the door, leading me outside. I follow him in a trance, still holding the items I collected underneath one arm, taking one last glance back at the only evidence of a life we created. I don't try to fill in the silence. For once, I have nothing left to say. I'm as lost now as I have ever been.

He leads me into the woods until we are in front of a fresh mound of dirt marked with smooth stones from the lake.

"You buried it?" I ask.

He nods.

"When?"

He points at me and then rests his head on his hands. *When you were asleep.* Sam motions towards it. I hesitate, but finally I kneel at the tiny bump of earth.

"Did the animals—?" I ask, without looking back. I don't want to know. I give a few tears, but it's all I have left. There's no time for lengthy requiems.

I stand up and give Sam a nod. He leads me back to the main house, and up the stairs, towards his bedroom, but we stop short of that destination. Instead, he turns the knob to the room that was locked and this time it rotates. The door pops open and he gestures for me to go ahead.

The room is a disturbing contrast to the barren organization of the rest of the house. The walls and windows are covered with layers of colorful tapestry. He clicks on a lamp, illuminating the cave-like atmosphere. Over the tapestries are countless news articles, many of them foxed, a few still crisp. Framed photos rest on most available surfaces, likely the ones that seem to have been removed from the rest of the house.

The dread dripping over me pools in my stomach. This is a room of insanity. If I could see into Sam's mind, would this be what I see? Is this the chaos underneath the exterior of calculation and unwavering power?

I look back at him, seeking his permission to explore. For some reason, he's decided this is the time to give me answers. He nods, telling me it's okay.

I gravitate to an article tacked to a hanging quilt. I notice a few of the squares has the same fabric as one of my dresses.

HUNTER-RIDGEFIELD HEIR, 8, RUN OVER AND DRAGGED BY DRUNK DRIVER

Samuel Hunter-Ridgefield, son of Gloria Hunter, one of the heiresses to the Hunter political and business empire, and Andrew Ridgefield, Sheriff of the Sacramento County Sheriff's Department, is in a coma after being hit and dragged by a vehicle while riding his bicycle near their home. Sheriff Ridgefield is a beloved member of the community, coming from a long line of California politicians and philanthropists. The boy's mother is an heiress to the Hunter fortune. Her great-great grandfather found wealth during the Gold Rush and built a farming chemical empire…

HUNTER-RIDGEFIELD BOY AWAKES FROM COMA

MAN CHARGED WITH HUNTER-RIDGEFIELD BOY

ACCIDENT RECEIVES MAXIMUM SENTENCE

BELOVED SHERIFF, ANDREW RIDGEFIELD, OF
RIDGEFIELD FAME IS KILLED IN ROADSIDE ACCIDENT

ANDREW HUNTER-RIDGEFIELD, SON OF SHERIFF
TRAGICALLY KILLED IN ROADSIDE ACCIDENT 11 YEARS
AGO, ELECTED YOUNGEST SHERIFF IN SACRAMENTO
COUNTY SHERIFF'S DEPARTMENT HISTORY.

I know of these families, their names ubiquitously etched in museum wings, mentioned on the news in business or political dealings. Sam clearly has money, but he's someone who lives by the callouses on his hands, who wears torn jeans and t-shirts, and whose head is crowned in a mess of golden-brown ringlets. I never thought he was part of a political and industrial dynasty.

Some of the articles have unintelligible scribbles on them, words circled, some crossed out, as if a code is being deciphered. While there is so much I don't know or understand, a blurry picture of who Sam is and where he comes from begins to emerge. The scars that run along his body and face, products of a tragic accident. His access to money and land explained by his privileged lineage. And the most shocking and confounding revelation of all: the man who was tasked to save me, is my captor's brother.

Sam waits patiently as I move on to the photos. There is a picture of a blond boy alongside a taller boy in front of handsome couple. His hair has darkened with age, but those eyes, even on a small boy, could not be missed. They are his mother's eyes. A beautiful woman, with dark hair, and an elegance that oozes from the photo. His father, a tall man with a dominating posture, his hair lighter, but his eyes brown, like little Andrew. Sam's mom smiles for the camera, but she looks hollow, as if held prisoner. Mr. Ridgefield doesn't smile, though his squint into the sun might provide that illusion. Little Andrew's smile beams across his face—a little boy who has it all. But Sam, little Sam, before the accident, when his skin was still perfect and unmarred—he looks uneasy, tense. His father's hand is gripping one of his shoulders. It's not a gentle touch like that of his mother's. It's a reminder to stay in line. I browse the photos of the family that should have it all. Over time, there is less and less of the Andrews, and just pictures of Sam and Gloria. She looks increasingly disheveled as Sam grows into a handsome young man, though there seems to be the occasional photo were her eyes are bright again, her hair combed and twisted into a prim updo.

I've gathered as much as my eyes and brain can before turning back to Sam.

"He's your brother?" I ask, already certain of the answer.

Sam nods.

I walk over to him and take his hand. I run my fingers around the stitches on his arm. Last night he reopened his scars. He flinches at first, but then allows me. "This was all from the accident?"

He nods, darting his eyes away.

"I'm sorry that happened to you."

He shrugs.

"Why am I here? Why now? What's going to happen, Sam? I need you to talk to me. Please."

It occurs to me that reason he may not speak to me is not psychological, but physical. Damage from the accident, maybe. But it still doesn't add up.

He pulls out his pad, and this time he writes slowly, thoughtfully, not rushing in fragments as he often does.

This room is not mine, Vesp. It's my mother's. She died last year. She seems nice in the photos, right? Pretty. Gentle. But she was sick, and she wrapped me in her sickness. I was different as a child. I had a severe speech impediment. My father, the hero, hated me for what he saw as a weakness. He made sure to remind me every day. I was teased incessantly; my own brother was embarrassed by me.

And then the accident happened. Things got worse. My mother told me people were trying to kill me and she took me up here, afraid the teasing and taunting would get worse with my scars. My dad used to pull me out of my bed at night, he used to make me swim in that lake until I would almost drown and then he'd pull me out. That playground, he made me build those obstacle courses and run them for hours until I would vomit or pass out. He thought my mother was making me soft, so he had to make me strong. She put on a good enough act for him, he knew she wasn't well, but he didn't want to be bothered with us, no one did. Our families have an image, they have goals, and we were blemishes on that perfection. I wasn't allowed to leave the land here without her, have friends. My speech improved as I got older, but when I was finally about to go out there, I was so overwhelmed by the outside that I found it easier to hide my voice, especially when it came to women. I didn't want fucking pity. I didn't want people laughing at me. Around my brother and mother, though, I could speak almost normally.

When my father died, I realized I could sneak out at night and be like everyone else. That's when it started. That's when I realized that when I was out there, alone like that, I had all the power. It was like a drug, and when that drug came over me, I became someone else. I watched the lives I had missed out on, the ones I knew I would never have because I was not like everyone else—a fact my dear mother had reminded me of every fucking day.

When she died, I snapped. I did the things you see mentioned in the articles I gave you. I stopped just watching and prowling. I found my voice. It was hiding in the darkest part of me, where rage, power, and sex intermingle. I didn't care about how they saw me, because I was in charge, and my stammer would disappear. I didn't have secrets in those homes I took over, and with that burden being lifted off, so did the oppressive tightness in my throat, so did the heaviness of my tongue. It was always something, my dad watching me, the kids at school, the secrets I kept, something was always like an invisible hand, choking me, making it hard to breathe, hard to speak.

You said you wanted to know, Vesper. Now you do.

I read the note, sometimes reading the same line over and over, the information overload making it hard to process this story of isolation and rage.

I look up at Sam, and though nothing physically has changed, I see him differently. I am angry at him, and I am sad for him.

"Why did you come to my house? I know you were watching me, but why me? You didn't take the others."

He sighs, again writing down his answer.

Because I saw you with Johnny. And it made me remember what it was like to have someone who took care of me like that. The person I loved and hated most in this world. But even she wasn't you.

You were perfect. You were the person I wish I had had. You were the person I dreamed of.

"But you took me away from him. You understand? You hurt the little boy you saw as yourself."

I didn't plan to take you. I had never been so careless. But you make me act out of character. You make me a fool.

"What's your brother going to do?"

He gave me a choice. He said he would forget what he saw if we left town.

I chuckle to myself. "I was going to propose that myself," I say, realizing how ridiculous I sound as I say it aloud. Giving my kidnapper ideas on how to never be found again.

He scrunches his brow.

"Well, it's just that, if we were going to try being…normal, we'd have to start fresh. But I don't know, Sam. I honestly don't know with you. You have to understand what's happening to me. I feel like an idiot for saying this…but, I don't think you're all bad. I know what you've done. I know the pain you've caused, but I do see that boy. I see that inside of you there is still a gentle person…" I begin to sob, the knotted cluster of emotions tugging at what's left of my soul. "But how do I forgive myself for falling for you?"

He watches me cry in silence, his brow furrowed with concern and confusion.

Finally, he scribbles something on his notepad.

The only person you ever have to hate is me.

But I can't. I can get angry. I can become disgusted at times, but I can't hate him.

"You said the secrets make you stutter. But now there aren't any. I know it all. And I'm not running. I'll run away with you. I don't care what you sound like anyway. You should have known better than to think I would. And when things are clear, when my face is completely forgotten, we can get Johnny. You have to understand he needs me. He's the only part of my old life I can't let go of."

I wait for Sam's response. I know it's a huge gamble, asking him to help me kidnap Johnny someday. I know how crazy it all sounds. But I also know things are different now. I am different. So is he. And what once sounded insane, now seems like the natural progression of things. We were preparing to have a family. This can be that family. Sam looks away, the intersecting thoughts in his mind visible in his distant stare. Eventually, he nods pensively.

I sigh with relief, but deep inside I know I can't steal Johnny. I may find a way to see him again, from a distance or in secret, but I can't bring him into the madness. My asking was a way for me to come to terms to that. I can tell myself it wasn't my idea to leave him behind. Otherwise, it's not possible to reconcile my love for Johnny and this choice.

Silence falls upon the room. I think of the letter, about the invisible hand he speaks of wrapping around his throat and I grow frustrated. "You picked me because you saw me with Johnny, because I don't see people that way. I might know and accept more about you than anyone else. So why?" I take the wrinkled paper and wave it between us. "Why are you still writing me notes instead of just talking to me?"

He writes a small note on the pad, tears it off and hands it to me as he stands up, turning his back to leave the room.

Because you make my heart race, Vesp.

CHAPTER 30

VESPER

Sam flings the last of his bags into the truck.

"What about the animals?" I ask.

Sam nods and jogs to the barn. I follow closely as he opens the door and leads them out. He swats Beverly on her hind until she runs away. The goats take a few steps but linger nearby.

"Will they be okay?" I ask as we head back to the truck.

They're free now. They have everything they need here.

Sam points to the floor of the truck.

I look at him quizzically and he huffs before pulling out the notepad again.

You need to lie down until we are well out of town. People will recognize you.

"You know, you wouldn't have to write it down if you just spoke," I snipe.

He shoots me a stern look out of the corner of his eye before walking over to the driver's side. I freeze anxiously. I've never done anything like this. I feel like a criminal.

Sam stops short when he senses my hesitation. He takes a breath and walks over to me. I stiffen, wondering if the stress of recent events has shortened his patience. But he palms my face in his hands and locks his eyes on mine, tilting his forehead down to mine. He locks his gaze on me, so that all I see are those eyes. For so long, it was all I knew of him. It was my greatest source of terror and uncertainty. But now, I'd follow those eyes into hell. Hell is my home now.

I gulp. "Okay," I whisper. His hands travel down from my cheeks, to my shoulders, and then my hands. In an uncommon gesture of affection, he squeezes my palms. For a second I swear a see a glimpse of regret in his usually unwavering gaze.

He grabs his pad and writes something. His expression goes solemn as he shows it to me.

You need to understand. If we are discovered, I'm not going to prison.

"What do you mean?" I ask, the calm he coaxed washed away with the white waters of fear.

He grabs his pen, but then stops and looks me in the eyes again. He puts his fingers to his temple in the shape of a gun and pulls the trigger.

"No," I shake my head sternly. "I won't let you do that."

It would be better for both of us that way.

"They won't okay? We are gonna get out of here," I vow.

He nods solemnly and I crawl to the floor of the truck, where he's placed some blankets and a pillow for my comfort.

We drive around for a while, my view from the floor rarely changing. Sometimes I see nothing but the passing tree or a tall sign. Other times, nothing but sky and clouds. I figure I see the least when we are on the freeway. Sam keeps the radio on the stations he knows I'll like, and occasionally, he'll peek back to check on me and I give him a thumbs up. After a while, the anxiety subsides, and the steady rhythm of the car lulls me into a nap.

It's only when that steady drone is broken up by intermittent bumps and jolts am I stirred.

"How long have a I been asleep?" I ask, hoping to trick Sam into speech.

He doesn't answer.

"Can I sit up now?" I ask.

No answer.

I study the window, unable to see much from my angle except that we are surrounded by trees so tall I can't even see where they end. Their trunks are wide and a rusty brown. Sequoias. Though they nearly block the sky from view, I can see from the hazy rays of sienna peering through the trees, that the sun is setting.

The truck stops abruptly.

"Sam?" I ask, sitting up instinctively. He ignores me, slamming the door behind him as he steps out, and rummages through the back of the truck. That's when I get a better look around. We seem to be on a dirt road somewhere in the middle of a desolate forest.

"What's going on?" I ask, an unsettling feeling balling the pit of my stomach.

He walks over to the car and opens the door behind me. A pillowcase drapes over my head before I even have a chance to face him.

"What are you doing?" I ask as I attempt to squirm away from him.

He drags me out of the car onto the mud, throwing me on my stomach. He sits on top of me, pinning me down as I struggle underneath him. But I can't stop him from tying my hands behind me. He is a monster. This I always knew. But he wouldn't stoop so low. He wouldn't lie to me, make me think we could finally be free and then take it all away like this.

"Please, Sam…" I beg, the caustic tears of betrayal burning my cheeks.

I was so sure Sam wouldn't kill me. He needs me. I am the only person who knows him. I am his humanity.

But all I can see is black, and I wonder if I am already dead.

SAM

Once I have Vesper bound, I use my hunting knife to slice through her dress. A twinge of sentimentality flashes as I recall the way I ripped her nightgown the night I took her. But it's different now. My gut twists and turns in agony. I'm sick with regret as I strip her naked.

I gave her so much of the truth. I figured I owed her that much. She wanted my story for so long, and I could finally let her have it. I knew she wouldn't tell, because she wouldn't be alive for much longer. But in the tapestry of all that truth, I weaved little lies. Lies that tasted bitter against my tongue.

That my brother said we could both leave.

That the only reason I needed her to lie down in the truck was that I didn't want her to be seen, and not that I also didn't want her to see where we were headed.

That I told her I would kill myself so that she wouldn't be tempted to make a last minute run for it.

Finally, that I told her, not with words, but with my eyes, that she would be fine. That I would take care of her.

I tell lies all the time. I am a fucking lie. But she told me she had been thinking about running away with me. That she chose me. And I had to tell her that I could make that happen. That I could find her a new freedom, knowing the only freedom she would know is death at my hands—it's never pained me so much to deceive.

I am no different from my mother, promising to take Vesp away from the danger, when I am the danger.

"Sam, I thought you cared. I thought you wanted me. I thought we were going to be together," she sobs. For once, I'm glad I can't speak to her. I slice into a trash bag and slide it over her head. I don't want anyone to find her naked, but I don't want her wearing the clothes I made. Maybe they could find a way to trace them back to me, even if my brother tries to divert the task force.

She tries to run, but loses her balance and falls onto her face. It makes me sick to see the pathetic state she's in. To have fooled her so viciously. The one person who made me feel a little less like a monster.

I walk towards her calmly as she kicks her legs against the ground, desperately trying to slither sway from me, blinded and bound.

I pull her up to her knees, but she's limp, holding the posture of someone who has surrendered. Who has fought and fought and doesn't have another battle left in her.

She whimpers, but it's more like a hum under the mask—quiet, melodic.

I pull the gun out of my waistband and I press it to the back of her head.

"Please," she wails.

My finger massages the trigger, but my hand trembles ferociously. I grimace and take a deep breath, trying to focus my eyes through the blur. With just a little pressure from my finger, she'll stop existing. She'll have come into my life, upturned it, leaving me haunted by her memory the way I have done to countless others. Now I'm on the other side. I'm the person whose life will never be the same.

I've taken care of her for so long. She's been my ward. She has become my responsibility.

No.

That's bullshit. She's more than that. She is my obsession. She is my heartbeat. She is my prize. She is the only fucking one. She's not one of them. She's the other part of me. Killing her would be committing suicide.

So I drop the hand holding the gun to my side and bow my head. If I am going to kill myself, then let it be the way it's supposed to be. Not the way Scoot fucking demands.

"I'm sorry," I whisper, afraid to say anything more. Afraid I'll start to stammer. Because I don't get that rush of lording over her here. She controls me.

I walk in front of her, and pull off the pillowcase. Her eyes are wild and red. She's panting between the uncontrollable sobs. I drop to my knees to meet her eyes and I kiss her. The last kiss. The kiss that I'll feel on my lips for the rest of my miserable existence. Hiding. Searching for just a glimpse of that feeling again before I die.

It's gentle, our lips barely meeting. She doesn't kiss back, she's too confused. So I pull back, unable to walk away, just wanting to taste her one more time.

"You're leaving me here?" she asks, with the pitch of despair in her voice.

I kiss her again, this time taking her face in my hands, tasting her tears, feeling her lips quiver against mine.

I keep tokens of all the places I've been. People I've taken from. And that kiss is the token I'll remember her by. She's not like the others. I'll never give them back what I've taken. I reach into my pocket and clasp the little moon necklace I took from her around her neck.

"Please don't leave me alone out here," she pleads.

She can hate me, that's the way it's supposed to be.

I stand up and write her the last note.

Do what you have to do.

I watch her eyes study it. I make sure she digests it. Then I crumble in and put it in my pocket. I head back to my truck.

"Sam?" she asks, as if she still believes this is all a bluff. I've toyed with her head so many fucking times, she doesn't even know when it's real. "Sam!" This time it's shrill, there's anger peppered through her voice. "Sam!" she screams as I slide into the driver seat.

I drive on the path towards the service road, watching her chase me through the rear view mirror. She's covered in mud, with her hands tied behind her back, barefoot. Her pleas grate on my ears, but when I'm far enough away, her voice stops carrying. Darkness has settled and she's just a speck in my rear view mirror. I hit the brakes and turn back one last time. Just one more look. But I feel a dangerous pull. So I look ahead, turning my back to her.

PART
THREE

CHAPTER 31

VESPER

*M*y name is Vesper Rivers.
It used to be so easy to utter that sentence to strangers. I never thought about what it meant. All the fine details, the lines and the shadows that lie behind that name. Maybe because I was just a two-dimensional sketch of a person. Thick lines outlining my identity. A flat image.

But now, there are creases and collections of small, nearly invisible grooves that come together to create depth and space. To make a picture so complex that depending on the angle from which I look at myself, I see someone different every time.

Now, to say those words, to tell a stranger who I am, it's too much. It's too loaded of a confession. The park ranger will think he knows me, from the details in the news or the circumstances of my disappearance. But that's just me from one narrow angle. If he saw things from my side, he would be shocked.

So I wait, filthy, shivering, sipping a warm cup of generic tea, still wearing the hefty bag Sam shrouded on me, and over that a fleece blanket, waiting for the one person other than Sam who knows the things I know. Who I don't have to lie to.

A deer head floats on the wall across from me. A picture of the man who I first found running down the service road along where Sam left me, with his little girls and wife. This world feels like the artifice. The white-washed walls of my tiny shack, the lake, the unending forest—that was reality.

I feel their eyes. The local police, watching me through the titled blinds on the door that gives me a false sense of privacy.

I go through eight and a half cups of tea. One cup for every half hour I wait for Sheriff Ridgefield. It's all I would say no matter what they asked. I wouldn't give my name. I wouldn't say what happened. Only his name.

I'm staring at the half-drunken mug of tea when the door opens abruptly. Our eyes meet and I can see the veiled panic. He's trying hard not to let me see it. From the sallow color of his face, to his sunken expression, it's clear the sheriff hoped to never see me again.

He closes the door behind him. I look over at the half-turned blinds and he follows my gaze, twisting the pole to block out prying eyes. I grip my mug firmly as he tentatively pulls up a seat across the table from me. This is easier. This I can handle, not all the commotion of police and press, just me, a man, and a room.

"I came out here as soon as they called. You were dropped off far away from home."

He means the single-level I was snatched from, in a sunny suburban neighborhood. The place where my boyfriend proposed to me. But that's not home anymore.

I nod.

He's smart. He's not saying anything. He doesn't know what I know. But he does know I hold his life in the balance. I understand now, the gravity of Sam's secret. It's not just a family being humiliated and shamed. It is generations of reputation and wealth tarnished in an instant. It's this man's future vaporized in one breath.

> *Your brother.*
> *He took me.*
> *Every part of me.*
> *He gave me parts of him.*
> *Forced them to fit into me.*
> *Now I am stuck with them.*
> *Then he abandoned me.*
> *I am not the girl in the picture you have in your file.*
> *She has not returned.*

She's disappeared forever.

"Are we alone?" I ask.

He looks over his shoulder before leaning in.

"For now."

"Sam told me everything," I say. It's not a threat, it's not a pledge of allegiance to the officer of the law in front of me. It's just information.

It's instant, the way he goes clammy. His skin going from a pale yellow to a pale gray. He swallows sharply.

"But, I don't know anything," I add.

His chest sinks with a strong exhale.

I lean forward, centering my eyes onto his. They're nothing like Sam's. They're a reddish brown. It takes light for his eyes to shine. Sam's eyes seem to thrive in the darkness. "I don't know his name. I don't know where he took me. He never spoke. I was blindfolded the entire time. He blindfolded me and drove me around for hours before dropping me off. I'm sorry I can't be of more help."

I don't know why I do this. Why I protect the man who did the things he did to me. It's certainly not for the Andrew—Scooter— whatever his name is. I'm free now, out of Sam's influence. He all but gave me permission to tell my story. But if I tell everything I know, Sam will be locked away, and it will be the end. I'm not ready to tell our secrets. I don't want to share this view of me with the world. Let them see me the way the stories on the news say. I'm not done with Sam, even if he thinks he's done with me.

Sheriff Ridgefield sits there for a few moments, weighing all the shit that's been thrust on his plate.

"If you know nothing, then why did you ask for me?" His tone, it's hypothetical. As if to tell me this is what someone else will ask.

"I don't know," I shrug. "I don't know anything."

He sits back in his chair and blows out a huge sigh, wrestling with an invisible monster.

"Why are you doing this?" he asks skeptically.

I run my finger along the edge of the table. Dirt has impacted on its edges, like someone who has been living in the wild. They don't know how he bathed me, fed me, fucked me, held me. They don't know about the beautiful dresses and how they swirled when I danced to the music he brought me, how these once manicured hands flipped the pages of books he gifted me.

"Even you wouldn't understand," I mutter.

He leans in, his face pained. "I had no idea, Vesper. Please understand that. I never thought he could do that."

I nod.

"I can find ways to make sure you are taken care of …to make up for your …suffering."

"I don't want it. You're just going to have to trust me."

"Why are you protecting him?" he asks. "How can I trust you won't wake up tomorrow and tell everything? If I cover this up, I am sinking further into this pile of shit, you understand? All my chips are going into this. Is this what you really want?"

"This isn't for him," I assure the sheriff. "Or you," I add, looking at my dull reflection on the pitted chrome poster frame behind him. "If you want to tell them, you go ahead. I can't stop you."

He scrunches his brow. "I'm going to take you to the hospital and then I'll interview you there. I'll transport you myself. It's a bit of a mess here. The police here want credit for finding you since you were found in their jurisdiction. Fucking Keystone Cops. So, I'm going to have to step out and do a little magic here."

I nod, sipping the cool, bitter tea as a distraction.

"Vesper. I have a family. A little boy and a girl. Please." I don't blame him for believing this is too good to be true.

"Does my family know?" I ask. My return has seemed so abstract, this room a place of limbo. I didn't even think about them until he mentioned transporting me.

He looks down. "The station called your parents, no one answered. We called your fiancé and he said they are out of the country and he'd try to reach them. He'll be the one meeting you to take you home."

A reunion with Carter looming, and I feel nothing.

I remember once watching the news about a girl who had vanished. Her parents left the porch light on for her every night hoping she would return. They wouldn't move from the house for decades, afraid they wouldn't be there for her if she came back. Of course, she never did.

My mother is far away. In that way, things haven't changed.

And there's something oddly comforting in that.

When I see Carter after they examine me, I cry. I didn't think I would until that moment. I hadn't shed a tear since I rejoined the world. Not even as I was interviewed; recounted the things that had been done to me by an anonymous man. He had blindfolded me. He had always worn a mask so even during the few times I could see his face, I had no details. He never spoke. All I knew was the color of his eyes. *Brown*, I told them.

I watched beads of sweat trickle down Sheriff Ridgefield's temple, belying his cool demeanor. On the way down, in the car, we didn't talk much. But we had decided that my insistence upon choosing him came from the fact that I saw his name in the newspapers I used as a toilet in the basement.

The car was stuffed with tension. That used to make me nervous and chatty, wanting to fill in every jagged crevasse of silence so everything would feel round and smooth. Now, the tension of silence seems so trivial compared to the terror I have survived.

I refused to let the doctor perform a gynecological exam. She insisted, even had the Sheriff come and try to talk me into it. He did--though I'm certain this was good news for him--but I grew hostile. I wasn't going to let anyone invade me. They'd think it was because of the trauma. That's what I want them to think. But it's because I hold a secret inside of me, one that only Sam and I share.

"Vesp," Carter whispers tenderly as he rushes towards me. His eyes gloss with emotion and that's the moment when I erupt. I was devastated when I lost my grandmother. I cried for days. But after a while, the sharpness of the pain dulls, and you try not to think of the person. That helps the pain recede. Eventually, you stop thinking of them because you realize that's the best way for the pain to stop. Then one day, you can think of them, you can speak of them and it doesn't always stab at your heart and take your breath away. You think you're safe. I remember I thought I was. About two years passed since she had died. I had moved on. And then I was cleaning my room when I found a picture in one of my drawers. It wasn't a good one—the angle tilted, she's reaching out for something that's out of the frame, my leg is peeking into the shot on the floor beneath her.

I'm probably sitting down, playing with something. It's of no significance, the photo. Nothing momentous. No one is posing. She's not even smiling. It's probably why it was discarded in a drawer. And yet, when I saw it, when I was unable to brace for the memory of her, for the void—grief shocked me and I found myself in tears.

I had done the same thing with Carter. Pushed him into the recesses of my thoughts. I had forgotten him and the future I had envisioned. When I see him, the grief breaks out of its restraints and takes hold of me. This life, the one I have been redeposited into so mercilessly by Sam, was dead to me. I mourned Carter, this world, and now I'm somehow supposed to believe any of this is real. None of it was ever real, not if it could be taken away from me so easily. Seeing Carter is just like finding that photo. It doesn't bring him back to me. It only brings back the pain.

He wraps his arms around me, but I'm not ready for his touch. His arms are long and lithe, not firm and forceful. He smells of his cologne and the sterility of his hospital, not of man and forest and shampoo lingering on damp hair. Carter is the stranger now, but I know that it's wrong to feel that way, so I let him take what he needs.

After I finish another round of questioning, Ridgefield leads us out a backdoor. I haven't seen them, but it's clear the press is beginning to accumulate outside. He gives me a knowing nod, and a gentle reminder that they will call me with progress and that they may have more questions. I thank him, and Carter places me in the passenger seat of his car as if I was fragile as a glass ornament.

CHAPTER 32

VESPER

The apartment Carter leads me into is unfamiliar. Not in the abstract sense. When I was taken, he was living with his parents, saving up for his own place. It looks like he moved on with that plan.

"I thought, maybe, going back to the house so fast wasn't a good idea," he says meekly.

"It's nice," I mutter, eying the stark interior.

"I haven't had much time or need for decorating. I'm always gone anyway. Maybe you can help me with that," he suggests, his voice tickled by a tense chuckle.

I give him a tight-lipped smile. I thought I was chatty. It seemed so amongst Sam's silence. But now, I have so little to say. I'm used to long stretches of time without a sound, and now voices seem unwelcome, invasive.

"Are you hungry? I can whip you up something to eat."

I am. Starving. More importantly, I want to give him something to do other than study me, wondering how he can approach me without shattering me into pieces.

"Sure. I'll take anything. I'd like to take a shower though."

"Of course, of course!" He hastily leads me to the bathroom, leaving me with a towel and instructions on how to get the perfect temperature using the fickle shower knob.

I lock the door behind me. A ritual I suppose. The click reminding me of the heavy latching sound every time Sam left me in my room. A punctuation. Once telling me I was safe, then as time went on, that I was alone.

The police took my hefty bag and left me in a paper gown. I watch myself in the mirror as I pull it off. My hair is so much longer than when I left, my already slender body, thinner. I run my fingers along my belly. There's no outward evidence of what I once held inside of me. And even though it took me a while to accept the idea of him or her, I came to feel like a mother, to feel sadness at what never was. And no one can ever know. Not even Sheriff Ridgefield.

Sam knew I couldn't come back and he let me go anyway. Dropped me into a world that couldn't possibly understand the choices I had made. Changed the shape of me, and then tried to shove me back into a space where I can no longer fit.

I slide into the warm water of the shower. I close my eyes and remember when he first took me in the cabin shower, when without words he showed me I made him weak.

I slide down the cold wall of the shower and sit on the floor. I let the water rain over me and I sob. I'm scared. I don't know how much more I can survive. I embraced him. And he ripped my arms from him and let me fall. He's out there. I know he is. And someday I will find him. I will thrust him from his life the way he took me.

VESPER

"I'm sorry, I thought I had more in the fridge," Carter says as I sit down in front of a grilled cheese sandwich, cut diagonally. "It's so late, nothing is open."

"No, this is great," I insist. I take a bite and look up. He's just standing up against a wall, staring at me. When he sees me looking back, he snaps out of it.

"I'm sorry, Vesp. I just…I just can't believe you're back."

"Me neither."

"You know, I never gave up on you. I mean, I knew logically what the statistics were, but I knew you, too. And you are strong and so good…and…that's why I still got this place. I thought, if you came back, if you wanted, you'd have someplace to live that wasn't that house."

I stall with a bite from my sandwich. I don't know what to say. I am not strong. I didn't fight hard enough. Or did I? Did I fight so hard to survive that I became someone else?

"Thank you," I reply.

"And I just want to say I'm sorry. I'm sorry I couldn't protect you. I tried so hard to break that door down. To get to you. And I heard you. I heard what you said. What you did to protect us. I'm so—"

"Don't. Please. Don't do that. You have nothing to apologize for."

He frowns and nods a few times, holding back his despair.

"So where is my family?" I ask, ready to broach the painful subject.

"Brazil, in the Amazon. I called the resort they're scheduled to go to when they return from their excursion, but they will be out of reach for a few days until then."

I snicker. "She took Johnny to the Amazon? She's insane. Well, at least this has forced her to spend time with him."

"Yeah." Carter's eyes flitter away from mine nervously.

"What?" I demand.

"Listen, this is a lot to come back to. You should just rest up for today, we can catch up tomorrow."

"Carter, fucking tell me," I snap.

He takes a deep breath, swallows, and bows his head. "Johnny doesn't live with your mother anymore."

"What?" I pry indignantly.

"He's in a home for people with disabilities."

The news knocks the wind out of me like a kick to the chest. I feel sick. Sick that not only was I forgotten, but that he was too.

I shoot up to my feet, staggering to the bedroom.

Carter shuffles from his post against the wall and races to meet me.

"What are you doing, Vesp?" he asks.

"I'm going to get him. He can't be in there. I didn't do all this for him to be shuttled into a home! That selfish bitch!" I cry.

"I don't think that's a good idea."

"Of course you don't. You never wanted him around. No one did!"

His shoulders sink. "That's not fair, Vesp."

"I can't let him rot in there. He has a family. He's not a fucking plant. He's a human being who needs love and attention!" I shout, marching past Carter, who shuffles again to block me.

"Vesp, I know the place. He's in a good place. He's getting a lot of attention. He's getting specialized treatment. It's a good place."

"He needs me," I insist. "He needs me!"

"What are we going to do? Break him out? You aren't his legal guardian."

"I'll do what it takes," I sneer, sidestepping him.

Carter grips my shoulders, I shudder at his touch. It feels like a betrayal to the person who took so much away from me.

"Please, just listen," Carter pleads. "You just got back and you need to take care of yourself. He's in a safe place, a good place. Soon, you can visit him. But you are in no shape to take care of Johnny. You need to take care of yourself for once. He's been through a lot, too. You can't just waltz into the home and pull him out of there. Do you understand how much that would confuse him? And what about you? You have been gone for almost a year. You haven't even been back a day. You need to focus on yourself. If you care about Johnny, you will leave him there until you know in your heart of hearts you are truly ready to take care of a special kid like him."

The cold splash of reality smacks me in the face. I don't know how to live anymore. Not without Sam taking all the responsibility away. He dressed me, fed me, entertained me. He took care of me the way I took care of Johnny. And like Johnny, I am going to have to learn it all over again.

I sob, "I was supposed to save him." Carter embraces me, and for a fraction of a moment, I recall the warmth of his hugs. "Everything has gone to shit." I left Johnny just like Sam left me. Maybe it was an act of mercy when Sam released me, just like my decision to pull Sam out of the house, but both had unintended consequences.

Carter holds me up as a rush of tears takes over my body. But I only let the moment last a few seconds, damming the tears back inside, pulling myself out of Carter's grip suddenly.

All this time, I kept thinking I had changed, while somehow everything around me had remained static. But the world doesn't wait for you just because you were kidnapped. Just like woods with those structures Sam and his father built as a child, it just grows over the memory of you.

CHAPTER 33

VESPER

"I should just stay here," Carter declares as he puts on his wristwatch. "They'll understand. Hell, maybe I should just take some time off."

"No," I protest firmly. "That's ridiculous. You cannot derail your life like that. I appreciate the thought, I do. But I won't let that happen. We can't let this change things."

"I can't concentrate knowing you're here alone. At least we should wait until your parents return."

"It's been four days. They'll be back soon enough. I'm just going to sit here all day anyway. There's a police car watching. If you want things to get back to normal, we have to act like it." I stand up from my chair and take a few steps closer. I can feel his need. He wants me to touch him, kiss him, but I can't. I'm still not here. "Don't put this on me. I can't be responsible for this. Please, just go back."

"Okay, well I am going to call you every hour to check in."

"Fine."

"Okay," he says with cautious resolve. I follow him as he heads to the door. He turns to face me and sighs. "Okay," he says again. "Bye."

"Bye," I reply with a wistful smirk.

He's stiff, like invisible arms have bear-hugged him. I can see the tightness of his body, resisting the urge to hug me. I should reach out, tell him it's okay to touch me, but I don't. I can't.

"I'll be fine."

He nods and leaves.

I wait until his footsteps disappear, and then lock and chain the door. I flip around and press my back against the door, gasping for air. I can finally breathe. It's only been four days, but Carter is suffocating me. I should want that constant attention, but it's not the kind I craved, the kind Sam was able to give. Carter's is cautious, gentle, and awkward. I have to be easy on us, I understand that, but I just need to have room to myself. Not only retreat to the bathroom where I take extra-long showers so I can sob on the floor.

I head for the window and look out to the street. A lone patrol car sits outside. Sheriff said they'd be there for the next week, both at Carter's and my mother's house, making sure no one returned. He has to pretend he wants to solve this. I think he's gambling on Sam being too smart to turn up so quickly. I turn on the TV. There are some daytime soaps on so I turn the dial. My face, it's there. A picture of an unfamiliar girl. I panic and turn the dial again before I can hear a word of what the news has to say about me. I change the dials to the last channel, then back. By then, the news has moved on from my story. But I can't quiet my mind, so I switch it off. I meander throughout the small apartment, touching things as if they were rare artifacts.

I hear a noise in the hallway and I freeze. Is it him?

I run to the door and look through the peephole, a neighbor is entering her apartment. I look down at my arm and see all the baby hairs are raised. I run to the windows and make sure each one is locked, shades drawn.

I jiggle my head as if trying to dispel the contradicting thoughts. I want him still. I hate that I do. I'm scared and yet I want him to come to me.

He is my greatest threat, and so, until I am back on his side, I will feel danger looming. Being with Sam, having him on my team, is the only way I'll feel safe again.

I spend the next hour jumping at every sound and tidying up things that don't need tidying, until restlessness overrides fear. I throw on a shirt of Carter's and a pair of pants he picked up for me from my house. I tuck my hair up and borrow a pair of his sunglasses.

I stare at the door for a minute, contemplating if I should breach this safe zone. It's been four days since I stepped outside that door. I wish I could just go to the lake. It's quiet and open and I'm not trapped between walls.

Stop it, Vesp. You're not going back. Do this. You need to do this.

I grip the knob tentatively, holding it with a tremulous hand. *You can do this. Turn it. Do it.*

I close my eyes and bite my lips together, taking a choppy breath. Drawing the jittery energy out of my body. Summoning strength.

The screech of the telephone jolts me back. I'm gasping again, ripped out of the hypnotic calm into which I had lulled myself.

It rings three or four times before I realize I am supposed to answer it. It's my responsibility now that Carter's gone.

"Hello?" I answer.

"It's me," Carter says.

"Hi."

"Sorry, I was a little delayed catching up this morning. Is everything, okay? How are you doing?"

"I'm fine. I promise. Just as you left me," I assure him. "How's your day?"

"Good. Like I said, it's hard to be here knowing you're alone,"

"Like *I* said, don't worry about me. Okay?"

"Okay. I'll call you in an hour, this time I'll be on schedule."

"Alright."

I hang up the phone, now determined to go right out that door, so I can be back in an hour for Carter's next call. I march towards it, my body pushing through doubt as if it were a physical force field. This time, I grip the knob and turn it purposefully.

The phone rings again.

I huff this time, annoyed by Carter's hovering just as I found some hidden courage. I trudge back to the phone and pull it off the receiver.

"Hellooo," I say in a melodic voice, disguising my annoyance.

There's no response.

"Carter?" I ask.

Breathing. That's all I hear on the other line.

"Carter, is that you?" I ask, convinced there's a bad connection.

The breathing continues, it's so light that I can only hear it because of the dead silence of the home.

My lips tremble as I force out what I can.

"S—Sam?" I ask.

There's a click. But I keep the phone to my face, waiting for something. Anything. Until the phone goes off the hook, blaring that aggressive tone into my ear. I barely slide the phone back on the hook, and plod to the bathroom. I turn the screechy knob until the shower is loud enough to drown out every little sound that scares me, and then I sit on the toilet lid and wait for Carter to return.

"I'm taking you out to dinner," Carter proclaims as he undresses from his work clothes.

"Oh…I…uh…"

"It's been six days. I don't want to push you, but let's try, huh? The press have given up outside. They think you're somewhere else."

I think back to how close I was the other day to stepping out on my own. How that mysterious call was like a perfectly timed reminder of the life I had just left behind. It was him. It had to be. All day and night I wonder what he meant. Was it a way to tell me he still thinks of me? Was he taunting me?

Every time the phone rings, I jump. I wait nervously for Carter to answer it, afraid if I take the initiative, I'll give away the secret. But so far, nothing has been out of the ordinary. And I haven't entertained the thought of leaving, thinking he'll call when I'm gone, and I'll miss some sort of chance at closure.

"We'll go somewhere quiet and fast," Carter insists.

He strips down to his briefs. It strikes me how it's the first time he's disrobed in front of me since I have come back. I remember what I found attractive about his body: how long he is, how the lines from his abs travel down to his hips like a long-winding road.

"Your mom will be back in a couple of days. I know that's a

lot to deal with and I just think it'll be good to remember what it was like to let loose a little."

I mull it over for a few seconds. "Alright."

"Great!" he says, losing himself and plopping a kiss on my forehead. I don't mean to, but I stiffen. He pretends not to notice, but I know he does.

"I'm going to take a quick shower," he announces, walking away with his underwear still on. He gently closes the door behind him and I let out a big sigh, collapsing back onto the bed.

The phone rings.

My breath stops for a moment. I want to run, I want to race to the phone, but Carter could come out to answer himself and I don't want to have to explain my sudden enthusiasm.

It rings again, Carter doesn't open the door, so he must already be in the shower. I walk over in between the third and fourth ring.

"Hello?"

Silence.

"Hello? Is anyone there?" I ask, my throat stuffing with emotion.

"If it's you, please say something."

A sigh.

"How could you leave me like that? Why did you?" I hiss. "Answer me, please? I know you can say something. After everything, at least give me that."

Nothing. Not even the courtesy of an answer.

"You dropped me off like some discarded pet and then intrude into my life? What is it that you want? If you meant to let me go, then let me go." I don't mean it, but I know it's the right thing to say.

Silence.

"Damn you," I growl, just before there's a click on the other line and he's vanished from my world again.

I hang up the phone, wiping my tears with the sleeve of my shirt. I check the bedroom mirror to make sure it's not obvious. Carter will want to know what happened and I don't want to deal with it.

We are seated at Ten 22, a restaurant I used to—and I guess still—love.

Carter is beaming. He thinks this is a breakthrough. I'm trying to be present, but all I can think about is that call. How I hate him and miss our quiet, mad world. How everything around me seems like a prop set. Like I am doll placed in a dollhouse and everything around me feels a little less real than what I had before.

The drive to the restaurant was quiet, but as we're seated, I become aware of all the commotion around me: forks clanking, laughter, plates clapping against tables. Eyes. So many eyes. I feel them staring at me…wondering—

"Do you want something to drink? Vesp?" Carter asks.

I look up and see a half-concerned look on the waiter's face. A waiter I didn't even notice was at the table until that moment.

"Uh…water's fine."

"We'll also have some chips and guacamole to start."

I try to drown it all out. But everything is amplified. I have lived in silence for so long, nearly every sound I have heard for the past year the result of a calculated choice.

"You okay?"

"Please don't ask me that. Ask me anything but that," I groan.

"Um, ok…how was your day?"

I snigger. "Well, I sat in your apartment and watched TV and stared at the walls."

"Sounds like a fun time," Carter quips.

"Yeah," I sigh, running a hand along my face and hair. "How about you?"

As soon as he begins, I check out. *The call. What does Sam want? Those fucking women across from us need to shut up. They're so loud. Their laughter, it sounds mocking. Is it about me? Do they know my face from the news?*

"Vesp? Vesp?"

Carter's voice lures me back to him.

"Yes?" I ask.

"Are you—" he stops himself. "Sorry. Sorry," he adds, waving his hands apologetically. "You look beautiful, by the way."

"Really?" I ask. I don't feel it. I feel hollow and like everyone can see the emptiness on the outside.

"Yes."

"Have I changed? From the last time you saw me?"

"No, I mean, your hair is longer. But you're you. You still have that smile, those eyes. I used to like looking at you, but now I appreciate it all even more."

"Thanks." I let out a gentle smile, but I know that's not true. I have changed. My smile and my eyes haven't. But I have. Carter has to know this. At least somewhere in the back of his mind. I can understand not wanting to admit that the person you loved is in many ways a complete stranger.

"What about me?" he asks.

"No, you're the same. Your hair is shorter though."

Carter grins. He looks down at the table in a moment of hesitation before looking back at me with determination. "Listen, I don't know if this is good timing. But, I just feel like—Listen, I want to give you something." He reaches into his pocket and pulls out a box. I recognize it instantly, his hand holding it just like he did the night I was taken.

"I want you to still have this. I want to pick up where we left off. I don't want some madman to steal this from us. I waited a year and I'll wait however long it takes you until you're ready. The last night I saw you before I almost lost you, it was with the knowledge that you were going to be my wife. And I still feel like that's true."

He takes my hand, and I don't fight him, letting him slide the ring on the finger that had abandoned it. It fits a little looser now.

"We committed to each other that night and that meant something to me. Still does."

"Me too," I whisper.

The women across from us break out into a frenzy of cackles and I startle.

Carter looks worried, but I brush it off and focus my attention back onto him.

"I want this too—"

Another loud eruption from them. It's winding me up, making me anxious. I just need them to shut up. Suddenly trumpets begin to sing. A fucking Mariachi band? I don't remember this place ever having that before. Everything has changed. All these little things. But they aren't so little when you add them up.

My heart thumps against my chest in a futile attempt at escape as all the sounds around me start to blur like movie film gone bad. Then there's a crash, it splits all the sounds apart: the hyena-like laughter of the women, the mariachi crooning away, the rambling voices. I hone in on the crash and see a man helping the waiter with the glasses in a hurry, before heading for the exit.

Is that him? Is that really him?

I mouth his name. Like seeing him is a siren's call, I stand up from the table and follow him towards the door.

"Vesp? Vesp! What are you doing?" Carter asks as he grabs my arm. I look back at Carter and yank it away, by the time I turn back the guy is already gone. I run to the door and push it open but he's gone.

"Dammit!" I snap.

"Vesp!" Carter calls as he joins me outside. "Can you please tell me what's going on?"

"It was him! He was just here!"

"What? Who?" Carter pauses before his moment of realization. "You mean the person who took you?"

I take a frantic breath thinking of an answer that will satisfy all the lies I've told to Carter, but I don't have the energy to keep it up right now. I can barely breathe.

"Did you see where he went?" Carter asks.

"No, you stopped me and I lost him."

"We should call the cops then."

"No—no!"

"Why not?"

Because I lied to them about everything. Because now that it's quiet out here and all the noise and music and laughter is gone, I'm not even sure it was him. I didn't even see his face. And even if I did, I told everyone he had a mask on the whole time, so how would I know? And, the most twisted reason of all, I'm not ready to hand him over. He's mine.

"You promised me it would be quiet!" I jab. It's manipulative. It's not me, using his guilt against him, but it's the only way I can stop his prying.

Carter responds with an apologetic stare, his mouth partly agape.

"I—I'm not even sure if it was him. I'm sorry. I think I just had a freak out. Never mind."

"Hey," Carter rests his hand on my shoulder. "Let me get the food to go, settle the check, and we'll go home, okay? Why don't you come inside? I can't leave you alone out here."

I massage my temples, trying to ease the tension between my ears. "I'm fine. It's too loud in there. I'm fine."

"Okay," he says softly.

I wait outside in the parking lot observing the occasional person or couple coming or going. It's calm here. Here I can take a breath. I don't think that person I chased after was Sam. I don't even know why I did at the time. My nerves finally settle, the light breeze blowing against me on this warm night aiding in the task. I take a deep breath and close my eyes for a moment. Reminding myself this is just the beginning. Things will get better. They have to.

I open my eyes just as a couple is exiting from their car. The woman is older, maybe mid-forties with leathery skin from too many years sitting out in the sun. The man with her is tall with thin, streaks of bright blond scattered throughout his crown as if he spends his days surfing. He follows her to the walkway that leads to the front door of the restaurant, where I am standing off to the side.

The woman glances up and me, and then she does it again. Her brow furrowing. She recognizes me. I give her an uncomfortable smile and look off into the distance. She passes me, but just as she's about to go in, she stops.

"Excuse me, but are you the girl from the news? I just had to ask."

I expected this might happen. My face had been on all the local news for weeks when I was taken, and then again upon my miraculous return. What I didn't expect was how intrusive and violating it would feel for some random person to ask me about it.

What fucking business is it of yours? "No," I answer.

"Oh, sorry. I just had to ask. You look a lot like her. You know the one that I'm talking about. Right?"

I know. The girl in the pictures. She's gone. She can't even go to a restaurant without seeing him. I look down and fidget with this stupid piece of hair that keeps blowing in my face. "Yeah, I've seen her," I reply as I tuck the long strand behind my ear.

"It's just amazing she escaped. But poor thing. I can only imagine what she went through."

Then don't. Anyway, you couldn't possibly. And you have no fucking right to ask.

"Susan," her husband huffs, a man who is clearly exhausted by his wife's constant need to chat with strangers.

Just then, Carter comes out from the door, observing the scene curiously.

"Come on, Vesp," he waves at me, trying to bail me out of the conversation he knows I am not interested in having.

The woman's eyes brighten as she hears the name.

"Oh my goodness, you *are* her." Her eyes go wide in awe as if she's discovered some rare gem.

"Sue!" her husband calls again, this time holding the door open to express his urgency.

I've run out of the thread of patience. Holding myself together, lying, adjusting to a world that was once familiar but is now a lie. This woman has tugged on a loose thread and has forced my facade to unravel.

How dare she? Doesn't she understand what she's asking? When she asks if I am that girl, she's asking me if I was kidnapped, raped, impregnated. She's asking if I miscarried that man's baby. If I still love my fiancé. If I feel guilt about my brother being stuffed in a home. Why my mother hasn't dropped her trip to come home yet.

"Who the fuck do you think you are?" I hiss.

She leans back in disbelief. As if *I* am the rude one. As if *she* has the right to be offended.

"Excuse me?" she asks. "I was just trying to wish you well."

"You have no right to come up to me and ask. My life is none of your business, you blithering dried up piece of jerky."

Finally, the woman shuts up, frozen in shock as I shoulder past her and towards Carter, who is now close enough to hear my rebuttal.

He's shocked too.

That's not Vesper Rivers. At least not the "before" version. She would have never lost her patience or insulted that woman. She would have gone out of her way to make the blabbing, rude woman feel comfortable, despite how uncomfortable that woman made her feel. She would have made sure everyone was understood around her, because she could absorb the insults, she could handle the hurt feelings, so long as no one else would have to.

I flounce past Carter right to the car. He chases after me, calling my name, but I don't stop until I am at the passenger side door. He gets in and unlocks my door. I sit with a thud, a physical protest to I'm not sure what.

"Vesp, what happened out there? Did she recognize you?" he asks.

"Don't worry about it. I'm fine."

Carter shakes his head. "You keep telling me not to worry, that you're fine." He shifts in his seat to lean towards me. "You think I don't know you? That I don't see you're hurting? I know you've been crying in the bathroom. I know you're scared still. But I can't help you if you don't talk to me. I've been giving you space, but I need to understand. What happened to you?"

The question has been lingering in his eyes since I came back. He watches me, as if the story was written on my skin and if he could just study it then he would understand. I haven't told him anything he didn't already know—that I was taken. Because even the version he would expect, the one he would want to hear, it's going to change the way he sees me forever. He'll know that some man fucked me like his personal plaything for months. That he stripped me, tied me up and starved me, so that I had no choice but to give in. That the man in the mask fucked me in places and ways I never let Carter explore. That he came in me just as many times as, if not more, than Carter ever did if I add it all up. Because he was insatiable. He craved me like a starved predator. But I don't even think I can tell that story without the thrill of it all sneaking its way onto my face, making my chest heave with fear and excitement, without getting wet.

And he'll know I grew to crave the man in the mask as much as he craved me. I'll lose Carter because he'll see I'm lost. The hunted is not supposed to yearn for the hunter. What Sam and I have is unnatural. It's aberrant. It's abhorrent.

"You don't want to know…" I rasp.

"Tell me what happened. You can trust me," he says, brushing away a tear. "You know I am trained to hear this stuff. I can take it. You don't want to see anyone, but you need to talk to someone. You can trust me." The outside of his hand caresses my cheek, and he finds that strand of hair that keeps escaping and tucks it back for me.

I'm sick. Sam's made me sick. Because just thinking about what I would tell Carter about him—the flashes of his feline eyes, the curves and lines of muscle along his naked body, the scars, like he has been so close to hell that it singed him—I'm throbbing all over; awakened.

I can't tell Carter what happened, not even in curated doses. So I do what I learned from the devil: I lean in and kiss Carter. Not softly, not seeking permission. I take. I won't give him a chance to wonder if this is the right thing. I'll make him feel so good, he'll stop caring about what matters. Just like Sam did to me. I give the affection he has been desperately wishing for when his body stiffens in my presence, holding back the urges to touch me.

I do it to distract him from the questions. To pretend I'm fine. I do it, using Carter as a milquetoast substitute for Sam.

"Stop, Vesp," he moans, but he doesn't push me away.

I climb on top of Carter, in the driver's seat, and between my legs, I feel that it's working. That he won't ask me any more questions tonight. I just hope I can do this without changing him the way Sam changed me.

CHAPTER 34

VESPER

Forks and knives clink against burnt orange Fiestaware as we sit in silence around my mother's dinner table. She's back. Finally. We picked her and the doctor up at the airport, where she put on her best show of an emotional reunion. She was so excited to have me back. So excited, in fact, that she made sure to finish out her trip in the Amazon, staying the two extra days after she got word of my return.

She embraced me at the airport, all refreshed and tanned, false tears of joy blurring her eyes. My whole life I thought she cared. I thought she did but just was built from a different material. Maybe, whoever my dad was, I got his painfully strong empathy. But no. I don't think she's capable of it. She's responsible. She would never have left me on someone's porch with a note pinned to me, but that's all I was—am—to her, a responsibility. It's why she put Johnny away. Carter may think it's because it's for the best, but her motivations aren't like Carter's. If it's for the best, that's a convenient side effect.

I let her hug me, I let her fill the car with talk of the trip as I stared out the window and watched the world pass me by. A lump formed in my throat, recalling the way I watched what I could from the windows the day Sam let me go.

Let me go.

Anger has begun to wear off to something else. I could have

turned him in. He told me everything about his life. He could have murdered me in that forest and no one would have ever known. But he let me go. I think I am supposed to appreciate that. I'm trying to. But it still feels like he abandoned me.

"Is it not good?" she asks.

"Hmmm?" I look up from the London broil and peas I have been scattering along the plate. It's just okay. "It's good," I answer before she can answer.

"I got it because I know it's your favorite," she says, like she's trying to prove we have this special bond.

"My favorite is strip steak." I enjoy the way she uses her napkin to wipe her mouth and shifts in her seat when I say that.

"Well," she sighs, tilting her head, a little nod to the less than warm greeting I have given her, "I was expecting a little more excitement for us to all be together."

Ha! Things like this are supposed to bring families together, right? Because I have never felt further from anyone at the table.

"Not everything exists to make your life that much more pleasant," I snicker.

Her fork and knife crash to the plate in protest.

"That's not what I meant."

I just keep looking at the limp brown meat and dull peas. Orange is a terrible choice of background for these colors.

"Carter, I picked up some fantastic cigars on the trip. Why don't we share one in the backyard?" Peter, my stepdad, asks.

Carter looks over to me, waiting for a signal. I can feel it, but I don't look up. "Uh, yeah sure," he accepts hesitantly.

Once the men leave the room, mom dives right in. "Listen, Vesper. I can't imagine what you've gone through but—"

"You haven't even mentioned him. Not once, not his name," I seethe, still looking at the plate.

"What?"

"Your son."

She lets out a sigh, like she's been holding this one in all night, wondering when she could let it out.

"Honey, I didn't know how to bring it up. You don't seem in good spirits. I didn't want to upset you."

I laugh sarcastically, finally meeting her eyes. "You put him away. You got rid of me, and then you were finally able to do the same for him. I bet you were *thrilled* when you heard I was back."

"How could you even say such a thing? You really think that? That I didn't want you back?"

"Who the hell waits over a week to come home when they find out their kidnapped, presumed-dead daughter has resurfaced? You think that's normal?"

"You know there were circumstances. We were in the jungle!"

"And what about when you returned? You finished out your trip!"

"I don't have to listen to these cruel accusations. The flights were booked."

"Then don't. But don't lie to me. I've been through too much. I've seen too much of the truth to be lied to like some idiot."

She shakes her head for a moment, her mouth curled into a deep frown. "You know you've always seen things in such simple terms. Not everyone is an angel like you. Not everyone is capable of giving that kind of constant sacrificial love. We all aren't wired like you."

"I'm no angel, mom."

"Then what gives you the right to sit there so smugly and judge me? I've done my best. I was alone with you. And I think I did a pretty decent job of raising you. And with Johnny, I just—I can't handle him. When you were taken, I couldn't handle it all."

"So you ran away, like you always do—" The lump in my throat returns unexpectedly. Not because of her, but because of Sam. He left me just like she did.

"I don't know what you want, Vesper. Was the world supposed to stop moving because you were gone? Was I supposed to stop living?"

"You said I was dead a few weeks in. You didn't even give me a chance," I scold. "You can justify it all you want. But just be honest with yourself. You were glad to be relieved of the burden for the first time in decades. To be that woman in the commune fucking every dick she could find."

Tears fill her eyes and she shoots up from her seat, marches over to me and slaps me across the face.

I stand tall. "You think that hurts? You think that's pain?" I grab the steak knife and hold it to my forearm.

"Vesper!" she shouts.

"I could do this and I wouldn't even feel a thing!"

I hear the suction sound of the sliding door to the backyard opening. Hands grab for my arms. I wasn't going to do it. I was making a point. But the way they all look at me, it's like they finally see I'm not me.

I'm not the girl put here to make them all feel better. To make their lives easier. Not anymore. I am difficult. I am unwieldy. Nothing fits and I am always uncomfortable, tugging on odds and ends, trying to get things to fall into place. I've seen and felt things that make pleasantries seem trivial.

They see the trouble I have become and I can tell they don't want this. They want their sweet, compliant Vesper back. Now they feel obligated. Just like my mother always has. But they don't *want* this.

I don't want this.

I wake up with what feels like a hangover. Except I didn't drink. I trudge out of the bedroom and see Carter pouring himself a cup of coffee.

I moan to myself, everything aching with the recollection of the ugliness of the night before.

"Well, that was a disaster," I say.

Carter's face is tense. "Vesper, I think you should see someone."

"See someone?"

"Yes. A therapist. You have been through an ordeal and I think you are having a hard time adjusting."

"Carter, it's been hardly two weeks, give me some time."

"I understand, and that's my point, now is the time to get help. The sooner, the better."

"I don't need help."

Carter puts his coffee on the counter and releases all the tension in the room with an exhale. "Look," he starts before taking a few steps to me and cradling my shoulders in his hands, "I understand there are things you may not be comfortable discussing with me, or your mother, or anyone you know. That's why an objective person would be ideal. They won't tell and you can just sort out the things you are feeling."

"I know how a therapist works, Carter. I was a semester away from being a nurse."

"I know you do, I'm just trying to make things clear for you. I feel like you think we're all against you. You've been defensive. And I wonder if it's because you've got all this stuff inside you are trying to protect. Like a shell. It's made you hard. And I understand these things do. I just want you to have someone you don't have to be hard with, a safe space, and then you can get back to living your life. Maybe finish school."

"I'll think about it," I say. I don't know if I want any of that. Nursing was once this trophy on a pedestal I was climbing towards. But as of late, that goal seems unappealing.

He gives me a tight-lipped smile. Hope.

The phone rings.

Carter, rubs the top of my head, gazing at me wistfully, before turning to grab the receiver.

"Yee-ello."

He scrunches his brow. "Hello? Hello?" He grunts and hangs up the phone. "Wrong number or a bad connection," he informs me.

"Oh," I respond casually as I pour myself some coffee, my stomach rolling with disappointment at the missed opportunity to scold Sam.

"Why don't you get me some recommendations from your colleagues and I'll see about setting an appointment?" I'm not sure how truthful I'm being, but I don't want Carter to worry about me. He lingers when he does.

"Okay, I'll do that. I gotta run." He kisses me on the top of my head and spins to make it towards the door. "Oh, and I do want to say, not that I am condoning the whole angry bit you had going on last night, but it was nice to see you stand up to your mother for once. I'm just thinking it could be more productive and less scary."

I laugh, rising my mug to him for an air toast. He leaves. I wait a few seconds, putting the mug down quietly and tiptoeing towards the door to listen for footsteps. Silence. I link the chain on the door. Then I go back to the phone and dial 0.

"Hello, operator. I just received a call on this line and I was wondering if you could tell me where it came from? I think it was a friend and I lost her number."

"Ma'am, I can't trace the call, do you have a name and city?"

"I...no, she moved, I'm not sure where."

"You don't have your friend's name, Ma'am?"

The impulse fades with her inquiries and I hang up, realizing how dangerously close I was to opening up something I shouldn't. But I have another idea, I don't know what it'll bring me, but I know it'll satisfy this hollowness, at least temporarily. I grab the keys to my car that I retrieved from my mother's yesterday. I told Carter I wasn't interested in using it any time soon, but it was wise to have it around in case of emergency. I lied.

CHAPTER 35

VESPER

My first stop is Las Palmas House. The edifice does not have the sterile appearance of a nursing home like I had imagined. My plan was to make a trip this weekend to visit Johnny with my mother and stepfather, a grand reunion of sorts. I'm not on the permitted list of visitors yet so I needed to wait for her to return. I think it's safe to say based on our dinner, my mother and I won't be spending time together this weekend, so I hope that today I can at least catch a glimpse of him, and maybe if I'm lucky, they'll let me see him. I can't wait any longer. I just need to see that he's alright.

It's a pretty brick three-story house. Carter had gotten a pamphlet for me from the hospital. It's small, housing no more than twenty children at a time. They have access to physical, occupational, and behavioral therapy. I refused to believe anything strangers had to offer could be more than what I had to give, but as I stand in front of this peaceful abode, rose bushes flanking the front door, amidst the sounds of children playing, it appears like a fine place for a child.

I follow the sounds to the back yard, surrounded by chain-linked fence like a school yard. There's a playground; kids of various levels of physical ability play. Some sitting in wheelchairs, some zig zagging about. Then I see him. He's holding a ball between his arms, tossing it to another boy in a wheelchair. He misses. It's hard to aim without the full use of his hands. A woman smiles and mouths words of encouragement as she picks up the ball. The boy in the wheelchair tosses it back to Johnny and he flings his arms together and catches it. I cover my mouth, stifling a tearful gasp, celebrating with tiny hops of joy as I link my fingers through the fence. I've never seen him catch a ball like that before. His smile beams. He looks taller, and his face has changed, already showing signs of the angles his jawline will take someday.

"Hello," another woman greets with polite suspicion.

"Oh, hi," I answer, straightening myself out.

"Are you a family member?" she asks.

"Yes. I'm Johnny Rivers' older sister. I'm sorry, I'm sure this seems odd. I don't think my name is on the list for visitation. My mother was out of the country and I know you have certain hours to visit. I've been—gone—for a long time. I just couldn't wait any longer."

A look of realization appears on her face. Her skin has a flawless mocha sheen that almost sparkles in the sun, and her bright hazel eyes warm towards me.

"Actually, I spoke to your mother this morning. You're Vesper, right? That's a nice name. She made sure you could visit him."

The knot of anger in my stomach I had been holding towards my mother unravels a bit. We're all a little good and a little bad. We're all just trying to figure out this life.

"He has therapy in about fifteen minutes. You can come play with him if you'd like."

She motions over to the entrance to the playground, we meet at the gate and she lets me in. I don't know how to approach him. He was told the man took me and I went to sleep. Will he be confused? Or will this whole thing have been a small blip in time for a child who seems to have had so much going on while I was gone?

I take a breath, trying to keep the tears down before approaching him from behind and gently tapping his shoulder. He spins, the ball still in his arms. We he looks up at me, he freezes and he drops it. It bounces in the small space between us. His blank expression becomes a frown and he begins to cry, burying his face into my stomach as he grips me.

"Johnny," I whisper. "It's okay. I'm back."

He holds me tight, only loosening so I can kneel and look him in the eye.

"Are you sad?" he shakes his head.

"Happy?" he nods, wiping a tear with his forearm.

"I'm happy to see you too." I've already forgotten about holding in my emotions as my tears match his. "I'm sorry I went away."

Johnny nods.

"Do you like it here?"

He smiles and nods many times. I can tell he's doing so well. He has other kids to play with and even his balance and strength have improved. It's humbling to accept that maybe I needed him around more than he needed me. He drags me to his friend, Thomas, who also seems to have cerebral palsy, but can still speak. He has a best friend. Someone like him. Someone who understands what he goes through every day in a way I can't.

I toss the ball with Johnny and Thomas until it's time for him to go to therapy. When I leave him with promises to return, he's smiling. He's safe. It was all worth it. No matter what happens to me, he'll be okay.

The library is nearly empty during this time of day, so the librarian seems happy to help me when I tell her I am doing some research for a real estate class I am taking.

She is all too eager to assist me in pulling records, bound together into books several inches thick. My search begins for property owned by the Hunter or Ridgefield family. It would have to be large, possibly designated as farmland. Somewhere quiet. Isolated. It turns out there is a lot of land to go around in that family. There are many Hunters and Ridgefields and many generations of land ownership.

Hours later, I am able to narrow the field down to less than a dozen properties according to size and distance. But I need more detail. My stomach rumbles as I look up at the clock. I have to get back soon, Carter usually comes home late, but sometimes he arrives early and surprises me.

But I can sense how close I am to finding where I was held. Where I began to form a new life. Finally, I have an idea. The librarian points me to the maps section and I begin to scout the addresses. My idea is to see if any of them indicate bodies of water. I am a complete novice at this, and while the pond seemed enormous to me, maybe it doesn't register large enough to be depicted on a map. About five properties in, and my ingenious idea seems to be worthless.

I gnaw the tip of my pencil, and stretch my shoulders, which had gone tight and sore from hunching over maps and books with the coiled tension of a predator.

I search the map for the next location, 1021 Redwood Lane, Villa Buena, CA. I squeeze my eyes shut a few times, tired and blurry from scanning maps and real estate records, and as they refocus, I find it. I trace my fingers along the paper, and even though it's just flat shades of ink, it all feels so familiar. I try to figure out its boundaries, coordinating with the land ownership records, and that's when I see it, a pale blue irregularly shaped ellipse. Water. According to the scale on the map, it's about the size of what I recall my pond to be.

I don't even have to look at the other locations. I know. Suddenly I can see the layout. Using the weeks and months I counted the steps between my shed and the water, I can narrow down where I stayed, where the house likely is. Where the barn is. My heart punches against my chest, stealing my breath away.

It's real. This place is real. It had almost begun to feel like it had only existed in my mind. Even in this short time, parts had faded the way a dream does if you don't recall it instantly upon waking. With shaky hands, I pile all the books and documents in a messy heap, crumpling the map and sliding it into my bag.

I look up at the clock and gasp. It's already eight o'clock. Carter's probably called the house twenty times and he's probably back. I run out of the library and speed home.

I open the door quietly, pretending my absence is nothing out of the ordinary.

Carter is on the phone, pacing back and forth, he whips around and pinches the bridge of his nose in relief when he sees me. "Never mind, she just walked through the door. Yeah. Okay. Okay.

Bye."

"Who was that?" I ask.

"Your mother."

"Why would you call her?" I snap.

"I've been calling all day. The first day they pull the patrol car off this place and you take off. It took everything I had to wait and not call the cops before I could get home. And you're gone. No note, nothing!"

"I'm sorry, I lost track of time," I say, tossing my bag, heavy with secrets, beside the door.

"Where were you?" he asks. The question annoys me more than I would expect. Ever since I returned, he's been more of a babysitter than a boyfriend and it's starting to wear on me.

"Do I have to report everything to you? I am an adult you know."

"Last night, you held a knife to your arm and threatened to cut yourself. Then you disappear today. What am I supposed to think?"

"I wasn't going to cut myself," I exclaim.

"That's not normal behavior."

I snigger. *Normal.* Is he expecting me to be normal? "You're right. It's not normal. I'm sorry that my return is so inconvenient for you and everyone else. I am sorry I came back and upturned your lives. I'm sorry everyone has to accommodate my strange and unusual behavior. I am sorry this has all been so hard on you," I lament sarcastically.

"Don't be like that, Vesp."

"I wasn't ready for this. For any of this. I thought I would never see any of you again. I didn't know I was going back home until the moment it happened. So forgive me if I need a little bit of an adjustment period. And that includes some time to clear my head and not be looked at like I'm some unhinged person. I am not the one who did this!"

"That's not what I meant."

"What have you sacrificed? What did you tell him when he asked you?"

"Asked me? Who? What are you talking about?"

"You know, when he gave you a choice…" I hint, not

wanting to unleash the elephant in the room that sits beside us, quietly, taunting us.

I shouldn't do this. It's not fair, but it's always been at the back of my mind, eating away at my resolve from the very beginning. When I was given a choice, I put my body on the line. I wouldn't let Sam hurt Carter, so I told him he could have me.

"When he asked if you'd take the punches or let him—" I can't say it. There's so much shame weaved into those words.

"Let him what? What are you talking about?!" Carter snaps.

"Let him fuck me!" I shout. It's cathartic, spilling out the hidden sickness inside of me like that. I've tried to protect Carter, but it wasn't working.

Carter braces and for a moment it looks like he'll be sick. I watch him search his memories. "I don't know what you're talking about Vesp. You mean that night?" His eyes glaze over with tears and now I'm going to be sick. "You think I would have let him…" he chokes up, "do that to you? You think I would have given him permission like it was mine to give?"

The hurt on his face is so vivid, I can't bear to look at it. I can tolerate my own pain better than his.

"He told me—"

"He's a liar!" Carter shouts. "I'm sorry. I need—I need air," he says between heavy breaths.

"Carter—" I call to him apologetically. But he's already heading for the door.

"I just need to take a walk," he says.

He leaves and I stare at the door in silence. I didn't believe Sam when he told me. Of course, Carter wouldn't have done that. But part of me wishes he had. It would be easier somehow. I stare at the door for forty some odd minutes, perking up when I hear the key unlocking the door.

I stand at attention when Carter enters. He doesn't look well. He's pale and his eyes are pink and puffed. What I asked was cruel.

"I'm sorry for what I implied earlier. I had some elaborate speech in my head, but really I'm just sorry, Carter."

Carter dips his head back, running his fingers through his hair, messy from a long day. We're both already so tired. His chest and shoulders drop as he rubs his hands over his face.

"I'm sorry I didn't protect you, Vesp. I'm sorry if I'm smothering you. I just—I feel like I failed you and—"

"No. No…" I insist, running over to him and grabbing his hands. "I didn't mean it. I was just feeling attacked and I said it to attack you. It was disgusting. Like I said, I am not the one who did this. Neither are you."

Carter bows his head and sighs. "You're right. I still think you should see someone and I collected some good names, but I didn't mean to pressure you. It's just that, I've been waiting so long to have you back and it's like you're right here in front of me, but I can't reach you. I've thought about how amazing things would be when you came back, and I didn't realize how painful this would be. For you. It's selfish of me to expect you to come back and pretend that past year didn't happen. I'm reliving it, too. The cops came to my job to talk to me, looking for new information, anything I could have remembered since the many times they questioned me right after you were taken. I didn't mention it because I hate bringing that night up. But it made me relive it, and it's fresh again and I feel like he's right around the corner to snatch you. I want to help, but I have nothing and I feel so fucking ineffective. That fucking bastard—"

I shake my head, regret pinching my chest. "No. No. Carter. He let me go. He's not coming back for me. I understand this is hard on you. And you are being amazing. Maybe too amazing. I want us to enjoy each other. You calling every few hours, constantly worrying. That's not healthy for you. I didn't expect any of this. To be honest, I had assumed you moved on long ago. I thought I was forgotten."

"I'm not your mother, Vesp."

"I know," I mutter under my breath. I think about the map sitting in my purse, how despite this understanding, loving man in front of me, all I can think about is finding that location. He may not understand it, but going there is something I have to do. I have to leave that place on my own terms.

"What do you say we just eat something, and enjoy the weekend? Let's just enjoy each other in the present. It's been a long week for both of us I think."

"I think that's a great idea. In fact, why don't we go out to eat for a change?" I suggest.

At first I'm not sure if I have the right place as I drive along the dirt driveway. But as it curves and I see a peek of the barn from behind the trees, I know my theory was right.

I waited two weeks to come here. Two long weeks. I always hated that saying: long weeks, days, minutes. A minute is a minute. An hour is an hour. But now I understand that's not true. Not when you've been lying naked in a cold basement, starving, thirsty and seconds seem to freeze endlessly. Not when you're in the arms of the cruelest man you've ever known and he feeds you pleasure, direct, like a shot of heroin, and those minutes count down, accelerating in speed like a free fall, so that you hit the ground with a painful explosion when it's over all too quickly.

I had to start focusing on my time with Carter. Rebuilding things. Letting him in again. I had to get him to trust me. That way he wouldn't call home every hour, so he wouldn't notice a long day trip like this.

I should be scared. What if he's still here? But I'm not scared anymore. I am many things, but I am not fearful. I grip the steering wheel tightly. I had been so focused on finding this place, I didn't even think about what I'd do if I was right. I think at least some part of what Sam told me was true—his brother wanted him gone. The man had to feel like he did at least one thing right, and getting his brother out of town was some sort of action.

I park on the vast green between the barn and the main house. I step out, my shoes crunching against the dry grass that's already several inches taller than when I was last here. The barn catches my attention. I creep towards it with the possibility someone could be on the property. If Sheriff Ridgefield ran into me here, he'd have a fit. When I open the door, the sound of buzzing becomes apparent; I follow it to the dried pool of Sam's blood and a horde of flies circling it.

The barn door softly creaks behind me and I startle. I hide inside a stall, listening for sounds, my heart beat pulses in my skull as seconds pass without a sound until a horse nickers. I step out, cautiously making my way to the entrance to find Beverly with her head peeking past the threshold of the barn.

"Heeeey girl," I coo. She huffs as I come close and rub the side of her golden muscular neck. "You look good. Freedom suits you." The goats are nowhere in eyeshot, so I continue my mission, walking past Beverly towards the house. She follows me, like I'm some warped version of a Disney princess, stopping at the porch steps. The front door is unlocked; the screen door wails in protest as I pull it open, powerless to protect its owner's secrets.

It's exactly as we left it. Almost like we never did. I wonder if he intends to return someday. I walk up the creaky steps to the room, the one that held his psyche, just like a dark corner of his mind. The colorful tapestries and articles still line the walls. There wasn't enough time before to read them all. To digest.

I pull the articles one by one. I observe the pictures of him as a child and his family. He looks different now, but it hurts to see his face. To see a boy who was forgotten up here, alone with a madwoman. I hate that I feel for him, but I can't control it any more than I can control the need to breathe.

There's a black and white picture of him. He's so tiny in it. It's from before the accident. He's on a quaint tree-lined street. The kind kids could play on without worry, where mom could easily step out the front door and call you in for dinner. I didn't really have that. I didn't grow up like most kids. Only the occasional visit to my grandmother allowed me a glimpse of that life. She lived on a street like that. In a house like the one to the left of Sam in the photo. I look closer. *98.* I can barely make it out, but because it's stamped in my mind, I know it when I see it.

I shake my head in disbelief. I don't remember him. But then again, I didn't know many of the kids there. Did he remember me? I want to ask him. I want to talk to him. I want answers. But I will get nothing. The realization makes me uneasy. Like this was all destined. Like I have been meant to be here in this spot since I was born. I set the picture down and yank on one of the tapestries, exposing a portion of a clean wall made of dozens of white washed wooden planks. Then another, and another, trying to tear away at the insanity until paper and piles of colorful fabric are crowded around my feet.

I look around the room, once the symbol of a dark and crowded mind, now bright and open. Except for one imperfection. One of the planks looks irregular—shorter and not lined up like the others. I walk up to it and press against it. It wobbles, but it's rather firmly set in. I run to the craft table and grab a pair of scissors, jamming one side into the space between planks and prying it away from the wall. Once I jimmy it, it falls out with ease. In the wall rests a box. It looks old but pretty, like most of the things in this house, made from a tan wood with carvings along the top. I pull it out and rest it on the craft table, opening it up. It's lined with a hunter green felt and inside are dozens of random objects. Jewelry and photos and odds and ends I can't quite place. Then it hits me: It's his trophy box.

I step away from it like it's infected. Suddenly I don't feel so special. I am forced to confront that I am just another victim in a long line of victims of this predator. He collected pieces of us. And I have no doubt that if he could have placed them proudly up on his walls, he would have. Smiles radiating from these pictures, stolen. Lives interrupted.

I raise a shaky hand over my mouth as tears flow down my cheeks. It hurts in a way that I didn't expect. Like when you find a love letter from your beloved to someone else. A betrayal. A deceit. He never told me he wasn't that man, but he showed me something different. And I believed him. I did. I couldn't believe in the handsome guy who wears his pain on his skin and that person behind the mask. They couldn't both exist in him. One had to die. Just like the old me dried up and withered to make room for the person here now.

I pull something out of my bag and place it where the box was. A message of sorts to Sam. Then I slam the lid down on the box, unable to stomach it for another second, latching it closed. I need to keep this, as insurance, as a reminder.

CHAPTER 36

SAM

She took the fucking box. It shouldn't make sense. There's no way she could have known where the house was without doing some serious legwork. And yet, she found it. She's thinking about me as much as I think about her.

I left that house in a hurry. My thoughts twisted about what to do with Vesp. I was going to kill her. I was. I would dispose of her and come back to the house to clean up after myself.

She always fucks up my plans. And the next thing I know, I am dropping her off a mile away from the park ranger's station and I'm running. Because she could turn me in. She could tell them what I look like, my fucking family history, the make and model of my truck. At that point, physical evidence would just be icing on the cake. I had to give myself a head start. I did what most fugitives do, drove south, stopping at a diner around LA, hoping to catch some news on the small fuzzy television screen behind the counter.

"Coffee?" a waitress asked, chewing her gum like a horse as she slid over the apple pie I pointed out on the menu earlier.

I nodded.

It's weird. I think I could have talked to her. I might have had a little hang up here or there, but I finally don't fucking care. I don't care what anyone thinks of the way I sound. And I don't have that invisible hand of the secret clenching my throat the way it once did. I was running, but I had also come to terms with it being the end. With this bitter diner coffee and apple pie being my last meal. With the world knowing who I really am. There's a peace in that. I hear that's what it's like when you know you are going to die. A calmness takes over.

I could have talked, but I didn't want to. I'd save my breath for Vesp if I ever saw her again.

Finally, the evening news started and the top story was no surprise to me.

Missing Sacramento area woman Vesper Rivers has been found in Sequoia National Park today. Authorities need help locating this man.

I took a sip from my mug, waiting for the perfect rendering, or even better, a photo of my face to appear on the screen. For the waitress to freeze and slowly look over towards me and look for an excuse to make a phone call.

A rendering popped up, a different version of the same shit.

I lowered my coffee down to the counter, and sliced my fork into the pie.

A face shrouded in a mask. Just eyes peering out.

A bulleted description: Male, 5'10", Brown Eyes

I snickered to myself and it caught the waitress' attention, but I didn't give a shit. She could look me right in these eyes and see I'm not that man.

Vesper fucking did it. She protected me. There's no way my brother could have covered this without her cooperation. I stood up, buzzing with energy and slapped a five on the counter, shaking my head to myself. Mister Ed eyed me as I walked out.

I'm free. I'm fucking free. But as soon as I stepped out into the dusty air, hunger stole my relief. I was prepared to die. To stop existing. But now that my plan had truly worked, and I had made her into someone who would do this for me, I couldn't have her. What the fuck was I supposed to do now?

I made my way to the pay phone outside of the diner and pulled out a few yellow sheets from my pocket. I ripped them from a phone book before I left town.

Peters, Dr. Richard

I slipped a dime into the phone and pounded out the numbers. I just needed to hear her voice. I didn't have to say anything. I just needed to know she was there. She had to know that I didn't stop craving her. That she did good. This was her reward.

The phone rang about five times. I slammed it and the change jingled down. I collected it and inserted it back in the slot. This time I looked at the other page. The one that made my hand tremble with rage and disgust. Mr. Perfect. That's the only other place she would be.

No answer. She's probably still at the station. I headed to my car and back onto the road. My truck lights illuminated a sign half-covered with shrubs that said: L.A.15 miles.

And that's how I ended up in L.A. I laid low for a couple of weeks, just to make sure this wasn't all some elaborate ruse. But I couldn't resist hearing her voice. Her practically begging me to save her from the mundanity of her ordinary new life. She understands now, she wasn't a prisoner with me, she's a prisoner out there, shackled by the expectations and relationships she thought she needed. I can't go back and take her again. That's not how this works. I'm not a knight in shining armor. I am Hades. I split the earth open and suck her under. I give her my seed, which she accepts despite her protests. Now I am her home. She has been released back into the world, but she will realize she inevitably must return to me. She can only survive this by inhabiting two worlds.

After a few weeks I head back north (fuck Scoot) to clean out the fucking farm of anything untoward before hiring a crew to empty it out, and I come back to my mother's room, looking like a fucking tornado ran through. Where that box once was, the copy of Green Eggs and Ham I gave Vesper.

She has the box. It's full of objects, but that thing lives and breathes and I'm not sure she can handle having something that powerful in her possession. She'll find many things in there, but there's one thing she won't find- any trace of her. As I stare at the empty hole, I reach into my pocket and pull out the folded photo. It's worn in that spot, the fold line splitting her right down the middle. I run my hands along the groove, down to her smile, and her neck. The image of her necklace is nearly eaten up by the crease. Sometimes I wished I had kept it, so I would still have a piece of her, something other than memories that fade over time like this beat up image.

"So I'm thinking we should go someplace. Take a long weekend," Carter suggests as he passes me a wet dish to dry.

"Oh yeah?"

"Yeah. Maybe we go…" His eyes widen up. "Why don't we go to Tahoe? You've always loved it there."

I did. But now, the trees, the water, memories of losing my necklace, it'll all bring me back to him. I would have loved this idea before Sam.

"Sure." I try to paint over the hesitation with a broken smile. But Carter senses it.

"We don't have to go there. We could go anywhere."

"No. No. That's a good idea." I don't want to complicate things. I've changed so much and I don't want to add to the list. I don't want to have to explain why suddenly my favorite place doesn't make me squeal with enthusiasm.

I can sense Carter doesn't believe me.

"Actually, I'm really excited," I say, doing a better job with the fake smile. "I think the fresh air and openness will be perfect. Do you want me to make the plans?"

Carter's eyes brighten. "Sure. Yeah, it's all yours. I'd love that."

I'm trying. I'm trying so hard. To accept that this is the life I am supposed to want. Carter is the man I am supposed to desire. I'm trying to rewire myself. But it's hard when a box full of victims sits at the bottom of your underwear drawer.

I don't know what to do with it. Right now, I use it to remind myself that this is where I am supposed to be. That for all of the gentle moments Sam shared with me, that box is who he really is.

But like Sam, the weight of the box sits on my soul, and always in the back of my mind, knowing it's there. It steals the moments I have in the present. I have to do something about it. Maybe this whole thing was a mistake, covering for him. I don't think I can live a normal life unless I let him go completely. I can't keep him and this life. I can only have one. Maybe it's time to let the cops have him.

Carter decides to step out for some errands, leaving me alone in the house for a while. Like I always do, I go to the drawer and open the box, going through its contents. There are so many pieces in here. So many lives.

I think I have to do it. I have to call the sheriff and tell him we can't go on like this. I don't want to blindside him. I glance at the clock. He should be in this early on a Friday. I stuff the box into my bag and leave Carter a note.

Sheriff Ridgefield wanted me to come in for some questioning AGAIN. I'll be back ASAP.

The station is only a few minutes away. He's standing right by the front desk, intently talking to a man in a brown suit, who I know is from the DA's office.

I stand barely in his field of vision, not wanting to intrude, but wanting to be noticed. It only takes a few seconds before he spots me. He places his hand on the man's shoulder, gives him a nod in my direction. They shake and he makes his way toward me.

He's handsome, but it's a different type of handsome. He's more clean-cut and fatherly in his demeanor. He carries a lot more weight in his step. He's not that much older than Sam, but he looks far more mature. Sam looks like he'll look young forever, even with the rough scars and the stubble. Maybe it's the job. Maybe it's having a conscience.

"Vesper, why don't you come into my office?"

I hold the strap of my bag a little tighter to my side and follow him. I feel like they all know. They can all feel the evil permeating from the bag.

We've seen each other a few times since the first time, mostly so I can "help" by answering more questions. It's weird walking through the station, sitting there, answering questions, knowing that the man in charge already has the answers and this is all for show.

"Coffee, water?"

"No thanks," I say.

"Have a seat," he gestures to the chair opposite his side of the desk.

I sit. It's always like this. Formal, procedural, the secret unspoken since we've made the agreement. But I'm here to break that wall.

"My secretary said you weren't home when she called. She left the message with your boyfriend. He said you were already on your way. That you had spoken to me, but I know that's not true."

"She just spoke to Carter?" I ask, trying to make sense of the miscommunication.

"Yes."

"Why did you call?" I ask.

"Why were you already on your way?" he retorts, leaning his elbows onto his desk.

I hug the bag closer to me. I don't think I should share what I have until I know what he wanted.

"I…um…I'm concerned. I just needed to talk to you. He's been calling me."

Ridgefield sighs and rubs his forehead. "Fucking idiot." I resent that he calls him that. "Have you told anyone?"

"No."

"Not even your boyfriend?"

"No."

"Good. Then it's just between us and we keep it that way. You should change your number and make it private. Tell your boyfriend you'd feel safer that way and you're sick of reporters."

"I just thought you should know because of the investigation. It's fine."

He sits back into his chair and sucks his teeth. "You don't want to make him stop? Remind me what's going on here, Vesper. Why are you doing this? I'm glad, but I can't quite ever be at ease. I'm losing a lot of sleep thinking you'll change your mind."

I wish I could articulate an answer. I can't even promise him I won't change my mind.

"Did you ever really know Sam?" I ask.

He lets out a huff. "At one point I would have said I did. Well, maybe not really knew him, but I understood a part of him. I can honestly say right now, I have no fucking idea who he is."

I glance at a picture on his desk. His little family. So perfect. So normal.

I spot the young boy standing in front of the sheriff with an innocent smile adorning his cherubic face. "Wow, he looks just like Sam when he was little."

Ridgefield's face tightens, like I've poked at a sore spot.

"Yeah, identical," he laments. "Did you?"

"Did I what?" I ask.

"Ever really know him."

"I think I did. It would be easier if I hadn't. It's hard to betray someone you know."

He nods. "Or someone you thought you did."

"So what did you want to tell me? Or did you just need reassurances?" I ask.

"Actually, I wanted to reassure you. This will all be over soon."

"What do you mean?" I inquire, a knot of uneasiness bubbling in my stomach.

"Someone confessed to your kidnapping."

"What?" I ask, in complete befuddlement.

He pulls a file and opens it, placing a picture in front of me. A dark-featured, middle-aged man stares back at me.

"The Northern Woods Killer," he states, stabbing his finger onto the center of the decrepit man's face.

"But it wasn't him. You know that." As if the Sheriff needed to be told that.

"This will make it all go away. So that you don't have to worry about anything coming to haunt us."

"I don't understand."

"He's a serial rapist and killer. A trucker leaving vics and bodies all over the state. We have him in custody. He's been linked to twenty-six bodies all over Northern California, and he's confessing to at least fifty."

"Why would he? I don't understand."

"He's agreed to give us information about additional crimes for a plea. Guys, they sometimes do that, they confess to a bunch of things. Sometimes for notoriety, sometimes to confuse us. But he has a small house that works for the scenario. He doesn't have friends or family. It's conceivable he could have had someone locked up and no one would have known. He told a good tale. He knew things only the kidnapper would know."

"How?"

"There's ways when you're questioning…to plant seeds."

"But he's innocent."

"He's not innocent, Vesper. He killed over two dozen people. Innocent girls who never hurt anyone. The fucker signed a confession saying he took you. We can actually close this case. He'll be in jail until he dies anyway. So everyone can be satisfied this case was closed."

"I don't understand. What about the other crimes?"

"You let me take care of that. There's gonna be some egg on my face, but nothing I can't salvage. Oh and Sam's place is on the market now. I checked myself. Once it passes hands and new people move in and bring their stuff in, it'll be impossible to retrieve untainted evidence."

That last bit of news stings--the thought of Sam being truly gone. "This doesn't feel right."

"This, right there," he points a finger at me, "is what's going to give me a heart attack."

I roll my eyes.

"Vesper, this man is a brutal murderer. He is a danger to society. And the disconcerting truth is, California is rife with these men. It's the Wild West out here sometimes. If I trump a charge on him, it's doing the world a favor."

"Have you done that before?"

"Vesper, I promise you, never. But I'm in an impossible place. We can't just seem satisfied with no answers. We both have to look like we want someone to pay for this. If we don't close this case, I can't keep stopping others from snooping around, finding something I couldn't hide. And I want us all to move past this. You—" he leans in with a hushed tone. "You didn't want to turn him in. I never forced you."

I'm glad I kept the box a secret. Something tells me if I handed it over, it would find its way into an incinerator. Suddenly Sheriff Ridgefield's constant need for reassurance worries me. I'm an inconvenient loose end and maybe Sam's not the only one capable of doing bad things.

"You're right. This works out perfectly. So we can all move on."

"Vesper, I need you to understand. You've saved my family. If you need anything. If you want to leave and start over somewhere, or just need a hand, I have ways of helping."

"I appreciate that," I say, coming to my feet, feeling like the walls of this office are going to move in and crush me.

Sheriff leans back and crosses his arms holding a sly smirk. "So you're really planning on never telling me?"

I pull my purse close to my side. "Telling you what?"

"How far along are you? You're not showing, but Katie didn't show with James until she was six months."

"What?" I gasp.

"You're protective of Sam. You wouldn't let the doctors examine you, but they took your blood, urine. Did you think I wouldn't know?"

"I promise you. I'm not," I declare through tremulous lips.

"We need to trust each other if we are going to pull this off," he says, leaning forward. "You understand if a child comes out of this, and it looks like Sam with those fucking eyes or the blood work doesn't match with this Northern Woods fella, this could bite us in the ass. Like I said, there are ways we can take care of things. Quietly."

"There is no baby," I insist through a clenched teeth, rage bubbling in me at the thought that our dead baby is such a convenience to him.

My gut twirls with a feeling of dread that I'm not sure why I didn't feel sooner around this man. Maybe it's the uniform he wears, the one that tells us all that he's one of the good guys. Just like how Sam's mask told me he wasn't. But sometimes those costumes deceive us. Sometimes the man in the police uniform wants you dead. Sometimes the man in the ski mask saves your life. I don't think Ridgefield ever intended to see me alive. I knew who he was. He doesn't trust me. And unlike Sam, I have no motive in Andrew's mind to keep the secret.

The present danger is in the sheriff, not Sam. So I choose to say something that isn't just a shallow reassurance. It shouldn't be true. I'm supposed to be moving on. In fact, as I prepare my words, my throat gets heavy and clogged and it almost pains me to say it. But it shouldn't hurt so much if it's just another lie.

"You want to know why I won't tell?" I ask, leaning my hands onto Ridgefield's desk.

He gives me a subtle nod.
"Because Sam is mine."

CHAPTER 37

VESPER

Tahoe is next week. I've been doing my best to give this life a try. Sam's box sits there like a twisted version of a comfort blanket, assuring me he still exists. Whenever Carter is not home, I go out to the park, library, anywhere away from the phone so I am not tempted by his random calls.

I can feel it growing slowly around me, like ivy. This new life trying to take root and rebuild itself over me. I can't be her again, the girl before all this, but maybe I can smother everything that happened and find a place where I can exist here.

I left the sheriff's office a month ago with news that someone else would be taking the fall for Sam's crime. That guy was plastered all over the news shortly after. A press conference was held. I watched it with Carter as he held my hand. But I pulled it away and left the room. I couldn't watch the lies. I couldn't sit there while Carter thought that was the man who had me.

But if I can just stay away from the temptation of him, the way an alcoholic stays away from bars and liquor stores, maybe I'll think of him less. Maybe I'll forget.

On this morning, Carter seems in a rush to get out the door. He's got a lot to take care of this week before we leave. I turn on morning news and I can't escape Sam. His brother is right there on the screen: *Sheriff Ridgefield announces his run for mayor of*

Sacramento.

They talk about how he's taking advantage of his recent success in my case and the Northern Woods Killer.

I snicker at the TV.

"What is it?" Carter asks as he puts on his watch.

"Oh just that the sheriff is running for mayor."

"Why's that strange?"

"I don't know why. I just find it funny they consider me a success story. They didn't find me. He let me go. I don't know how he saved face telling the world it was The Night Prowler who took me if it was this guy. Not to mention that means that Night Prowler guy is still out there. A convenient fact everyone seems to forget."

"If?" Carter asks.

"I'm just saying, I don't think the Sheriff comes out looking as sparkling as he thinks."

"But they put the asshole who took you away for life, right?" he says, kissing me on the top of my head.

"Yeah."

He glances over at the TV. "You don't like that guy, do you?"

I shrug.

"You okay?" He's being thoughtful, but I can tell his mind is already out the door. Understandable.

"I'm fine."

"Okay. I'll see you tonight." It's actually comforting he takes my word for it.

Carter's gone within a minute and I start the shower to get ready for my day of avoidance. But now Sam's on the top of my mind, so that no matter where I go, he'll be there.

You'd think the shame would keep Andrew Hunter-Ridgefield from running for office. But no, this is exactly why he wanted this. It wasn't to protect Sam, it was so his own ambitions wouldn't be sidetracked. He stands up on the podium, with his little family and his expensive suit, and he claims that he cares about people. Well I have a box with 82 lives—homes that were broken into, people terrorized and violated—that prove otherwise. But I am just as guilty. I could go to the FBI. All the scenarios run through my mind when the phone rings. It's too early for Sam. Unless this is a new strategy since I'm gone all day now. Or maybe Carter is calling because he forgot something. I have to answer.

When I do, I know within seconds it's him.

"I have your box." I pause for a response I know I won't hear.

"Your brother is the big winner in all this. Did you see on the news? He's running for mayor."

Nothing.

"Is this ever going to stop? You don't want me, Sam. I wouldn't be here if you did."

I hang up before I can say anything else stupid and I get ready as quickly as I can so I can go somewhere he can't reach me.

I spend my day in the library, flipping through pages that don't interest me. I'm restless today, full of secrets and emotions I can't let out. I have to do the opposite of what I feel urged to do. So I decide to stop by and surprise Carter for lunch. He's a TA and usually in the TA lounge between classes, so I drive over there but don't see him. Someone tells me he's in one of the lecture halls, wrapping up a class.

I find the hall; a door is propped open. I walk towards it and hear his voice conversing with another. She's emotional. I stop before they can see me and peek just over the corner. A strawberry blond with feathered hair and big glasses stands in front of him. She's bracing her books across her chest. That's all I can gather before I have to hide behind the doorway.

The acoustics of the lecture hall make it easy to gather most of the conversation, even from the top tier.

"I don't understand…you said this would be temporary. It's been almost two months, Carter."

"You don't understand. She's been through a lot."

"So that makes this okay? Just be honest with me. Do you love me?"

"Of course."

"But not more than her."

"Can you please understand the position I'm in? We were engaged before she was taken away. It's all very confusing."

"Well, it is for me too. One day, I'm practically living in your place. You're telling me you love me and how you can finally see a future with someone else, and then the next you get a phone call and tell me I have to pack my things. That she's back and you have to make sure she's okay. That was all you were going to do. Make sure she was okay. But now she's living there, and you are going on vacations—" She stops to sob.

"I'm not the kind of person who leaves someone when they're down."

"So what? It's your responsibility to take care of her forever? You keep saying she's not well, but she doesn't want to go to therapy. You say this is just something you have to do, but—I don't even have to ask if you are having sex. I can't keep waiting. Just let me go," she begs.

"I can't tell you to leave. I still care about you."

"You have to make a choice. Either you start a new life with me, or you just take care of someone who I'm not even sure loves you anymore. But I won't keep waiting here, sleeping alone at night while you try to fuck her pain away. It's sick, this whole thing."

That's about all I can take before I turn and rush out of the building, tossing the lunch in the garbage as I wipe away tears. None of this has ever felt real. Because it wasn't. I kept telling myself I could make it more real than the life I left behind, but now I know it's not possible. Because Carter is faking it too. We're faking it for each other. We think that the other needs us. But we're holding on to an illusion.

I've only ever felt so completely desired by one person. This world found a way to move on without me. I was dead. Coming back has only thrown it off kilter. We all keep trying to find our balance, but it wobbles on its axis like a top spinning on its fragile tip, waiting to topple over.

My mother did her duty, she got me to adulthood and she's ready to get back to the life she stepped away from.

Johnny is thriving without me. And even if my mother would let me, I'm not the girl who can take care of him anymore. Not the way I once could. I can barely do it for myself.

And Carter, sweet Carter. I don't blame him. I'm not angry with him. He deserves someone who would cry and beg for him like that. Not someone who answers the phone to her kidnapper. Who protects the man who disrupted our lives. Not someone who has to try so hard to love him.

Ever since I returned, I have felt unsettled. Always uneasy. I'm not safe. And the only way I can feel at ease again is to go back towards the flames. Go into the fiery building and let it overtake me. I might turn to ash, but at least I won't live in fear of being burnt.

I may have a purpose. But it's not here anymore. It may not be a happy one. But my story doesn't happen here. It happens with Sam. Sheriff Ridgefield might think this is over, but this isn't over until I say it is.

I run into the apartment I share with Carter and grab a pen and paper.

Dear Carter,

I can't thank you enough for the love and support you have shown me. Before and after I was taken. You deserve a life full of love and devotion. And I can't do this. I have to leave. I have to start somewhere else. Maybe one day I'll come back and we'll see each other. But you should move on. Take someone else to Tahoe. It's not my place anymore. I'll be fine. I just need to go my own way for a while. Please don't look for me. I'll be back when I'm ready. I'm sorry. I'm sorry about everything.

Love,
Vesper

I grab my bags, Sam's box shoved safely at the bottom of one, and try to find something real.

CHAPTER 38

VESPER

I've been sitting in this diner for about two hours. I'm on my fourth cup of coffee and my runny eggs sit there, cold. I have to eat them. I don't have a job and all I have to live on are the savings I had before I left, money intended for nursing school tuition, and some money my mother, well really my stepdad, threw my way to help me get on my feet. It's enough to last me a few months, but letting this nutrition sit on the plate is foolish. I try to will myself to take a bite, but I can't. I'm closer to him. I can feel it.

"Need a refill?" the waitress asks. She's been patient with me taking up this table. But that's what people do in diners, right? They either come for a quick meal, or respite from something, a place they can come to sit for a cheap escape.

"Sure." I reach for the cup to hand it to her, but it's shaky. I've had too much caffeine and I'll keep on drinking. I feel resolute to do something, but it's one of two somethings and one is the one I want, the other is the one I should. We can go back to the quiet mornings under the California sun, when I'd read him books. Or the afternoons in the water, but this time it could be the beach instead of the lake. At night we could listen to music. Our world would be quiet, it would be just us and it wouldn't be so loud and full. And he could do what he wanted with me, because I'd let him. I'd let him devour every inch of me like I was the sweetest thing. Like I was the only thing that could curb his hunger.

Or I could do what the lives represented in the box in my bag demand—find him, ring his doorbell at night and when he answers, shoot him in the face. I'll walk away the way he does: into the night. There will be no discernible motive. No reason for the police to trace his murder to me.

Then I'll dump the box and the gun in the ocean. I'll find a motel and because I will have killed the only reason I had left to live, I'll take a bunch of pills and go to sleep.

Both somethings pull at me. They weigh equally and opposite, each making the other unfathomable. So that I am affixed to this spot, anchored by the choice I need to make. And when I can't think about that any longer, I replay the conversation that got me down to LA.

"What are you doing here?" Sheriff Ridgefield asks as he looks back over his shoulder into his house. During my research, I was able to figure out where he lives, in his and Sam's childhood home. It's the nicest house on the block, with a bright green lawn, and rose bushes.

"I need to talk to you," I respond without shame or hesitation.

The high-pitched scream of a giggling child carries out the front door. Ridgefield looks back again, rolls his eyes and sighs. "Fine." He leans back and shouts to his wife that someone is here from work and he'll be back in a few minutes.

"You shouldn't be here. Is this about money?" It's insulting, that he'd think I'd be here for something so trivial.

"No."

"Then what?"

"I need to know where Sam is."

He barks a mocking laugh. "What? Why?"

"I have my reasons."

"We are so close to being done with this. Why would you want to go to him?" A woman walks by with her poodle and waves at us, there's a curious look in her eyes. He smiles tightly and waves back. He leans in and hisses "Are you insane?"

"You are no one to judge me."

He shakes his head. *"I may have done something awful, but I didn't ask to be caught up in it. And you had your chance. You definitely didn't lie to protect me. You didn't even know me. You protected him or yourself, or I don't know who."*

"I didn't come here to discuss this. I just want to know where he is. At least point me in the right direction."

"I don't know. He's dead to me."

"So you expect me to believe a cop, who banished his dangerous brother out of town, isn't keeping some sort of tabs on him? I may not be well, but I'm not stupid, Sheriff."

"I'm not going to lead you back to him."

We stop at the corner of the block as we reach this impasse.

"What was your plan for me?" I ask him.

"What do you mean?"

"I mean, Sam told me you said he should get out of town. That we should. But he left me. I know he didn't want to. It doesn't add up."

"So that's what you want to find out? Why he left you? Christ, Vesper, let it go."

I shake my head at his callous trivialization of my ordeal, but I don't let it distract me. "You were going to let him take me. That's what he said. That you would have let us disappear. But then he left me. It doesn't make sense."

"I...uh...what are you getting at, Ms. Rivers?" he asks, frustrated.

"I think I know why. Because it was the only way he could save me. You let him go. So that part was true. But there's no way you'd let him take me. My face was everywhere. I was a liability. If your brother was spotted with me, that would be too risky. I know he took me out into the woods to kill me. I could feel him agonizing over it. I could feel the barrel of the gun against my head."

He can't even look at me now. It's all over his face. The guilt. I took a gamble, making the accusation. It was a hunch. I could have been wrong, but he doesn't have to say a word to convince me I'm right—that for all of Sam's wickedness, it was his cop brother who wanted me dead and it was Sam who risked everything so that I could live.

Sam knew the one way to keep me safe was to bring me out

of the shadows and into the light. Once I was in the park ranger's office, I was too high profile to disappear again. Sam knew his own life might be destroyed in the process.

He let me go anyway.

"You need to go. I'm not leading you to him. You may think I'm the bad guy here, but this is to keep you safe."

The old Vesper would have taken the first no. She would have not wanted to inconvenience or pressure someone. She would have seen the look on Sheriff's face and somehow felt guilty for confronting him with the truth. But now, I won't leave here until I have what I want. I didn't come here with a request. This is a demand.

"Andrew, right? Can I call you that?"

"Yeah," he confirms skeptically.

"I don't have anything left. People like me don't come back home. We die. Or people think we have. But we're not meant to come back home. And I am here, and I'm not supposed to be here."

"You just need to give it time."

"I feel suffocated by all this freedom. All these choices. I don't feel safe without him."

"He's the one that made you feel that way."

"He is. And there's only two ways I can feel safe from him. One is to be back where I was, and the other—" I stop myself from telling an officer about murder. He's not my friend. I have to remember that.

"What are you trying to tell me, Vesper?" He's becoming agitated.

But I can't tell him any more of my secret thoughts. The shame of wanting a man who has done the incomprehensible to me. How I agonize over every decision I have made since Sam drove away.

"I have it, Andrew. His box of trinkets. I bet you thought he took it with him when he cleaned the place out. You must know about that. All the little things he took from us. All the mementos. Like this..." I reach down and hold the moon charm on my necklace between my fingers. It used to mean so much to me. I didn't think it could symbolize any more than it already did, but now it's overflowing; loaded. It holds so much that I feel its heaviness pressing down on my neck every day.

He doesn't say anything. He just waits there with his arms crossed, lips pressed into a tight line, as the occasional car passes or child runs by.

"I have it. You have to understand that I have nothing left. And if I can't get to him, then the only way I can bring him to me is to tell everything I know. To go to the FBI and hand them that box and tell them everything."

"You wouldn't."

"I don't want to."

"Is this a threat?" *he asks, his brow glistening with sweat.*

"If something happens to me, it will be found. And then there will be more questions than you can answer."

"When is this going to end? I thought we were going to forget this?"

"It ends when you tell me where I can find him. So I can end this myself. You had your reasons for lying and I had mine. You can go back to your family and I can finish what was started."

"What are you going to do when you find him? Kill him? You think Sam's gonna let that happen?" *Andrew is tight, trying to hold in the sleepless nights, the betrayal, the frustration. He jabs his finger at his temple.* "He's smart, Vesp. He's evaded us for years. You think he's going to trust you? And if you kill him, that puts me in the same spot I was trying to avoid, having our name on the news."

"I promise you telling me won't come back to you. This isn't even about you."

"You're nuts. This conversation is over. If you go and see him, try to attack him, it's you who will end up dead," *he snipes through gritted teeth. Sheriff turns abruptly and walks away, leaving me without options. I played all my hands and he's called my bluff.*

He makes it about twenty feet away, before looking side to side and stomping back over to me. "You know what? You want to go find him, you want to put yourself in danger? Fine. But I want that box."

"I don't trust you."

"Well I don't trust you."

"Just tell me," *I say.* "And you won't have to see me again. Ever. I don't want money. I want to know where he is. And that box will be in the ocean or in a fireplace once I have him. If he kills me, *it'll be safe with him. I have no reason to want that thing to come to the light of day. Not unless you give me one."*

He pauses for a moment. His lips purse a few times because he knows he's getting a raw deal. But he knows he owes me. He almost took my life from me. The least he could do is give me this.

I give him a little extra push. "I'll find him. Now you can either direct me, or I can snoop around."

He sighs and looks at his watch. "Shit, Katie's going to kill me." He looks back up at me. "He's in L.A. At least the last time I checked. I thought I wanted to know what he was up to, but the truth is I don't. Because if he hasn't stopped...I can't know. I can't—" his voice catches. Andrew Hunter-Ridgefield is a cop, through and through. There's something in the way he walks, a pride, an honor. I can tell this—what we've done—it's like a parasite eating him from the inside out. His need to protect his family and the very badge he has worked for going against the very thing that badge stands for.

"Thank you," I say, "And this is goodbye. Really."

"Yeah," he replies sarcastically, taking a few steps back, keeping his eyes on me before turning and leaving me standing there alone on that corner.

I take a sip from the fresh mug of coffee and my eyes train up to the fuzzy small screen behind the counter. There's a sketch of a man with a mask on the screen. Like moth to a flame, I hover over to it, nearly bumping into a waitress. The one behind the counter turns to look what has me so interested.

"Oh the volume on this thing is broken. Have you heard about him? It's scary."

"Who is that?"

"Nobody knows, it's this guy that's been breaking into homes and killing people."

"Killing people?" I repeat, my stomach and heart swirling in a sickening fashion. This can't be him. Not my Sam. Sam doesn't kill.

But just like I feel I'm closer to him, my gut clenches almost painfully, telling me something.

I turn around just as a man leaves the diner and his paper on the booth where he was sitting.

It's on the third page. The story of a predator who has claimed his third and fourth victims. No rape, just an invasion and murder. They don't have any leads. He's smart. He wears a mask, likely stalks his targets, and he's athletic. He gets in and out of the neighborhoods on foot so he's gone before the cops are even called. His eyes are a striking blue or green.

I cover my mouth as acid works its way up my throat. Sheriff Ridgefield said it, Northern California is crawling with killers; dead bodies with no justice. It can't be much different down here.

But I look at the dates of the attacks, and I just know. And the choice I have to make becomes perfectly clear.

CHAPTER 39

SAM

Blood. It's something I've never had to deal with before on a hunt. Now it's everywhere, in my hair, soaked into my clothes, in my fingernails. It's messy. A variable I don't like. But I've lost it. Ever since I left her, the urge has come back. And it's strong. I'm alone again. Unattached to humanity.

I'm angry that I've felt what it was like, to have it, that thing I craved, I stole—and now I'm back to where I started. She was my medication, she was my sanity. A missing cog in a machine that suddenly made it work without a squeak. And now it's gone and the whole fucking thing has gone haywire.

I tried to recreate the thrill of the hunt. But each time I go into a new home, it feels flat. I can't get back what I've lost. And then I'm filled with that wrath that has to go somewhere, but I can't keep cutting myself. I'd only do that to protect her. So it goes out, in a flurry of blood and screams until the house is as quiet as it was when I first breached it.

I know she still wants me. Before I let her go, there was always that doubt, that it was all a manipulation. That she was the one playing me. But the way her voice quivered on those calls when she asked me why I left, the way she filled me in on things, as if we're having a conversation, except her voice was pleading—for me to take her away, back to our little world—It is real.

But I can't go to her. I can't take her away again. This has to be a choice. She has to come to me. And if this is what I have to do to smoke her out, I'll do it.

This is my love letter to Vesper. I write it in their blood.

VESPER

It's a sunny day in LA. The kind of sun that makes you smile when you rise. It's warmth gently heating you to your core, softly baking the skin. The day when I kill Sam.

I stuff my belongings into my bag, over the box of tokens, and leave my motel room, heading over to the nearest pay phone. I open the phone book, first to Ridgefield. There are seven listed. None with the first name Samuel. I flip over to the H's. No Hunter-Ridgefields, many Hunters, none with his name. The phone book is old, so I pick up the phone and dial the operator.

He could have hidden the listing or changed his name. But why would he? He has nothing to hide from. Only two people know his secret, and we share it with him.

The operator answers, uninterested in the magnitude of this inquiry. She doesn't understand what she's doing. Who I am. What I've been through. What I am about to do. She finds the one Samuel Hunter-Ridgefield in the directory and provides his number and address, not understanding this is a death sentence.

I stare at the address, written on my motel receipt, my hand trembling. From the moment he left me, I had imagined we might see each other again. But not like this.

The taxi leaves me a couple blocks away from the address at my request. I need the time to walk and build the nerve. I can't just step out of the car and onto his front door. It's a nice neighborhood, filled with families, and it builds my resolve. This monster lives among them and they don't even know it. They don't know he could be watching, waiting to bludgeon them to death like he has four other people since he has arrived. I caress the gun in my pocket, bearing a little bit of its weight so it doesn't make an imprint through my thin sweater.

I could still turn around and go to the police. There is still time to change this story. But it doesn't feel like a possibility. I am invested in every possible way. If I have to kill him—the little boy who was always different, with the stutter and scars, locked away by a crazed mother and a family with too much pride to admit imperfection—I won't drag him out there like a spectacle. I'll do it quickly. Mercifully.

My stomach roils when I see the number on the mailbox. 445. I stand on the path to the front of this quaint home, and stare at the door. I'm shaking everywhere, unable to stop the uncontrollable jitters. I can feel him, throwing off my equilibrium, pulling me out of my orbit.

I take one deep breath, and proceed to the door, my hand firmly gripping the small revolver.

I take each of the three steps up to the door carefully, as if they were made of thin ice and could crumble underneath me. Then I stand in front of the door, holding in the volcano of emotion that rumbles in my skull and chest, wanting to burst. I raise my fist to knock, and before I can, the door opens.

All the blood drains from my head, a heady feeling taking over me as my eyes lock on his for the first time since the day he fed me lies so he could kill me. The day he put his own life at risk so that I could live.

I should have known. It was too easy to find him. Sam was never in hiding. He was in waiting.

He stands there before me, his faded red t-shirt clinging to his sweaty chest, his ripped jeans snug against his frame, his face, beautiful, yet corrupted with scars, and his eyes—eyes like a nocturnal creature that has hunted and tortured, that has killed me and brought me back to life—they stare into mine. There is no uncertainty in them. This is exactly where he expected to find me one day.

I grip the gun, willing my arm to pull it, but it locks up. I'm frozen by the sight of him. Distance was my power, proximity is his. Now that I am here again, I want to drop down to my knees and cower before him like a subjugate to her king. It's beyond rational thought. It's been trained into me. It's conditioned into my mind, body and soul.

I want to be in his favor. I want to be good.

The temptation of the carnal is too strong to be subdued by abstract concepts of right and wrong. The only real thing is him, here, right now. I know what he's done, but this person before me, calm and assured, he's not the wild person behind the mask. That's someone else.

My hand lets go of the gun and I slide it out of my pocket.

"Sam—" I utter, a whimper.

I don't know what I am supposed to say right now. And I've learned not to expect words from him. He takes the hand, the one that a moment ago was just holding a weapon, and pulls me into the house. The door slams behind me as he pushes me up against a wall, so hard it beats the breath out of my chest and the bag hanging on my arm falls to the floor. I see flashes of the danger he poses, the bright sun reflecting off of the pale aquamarine just like it does the sea— beautiful and deadly. How many people have been seduced by the endless ocean, thinking they could conquer it, and were never seen again?

My heart rages in my chest, taking me back to the very first night he had me. His lips tremble with a hint of a snarl. A faint sound—almost like a purr—rumbles from his throat. Like a predator, he pounces.

It's repugnant, the way I feel when he presses himself against me. The fact that my body lights up like a pilot switch, giving into everything I shouldn't want. That I can forget everything inconvenient just so I can feel this moment in its purest sense. I can close my eyes and be that girl who didn't have a choice but to enjoy this, for her own survival. I can tell myself I'm in his house alone, and I have to let him have me. But I know I passed that point a long time ago.

The way his lips taste my lips, my collarbone, the curve of my chin, my shoulders. The way his teeth graze parts all over, instantly brings back the high of being craved by a man so dangerous, having a power over him that I know no one else has, no matter how many tokens are in that box.

I make the decision at that moment not to be a victim. I came here, I had the gun and I didn't use it. The very first night he gave me a choice. And now I am making another. I grab at him, pulling at his shirt so I can feel his skin again, hot and slick with sweat. This can't be wrong. The way I feel like I belong here. The way out there, I feel unsettled. But here, pinned to a wall by the most dangerous man in L.A., I feel like I'm home again.

Tears run down my face as I abandon every principle I ever stood for. I don't just abandon them, I scorch them. I blaze them to soot. Sam pulls off the sweater I'm wearing and then at my dress, so the top falls down and its weight pulls the rest of it to the floor.

I manage to yank off his shirt, and I taste him—his sweat, his smooth skin, and then his rough skin, like those maps I played with as a child, where you could feel the rugged topography lift off the paper like braille. I'll take it all, the soft and the jagged.

Little dashes of paint and plaster stain his skin. It feels familiar. The way he used to come to my place after a long day of working to bring me food. I could tell he was tired. But he took care of me still. I'd study them for clues about his life out in the world, hoping they could aid me somehow in an escape, but now, it's fondness I feel looking at them.

I bury my face in his neck, inhaling his faint musk mingled with soap. A rush—like all the blood pooling down at my feet and rising up through my head—inundates me. Seeing him, feeling him, tasting him, smelling him—I am right back to that last day, like he never left. Like nothing exists except us. Like right and wrong is something outside of us. It doesn't matter here. Everything we were and did doesn't matter when it's just us. We become renewed.

He turns me away, pressing me up against the wall, biting the back of my nape and shoulders. We'll do it like the animals do, because he's not a man, he's a savage.

"Say it," Sam growls.

"Fuck me," I plead. I need to stop thinking. I'm still thinking. Still wrestling. When he's in me, it'll stop, it always does.

He doesn't hesitate to burrow himself into me. I grip at the wall, then reach back for him as he pushes in and out. The thinking stops, then I can just feel. *Smell. Touch. Taste.* I just am. The world shrinks to him. To this very moment. Nothing else matters.

I let go. It feels so good to let go. He pounds against me. He is not gentle. He is not tentative. He's hard as stone inside of me. I know no one else does it for him like I do. I know while I've been with Carter, all this time, Sam's been with no one else.

So it doesn't last. No, he's pulsating inside of me, his groans brushing against my ear with little wisps of his breath. I stay plastered against the wall, my breasts touching the cool surface with each inhale.

Sam takes me by the hand, without a word, to the bathroom. He leads me into the shower. He soaps me up, running the slippery hands along my breasts and stomach, over the mounds of my ass, sliding his fingers between my thighs to clean me. He fucks me again, against the tile wall, and this time he lasts longer and I come and come. And it's like the last couple of months didn't even happen. I should be scared, but I'm not. There's no reason to be scared of Sam when he's getting what he wants.

CHAPTER 40

VESPER

I wake up, my head pulsing with indecision. It takes me a second to see as I rub my eyes, coaxing them open against the blinding light of the mid afternoon sun. My breathing stops for a moment when I see Sam at my side, facing away from me, his golden skin swathed by a crisp white blanket, slits of sun peeking through the blinds dashing across his skin. This is real. This wasn't a dream. The most restful sleep I've had since I rejoined civilization couldn't have been precipitated by letting go of that gun and taking his hand.

I watch Sam—quiet, still. His breath is too shallow to be heard over the humming of the fan pointed at us. The room is plain. Just a bed and white sheets. A small table by his side. A standing fan. He's new here. This place doesn't have the generations of history the ranch did.

But I can't let him keep doing what he's done. I have to stop him. And in his sleep, he can't look at me with those eyes. He can't take my hand, or kiss me. I can't see those marks on his face and feel for the boy who never knew what it felt like to be accepted by those who should have loved him the most.

I look away from him to the open bedroom door. Down the long hallway is the front door, where my bag and clothes still lay. They are in a heap, some of its contents spilling over: a couple of shirt sleeves, a piece of paper, the glinting hint of a gun. And hidden under all that is a box. A box I have to keep in the past. No more pictures, no more souvenirs.

I don't want to do this. But I didn't put him away and now it's my responsibility to stop him. I look over again at him, biting my lip to stifle my emotions. I want this to be us. This right here. Quiet in bed. Just the two of us. But there is a part of me that never died, and she can't let this madness go on. I lean close. To feel him. To make sure he's asleep. His chest rises and falls in the familiar way I have seen so many times in that shed he built for me.

I wince as I slide out of the bed. Pursing my eyes shut at each little creak, each time a plank of wood moans under my feet, until I am crouched in front of my mess. Until I have the cold gun in my hand. I walk back, this time my stride is more confident, making me lighter on my feet and suddenly all the little noises don't creep up. They don't scare me. This is the only time I can do this. The only time I can atone our sins.

I raise the gun up, showing me that the sudden spurt of confidence was false. It trembles, aimed five feet from the back of his head.

"If you're going to do it, Vesp, do it," he says.

The cold shock of hearing him speak like this for the first time makes me go rigid. Hearing it purely. Without sex, without violence, without anger. It's raspy, but there's a softness to his tone.

"I—I know what you've done here. I can't let you..." My voice trails off. This shouldn't be so hard.

"You have a choice to make, Vesp. Because I won't—can't—stop unless you do something. You can pull that t-trigger and end it all right now. And you will be alone. You will have to go back to your mom and that pretty boyfriend of yours, and you will have to s-spend the rest of your life pretending. You couldn't even bear it for a couple of months, but you'll have to for the rest of your life."

I close my eyes, shaking my head, sobbing. When I open them, he's still in his spot, unmoved, his back still facing me. Doing me the favor of making it easier.

"Or, you can stay here with me. B-because when I have you, it works. You are the object of my obsession. You are the world. My—my holy grail. And if I have you, I don't even think about anyone—anything else. And you can be here with me, and you will be doing a good thing. For everyone. For yourself."

Sam speaking to me, alone, is enough to leave me stunned. I finally broke through. This battle we fought all this time—he's letting me have this victory.

"You're speaking," I mutter.

He bobs his head in acknowledgement.

"Why now?" I muster through the tears.

"Because I'm free with you."

I maintain my wobbly aim at him, and he puts a hand up to show he won't hurt me before slowly turning to face me. "I can't stop myself unless you do something. You either pull the trigger or you stay with me. Death or life. So—so it's okay."

"I—I could go to the cops. I could tell them the truth."

"Vesp, you know I won't go with them. But I won't stop you. I wouldn't—wouldn't hurt you."

There are only two options. I kill him —directly or indirectly— or I let the past die.

"If you won't stay, then I don't want to live anyway."

"Why? Why am I different?" I need to know. That's the only way I can believe he'll stop if I stay.

"I saw you with Johnny. I always wanted someone like you when I was l-little. I've dreamt of someone like you m-my whole life. And you would've been the same way with our boy."

"Boy?" I utter. We were going to have a little boy.

"You needed me to save you."

Sam turns away again, giving me room to make the choice. I can take him out of his misery and live in mine. Or, I can forget the man in the mask, and chose the one before me, the one who I know would die for me. And I can find some sort of peace in that.

I slide my finger along the trigger. Toying with the idea of pulling it. What would happen then? His victims would never know. They would never get any closure. Unless I leave the box here with his body. Each souvenir could tie back to the people he's hurt.

I pull a hand away from the gun for a second just to wipe my blurred eyes.

Right. Sometimes the choice is so clear. But for the past couple of years, my heart and my mind have not agreed. And here in this moment, there are two types of right. The one for everyone else, and the one for me.

You don't stare the devil in the eyes and come out without some of his sin. You can't beat the devil without becoming like him. You can't appeal to his kindness, so you have to learn to play his games. You lie, you fuck, you manipulate, you fight, you hurl insults, until you do whatever it takes to win the battle. Every time you do those things, you understand him a little more. Until finally, he becomes your ally. You think you've won, that you've made him more like you. But the truth is, it's the other way around. So that even when you win, you've lost.

Sam waits, patiently, as if he has already come to terms with both fates.

But I'm not a killer. Each step closer I get to doing it, the harder it becomes. So that leaves me with only one choice. He must know that. Just like all the other choices I had with him, there was only ever one option. It's the very reason he wants me above anyone else. I am that girl he saw with Johnny. I don't hurt people, I nurture. He wants someone all to himself. I want to be the complete center of someone's universe for once.

I offered myself as the sacrifice. That's what got me taken in the first place. And if it means saving others, I'll do it again.

I firm my grip around the gun, stiffening my arms in one last show of strength, and let them fall at my side. This time, Sam, the athlete that has outrun bystanders and cops on foot dozens of times, rolls over and is in front of me in a flash, but he doesn't lash out. No, he softly strips the gun from my hand. He opens the revolver and shakes the bullets into his palm before tossing them onto the bed.

The same hands that he has used to hurt me, he uses to hold me up as I weep with my entire body.

"Shhhh," he whispers, stroking my head. "No one loves you like I do."

Love. I never dared use that word with him. It felt too perverse. But if what we are doing for each other isn't love—if letting me live at the almost guaranteed cost of his own freedom isn't it—if lying to the police and my family to let Sam live out his life isn't— then what is?

He caresses my hair as I melt into his chest. I have tamed him. He is mine and mine alone. I will keep you all safe from him.

"I know," I answer, softly nodding against his warm chest.

It feels good—the way floating in that lake would make me feel light and easy—to let go of that weight. To take that final breath and let myself sink down so far, that I realize I don't want it all to end. I want to live. I want him. I choose him.

SAM

It's going to take her some time to get used to it all, but she will, just like she did before. I know I am a lucky man to have her, and I'll make sure she never regrets it. I wasn't lying about the promise I made. I don't need to hunt anymore. I've gotten my prize. I had to show her my commitment, even if it meant she heard my flaws. I wouldn't know until I spoke, whether I would sound like a babbling incoherent idiot or not, but living in truth truly is the greatest remedy. It'll only get better, speaking to her, the way it did around my mother. Though the night will always be my home, I finally have a place in the sun with Vesp.

It's funny how I can finally speak to her, but we spend most of the afternoon in bed, staring at each other. I wipe the tears from her glowing cheeks. I watch her settle into the decision she made. As each minute passes, she seems easier. This is what she wanted. She just needed permission to want it. Vesper is good. I needed to make her feel like this was a good thing. That by putting that gun down, she was still protecting people.

I've decided, with Vesper's approval, of course, that I'll be grilling up some burgers for dinner tonight. God, I feel good. I feel…happy. It was a long shot, this whole thing, but in the end, it all paid off. Planning and focus always does.

I fumble around with the charcoal so that it perfectly frames the box. For so long, it was my only way to feel connected to the thrill of those moments. But they weren't real, now that I have something that is, I know this. Every time I used to open that box, the memories got a little foggier, the emotional connection a little weaker.

I squirt an obscene amount of lighter fluid on the thing and the surrounding charcoals, and throw a match in. I jump back as the flames shoot up. I keep the fire going, sweat pouring over my brow as I use a grill fork to open the box and add fuel to the contents. A smiling picture of a couple I don't even remember curls as the flames overtake it.

I look over at Vesper, sitting on a chair on the back patio. She looks troubled for a moment, and I get it. She's a sweet thing. That's what I saw in her that day. She was the embodiment of I had always dreamed of: a person--a spirit--kind enough for both of us. I'll help her reconcile it all in time.

I wave at her and it breaks her distant stare. She gives me a smile that lets me know her mind is in a million places, but she's here, and that's all that matters.

I said I would do it. Piece by piece. Break her down, and build her up again. Until she was rid of all the things holding her back from me. I never lost sight of that, even when things looked dire.

I'm not a killer. Not really. Not unless I have to.

But if there was anything I knew would finally push her to make a choice, the hard choice, to commit instead of wavering, it was that.

I didn't have her at the ranch. I didn't have her until I let her go. Until I bloomed into the monster that she felt only she could save.

I meant what I said. You're all safe now. You can thank Vesper for that.

EPILOGUE

VESPER

"Look at him out there, playing with Johnny," mom says, glancing out of her kitchen window. It's not the house we used to live in. She decided to sell it. Too many bad memories.

"Yeah, he's so good with him," I add wistfully. It always tugs on my heart in a painful way, in the way something can be both beautiful and sad, watching Sam with my little brother.

I look back at my mother and she's looking at me with a smile—you know—*that* smile. The one where they want you to see they are happy to watch you in the moment.

"What?" I ask sheepishly.

"Oh, it's just, I'm happy for you is all." She folds her arms and takes a breath. "Listen, I know I haven't been the greatest—"

"Mom, don't."

"Let me finish, Vesp." She places a hand on my forearm as my arms cross my chest. "I know I haven't been the greatest mother, but I have always wanted the best for you. I just wanted you to be happy. When you left like that—I worried so much about you. That I had lost you forever. But I understood you needed to get away from that house, and even Carter. Hell, probably mostly me. I'm just so glad you're feeling better. And I am happy that you found a nice guy like Sam."

"Thanks mom. He likes you, too."

I couldn't stay away from home forever. I love my brother, and even though my mother has decided to keep him at the home, he still needs his family. Sam understood that, and he was in total agreement.

So after a few months in L.A., I came back. Told my family I met a guy. Not just any guy, a Hunter *and* a Ridgefield. Someone with a great family and money. Someone who adores me. Someone who would never let me go. Carter moved on like I knew he would. And now he wouldn't have to feel guilty because I found someone, too.

I spruced up the little house in L.A. so that now it's a home. We thought giving Andrew his space was the right thing, even if we could force our way back to Sacramento. So we take the long drive up as much as we can to visit Johnny.

Johnny makes a heaving sound, his version of laughter as he races into the house. I only hear it when he plays with Sam. Sam catches up to him, scoops him up and he gurgles with laughter. A flash of the first time he held Johnny comes to mind. But he's different now. And even then, it was just an idle threat.

"Alright guys, it's time to sit down for dinner. Where's your stepfather?" Mom asks as she wanders off to find him.

Sam sets down Johnny, who comes over to me and embraces my thigh. I rub his head. "Go wash your hands," I tell him. He shakes his head no.

"Now, my sweet boy," I order.

He huffs and leaves for the bathroom and it's just Sam and me.

"You're beautiful," Sam mouths to me.

I smile. So much of what he used to be already feels like a distant memory. But it's always there. In the back of my mind, it lingers.

As if he can feel the thoughts stealing my joy, he leans in and kisses me. His lips, they replace the doubt. They graze my cheek and then my ear as he leans in and whispers. "You make me so hard.

Always. I never stop thinking about you. Even when you're just out of sight. I wonder about you, always."

That's his danger. That's his appeal. It's always just beneath the surface, the hunger he has for me. The pretty devil with the clear eyes.

"Alright!" My mother announces as the family comes into the kitchen and we pull away, looking like two lovers having a sweet, secret conversation. "Let's eat!" Sam puts on the most innocent of smiles. I know now how he was able to go undetected for so long. How he can summon darkness so strong, there aren't even shadows, and suddenly turn bright and sunny. How he can go from bafflingly complex, to sweetly simple.

We sit down for a meal. My mom's on a new religious kick. It'll pass, it always does. But she prompts us all to bow for prayer. I comply but shortly after she begins, I open my eyes. Amongst the bowed heads and closed eyelids at the table, there's Sam with his hooded gaze, and those glowing eyes, fixed on me.

SAM

I watch Vesp, sprawled on the bed, a sheet perfectly draping over her breasts and buttocks, her long hair fanning across the pillow. Then I look outside the window I'm leaning against. It's late into the night. The night still belongs to me. It will always be my home. But now, it's to watch her. Still. Perfect. Mine.

Every day is perfect. I get to be like them. Except we're not like them. No, this is truer. More crazed. We hold secrets that are as destructive as atom bombs. My brother, the only other keeper, is running for mayor now and very much in the lead, further cementing his pact to protect the family name.

My promise to Vesp isn't hard to keep. I don't want to go out there anymore. She feeds the ravenous animal that lives inside of me.

Now I finally have the family I never had. A little brother who I can treat the way Andrew never did me. A mother, who for all her faults, is nothing like the woman who locked me away in her secret shame and fear. You might not approve of what I did, but you can't tell me it didn't work.

Vesp rustles, feeling for me with a half-smile. She opens her eyes when she doesn't find me. "Mmmm," she says as she opens her sleepy eyes. "What are you doing?"

She knows. "I'm watching you."

She motions for me to come into bed. I look outside the window one final time, It all seems like he was someone else. I slide in, and take her in my arms. She closes her eyes and almost instantly falls asleep again. I made that happen. I made her love me. I made her feel safe in these arms.

Don't tell me this isn't love. When you love someone, you'll do anything—lie, manipulate, kill (even yourself)—to keep them. You just aren't willing to go that far. When I let her go, that's when I knew what this was. I'd never felt it before. And I knew this couldn't be the end. There were moments it felt that way, when I thought she wouldn't come back, but just like from the very beginning, I knew I had to be consistent. I had to do whatever it took to bring her back to me.

Love isn't flowers or poetry. It's this. Ask yourself. Has anyone ever loved you the way I love Vesp? Can you say anyone has done for you the things I've done for her?

Carter was a breeze. Soft and comforting. Safe. But it doesn't move things, it doesn't shake things. I am the storm. Strong and violent. Dangerous. I will tear down anything in my path to have her. When I roll through, you see evidence of me all around. You will see branches broken, windows shattered. I will move obstacles that seem insurmountable.

I have to be honest with you now. I let her go is because I knew I had done my job. I knew she wouldn't snitch. I knew she would come back to me. As sure as I know the sun will set every night. But still, I had to test her. Even if that meant putting my own life on the line. It was her final exam, and she has been rewarded.

And none of that makes this any less real.

THE
END

SOCIAL
MEDIA

FACEBOOK:
https://www.facebook.com/strappednovel

TWITTER:
https://twitter.com/NinaGJones

INSTAGRAM:
https://www.instagram.com/Ninagjones/

OTHER WORKS
BY NINA G. JONES

STRAPPED SERIES
(*Erotica/Suspense*)
STRAPPED
STRAPPED DOWN
UNSTRAPPED

GORGEOUS ROTTEN SCOUNDREL
(*Standalone Erotic Romance/Comedy*)

DEBT
(*Standalone Dark Erotic Suspense*)

IF
(*Standalone New Adult Contemporary Romance*)

SWELTER
(*Standalone Erotic Romance*)

Made in United States
Orlando, FL
22 April 2023

32358760R00207